DRAKONIA SERIES
BOOK 1

THE DRAGON'S FLUTE

RYLO KINN

Prologue
In the Beginning.

In the beginning of time, on the planet Earth, creatures we now call the Mythicals roamed the planet. For centuries, the balance of true bliss endured.

Suddenly, without warning, the heavens were ravaged by the dark power of evil. A war between angels and demons lit up the night sky creating a chaotic abyss. In the end, good prevailed and evil had successfully been imprisoned within a black sphere known as the Darkstar.

The arc angels had entrusted this sphere with the wisest of all Earth's creatures, the eternal living elves. Respen, Eldrin and Nym, the Elvin elders, became the guardians of the Darkstar and the special scroll upon which had been written certain magic words. These words were the key to unlocking the Darkstar and releasing evil once again. For hundreds of years the Darkstar tried desperately to manipulate the elves into giving it release but the elves were resistant to such temptations.

All was well until the dawn of a new creature whose greed for power poisoned the Earth. That was the dawn of Man. The Darkstar spread its word to mankind and the will of the weak surrendered to its call.

It manipulated its new allies to seek out a powerful demon, an entity of great evil known as Baelin. It was Baelin who led the vast army of men with promises of great fortune and power. Baelin hunted down and decimated the Mythicals in his desperate search for the location of the Darkstar.

After multiple interrogations, they had found it. Baelin and his troops then marched into battle upon the Elvin castle. Aware of their fate, the Elvin elders gathered into the courtyard where they bowed on their knees and prayed to the creator.

Inside the castle, Baelin raised the Darkstar to his human army with great glory. But the old demon knew. Without the scroll, the sphere could not be opened. They tore the castle apart without success.

It was time for Baelin to deal with the Elvin elders who still knelt in the courtyard—the elders, whose prayers had not been answered by God. Instead, a spirit appeared by the name of Malshidiel, the angel of innovation and new beginnings.

Just a ghost to Elvin eyes, Angel Malshidiel spoke. It explained to the elves that it was here to take them to a parallel dimension on a world where they would be safe. It was a place much like Earth, a planet named Drakonia.

A vast black void appeared behind the angel, followed by others across the globe. Uncanny creatures from far and wide were attracted by its desirable energy. The void guided all to the place of promised sanctuary and fertile lands.

Malshidiel reclaimed the scroll from the elves and faded into the void. All Earth's creatures (now Mythicals) followed.

Not far away, Baelin observed a red dragon flying over the Elvin castle. He followed and witnessed the angel's doorway. Before the dragon could enter the void, Baelin hurled the dark sphere toward her. Its impact, like a bolt of lightning, tossed the red dragon through the black void and became absorbed into her scale-like armour. The gateways closed and all the Earth's uncanny creatures were gone—only to be remembered as tales of fiction.

Now on Drakonia, Angel Malshidiel flew over its only vast continent with wings of silver feathers reflecting the moonlight like carved crystal. Malshidiel was looking for a place to call home.

Elsewhere in Drakonia, the injured red dragon flew as high as she could. But the Darkstar had already become imbedded deep within her. Its toxic spirit would soon overtake her. Her wings seized up as she spiralled downward out of control. She then crashed into Drakonia's highest mountain peak.

Frantically, she searched for sanctuary. She crawled deep within a cave before finally collapsing on the ground. Her eyes faded into unconsciousness.

Malshidiel landed gracefully. Its dark glowing blue eyes scanned the area until it recognized its location. It was the southern tip of Drakonia's only continent. It was a narrow piece of land extending a few miles from the continent. Other than its one entrance, its perimeter was a bottomless ravine where even the vast ocean surrounding it could not ever fill it up.

Malshidiel raised its hand, and a giant castle began to take form close to the mighty ravine. Then, a thick enchanted forest about two miles wide grew instantly separating the castle's land and protecting it from the rest of the vast continent.

When the forest was complete, the angel was pleased to see a native Drakonian man walking out of the newly grown Mystique Forest. The curious mortal walked up to the angel in disbelief. This Drakonian had passed the angel's test by exiting the Mystique Forest unharmed…a difficult task indeed.

Malshidiel watched this one closely. He was different from the humans of Earth. He was different from the humans of Drakonia. He stood before Malshidiel bleeding from the forest's venomous vines. This was no ordinary venom. It was a venom that would kill all whom the forest deemed unworthy.

The Mystique Forest had embraced the Drakonian's heart and soul. Its poison became his cure while opening the locked doors within his mind. He was reborn with psychic enlightenment.

Moments later the mortal's mind began to expand. Then Malshidiel explained.

"The forest has given you a special gift. What is your name?"

"My name is Mikel Duren." replied the young man.

"You are now Lord Mikel Duren. You are a guardian knight of I, Malshidiel. Listen to me, young knight, and listen well. The forest has just opened your mind to endless possibilities. This honours you with psychic capabilities beyond your imaginable dreams. You have enhanced instinct and gut feeling, strength in body and mind and increased healing capabilities. You'll be able to feel the presence of living energy…to read minds and empathize, if so desired. You'll be able to speak telepathically to animals or to others who share this gift and, in your sleep, the strongest of you will have prophetic dreams."

Lord Duren staggered as his mind continued to expand.

"In exchange, Lord Duren, you are to protect my castle while I rest and replenish my exhausted energy."

Lord Duren gazed at the towering castle still trying to accept all that had been bestowed upon him.

"Within this castle hides a powerful scroll. This scroll holds the key to unleash all evil. You must protect this scroll."

"In time, a gifted knight will be born into this world—one chosen for me. This knight will awaken me using this talisman as the key to open my subconscious tomb. The chosen will unite with my spirit giving me the ability to walk this world in a solid form. Together we will lead the Earth's creatures to battle the Darkstar and destroy it once and for all."

Malshidiel handed Lord Duren the talisman key. The talisman key, seven inches in diameter was a circular pendant showcasing a five-pointed star called the Pentacle. Lord Duren immediately recognized that the design of the talisman offered the ability to separate in two.

The silver spirit handed the new knight a thick book titled, *The Book of Malshidiel*. Then it explained, "This holds all the knowledge to becoming a Knight of Malshidiel. It contains important spells and recipes, training for combat, survival skills and understanding the philosophies behind your power. Study this thoroughly."

Lord Duren could not help but feel the presence of the forest from whence he had emerged. A comforting aura surrounded that feeling. Malshidiel continued.

"The Mystique Forest not only protects this castle but will be the judge of others selected to join your knighthood."

"Others?" questioned Lord Duren.

"Yes, others over time will follow your footsteps and an army of our kind will help protect the castle and defend the Earth's creatures."

The young knight took in all that was bestowed upon him. Then willingly he accepted this enormous responsibility.

Malshidiel moved toward the castle. Then it looked back at the new knight feeling the Drakonian's mind opening at an unusually fast pace.

"Young knight." He shouted in an assertive voice. "Remember, with all of the power you have gained and all the knowledge you've received, penetration of a major organ or decapitation means you will die."

"Am I immortal?" asked Lord Duren hesitantly.

"Immortality is a burden you will never have to endure. However, you will age gracefully."

With that said, the angel absorbed into the castle leaving nothing but a deteriorating mist of reflective colours.

The young knight stood motionless in astonishment. His entire world had just been turned upside down or was that right side up? Within his confusion, a unicorn exited the Mystique Forest sneaking up beside the young knight of Malshidiel. Lord Duren turned his head toward him. Then the unicorn smiled and simply asked, "Hi, I'm Dirge, what's your name?"

Overwhelmed, Lord Duren turned his head away from the friendly steed and thought to himself, "Now I've seen everything."

The unicorn read his thoughts. It then simply replied, "No, this is just the beginning."

One thousand years later. . .

Chapter I
The Hope for Peace.

On a cold, windy day with dark clouds shadowing the sky, King Cronos Sarius of the Arkonian Kingdom waited impatiently at the front entrance of his castle. As the winds grew stronger, the King nestled deeper into his fur robe anxiously awaiting the arrival of Lord Hirum Drakus. He was the current leader of the Knights of Malshidiel now commonly known as the Komalsh. He was the only Ambassador of Peace the lands could offer.

As he was waiting, a young girl no older than sixteen dressed in grey robes approached the King. Removing her hood, she revealed her soft light brown skin and long, straight, snow-white hair. Freckles surrounded her dark green eyes and those eyes stared reassuringly at the King. As always, she was guiding him to ease.

"Your majesty," she smiled. "Do not fret for he will arrive. The awful weather must be delaying him."

"Oh, young Savita Cosmos," replied the King. "Such a pleasure it is to have the presence of the most powerful sorceress in all of Drakonia."

"Your words are too kind, your majesty," smiled Savita. "I have trained hard to follow my father's footsteps."

"Indeed, you have," acknowledged the King. "And what of this I hear about you following your mother's footsteps by challenging the knighthood of Malshidiel?"

"Well, your majesty, I believe in the importance of the Komalsh, and I intend to honour my mother's legacy. It would fulfill me completely to continue my belated parents' beliefs. They sacrificed their lives so that many could live in a better world."

"Well, Savita. From what I've gathered from Lord Drakus, you've become a promising young prospect. In fact, he's mentioned you as a promising future for the Komalsh."

Savita stood humbled. She stood proud.

"I am half Arkonian, your majesty, and there are no limits to our dreams or our capabilities."

The Arkonian King smiled at Savita.He stood humbled. He stood proud.

"Your majesty!" alerted a guard pointing to a carriage rolling in through the front gates.

The King smiled with anticipation. "It appears our guest has finally arrived."

A carriage, flat-black in colour and hauled by six majestic unicorns, pulled up to the castle's front entrance. The two Komalsh who steered the wagon, Lords Tobias and Pellerin, leaped down from the carriage with the finesse of cats.

Lord Tobias, an elderly knight, and Lord Pellerin, the youngest of the Komalsh, looked toward King Sarius and bowed their heads in respect. They then proceeded to open the carriage doors.

The six-foot-two, 220-pound Komalsh leader exited the carriage in a rather clumsy and wearied way. He wiped the sleep from his dark-green eyes and released a prolonged stretch. His Dosanian heritage was reflected by his dark skin which had been weathered slightly from his thirty-eight years of age. His long hair and beard, once solid brown, was now highlighted with grey and silver.

Slowly making his way up the stone stairs, his body limbered up. "Your majesty, forgive me for my tardiness but my schedule and the weather have not been accommodating."

"No forgiveness required, Lord Drakus, for your presence in this time of need is a gift in itself."

Lord Drakus held out his hand in friendship. "Please, spare me the formalities, my friend, and call me Hirum." The King returned his handshake. "You may call me Cronos."

Lord Drakus turned his attention toward the sorceress Savita and handed her the Komalsh religion's most precious book, *The Book of Malshidiel.*

****

The Book of Malshidiel was originally handed down to Lord Duren by Arc Angel Malshidiel. The tradition was then continued by handing it down to each of the Komalsh leaders over the past thousand years.

****

"You must memorize this book, Savita. The time has come for you to challenge Malshidiel's knighthood." Savita was overwhelmed with excitement. However, she could only reveal a short burst of joy. "My lord. I'm only sixteen years old. The average apprentice's mind isn't fully developed until eighteen years from birth. To challenge the Mystique Forest prematurely would surely result in failure. The consequences could lead to insanity or even death."

"Read the book, young sorceress, and you will understand, as I do, why you are, without a doubt, ready."

Savita accepted the ancient manuscript. Astonished by the immaculate condition of its thousand-year appearance and taken away by its historical significance, she grasped the book into her arms feeling its energy. Holding it away from her body, she quickly glanced through some of its ancient text.

"Among the chapter of spells, you'll find the one you had been so curious about, Savita, The spell of Gorgon."

"Really!" she squealed enthusiastically. "Do you mean Medusa's ancient spell that placed a curse on the Earth women? I have read so much about Medusa."

"Yes, I believe it's the forty-second page in," guided Lord Drakus.

Savita browsed through the pages. It was hard for her to contain her excitement for its knowledge.

"Very well then," interrupted King Sarius. "Shall we continue toward the conference room? All the rulers of Drakonia and their accompanying wizards are anxiously awaiting your arrival. World peace is within a stone's throw away, Hirum."

Lord Drakus replied with an eager nod and then turned to his two Komalsh guarding the unicorn-pulled wagon.

No words were spoken. Only thoughts were sent. "I sense a darkness near by." The Komalsh lord turned back and spoke as he glanced across the shadowed sky. "Even the weather seems edgy. Perhaps the two of you should scout the castle just to be on the safe side."

"As you wish, my lord," returned Lord Tobias, the eldest of the two.

Lord Hirum Drakus joined King Cronos Sarius and Savita Cosmos. The three entered the castle and headed toward the conference of peace.

****

Inside, the Arkonian castle was warm and dry. Being a cold wet season, the conditions indoors exemplified a modern technology in the art of the castle's construction.

During the Dragon Wars which ended six years prior, the Arkonian Castle had received an extensive amount of damage. To raise morale, King Cronos Sarius worked alongside his people and together they erected the most modern and advanced of castles. The rebuild was highly praised by Drakonian nobles.

In memoriam, the King had engraved the names of all Arkonians who had given their lives defending their kingdom during the long battles of the Dragon Wars. Savita's parents were among them.

****

"Has my niece arrived?" inquired Lord Drakus.

"Little Milita arrived ahead of schedule, my lord," answered Savita. "I believe her Dosanian guards were concerned with the weather and left earlier than arranged. She is currently in your assigned chambers, my lord."

"She means a lot to me and our future," stated Lord Drakus in a fatherly, protective kind of way.

"I understand," smiled Savita.

They made their way through the castle corridors. Before arriving at the assembly room, they walked along a narrow hallway. It was illuminated by candles with mirrors strategically placed to enhance the lighting. As they approached the end of the long hallway, Savita questioned Lord Drakus about his solution to bringing peace to the fifteen kingdoms of Drakonia.

"Well, Savita," replied the optimistic Ambassador of Peace. "I will start by proposing a barter and trade system amongst the kingdoms. This will, hopefully, begin the healing process caused by the scars of the Dragon Wars and create the beginning of trust which I feel is the most important issue in making peace."

"Unfortunately, this will only go so far," continued the lord. "You see, the Komalsh leader before me, Lady Raine Shade, had been awarded a special book from a rare and most prestigious breed of dragon, the Silverback. This volume containing dragon sorcery titled, *The Book of Dragons*, was comprised of fifteen chapters of powerful spells. After receiving this gift, Lady Shade concluded the path to peace was through dividing the book amongst the kingdoms, creating equal power and strength. This would instill fear toward attacking one another causing what I believed to be a crude and forced form of peace. Nevertheless, her idea backfired and now the greed to capture each other's chapters of power, fueled by religious conflict, has become the cause of this Drakonian war. After softening the hardened will of the kingdoms with my trade system, I will then propose that the chapters be reunited and stored safely in Castle Malshidiel."

The King entered the conversation to clear what he saw to be confusion in Savita's eyes. "You see Savita, *The Book of Dragons* is cursed."

"Or blessed," defended Lord Drakus.

"With a spell that prevents any recollection of its contents," continued the King. "It neither can be duplicated, nor could it ever be recalled even after you've just read it."

"Brilliant defence mechanism, I might add," Lord Drakus defended again.

"So once the book has been recovered it will no longer be the cause for war," finished the king.

Savita saddened while recalling her last memories of Lady Raine Shade. The lady was a loving woman who, after the death of her parents during the last days of the Dragon Wars, adopted Savita as her own. She raised her through her most complicated of times. King Cronos Sarius also shared a moment of silence for the loss of his beloved cousin. Lord Drakus could sense the sadness. Lady Raine Shade's passing was hard on all the hearts she touched.

At the end of the hallway, they arrived at a large eccentrically carved wooden door. Beyond this door awaited the leaders of the fifteen kingdoms who survived the unimaginable onslaught during the Dragon Wars. Lord Drakus straightened out his cloak. "Let us begin the long process to peace."

The guard opened the door and the three entered the conference room.

In the middle of the conference room stood a large round table surrounded by ten kings, five queens and their wizards for counsel. Around the room, walls were decorated with Arkonian artwork—their soothing colours complementing the subject of manifesting a calm environment. Statues were also on display recognizing past philosophers who had contributed to the peaceful Arkonian lifestyle. All of this was purposely portrayed adding to the effect which Lord Drakus would work so hard to achieve. Opposite the entrance doors on the far wall of the assembly room were three six-foot-high by three-foot-wide open windows. The winds blew hard beyond those windows guiding in a roll of thunderstorm clouds. They warned of a lightning storm to follow.

A mumbling debate surrounded the table. Tension had been created earlier between King Roche Mordecia, the sixty-year-old ruler of the Sinasian Kingdom and King Sayth Arrasidia, a sixty-five-year-old man who ruled the Thorenite Kingdom. Their eyes locked in a staring showdown. Their hands remained gripped to their swords. Lord Drakus could feel the tension.

****

King Roche Mordecia ruled the Sinasian peoples, a group of Drakonians that was cursed decades ago by the spell of a dark witch. This curse caused them to continuously release sexual pheromones which would arouse and seduce anyone of their sexual preference. This love curse was not controllable by its host and often the cause of conflict for more than obvious reasons.

King Sayth Arrasidia ruled the Thorenite peoples who were a battle-driven breed of Drakonians. They lived and died by the sword. Diplomacy was not one of their stronger attributes, but they understood the importance of unity and respected the Komalsh for initiating peace.

Earlier, King Arrasidia's wizard, Saydeez, had stepped too close to King Mordecia and inhaled his cursed pheromone. This sent Saydeez into an uncontrollable sexual frenzy as she seduced King Mordecia before the eyes of all the prestigious guests. This humiliated the Thorenite King provoking the warrior inside him. All had subsided by the time King Cronos, Lord Drakus and Savita stood before the table. Thankfully, the commotion had now wound down to nothing more than the exchanging of dirty looks.

****

The room fell uncomfortably silent. All eyes around the table focused on the Komalsh leader. Lord Drakus had prepared a speech. He was experienced in public relations. He never liked it.

"I would like to begin this conference of peace by thanking each one of you for your participation in these crucial times. I would also like to take the time to give special appreciation to King Sarius for allowing us the use of his castle for these proceedings."

All the attendants of the meeting bowed their heads toward King Sarius with respect and gratitude—all, that is, except King Dag Kaloun.

****

King Dag Kaloun was a 25-year-old king who weighed just over 160 pounds. He was not a large man by any means but made up for it with his ability to lead in combat. His tactical strategies were unequaled, but to the rest of Drakonia he was better known for his ability to complicate, especially when it came to a unifying Drakonia on peaceful terms. He was a miserable man who didn't care for anything outside his kingdom walls but, as disliked as he was by all other kingdoms, the Drake Kingdom possessed the largest army in Drakonia. The Drake Kingdom was an ally most necessary. If the peace conference were to succeed, King Kaloun and the Drake peoples were a much-needed piece of the puzzle.

Lord Drakus knew this. He didn't like it.

****

King Dag Kaloun stood motionless. His body language displayed volumes of distaste toward his fellow colleagues. Even his wizard, Sesh, sat there grooming his fingernails oblivious to his surroundings.

The King of Arkonia and host of the proceedings rose from his throne. "I will spare the pleasantries, my fellow leaders, and get to the matter at hand. As you all know, before our kingdoms were formed, the Komalsh maintained peace throughout the lands and protected the villages where our peoples lived. A thousand years ago the Komalsh protected the Drakonians by keeping the most vicious predators, the Nomaydens, away from their villages."

****

The time of the Nomaydens was only remembered in history books. Yet to this day, the name, "Nomayden" was enough to send a shiver down any historian's spine. They were ruthless humanoid creatures who fed on flesh. They stood four feet tall with black scaly skin. They had bat-like ears and cat-like eyes. Their claws and teeth were razor sharp and they preferred to eat their prey alive.

Lord Duren, the first Komalsh leader and sole Drakonian ever to meet the Arc Angel Malshidiel, spent most his life protecting Drakonians from these native creatures. In the end, Lord Duren imprisoned the Nomaydens within a deep cave in the largest mountain of Drakonia. With the help of the Elvin elders, he placed an enchanted door over the entrance to the cave imprisoning these viscous predators. To this day the entrance is known as the Door of Duren.

****

"Do you recall," continued the King of Arkonia, "not six years ago when the courageous Komalsh leader, Lord Radik Shade, ended the Dragon Wars sacrificing his own life in the process?"

The King paused for a moment with a sad expression toward Savita Cosmos and then continued, "and do not forget the others who died with him."

Savita bowed her head in memory of the loss of her beloved parents who fought and died alongside Lord Radik Shade in that final dragon war.

"The Komalsh were created to prevent the Darkstar's awakening. The Darkstar is the prison of great evil! The key to unleashing it is written on a scroll—a scroll entrusted to the Komalsh by the Arc Angel Malshidiel!"

The King paused, allowing his audience to process his words.

"You see, my fellow colleagues, I address you today with my faith in the Komalsh and their ability to lead us in the direction of a new world order by appointing Lord Drakus as Ambassador of Peace and empowering the Komalsh to legally police and protect our new way of life."

The King gazed around the table with eyes widened in promise. Then, respectfully, he returned to his seat. The overlapping of conversations filled the room with incoherent babbling until order was regained by King Sarius. He next insisted that questions be directed to Lord Drakus for all to hear.

The first to speak up was the Tarnian leader, King Ses Thel, a good-hearted, 34-year-old fellow who had always sided with the Komalsh.

"Lord Drakus," he addressed. "If we were to accept you as our ambassador, what would be your plan for attaining peace?"

Drakus rose from his seat and glanced across the table toward his prestigious audience. Then he answered the question like he'd rehearsed so many times the night before. "In order to attain peace, we must first become friends. We need to create trust."

Nods of agreement surrounded the table.

“My first initiative is to propose a barter and trade system amongst the kingdoms.”

Savita rose from her seat and handed out the written documents Lord Drakus had prepared earlier.

“Within these documents are rules, regulations, and laws of our new trade system. We’ll start with planned events where two kingdoms, policed by the Komalsh, will meet in either castle to negotiate trade. Opening our doors to one another will create the opportunity to share similarities and differences among our cultures. Eventually, we hope to surpass our differences and develop a common respect for one another. Our short-term goal will be unescorted trade of medicines, food, technologies and so forth. The list of goods and services to be traded will expand based on the needs of our peoples.”

Lord Drakus glanced across his intrigued audience. He then concluded his speech. “A unified Drakonia will benefit all it’s people.”

On the last word spoken by Lord Drakus, the Sykanian wizard, Malores Barnett, interrupted with outrage.

****

Malores was a mystically unpredictable 25-year-old wizard whose complexion was pale and haggard. His hair was black as night. His eyes were haunted with guilt. It didn’t take a psychic to see he hid many skeletons in his closet.

****

“This is the road to weakness your majesty! We are the most advanced of all kingdoms and could never benefit from such an outrageous unification!”

The Sykanian King, Hyram Hexity, raised his voice toward his undisciplined wizard. "You will shut your mouth, wizard! You have spoken out of line too many times as of late! Your greed for power has poisoned your mind and it's making me sick to my stomach. I'll do what's best for my people, wizard!"

The King of Sykania turned his disappointed gaze into a wrinkled smile of acceptance. "You have my approval, Lord Drakus." Then returned his glare to his wizard, Malores, who cowered back down into his seat. Malores cast a bitter look of disappointment toward his king and anger festered within him. The Sykanian wizard glared at the old fool with his fists clenched while muttering to himself in disapproval.

While King Hexity spoke his approval of the new trade system, King Dag Kaloun of the Drake Kingdom also built up an uncontrollable urge to speak his frustrated thoughts. With little self control he exploded verbally, "What is wrong with you people!?" he shouted nastily while rising from his seat.

King Kaloun proceeded to pace around the circular table waving his hands about while lecturing to the other rulers. "Give your heads a shake!" he continued by pointing to Malores. "The dead-looking wizard is right!" Malores took a mirror off the table and looked at his reflection. "Dead looking?"

"What will happen next? I'll tell you what will happen!" continued King Kaloun. "At the end of all this the Komalsh will be all powerful with complete control over our kingdoms. No individual group of Drakonians should ever be entrusted with that much power nor that much responsibility!"

"He's right!" interrupted Malores while placing his mirror in his tunic. "Next thing you know, they'll be wanting us to return our chapters from, *The Book of Dragons*!"

"With all due respect," interrupted King Kalem Turek.

****

King Kalem Turek was a rather large man who ruled the Dosanian kingdom. The Dosanians were a race of dark-skinned peoples who brought justice and order to their region. They are a noble race and have been allies to the Komalsh since the birth of their kingdom. Dosania was also the birthplace of Lord Drakus.

****

The agitated King Turek spoke in a deep voice. "We, the Dosanian people, have great faith in the Komalsh. They are not only blood brothers to my people, but they're also a creation of Malshidiel, an arc angel sent from God. They are advanced Drakonians born, bread and trained to uphold peace and order. What more do you want?" finished King Turek with a tone of confusion.

King Mordecia of the cursed Sinasian peoples rose from his chair and, with calm respect, questioned King Turek's statement. "What you are talking about, King Turek, is a thousand-year-old bedtime story that was used to help put our children to sleep."

Seizing the moment, King Kaloun intervened. "That's right! It's not real! For all we know, the Komalsh made this all up to manipulate us…to control us!"

The dead-looking wizard, Malores, also added his opinion. "Really! Has anyone else but a Komalsh read this, Book of Malshidiel? For all we know, it's a book of empty pages…or even worse, a book of dark magic!"

King Hexity slammed his fist on the table. "Not another word, wizard!" The King pointed toward Malores' cowering face. "As soon as we return to Sykania, we will be re-examining your role as wizard."

Malores sat back silent and stewed in his disfavour.

King Dag Kaloun laughed at King Hexity. "You shouldn't dismiss him, you fool! You are a pathetic old man. The dead-looking wizard is far wiser than you!"

King Hexity tapped the pommel of his sword. "I'm wise enough to know how easy it would be to gut you like a pig."

King Dag Kaloun sat back in his chair with distaste. "A death threat at a peace conference. How fitting. Just as fitting as Lord Drakus here and his so-called connection through God's angel, Malshidiel, an angel who couldn't even prevent Lord Drakus' own wife from dying during child labour!"

Lord Drakus' patience collapsed. With an aggressive thrust from his hand, he telekinetically jolted King Dag Kaloun's chair out from under him. The chair shattered against the wall. Dag fell hard to the floor.

Quickly regaining his footing, King Dag Kaloun shouted accusingly to the Komalsh leader. "Did you do that!?"

Lord Drakus shrugged his shoulders.

"This is what you represent Lord Drakus? A misuse of power!" The humiliated king turned to the Drakonian leaders. "I, for one, do not agree with any of this!"

King Sarius stood before the table shaking his head while rubbing his eyes. He had offered his castle with great hope for a peaceful resolution—one which seemed to be deteriorating rapidly. But he would not give up. Using his prestige, he asked the others for their confidence.

"Fellow Kings and Queens of Drakonia, I ask for your support in these matters, and I would like to propose a vote giving embassy power of peace to Lord Drakus and the Komalsh."

The room buzzed with mumbled conversations. Most were convinced. Some needed persuasion. King Dag Kaloun of the Drake Kingdom despised it.

"Keep in mind, my prestigious guests, for this proposal to succeed we will need the confidence of all our kingdoms." declared King Sarius.

Inside, the room fell silent. Outside, a thunderstorm grew violent.

The Arkonian King bowed his head. His stomach filled with butterflies. Then he broke the silence by asking the inevitable question, "Who is not in favour of Lord Drakus becoming our Ambassador of Peace?"

Without restraint, King Dag Kaloun raised his hand ever so gently and answered, "The Drake Kingdom is not in favour."

He was followed by King Mordecia who raised his hand as the next speaker. "The Sinasian kingdom is not quite convinced. I believe these accords to be in order and have no doubt the Komalsh could police such a treaty. However, Lord Drakus has shown me by his undisciplined outburst that perhaps he's not the best suited for the role as ambassador."

Lord Drakus grimaced in frustration as the other leaders agreed to his assessment.

Queen Denham of the Konasian kingdom, whose red hair and fair skin was common among her people, questioned the Komalsh ambitions. “Lord Drakus, other than the Dragon Wars, the Komalsh have historically distanced themselves from Drakonian affairs. Lady Raine Shade first attempted Drakonian unification years ago. However, after her passing the Komalsh had become stagnant toward unification. Why the sudden interest in rehashing peace?”

“Well…,” answered Lord Drakus.

A loud crack of thunder echoed from outside the three windows. In that moment, the conference room doors simultaneously burst open and two wounded Arkonian soldiers staggered in.

“Your majesty!” shouted one struggling for air. “Lords Tobias and Pellerin have been murdered by two Komalsh assailants!”

“Komalsh!?” King Sarius sounded confused.

“It appears so, your majesty.” answered the Arkonian soldier. “They were both robed in Komalsh attire.”

Lightning lit up the three windows and thunder raged with vengeance.

“My King,” announced the guard, “we have them cornered in the south end of the castle.”

“My private library?” queried the King.

“Yes, your majesty.”

Without haste Lord Drakus ran out of the conference room and headed toward the King’s library. Trailing close behind him followed Savita Cosmos and King Kalem Turek of Dosania.

King Sarius ordered his kingdom on alert and then, accompanied by his two guards, left the conference room with their swords in hand.

Chapter II
The Three Windows.

Outside of the castle, bolts of lightning lit up the night sky and thunder ravaged the heavens. Back inside, Lord Drakus hurried through a maze of hallways undeterred by the storms violent echo. On approach to a staircase leading to the King's library, Lord Drakus drew out his two-handed Komalsh sword.

****

This weapon was an elegantly crafted sword with a long blade curved slightly upward towards the point. Halfway down the top of the blade to the hilt, a sharp serrated edge was fashioned.

The hilt of a Komalsh sword bore a design unique to each Komalsh. The blades of a Komalsh sword were forged from the strongest metal in Drakonia known as durenthium, a precious metal only found in the Mystique Forest. The durenthium sword has become the weapon of choice by the Komalsh since the day Lord Duren discovered it a thousand years ago.

****

Lord Drakus' sword glimmered from the hallway candles as he, Savita and King Turek ran up the last set of stairs and down the hallway toward the King's private library.

Halfway down the hallway, the walls were stained red, and blood had puddled on the floor. Savita covered her mouth, disheartened at seeing the lifeless corpse of Lord Pellerin. She knelt before the youngest of the Komalsh and guided his face toward hers. His eyes were vacant. Saddened, she looked up to Lord Drakus.

"He's dead, my lord."

Savita proceeded to inspect the body thoroughly. "It appears he had been stabbed through the heart. His death was quick," she observed assuredly.

King Turek placed one hand on Lord Drakus' shoulder. With his other hand, he pointed toward the library's entrance.

At the end of the hallway guarding the entrance stood a Komalsh with his sword pointed to the ground. Blood dripped down his blade and puddled on the floor. Hidden behind a black, hooded cloak the assailant waited patiently. Lord Drakus stormed down the hallway. His sword drawn firm within his grip. He stopped ahead of the faceless Komalsh and stared angrily into the bitter essence of his opponent.

Kings Turek and Sarius, Savita and the two Arkonian guards joined Lord Drakus with their weapons drawn. The mystery man gently removed his hood.

"Lord Siris?" drowned Drakus in confusion.

****

Lord Cretes Siris stood a couple of inches shorter than Drakus and about 30 pounds lighter, but this meant nothing. Lord Siris knew, as well as everyone there, even at the age of 30, Siris was renowned as the greatest swordsman in all Drakonia.

He was the Komalsh swordsmanship instructor, and he had learned most of his teachings with the Komalsh elite. Recognized as a popular hero among the Komalsh, Siris was easily identified by his laughter and arrogant humour.

He is the best and he knows it.

****

"I don't want to fight you, Lord Siris," spoke Drakus.

"I wouldn't want to fight me either!" replied Siris following his words with his erratic, cackling laugh—a laugh whose comical sounds normally spread joy to all within an ear's length away.

But not this time. The laughter was there but he wasn't. Siris had changed. Drakus could not only sense this but could also see it within his eyes. He looked edgy and disturbed.

"Let me spare you your confusion," explained Siris. "Lord Demonis and I come only to borrow a scroll. No one else here needs to die." A shorter less enthusiastic cackle exited his lungs.

"Lord Demonis is here?" Savita was bewildered.

"That's right, little sorceress," cackled Siris demonically.

"He's gone mad my lord," remarked Savita.

"King Sarius, what are they looking for? What is so special in that library?" demanded Lord Drakus.

"Just historical books." The King paused a moment and then recalled, "and the scroll of music for the Dragon's Flute. I kept it after the Dragon Wars as a keepsake. I figured with the actual flute buried deep within the rubble of the Avila Mountain range, the scroll would be harmless."

"It is harmless," assured Savita.

Drakus stared at Siris. "What has happened to you? Do you no longer value the Komalsh code?"

"I have a new code. A new order. One that doesn't involve wasting my time as a servant like you!" Siris was infuriated.

"Then we are enemies, old friend," scolded Drakus.

Siris' smile grew vast revealing three long scars down the side of his face.

****

These scars were compliments of a griffin he was gallantly trying to save. A griffin is an Earth creature that possesses the body of a lion and the head and wings of an eagle. Siris saved that creature's life.

Lord Cretes Siris was of Sykanian descent. He was a renowned Komalsh hero and mentor. The person who stood before them was only the shell of that man. Everything good about him seemed to be gone.

****

"You can not defeat me, Lord Drakus. You are aware of this, are you not?" cackled Siris. "Even if you could defeat me with swords, the door behind me is locked tight!" Siris raised his sword for combat. Without hesitation, Lord Drakus ran toward him. Just before their blades could clash, Drakus tossed his sword in front of Siris' feet. Siris watched the sword fall to the ground in disbelief. Then the Komalsh leader kicked his booted foot up into Siris' jaw and knocked him through the library door. Siris hit the library floor unconscious.

Savita knelt before Siris and checked his vital signs. "It appears you broke his jaw, Lord Drakus. He's unconscious."

Lord Drakus telekinetically summoned his sword to return to his hand. "King Sarius, take your guards and barricade the entrance. You are no help here."

"Savita."

"Yes, my lord."

"Find something to restrain Lord Siris' hands. His enhanced healing ability will awaken him shortly."

While Savita tied Siris' wrists, his broken jaw was already resetting into place.

Lord Drakus entered the library with King Kalem Turek and Savita following close behind.

Inside, the room was dark and quiet. Bolts of lightning flashed outside the library windows. Loud pounding thunder echoed through the castle and the storm's powerful winds whistled through the rafters.

"Sorceress," whispered Drakus. "We need light."

Savita raised her hands above her head with her palms facing upwards. Her body started to illuminate brighter and brighter. As she reached her full capacity, a blue flash burst from her glowing body and absorbed into all the inanimate objects within the room. The blue flash had momentarily blinded them but there was now enough light to see.

The three spread out along the room searching for Lord Demonis. Lord Drakus could now feel his presence. With a hand gesture he instructed Savita to follow along the right side of the room.

Although their vision had been sufficiently restored, some areas remained darkened in shadow.

Savita stumbled upon a person laying lifeless on the floor. Cautiously, she searched the body and discovered it had been decapitated. Savita could only assume it was Lord Tobias, the elderly of the two murdered Komalsh.
Savita vaguely recognized the silhouette of a person standing in the shadowed corner of the library. She quietly hid beneath a rectangular table. Holding her breath, she glanced over the table to take a closer look at the shadowed figure. There, on the table before her, displayed the head of Lord Tobias. The startled Savita staggered backward and knocked over a stack of books on the table behind her.

The silhouette hiding in the shadows laughed in a deep tone that would send shivers down the Grim Reaper's spine. Lord Drakus and King Turek cornered the shadowed man with their swords drawn. Recognizing the intruder, Lord Drakus began to negotiate. He commanded, "Surrender now Cable. No more blood needs to be spilled."

****

Lord Cable Demonis stood six foot four inches tall and weighed approximately 240 pounds. His skin was golden brown, his hair darker than night. This was the norm of all citizens of the Crassord Kingdom. His facial bone structure was most unusual with broad cheek bones and a blockish chin.

Demonis and Drakus were close friends. They graduated from Olemeeze together. Cable was also an outstanding member of the Komalsh and a natural leader.

Something had changed.

****

Lord Cable Demonis stood motionless with a lackadaisical expression. Drakus could sense the same dark spirit he had felt in Siris.

Demonis slowly recognized Lord Drakus. He seemed to lack focus and showed signs of confusion. The sight of Lord Drakus appeared to agitate him, and his expression turned to anger.

Drakus recognized the scroll in Lord Demonis' hand. It was the score of the music for the Dragon's Flute. He had found what he was looking for. "But why?" he pondered. Demonis placed the scroll within his robes and drew out his sword. With rage igniting within him, he warned. "I've created a new order, Lord Drakus—one which would rather die then serve Malshidiel!"

King Turek attacked Lord Demonis head on.

"Wait!" warned Drakus.

Lord Demonis reached out his empty hand levitating King Turek into the air. With a flick of his fingers, he threw Turek against the stone wall knocking him out cold.

Savita's hands lit up with an electrical current absorbed from the static of the lightning storm. Her sorceress eyes glowed white as she released the energy directing it toward Demonis. Demonis focused on the table displaying the severed head. He telekinetically tossed it toward Savita. Savita's electrical current left her hands and blew apart the table tossing her backward into a bookcase.

Lord Drakus confronted his old friend and ally. The two circled one another with their swords drawn while staring at each other coldly.

"What's happened to you Cable? You've changed!"

"Changed for the better, Hirum. I am no longer sheltered by the ignorant shadow of Malshidiel. I've been enlightened to the truth!"

"Your mind is poisoned, Cable! You've taken the lives of our own kind. You are a murderer!"

Drakus swung his sword down onto Demonis' blade and pressed him against the wall. "You will pay for your crimes," glared the Komalsh leader.

"Maybe, old friend, but not today." Demonis head butted Drakus momentarily blinding him. Then using his telekinesis, he slid a table across the room sweeping Drakus off his feet and knocking him to the ground.

Getting back to her feet, Savita reached into her robes and removed the book Drakus had lent her earlier, *The Book of Malshidiel*. With urgency, she scrolled through the chapter of spells.

Lord Drakus regained his footing. He raised his sword and blocked a downward attack from Demonis' blade. Drakus tackled his old friend to the ground. He got on top of him and punched him in the nose. The blow from his fist blinded Demonis' eyes with tears. Drakus raised his sword with two hands and thrusted down toward his opponent's heart.

Demonis, blinded by sight but not in mind, felt the blade thrusting down. With his free hand he slapped the side of the blade guiding it into the floor beside him. With his knee, Demonis lifted Drakus over his head and tossed him aside. They both got up and continued to clash swords violently. With a twist of the wrist Drakus separated Demonis from his sword and forced him hard to the ground. With his blade pressed against his foe's heart, he commanded him one more time: "Surrender, Cable, all is lost!"

Looking up from, *The Book of Malshidiel*, Savita stopped to admire her hero, Lord Drakus, as he stood over the defeated Lord Demonis. Staying alert her eyes also noticed Lord Siris. Freed from his bonds, he ran at Drakus' back with his sword held high.

"Lord Drakus, look out!"

Drakus turned around and collided swords with Siris. In moments, Siris' superior skill became apparent as he dominated the Komalsh leader. His offensive attacks enhanced by his psychic abilities proved to be dominant in comparison. Lord Drakus did everything he could to defend himself.

"Savita! I don't know how much longer I can hold on!" warned Drakus.

Demonis rose from the floor and joined Siris' offence. Lord Drakus was now fighting two of his elite knights.

Savita scrolled through the spell section until she found page 42—the page with The Gorgon spell and the curse placed on Medusa. With thunder crashing outside and lightning illuminating the room Savita shouted to Drakus, "The spell of Gorgon?"

"Just do it!" yelled Drakus who had been forced into a corner.

Demonis stabbed Drakus in the shoulder. Siris punched him hard sending him to the ground. Separated from his sword, Lord Drakus was defeated.

"Savita!"

Thunder roared through the castle and lightning lit the sky. Savita stared at Demonis while delivering the mantra spell. "Alla mestra fausohl grana. Alla mestra fausohl grana," her voice becoming increasingly louder with each syllable spoken.

Another roar of thunder filled the castle halls. Savita's mesmeric voice forced Lord Demonis to lower his sword and stare back into her glowing eyes.

"What are you doing, Cable?" asked Siris, perplexed.

Moments after eye contact, a flash of light filled the room and Demonis turned to stone.

Awoken from his head wound, King Kalem Turek rose from the ground and threw his dagger at Siris. With a swing of his sword, Siris slapped it to the ground. Savita drew her sword and joined the fight. Siris retreated to the library window. King Sarius and his Arkonian knights poured in from the hallway.

"Surrender, Lord Siris!" demanded Drakus, summoning his sword to his hand.

Siris stepped back getting closer to the window.

"We are on the castles highest peak, Lord Siris," reminded King Sarius. "If you jump out the window, you'll only land in a moat that surrounds it. A moat inhabited by Karnagins."

****

The Karnagin was a crocodile-like lizard whose average length is about 15 feet. Some have been recorded to be up to 20 feet long. Each of its four webbed feet have needle-like claws covered in tiny little thread-like hairs. Once their claws penetrate their victim's flesh, the hairs release a nerve toxin that is meant to subdue their prey. The use of the venom allows the Karnagin to take down prey twice their size. With their razor-like teeth and carnivore-like instincts, these heartless predators have taken many Drakonians as victims. Even the Komalsh keep their distance.

****

Lord Drakus lowered his sword. "Surrender now Cretes. It's over."

Lord Cretes Siris smiled. He gazed at *the Book of Malshidiel* within Savita's grasp and then swiftly turned back to greet Drakus' eyes. "Old man, this war has just begun."

Lord Siris reached out his hand and telekinetically summoned *The Book of Malshidiel* from Savita's grip to his own. With his trademark cackle, he leaped out the window and disappeared into the darkness.

Drakus ran to the window as forks of lightning lit the night sky. In those intermittent bursts of light, he watched as his old ally fell.

Siris, still smiling, waved insanely while plummeting to his demise. At the falls end, he hit the moat with a violent splash. The water exploded into a frenzy as a pod of Karnagins swam in for the kill. Moments later the moat returned to stillness.

"He committed suicide?" King Turek struggled for words.

"Lord Drakus!" interrupted Savita in astonishment. "You had better come see this."

Thunder echoed loudly throughout the castle.

"What is it Savita?"

"Feel the statue, my lord."

Drakus placed his hand on Demonis' stone imprisonment. It was warmed with life. He could feel Demonis as though he were reaching out to him. Bewildered by the sorcery, Drakus consulted with Savita.

"Can anyone with our enhanced perception feel his spirit?"

"It appears so," answered Savita.

"Then he must be hidden until we understand what happened to both him and Cretes."

Lord Drakus went back to the window where Lord Cretes Siris' had chosen to surrender to his demise. "You leave tomorrow on your first mission, Savita. I will inform you of the details come sunrise." Drakus paused in thought. "Savita, when you return from this mission you will start your journey into the Mystique Forest. You will become a Komalsh."

"Understood Lord Drakus," acknowledged Savita.

King Kalem Turek patted her on the back. "Congratulations, little one!" He spoke joyfully. "Your parents would've been proud!"

"Thank you, Kalem. But I lost, *The Book of Malshidiel*." Savita stared into her empty hands. "Lord Cretes Siris stripped it from me and now it is gone."

King Sarius looked out the window to Lord Cretes Siris' watery grave. "There's no way anyone could have survived. Even with the healing ability your kind shares, Hirum, the impact from this height would have left him unconscious long enough to be devoured."

Lord Hirum Drakus closed his eyes and searched the area with his psychic gift but never found any trace of Siris. Savita stared timidly at Drakus. "I'm truly sorry for not being able to hold onto the book, my lord."

"It is what it is, Savita. There are other copies of it within Castle Malshidiel. I was only hoping you could read the original text before entering the Mystique Forest."

"Then why the effort to take it from me?" she wondered.

"This wasn't premeditated, Savita. Lord Siris did, however, know the value of the original text. It holds knowledge not shared in the copies—knowledge only shared among the Komalsh leaders."

"Then why share it with me?"

"A question best answered another time."

Savita exhausted herself with guilt. "I feel I've let you down, my lord."

Drakus gazed at Savita intensely. "I feel there's a greater threat upon us. I need you to focus on the now."

"Yes, Lord Drakus," surrendered Savita.

Two guards entered the room escorting King Ses Thel, ruler of the Tarnian Kingdom. His expression frozen in disbelief as he addressed Lord Drakus.

"You must hurry to the conference room! King Hirum Hexity of the Sykanian Kingdom has been assassinated!"

A crowd had gathered in the conference room around King Hexity's body. Lord Drakus forced his way through and knelt beside the deceased. Both Savita and King Turek ushered the crowd back allowing space for his investigation.

The Sykanian wizard, Malores Barnett, was already kneeling by his majesty's side. He slowly placed his hand over King Hirum Hexity's face and gently closed his soulless eyes.

Lord Drakus searched the body. With brute strength, he removed a long arrow protruding from the King's chest and studied it momentarily. "This arrow tip is made from durenthium. This is the same metal used by the Komalsh. However, this design is quite different from ours and unique to one individual." He looked up to his audience and spoke a name not heard since he was young. "Fenka Rek."

"Who is that?" asked Savita.

"He's an assassin and a mercenary—a murderer really but not an ordinary man. His dark deeds are written in the history books as far back as the Lord Duren era. No one to this day really knows who or what he is."

Lord Drakus scanned the room for clues while continuing his history lesson. "Most of the history books from Lord Duren's time were burnt in a fire. What little we know of Fenka Rek is mostly urban legend. He is a phantom to most and the Grim Reaper to those who have crossed his path."

"It is certain whoever hired him must have paid handsomely. Somebody really wanted King Hexity dead." Drakus rose from his knee and continued the investigation. "Where was he sitting when this occurred?"

Malores pointed to the seat and proceeded to sit in the direction he was in. After a moment of speculation Lord Drakus proceeded to explain. "The trajectory of the arrow lines up from those three windows."

Drakus walked over and looked out the centre window. A similar arrow was embedded outside the stone wall. Attached to it was a long rope reaching into the dark depths below. Vision was limited until another magnificent fork of lightning stretched across the sky illuminating the ground below. There, mounted on an undead horse with its front legs thrusting toward the howling storm was Fenka Rek. He stared back up to Lord Drakus and when the bright flash of lightning faded into darkness, so did the prestigious assassin.

The always problematic King Dag Kaloun was outraged. His wizard, Sesh, tried desperately to calm him but Dag simply pushed him aside. "Any one of us could have been the target!" shouted Kaloun. "These Komalsh are too busy killing one another! How can we discuss peace under these circumstances? How could we trust them to police our peaceful treaty?"

Kaloun pointed to Drakus with intentions of ridicule. "You all saw Lord Drakus use his psychic abilities forcing me to the floor when all I did was speak my point of view! Should an Ambassador of Peace be allowed to oppress those with an opinion?"

King Kaloun waited a moment for others to process his words and then continued his rant. "What's to stop the Komalsh from using their powers to read our minds? Invading our own private lives?"

"It's against the Komalsh code," answered Savita calmly.

King Dag Kaloun walked up to Savita with his hands held high. "So is killing one another but I don't see that stopping them!"

Turning to the rest of the assembly, King Kaloun finished his speech with reverence and respect. “I, for one, will boycott these proceedings.”

The Arkonian King Cronos Sarius slammed his gavel on the round table. Its sharp echo captured everyone’s attention. “My fellow leaders, I propose we set these meetings aside until the Komalsh do a full investigation of these horrific crimes.”

The room filled with mumbles of debate. The Sykanian wizard, Malores Barnett, gathered himself to his feet with feelings of despair as he addressed his prestigious audience.

“The King is dead. Therefore, the Sykanian peoples must withdraw from these meetings until a new ruler is crowned. With the recent and tragic deaths of his wife and two sons, I will be forced to take on the leadership duties and responsibilities of our peoples until a new leader is crowned. Now, if you will excuse me, I have a funeral for which to prepare.”

Malores left the conference room escorted by his two appointed Arkonian guards. Drakus observed the Sykanian wizard exit the conference room thinking to himself that something was not right.

Savita recognized Drakus’ concern and joined his gaze at the dead-looking wizard. “My lord, the possibilities are endless. Without facts, we have only speculation.”

“Indeed. However, with speculation we can narrow down the possibilities, rule out the improbable and allow the facts to reveal themselves,” returned the determined Drakus.

“As always, you show leadership during a crisis, Lord Drakus. But who do you believe is behind the assassination and is it linked to Lord Demonis?”

“I don’t believe they are linked, Savita.”

“Explain, my lord.”

"This assassination was to prevent the success of the peace talks. The fallen Komalsh were here for the flute's music, and they were trying to steal it unnoticed. An assassination would have caused unwanted attention."

"Or it was a diversion?" corrected Savita. "Lords Demonis and Siris were the cause of us leaving the room for the assassination to take place."

"Perhaps it was two birds with one stone," agreed King Turek.

"If that's the case," feared Drakus, "and our fallen Komalsh are linked with Fenka Rek, then we have plenty to fear."

Drakus rubbed his wearied eyes. "I had ordered Lords Tobias and Pellerin to search the castle, Savita. I felt something earlier this day. Evidently, it was Lords Siris and Demonis' attempt to hide from my detection. Lords Tobias and Pellerin must have caught the fallen Komalsh in the act and died by their swords. Their blood is on my hands."

****

Lord Drakus had lost many close friends throughout the years, including his wife and child during a complicated childbirth. He had grown accustomed to only three stages of grief. He mourned for their loss. He blamed himself. Then he moved on quickly. Lord Drakus was all about the now.

****

"I still believe someone else hired Fenka Rek, and my suspicions start with Malores."

"Have you thought to read his mind," asked Savita cautiously.

"As inviting as that sounds, I will not break the Komalsh code." Drakus pondered a moment. "I must rest for now, Savita. I suggest you do the same. You have a big day ahead of you tomorrow."

"Yes, my lord," she spoke but she was without conviction.

"Are you okay, Savita?"

"Yes. I'm fine."

"Stay focused on the now, young one. The more you dwell on the past, the more you'll miss the present. Goodnight, everyone."

As the last person left the conference room, Savita remained behind. She stood by the three windows staring off into the darkness. The lightning and thunder had subsided, and the rains began to pour. She lowered her head and with one hand covering her moistened eyes she started to cry. "I'm so sorry I failed you, mother, and father. I lost the book. I lost it!" She closed her eyes and gasped for air. "I wasn't good enough and now even Lord Drakus must have doubts about me."

With her second hand helping the first she split the tears of failure down both her cheeks. Amid those tears she could hear a deep voice of hope speak out from the darkness.

"Savita."

A short stocky figure walked behind her and placed his hand gently on her shoulder. "Oh, young Savita," spoke King Turek. "Calm your thoughts, child. You are, indeed, your own worst enemy."

King Turek placed his arm around her. Looking into her dampened eyes, he continued to reassure. "I knew your parents well, and yes, they made their share of mistakes along the way. But they always made right where they had wronged. Just like you." Turek pointed his stubby finger and poked it into Savita's shoulder. The young sorceress gazed back into Turek's eyes as a daughter would her father.

"That's right!" continued Turek. "Your parents, especially your father, went through countless mistakes and follies before they were ever regarded as legends. But they always got back on their feet and made twice the right they had wronged."

Tears streamed down Savita's face as she hugged the King. His kind words stirred deeply within her.

"From the day you were born, your parents were so proud of you. Seriously! It sickened me how much they loved you. They wouldn't shut up about you—honestly. Savi crawled today. Savi walked today. Savi puked all over me today."

Savita giggled as the King's words lightened her heart.

"You see," continued King Turek, "your parents adored you. They were and forever will be proud of you."

"Thank you, Kalem, but I lost, *The Book of Malshidiel*. I'm such a loser. How could I ever be a hero like my parents?"

"Nothing wrong with being a loser," replied King Turek.

"What do you mean 'nothing wrong?"

"Listen here, Savita. There three different types of people in this world. There are winners, losers, and quitters. A winner endures from their mistakes. A loser makes mistakes but learns from them until one day they become the winner. A quitter, however, was too afraid to ever have tried. You see, Savita, before your parents were legends, they were losers. But never were they quitters."

"I understand," said Savita.

"Your parents loved you and that is why they sacrificed their lives. It was so you and countless others would live better. You see, they lost but they came out as winners. You are their reward."

Savita squeezed Turek with all her love. The King turned a dark shade of red. "Ah, the women love me!"

The two laughed together.

"Now then, how do you feel?" asked the King of Dosania with utmost concern.

Savita looked up to King Turek with her smile and glistening eyes. "Thank you for being there for me."

"I'll always be here for you, Savita." He grinned affectionately.

"Your father was a Dosanian. Your mother Arkonian. That is why your skin is not as dark as mine. You're the best parts of two different kingdoms yet, life has never been easy on you."

"Tell me about it," groaned Savita. "I never had any friends being different. They called me a half breed and countless other names."

"And now look at you. Drakonia's most promising sorceress and soon to be a Komalsh. The first in history to achieve both," said Turek with a smile. "I suspect you will have many more achievements as time moves forward."

Savita was humbled. "My father taught me to channel my anger into my work and studies. Evidently, I have a lot of anger."

The two laughed together. Then King Turek released Savita from his hug. "Feel any better?"

"I do, thank you."

"No thanks required," smiled King Turek while stretching his ageing body. "We will see you in the morning."

King Kalem Turek left the conference room.

Alone in the dark the young sorceress gazed out the window. Staring off into the stormy skies, she whispered a promise to her parents. “I, Savita Cosmos, will make the wrong become right.”

Pausing for a moment as if she were waiting for a reply that never came, Savita turned away from the three windows and retired to her chambers.

Chapter III
Children of the Komalsh.

In the early morning hour, birds sang to the rising sun, flowers reached for nourishing rays and the sweet, moistened air left little trace of last night's storm. Outside Savita's window the loud scream of frightened horses woke her from a deep slumber. Rising from her bed, Savita approached the open window. Her naked body bathed in the suns rays as she stretched her arms out to embrace the heat.

From her window, she could see a handful of anxious horses linked to a Sykanian carriage. Arkonians were frantically assisting a rather flustered Malores Barnett who showed little respect toward their hospitality. The wizard looked to be in a real hurry.

Savita dressed into her robes and left the room to search for Lord Drakus. In the hallway, she was confronted by a servant carrying a tray of food.

"My lady. The King's chef has prepared you a special breakfast, indeed."

With little interest, Savita shrugged her off but on the second glance hunger's temptation took over. "That smells delightful. What might it be?"

"Well, my lady, as showing good faith toward the Komalsh, King Sarius has joined the Dosanian Kingdom with a peaceful trade system among some of the Earth creatures. This breakfast consists of pork and chicken eggs—Earth animals farmed by the Kobolds. I insist you try a bite, my lady. I assure you that's all it will take." Savita bit into the morsel and was astonished by its flavor.

"As you may be aware, my lady, that although some Earth creatures are accepted in today's world, they keep tight amongst themselves. A hidden bunch they are. They do not trust people and I don't blame them. There's much ignorance in this world," said the servant nodding her head.

"This is true," agreed Savita as they continued down the hallway.

"The word is the Komalsh protect all the Earth creatures."

"Yes, it's their prime directive," confirmed Savita. "I hear this kind of food is served in great proportions at Castle Malshidiel," spoke the busybody servant hoping to gain more informed gossip.

"Indeed," replied Savita, "but I am not a Komalsh as of yet and they are quite tight when it comes to any information about their protected castle."

The servant peered around to look for any ears that dropped. "Yeah, I suppose so," she whispered in secrecy. "I hear even the Komalsh students train outside the castle in a small village called Olemeeze."

"Yes, and for good reason, too," replied Savita. "Not all students pass. It is one thing to graduate the Olemeeze School of Discipline and Training and yet another to pass the final test."

The servant escorted Savita to the castle's front exit and turned to her while asking with fear-filled curiosity, "Is it true about the final test? The Mystique Forest?" The servant glanced around again for eavesdroppers. "I'm told it's haunted by something unimaginable."

Savita stared uneasily into the servant's eyes and grasped her arm firmly. "I'm not a Komalsh," she whispered. Then left to stroll the castle grounds.

Outside the sun felt warm upon Savita's face. She closed her eyes and with a huge breath of fresh air rejuvenated her senses. Savita walked further out into the kingdom's yard. There were wagons coming and going through the wall barrier's main entrance. Guards and citizens scattered about crowding the Arkonian streets. Savita wandered aimlessly in search of Lord Drakus.

During her wander, the young sorceress came across an angered elderly woman wrenching on a young boy's arm. Quickly attending the commotion, Savita realized that young boy was Nyte, her adopted son.

****

Nyte Shade was a seven-year-old, blonde-haired Arkonian boy. He was the offspring of the famous Komalsh leaders Lord Radik Shade who lost his life ending the Dragon Wars and Lady Raine Shade who first initiated the peace talks. Shortly before his mother's passing, she had entrusted Savita with the raising of her boy. Savita did not take this task lightly.

****

"What is going on here?" Savita confronted his aggressor like any proud mother would.

"This little pest was caught urinating in the church's holy water!" shouted the disgusted elderly lady. "He and those little hellions over there have been taunting our church ever since their arrival!"

The elderly lady pointed 30 yards away to her two young terrors. Nyte's closest friends, Kris, and Terex, who, too, looked quite guilty. The lady turned three shades of red before she finally exploded aloud. "You're all going to burn in hell! Do you hear me? Burn in hell!"

"Who's going to burn in hell?" Lord Drakus calmly interrupted while comforting his belly from a monstrous breakfast.

"Am I glad to see you, Lord Drakus!" cried the elderly lady. "The Komalsh are God fearing worshippers, are they not?"

"Well, yes, and no," he waffled.

"This little pest has insulted God—insulted the creator himself!" she explained owning her vigilance. "He must pay the price and be punished!"

"What is your name ma'am?" Smiled Drakus pleasantly.

"My name is Ethyl." Replied the upset elderly woman.

Taking a breath to summon his patience, Lord Drakus proceeded to explain. "The Komalsh are believers of spiritualism, ma'am, not religion."

****

Lord Drakus wore a circular pendant around his neck showcasing a five-pointed star—The Pentacle. Its star points protruded through the radius of the circle.

Lord Duren had received this talisman from the Arc Angel Malshidiel a thousand years ago. This talisman was handed down from leader to leader over generations.

The stars five points represent the four elements: matter, energy, water, and air. The dominant upper point represents the fifth element: The Universe. The circle around the star represents life and the space between signifies the spirit world.

****

"What's the difference?" pouted Ethyl.

"The difference is," answered Drakus with composure, "our faith lies within the Universe. It is a spiritualistic energy which binds all life." Lord Drakus patted Nyte on the head and directed his smile infectiously upon the young child.

"If this boy doesn't change his evil way and follow the word of God, he will suffer eternal damnation in hell. He must be saved. He must be taught," instructed Ethyl.

"This confuses me," replied Drakus while rubbing his chin. "What God would create a lesser being and then threaten it with total damnation if that being does not only worship it, but does not worship it properly? And what god needs to be worshipped? To worship is to cater to the ego. Only mankind feels the need to be worshipped."

Lord Drakus paused a moment to gather his calm once again. He went on to say, "Our belief is to respect life, my lady. This can only be achieved by respecting all its creations equally. We are forces of energy within all life and death is only a transformation—a crossover to the other side. The universe is holistic."

Nyte stood awed by Drakus' words until an evil glare from Ethyl chased him behind Savita's back. Lord Drakus smiled to him with reassurance.

"What kind of rubbish is this?" retaliated Ethyl. "There can be only one religion for one God and that is us. We are the Klutafish. God himself chose us to tell the world of their evil ways. We must change everyone over to our side so we can all dance in the heavens rather than burn in hell!"

"There's no reaching her." Savita was clearly irritated by what she just heard.

"How do you know your religion is the right one?" challenged Drakus.

"It's not hard to read the book of god," rasped Ethyl.

"But don't you all read a different variation of the same book?" he questioned. "Let me show you something about human nature, ma'am." Lord Drakus pulled up his sleeve revealing his right forearm. On it was an outlined tattoo of an angel.

"What color is the angel's skin?" he asked.

Ethyl stared at it then answered, "Why, it's the color of your skin. It's black."

"That's right. It's black because my skin is black, I'm Dosanian. What color would the angel's skin be if this same tattoo were on your arm?"

"Well white of course."

"That's because your skin is white. And if this tattoo was on a Crassord citizen. Then what color would the angel be?"

"Golden brown." She cringed as she answered Drakus in a feeble attempt to hide the racial discrimination on her part.

"The point I'm trying to achieve is that it is human nature to perceive God in your own image. The same goes for the religion you practice. You weren't chosen by God. Your religion was chosen for you due to the geographical location where you were born."

"But the bible says we were created in his image," argued Ethyl, "so, God is white."

"Was your bible referring to our physical bodies? God is not a physical entity. Therefore, he has never had a body. Or could it be that your bible was referring to our soul's image?"

Ethyl gave Drakus a momentary look of confusion which was quickly followed by a glare that could send Earth creatures fearing for their lives. "Careful what you say, Lord Drakus. God is always watching."

"Well, that is something upon which we can agree." Lord Drakus smiled. "However, we like to phrase it as, you are never alone; god is always there."

Ethyl struggled to understand Drakus' positive demeaner particularly because of his inferior understanding of God's will. In response, she chose to regurgitate the words that were recorded in her memory since she was a child. "God will burn you in hell if you don't follow his rules. Only those who go to church will learn the path to heaven."

"We Komalsh do not believe in heaven or hell in an afterlife sense," explained Lord Drakus. "To us heaven and hell is right here right now. It's called life and it's what you make it. A person who follows a negative life lives a living hell. The ones who live a positive life transpire a life of heaven. Every soul goes to the same place when we cross over. Some just take longer getting there."

"That's the most ridiculous thing I've ever heard!" scowled Ethyl. "We follow the book of God to learn how to properly behave and condition ourselves. We earn our place in heaven. The ten commandments explain to us the difference between right and wrong."

"Everyone in the universe knows the difference between right and wrong," stated the lord.

"Young Nyte here didn't seem to know, did he? Perhaps the lack of time in church," winced Ethyl.

"He will ma'am," affirmed Drakus. "I assure you he'll be punished for his disrespect of your sacred water."

"Thank you, Lord Drakus," replied Ethyl satisfied with Nyte's conviction. She left while giving young Nyte Shade a final scowling gaze.

Savita smiled pleasantly to Ethyl as she walked away. "I don't like her, Lord Drakus."

"You don't have to."

"It's people like that who turned me off regarding religion."

"Do not use her or people like that as an example to define any religion. There are a lot of good people who follow different beliefs and who, in their hearts, utterly understand the meaning of God."

"I still don't like her."

"You still don't have to."

"What do you think, Nyte? Should I have turned her into a toad?" humoured Savita.

Nyte giggled a child's laugh. Then shrugged his shoulders hesitantly.

"Lord Drakus," queried Savita, "the bible from which Drakonian religions derive…well, I was told it came from Earth's future. If so, how did it get here?"

Drakus rubbed his eyes with one hand. "It's complicated, Savita."

Looking off into the distance, Lord Drakus could see that his unicorn driven carriage had arrived. King Sarius had gratefully donated two of his most trusted soldiers to replace the late Lords Tobias and Pellerin. Their bodies were placed in caskets and carefully strapped down to the back of the Komalsh wagon.

A six-year-old Dosanian girl with red hair exited the unicorn driven carriage and, with the innocence of a child, she skipped up to Lord Drakus.

"Milita, my niece. Come over here and give me a hug."

Without hesitation the little girl leaped into his arms. He almost toppled as she squeezed him about the shoulders as hard as she could with her cheerful little giggle and a big warm smile.

****

Little Mili's parents were killed in a robbery when she was just a baby. Their carriage was attacked by petty thieves. Her mother had hidden her safely within a compartment in the carriage. Her father's throat was slit, and he was left for dead. Her mother was raped and then brutally murdered. Both of her parent's lives were taken over a handful of gold coins and jewelry.

Lord Drakus found his sister's baby while tearing the wagon apart for clues. He adopted her as his own. He loves her dearly.

****

Lord Drakus looked toward Nyte Shade intently. He needed Nyte's attention to ensure the wishes of the elderly lady were carried out. "Now then, is this who I think it is, Savita?"

Savita went behind Nyte and placed her arms around him proudly. "Yes, this is my adopted son, Lord Drakus. His name is Nyte."

"I know who he is," said Lord Drakus. "He is the son of Radik and Raine."

Nyte held his hand out to Drakus. "Hello sir."

Drakus went down on one knee to compensate for his vast height and shook Nyte's hand firmly.

"You look so much like your mother," commented Drakus seeking eye contact with Nyte.

Nyte did not lift his eyes but stared at the ground. "I'm sorry for what I did to the holy water."

Drakus rose to his feet and placed his hand on his shoulder. "The apology should not be given to me young man. I would like you to apologize to the people whom you disrespected."

Nyte displayed awkward body movements. He could not bring himself to look Lord Drakus in the face.

"Young Shade, everyone is entitled to their own belief. We are all born into this world. That is our common ground. You must take advantage of this and learn from all walks of life. The more you understand the views of others, the more you'll find our differences aren't our spiritual beliefs. Our differences derive from the inability to empathize and understand another's. When you have walked in the shoes of those whom you've ridiculed, you'll find your ridicule was mistaken for ignorance. To be a Komalsh son, you need a worldly insight—one that will evolve as the shape of society does. But most importantly, you need to choose to be a Komalsh."

Drakus interrupted his pearls of wisdom with a soft laughter. "I must admit though, pissing in the holy water…that is kind of funny." Grabbing Nyte's shoulder, he roared an uncontrollable laugh. "Could you imagine the looks on their faces when they splashed it on their cheeks!"

"This isn't helping," interrupted Savita.

"Yes, you're probably right," agreed Drakus regaining his poise. "Just be yourself son. You're the only one that's going to be any good at it."

Nyte looked up to Lord Drakus with admiration. He wanted to be just like him.

"Next time, Nyte," continued Drakus, "I'd like you to show a tad more respect for other people's beliefs for two reasons. One—religion helps people cope with their very existence. It gives them direction and hope. And two—when you interfere with a person's direction and hope, you will feel their wrath."

"I understand, sir. I'll say sorry," promised Nyte.

Lord Drakus smiled reminiscently. "Your mother and father were my mentors, Nyte. They were also the dearest of friends to me."

Nyte stood silent. He never knew his father and was only two when he last saw his mother. All he could recall about her were faint images.

Drakus broke that silence patting him on the shoulder. “Now then, it was a pleasure to meet you, Nyte.”

“You, too, sir.”

“Savita, come walk with me,” instructed the Komalsh lord.

“I’ll be right back, Nyte. Sit tight and stay out of trouble!” Savita stared assertively at Nyte while walking off with Lord Drakus.

After they left, little Milita Drakus skipped up to Nyte Shade. She was dressed in white and tan coloured robes. Her straight red hair fell in long tresses down her back. Her skin was dark just like the skin of the Dosanians. Her smile was innocently contagious, and her eyes appeared as if to be filled with wonder. Without fear nor hesitation she introduced herself.

“Hello. My name is Milita.” She stood shuffling the flowers she had gathered that morning. “Well, do you have a name?” she pestered.

“Yes, I do, my name is Nyte.” He spoke hesitantly.

The six-your-old princess smiled and, with no intent for secrecy, told her story. “The other day my uncle Hirum and I…you know…Lord Drakus…” she bragged, “we were walking together along the outer edge of the Mystique Forest when a vine reached out and pulled me in. Uncle Hirum was scared. He searched all day for me! When I woke up, I found myself on the ground, so I got up and yelled for my uncle. That’s when a baby unicorn named Stormy led me out of the forest to a big castle.”

“I know this forest,” said Nyte. “I’m going to the school of Olemeeze where I’ll study to become a Komalsh.”

“Yeah, me, too,” explained Milita. “Except I have to study at Castle Malshidiel.”

“You can’t go there till you are finished school!” explained Nyte.

"Well, that's what I was trying to tell you. Uncle Hirum said the vines that pulled me in had a venom which gives special gifts to the Komalsh."

Nyte stood there astonished.

"My uncle was very scared because I was way too young to have my mind changed. Something bad could have happened. I could've even died! But instead, I felt very woozy for a long time and now I feel okay. My uncle says I'm special. He says I'll be alright and soon will be the youngest Komalsh in all of history!"

"Your parents must be proud of you." Said Nyte. Milita look saddened. "Uncle Hirum started looking after me when my parents passed away. He promised me he would be there for me forever."

Nyte's facial expression sank with sadness.

"What's wrong?" asked Milita.

Nyte looked into her green eyes and with a bitter tone replied. "My parents are gone, too. My mother left me a note saying she'll love me forever. But she never returned. Nothing lasts forever."

Milita put a half smile on her face then countered, "Love lasts forever, silly."

A tear slowly made its way down Nyte's cheek only to be stopped and absorbed by Milita's handful of freshly picked flowers. After carefully wiping the tears away, she revealed a gift. "I have something I want to give you, Nyte. Before my mother and father went to live with God, I would get sad at times. So, my uncle Hirum gave me a special gift—a magical ring that will conjure smiles and happiness."

Milita reached around her neck and removed a silver chain holding a ring. "Listen, Nyte. This enchanted ring is made from durenthium and if you hold it tightly enough, it will make you feel happy and put a smile on your face." Milita handed Nyte her uncle's gift.

Nyte placed it into his hand and squeezed it with all his might. Moments passed and nothing happened.

"It's not working. I don't feel very happy."

Milita smiled at Nyte, "Sometimes you need to let it warm up a bit."

Nyte paused for a second then a smile stretched across his face. He realized the ring had no magic. His smile was conjured by the trickery of Milita.

"I told you it would work!" giggled Milita. "Feeling better yet, silly?"

Nyte handed her back the ring.

Milita refused it. "I don't need it anymore, Nyte. I want you to keep it."

"Thank you, Milita."

"Don't worry about it, Nyte. That ring has made us both happy today. Perhaps it will bring you a smile when you most need it."

From a distance Lord Drakus hollered for Milita to return to the wagon and prepare for her journey.

"Where are you going?" asked Nyte. He wondered if he would ever see her again.

"I'm going to Castle Malshidiel. I'll remain at the castle where I'll study and learn how to use my psychic power wisely." Milita spoke her words with confidence. "Without the training, I could accidentally hurt someone, and I don't want that to happen. That would be awful!"

"Well, it was nice to meet you." The words were hard to express. Nyte was saddened to have made a friend who was now leaving to take a different path.

Milita reached over and kissed him on the cheek. She leaned toward his ear and whispered, "Don't worry, we'll meet again…I've dreamt it."

Milita winked at him without anyone seeing her. Then she skipped off to the carriage.

Holding the ring close Nyte waved to Milita as the unicorn driven carriage left the kingdom.

Savita returned to Nyte and started adjusting the wrinkles from his clothes. "Hey, my little man, it's time for me to leave."

Behind Savita, Lord Demonis' stone imprisonment was carefully being loaded onto a wagon by five Komalsh. These knights were summoned telepathically by Lord Drakus the night before—a rather common way for the Komalsh to communicate.

"I will return shortly," continued Savita. "For the time being, I've asked Terex's mother to escort you to Olemeeze. There, you'll start your first day of school and train to become a Komalsh."

Nyte stood saddened.

Savita placed her hands on his shoulders with sorrowed eyes. "I'm sorry. I realize you wanted me to be there for your first day."

"I wish my mom was alive."

Savita wrapped her arms around him. Nyte pulled away from her grip…then ran toward Terex and his mother, Ayesha, who just arrived.

While the three walked away, Ayesha turned back to see the unsettled look on Savita's face. Understanding what she must be going through, Ayesha smiled with a look of reassurance and then continued onward holding both boys' hands.

Savita held an empty feeling in her gut. She felt for that boy dearly.

****

Nyte's mother, Lady Raine Shade, adopted Savita after her parents died in the final battle of the Dragon Wars. They fought bravely alongside Nyte's father, Lord Radik Shade, who too died in that battle.

Savita had promised to do the same for Nyte—to become the adopted parent Raine was to her. But it was far from easy. The boy was crushed. It was clear that the boy felt disconnected and unloved.

****

"Are you ready to go, Sorceress?" asked Lord Dunlam, the appointed captain of the Komalsh mission party.

Savita entered the unicorn driven wagon. As they started on their journey, she looked back to the crowd where Nyte had disappeared. Her heart ached for her little man.

"Stay focused on the now," whispered Lord Drakus' voice in her mind.

Lord Demonis' stone prison was priority now. She could feel him reaching out to her. Prioritising her thoughts, Savita's parents entered her mind. She recalled King Turek's words. Then quietly she whispered, "Time to be the winner."

Ten years later…

Chapter IV
Olemeeze.

It was well past nightfall. Under the stars, the village of Olemeeze lay protected behind stone walls. As the hour approached midnight, most of the teachers and students had gone to seek their silent slumbers.

At the stroke of twelve, a cloaked knight riding a white unicorn approached the skookum entrance doors of Olemeeze. Using only her mind, the enormous doors began to open.

Upon entry past the doors, the mysterious visitor was confronted by two of the Komalsh elders, Lord, and Lady Dunlam.

****

Lord and Lady Dunlam were two gracefully aging knights who had chosen at a young age to devote their lives to not only the Komalsh but to each other. Even after retirement, they continued their roles as teachers in the great Komalsh School of Olemeeze.

****

"Welcome back, Lady Cosmos!" greeted Lord Bossel Dunlam before the stranger could reveal herself.

"Thank you, Bossel," addressed Savita lowering her hood. "It's good to be back."

Lady Savita Cosmos is widely known and respected to be one of Drakonia's most gifted sorceresses, however, Lord and Lady Dunlam have always been more impressed with her tenacity. At the young age of twenty-six, Savita has already earned her place as a high-ranking member of the Komalsh.

"What about me?" neighed her exhausted unicorn between gasps of air.

"Well, top of the evening to you too, Jinx," smiled Lady Elasia Dunlam whose enormous grin seemed to stretch out her ageing wrinkles.

"What in the Book of Dragon's are you doing arriving here so late? That's so unlike you, dear," said Elasia in a tone of worry.

"I ran into some minor difficulties going over the trade details with that troublesome King Dag Kaloun. Once again, he seems to be creating chaos out of every detail concerning these new peace talks. I swear, sometimes I'd like to wrap my hands around his scrawny little neck and put him out of his misery."

"Now, now, Savita," calmed Bossel. "Dag and the Drake Kingdom have been problematic long before you became important to the Komalsh. It would only be proper etiquette for you to let me strangle him first. I am the oldest active Komalsh you know."

Elasia rolled her eyes. "You're only two months older than me, you old coot!"

Savita's gentle laughter in response to the humour of her elders was overpowered by a sudden yawn. "Please, my friends, our travels have made my faithful companion and I wearied. If you don't mind, we'd like to retire for the night."

"Oh, but of course, Lady Cosmos. Allow me to escort you to your cottage," offered Elasia. "Bossel dear, why don't you find Jinx a place to lay in the stable. She looks exhausted."

"Absolutely," he replied happily.

"Thank you, kindly," neighed the tired steed.

Arm in arm, Elasia escorted Savita into the sanctuary of Olemeeze. With a mere thought she effortlessly closed the entrance doors behind them.

“You will rest your weary head, my dear, and tomorrow will bring another day,” smiled Lady Dunlam.

In the early sunrise, Savita awoke to the song of birds. Rested and renewed she rose from her cot and prepared for the day ahead.

Once outside her dwelling, Savita strolled down the main road of Olemeeze. Along this road nestled small cabins that were home to the school’s students and their families when needed. Four more blocks of roads and dwellings wrapped around this one in a tightly knit community. Being the main road through town, all the excitement took place here. Drakonians and Earth creatures alike were setting up shops selling and trading jewelry, clothing, and other hand-crafted items. As the morning grew warmer, the road filled with Olemeeze society. Savita walked through the centre of town greeting merchants as she made her way to an ancient two-story school building. She was on a mission.

****

The School of Olemeeze was an educational facility founded by Lord Duren and the Elves a thousand years ago. It’s gothic structure of Elvin design gave it a unique appearance compared to the blander Drakonian architecture.

After several hopefuls failed the challenge of traversing the Mystique Forest, the Elves decided to train the hopefuls from a young age. Their educational programs demanded a more disciplined and sophisticated Komalsh—one who was prepared for what lay hidden within the Mystique Forest.

The school had two floors. The upper floor was used for classrooms divided not by age but by groups of students who were evaluated to be of equal learning ability. The bottom floor was an arena with various training facilities and weapons used for combat and survival exercises. Lord and Lady Dunlam ran this school with the help of volunteer Elvin teachers. The rigorous preparation provided at Olemeeze combined the need to develop both physical and the mental stamina.

****

Savita approached the stone carved steps leading to the entrance of this historical building. As she stood there, she was in awe at its gothic structural design. She could not help but reminisce about her short time there as a student. A happy voice interrupted her thoughts. Savita looked to see Nyte Shade running to greet her. She noticed how grown up he seemed, especially while dressed in his dark green robes issued to each Olemeeze student. Surely, he was almost six feet tall now! His dirty-blonde hair fell long past his shoulders and his darkened blue eyes gave him a depth of maturity.

Nyte wrapped his arms around Savita. "I'm so glad to see you."

"Well, I couldn't miss your last day at school, little man."

Nyte looked at her, unimpressed. Almost 18 years old and she still had to call him little man.

"Lady Dunlam tells me you have the highest grades in your class," exclaimed Savita proudly.

Nyte smiled while downsizing it. "Well, I share it with a student named Kelar."

"Kelar who?" asked Savita curiously.

"Just Kelar. As a baby he was found on the doorstep of a Tarnian family with a note that read 'Kelar,' so his adopted family left it at that."

"Interesting," commented Savita. "The Kelasian people were the only recorded race of Drakonian who went by a singular name."

"Kelasians were also wiped out during the end of the Dragon Wars Savita," reminded Nyte.

"Yes indeed. However, it is possible he is of Kelasian descent."

"Perhaps, or perhaps the parents just didn't want to be found," countered Nyte. "Nevertheless, Kelar is at the top of the class with me."

"What of your friend, Terex? Terex and his mother Ayesha?" asked Savita. "How is he doing in school?"

"Well, Savita, he is passing. Not big on the books but excels at the combat and survival training so the teachers are closing a blind eye to some of his grades and are graduating him."

"I don't agree with that decision," muttered Savita. The very thought flustered her. "A Komalsh is nothing without an education. To prevent a fight is far more the Komalsh way then ending a fight."

"Don't underestimate him, Savita. He has a big heart and that is something no book could never teach."

"Is he still getting himself into trouble then?" inquired Savita.

Nyte chuckled in defeat. "I don't think he'd have it any other way."

"Indeed." Savita smiled.

"How about his darling mother? I owe her so much for all those times she took care of you while I was away."

With a saddened look Nyte told her the news. "Terex's mother passed away. She caught her death shortly after the winter solstice. I'm sorry you hadn't heard but it was a brutal winter. Terex hasn't been the same since."

"This is a tragedy, Nyte. I'm so sorry I wasn't here for him."

"It's okay. I never left his side," declared Nyte.

Savita placed her arm around him. "You are a great friend, Nyte."

"Yeah, well, he would have done the same for me. That's just what friends do."

Savita and Nyte entered the school building and went to the combat training room. Inside Lord Bossel Dunlam and his seven graduates stopped their sword-training exercises to greet their guest.

"Did you sleep well, Lady Cosmos?" inquired Bossel.

"Indeed, I did," She replied, feeling replenished.

"Excellent! We were just about to review defensive manoeuvres when it had occurred to me that I have only seven graduates and not eight. What brilliant excuse will you be sharing with us today master, Nyte Shade?"

"Well…," stuttered Nyte.

"Go on son. I do look forward to these."

****

Lord Bossel Dunlam never raised his voice at anyone. This year's grad class was a giant test of his patience. Their immaturity and undisciplined behavior raised Bossel's blood pressure on many occasions…but he never raised his voice.

In Bossel's professional opinion, none of these students were worthy of graduation.

****

"I misplaced this ring, sir." Nyte revealed a silver chain from around his neck holding a durenthium ring. It was the one he had received as a gift so long ago. It had a special history about it in that it was nicknamed the not so magical ring of smiles.

Lord Dunlam stood expressionless. He had become immune to his students and their justifications for being unavailable. "That is definitely up there among your most preeminent of excuses, Nyte. However, Terex's excuse of being unable to find matching socks still reigns first." Terex raised his fists over his head and with a smile nodded his victory.

"Do you realize, young Shade, that your mere trinket is insignificant to the knowledge taught here?"
Nyte raised his hand. "With all due respect, I am top of the class."

"Tied with me." reminded Kelar smirking in the background.
Bossel overheard and laughed. "Take a good look around you! That's not a difficult task to achieve!" The words were meant to slice the air harshly without raising his sword. Bossel held his hands behind his back and paced in front of the eight grad students. "Forty-two students started this year and you eight are all that graduated." Bossel's pace came to an end as he stared through his students with disappointment. "Graduating this class does not guarantee you'll pass the Mystique Forest. That can only be achieved by a disciplined mind. The minds that stand before me now couldn't manage their way through a corn field." Bossel was unimpressed with the lot of them, and he wanted them to know that their lacklustre attitude was a disappointment to him.

The old teacher rubbed his temples as if to remove a migraine headache. "Listen to me, class, and listen well. You are all great warriors and some of you are even smart but all of you lack discipline. I fear the forest will show no mercy on any of you."

"That's quite the pep talk, sir," chuckled Nyte.

Bossel scowled. "If it were my way, Nyte, I wouldn't allow any of you to graduate to the next level."

The room fell silent.

"But it's not up to me," sighed the teacher. "You see, for some unexplainable reason, Lord Drakus has the audacity to allow all eight of you misfits to challenge the Mystique Forest immediately."

The sound of relief circulated through the graduates. "I wouldn't get too excited! Your lackadaisical impression of discipline will make your stay in the forest quite unpleasant!"

The room fell silent again.

"The forest will eat you from the inside out! It will crawl within your mind and regurgitate your very identity!" The students' faces dropped. Savita hurried over to Bossel and patted him on the back while giving the students a reassuring look that everything will be fine. The class sighed with relief.

"Now, now, Lord Dunlam. No need to spread fear…that's the forest's job!"

The students' faces dropped again.

"Just look at these students, Savita. They won't survive the Mystique Forest. I honestly can't believe they survived school!" expounded Bossel.

"Lord Drakus has his reasons. He is our wise Komalsh leader," reassured Savita.

"He's never been a wise one," reminded Bossel.

Savita went before the class. Her gentle smile was good at defusing Bossel's unpleasant pep talk. Pleased by the reaction she received from the students; she addressed the class. "Hello students, for those who don't recognize me, I am Lady Savita Cosmos."

The class chuckled. Everyone knows of Savita the sorceress.

"I am a Komalsh and a sorceress. I have pledged my allegiance to Castle Malshidiel. I have sworn to protect the Earth creatures and the scroll to the Darkstar. It's a lifelong commitment but I assure you it is rewarding."

"Now then, of course I'm familiar with my adopted son Nyte Shade." Savita searched through the students. "I do know his two good friends Terex Gungnir…"

****

Terex Gungnir was from the Thorenite Kingdom—a brown-haired Caucasian man who stood six-foot-two and weighed 220 pounds. What he lacked in learning from books, he made up for in combat. He was strong and fearless.

Raised with honour and bravery, Terex was quickly recruited by Lord Drakus who foresaw his value when he was just a child.

****

"And Kris Tarius."

Kris smiled bashfully. "Hi Savita."

****

Like Nyte, Kris Tarius was from the Tarnian Kingdom. He was a six foot, 195-pound man with golden brown skin, brown eyes, and short, curly, brown hair. He was headstrong yet wise to the world. He read much philosophy, and it reflected in his everyday life. His loyalty to the Komalsh was only outmatched by his love for family. He was Nyte Shade's first and oldest friend…another student discovered by Lord Drakus.

****

"However," continued Savita, "I don't recognize the rest of you. Please feel free to introduce yourselves."
The first student stepped forward. "Hey there! My name is Trayke Basa and I'm at your disposal, my lady."

****

Trayke Basa was born of the Palianite Kingdom. A tanned, handsome, Caucasian man who stood six-foot-tall and weighed 160 pounds. He had long ravishing light-brown, shoulder-length hair and dreamy, blue eyes. His Achilles heel? Spirits and women. One might say he was an easy-going social butterfly whose sharp tongue and magnetic personality lured the ladies. Trayke was the pretty boy of the bunch.

****

Trayke introduced another student. "This is my best friend."

"Hi, I am Arias. It's an honour to meet you, Lady Cosmos."

****

Arias Jackyle was from the Konasias Kingdom. He was a tall, red-headed Caucasian man who stood six foot five and weighed 210 pounds. From weapons to instruments Arias could build or fix anything. Where most would see colours, he saw structure and design. He was an easy-going, good-natured person who only saw the positive in every situation. Diplomacy was his currency for getting along with everyone.

Both Trayke Basa and Arias Jackyle were also chosen by Lord Drakus.

****

A five foot ten, 150-pound woman forced her way to the front and reached out her hand. She had long shiny black hair and golden-brown skin. She smiled at Savita with admiration. "I'm Neasha Sentrix, my lady. I'm from the Fylosian Kingdom."

Savita held out her hand and returned the smile. "The only woman in this year's grad class? It must have been difficult. I'm so proud of you, Neasha."

"I can hold my own, Lady Cosmos."

Behind Neasha stood two men who showed little interest. One ventured closer displaying an arrogant smile. He stood five foot ten with a solid build of 170 pounds. He had very pale skin and his almost completely white hair was short.

"My name is Kolos Dreken, my lady." He spoke haughtily. "I am from the great Drake Kingdom."

Savita sighed as she pictured the problematic Drake King, Dag Kaloun.

"Well then," concluded Savita, "that must make you Kelar."

Savita stepped past Kolos and approached the remaining student. A Caucasian man with long black hair who stood six feet in height and weighed 180 pounds. Kelar stood broad-shouldered with a serious demeanor. Savita held out her hand in friendship.

Kelar shook hers firmly. "You're as beautiful as you are legendary, my lady." He raised her hand toward his lips and gently kissed.

Neasha Sentrix seethed with jealousy. She wrapped her arms around Kelar from behind and sensually kissed the back of his neck.

"This is a classroom not a brothel," reminded Bossel.

"Yeah, you two, go get a room," taunted Arias.

Then the rest of the students fell into a host of distasteful gestures by making humping and kissing sounds while laughing hysterically.

Savita found their humour immature yet uplifting. She took it to be a positive carelessness with the effect of being contagious for one another. In mere days, these students will challenge the Mystique Forest. Nervousness etched their faces, but these students weren't afraid. Their unconditional love for one another strengthened them as a pack—a friendship pack. Savita could understand why Lord Drakus put so much faith in this year's class. Individually, they seemed challenged but together they had potential.

Lord Bossel Dunlam thought differently.

"Lord Dunlam," commanded Savita, "I'm going to need your two most promising students to escort me to the Arkonian castle. They are to represent the future of the Komalsh at a time most needed. This will be the first peace conference with all Drakonia's kingdoms to take place in ten years. I cannot express the importance of this meeting nor the importance of proper representation."

Bossel never hesitated to choose whom he deemed fit. "Nyte, Kelar. You will join Lady Cosmos."

The two students were thrilled. A field trip was always welcomed…anything to get out of Olemeeze. Intrigued by recent rumours, Bossel queried, "I heard the Sykanian Kingdom will be revealing their new king at this peace conference, Lady Cosmos."

"New king!" humoured Savita. "He's been in power for almost five years."

"Disturbing, indeed, Lady Cosmos. This kind of secrecy can lead to no good."

"I agree, Lord Dunlam…Nyte, Kelar come with me. Is there something else bothering you, Lord Dunlam?"

Savita detected that something was off.

Bossel looked around at the students who were listening. He telepathically hailed Savita. "We need to talk before you leave."

Savita replied to Bossel in thought. "I'll see you out front after class."

Bossel returned his attention to the class. "Remember students, the rest of you are to finish with your homework. Tomorrow we will be on a field trip to the remains of the Kelasian Dynasty, the last kingdom destroyed during the Dragon Wars. This will be the last of your historical lessons."

"Lastly, your final test of challenging the Mystique Forest is scheduled a few days after. Are there any questions?"

The class went silent again.

"Good, class dismissed."

Nyte and Kelar followed Savita up the stairs to say her goodbyes to Lady Elasia Dunlam who was currently teaching a class for students between the ages of eight and ten.

When Savita entered the classroom, the students lit up with the presence of stardom. She was quite popular amongst the students of Olemeeze.

"Well, hello there, Lady Cosmos. Did you sleep well, dear?" asked Elasia with her contagious smile.

"Yes, I did. Thank you, Lady Dunlam, for your hospitality. I hope I'm not disturbing your class."

"Not at all dear. I'm sure the class would love your company."

Smiles and nods circulated the room.

"Besides, I was just about to read the final historical chapter to the Dragon's Flute."

All the children's eyes turned back to Elasia widened with curiosity.

"But since you are here, Lady Cosmos, perhaps you could read it for me."

"I'll do more then read it, Lady Dunlam." Savita turned to Nyte and Kelar. "Why don't you two go pack your horses. I'll meet you at the stable shortly."

Kelar and Nyte left eagerly with excitement etched to their faces. A road trip away from the school of Olemeeze was welcomed by any student.

"Hello class. My name is Lady Savita Cosmos. With your permissions I would like to enter your minds in order to share an important time in our Komalsh history."

The class, eager with anticipation, agreed to the terms and gathered around in a circle seated cross-legged on the floor. Lady Dunlam participated too.

"I want you all to close your eyes." Savita spoke softly. "Relax and focus only on my voice."

The students obeyed.

Behind the darkness of each child's eyelids, Savita brought light. In the cluster behind each child's thoughts, she brought silence. In the depths of each child's consciousness, she created an illusion of where the historical event transpired. They were now in a dream world guided by Savita.

The students could smell the summer air. They could feel the gentle breeze. Each one stared at their hands in disbelief. Although their bodies were cross-legged on the floor, their minds were where Savita had led them.

****

It is said that when you are in this state of mind, if you die, so does your physical form.

****

Savita's soft voice entered the minds of her listeners. "It was 18 years ago. The Dragon Wars had raged for years. By this time countless lives and entire kingdoms had been wiped from existence by these viscous dragon attacks."

"Nobody understood why the dragons started this war. Prior to this there had been the odd encounter but nothing of this magnitude."

"One night in his dream vision, it was discovered by the leader of the Komalsh, Lord Radik Shade, who had orchestrated these dragon attacks. It was an apprentice warlock named Kaylitan who possessed a powerful instrument known as the Dragon's Flute. Lord Shade's prophetic dream led them to Kaylitan, and a dragon named Trisadez."

****

Trisadez was a three-headed dragon who was banished from the dragon homeland of Jirasab for acts of hatred against its own kind. One head breathed fire. One breathed ice. The third lightning.

****

"Trisadez swore an oath to protect Kaylitan in exchange for his revenge against the dragons of Jirasab. Together with the Dragon's Flute, they rained havoc on Drakonia."

Savita created an illusion of the Dragon's Flute hovering before each child.

"Carved from a dragon's talon and cursed by sorcery, the enchanted flute possessed the ability to control dragon kind."

Savita's illusion created an agitated flock of flying dragons circling the students above. Anger and darkness filled the skies as dragons howled with hatred.

Savita went on, "Thee who play the flute control the dragons."

From the mist, a cloaked warlock appeared playing the Dragon's Flute.

"To this day no one knows how Kaylitan found this enchanted instrument."

Savita's illusion replicated the location where the final battle ended the Dragon Wars. The land formation transformed into a place on a desolated mountain. The children were awed by its rugged terrain overlooking the fertile flatlands below.

"This almost lifeless region of jagged cliff and mountainous rocky range," continued Savita, "separates the southwestern corner of Drakonia. This land is known as Jirasab."

****

Jirasab was an area of land reserved for dragons shortly after their arrival from Earth. The mountains which separated Jirasab from the rest of Drakonia were known as the Avila Mountain Range, after Lord Tone Avila, the first Komalsh to ever communicate with these complex reptiles with peaceful intentions.

During the reign of Lord Duren. Lord Tone Avila, with the help of Lord Jira Sab, convinced the dragon population to live beyond these jagged mountains in the marsh lands of what is now called Jirasab. Not only did the ocean and mountain range act as a deterrent to any Drakonians who poached dragons, but the marsh lands also provided the necessary food, water, and shelter for the dragons to survive.

****

"You see, class, continued Savita, "during this era, early religions had a strong grip on the Drakonian people and taught that their followers should be against the newly immigrated Earth creatures. They were afraid of what they did not understand. Their priests, who are now replaced by wizards for council, found it easier to convince their people that dragons were emissaries of the Darkstar. Knights who were eager to prove their faith and chivalry to God and their kings set out on quests to kill these so-called evil demons.

"Many dragons and knights lost their lives from this misdirection.

"Fortunately, the treacherous Avila Mountain range was too steep and jagged for any knight to cross. The treacherous waves of the ocean shores were too violent to safely navigate by boat. The dragons were protected."

In her mind's eye, Savita walked along the outer side of the mountain range and the students followed. She created a visual image of a fire, a warlock and a three headed dragon and then continued her story.

"In these desolate mountains, the warlock Kaylitan hid with his ally, Trisadez."

Five other characters appeared from the mist. They were shown sneaking toward the warlock who sat nestled by his fire.

"The five Komalsh you see preparing to ambush the warlock were the following. In front was our leader, Lord Radik Shade. Beside him was the sorcerer who dedicated his services to the Komalsh, my beloved father, Marlyn Cosmos. The Komalsh who stood beside them was my dear mother, Lady Mia Cosmos. The two who followed behind were Lords Hirum Drakus and Cable Demonis, the Komalsh's promising future."

A light disturbing murmur spread through the students as they recognized the renegade Lord Demonis.

"When Radik confronted the warlock," continued Savita, "he demanded his surrender. Kaylitan would not comply. Instead, he rose from the ground holding the Dragon's Flute. With the written music rolled out before him, he played its enchanted melody. The melody filled the sky with dragons. Its soothing sounds captivated the reptile's sensitive ears. Then, the melody turned dark, and the skies tinted with rage."

Savita added thunderous clouds to the illusion. The three headed dragon crashed through those clouds landing hard on the rocky surface.

"Trisadez!"

The students jumped back in terror including Lady Dunlam who laughed at herself afterward.

"The five fearless Komalsh separated into two groups," recounted Savita. "Radik Shade, Marlyn Cosmos and Cable Demonis attacked Trisadez while Mia Cosmos and Hirum Drakus confronted the warlock Kaylitan."

Savita focused the illusion on the warlock who played the flute.

"Lady Cosmos and Lord Drakus, with swords drawn, attacked Kaylitan head on only to be ambushed by a dragon."

The students jumped as a wingless Catalan dragon leaped out from a nearby cave. Her breath of flames and poison incinerated Lady Mia Cosmos.

"This unfortunate event took the life of my mother." Recalling the memory saddened Savita. "Lord Drakus, however, was shielded by Lady Cosmos enabling him to leap onto the back of the dragon whereupon he thrust his sword deep into its skull."

The frenzied reptile dropped to the ground dead. Savita turned the focus of the illusion toward the three-headed dragon, Trisadez.

"Radik's group waited patiently for Trisadez to make his first move—a wise decision, students, when engaging a multi-headed dragon. Often, we assume they will lead their attack with the middle and more dominant head. However, the unpredictable nature of these dragons demands a wiser approach."

"Trisadez's left head attacked unexpectedly and shot a bolt of lightning toward Lord Demonis. The impact sent him backwards through the air and sliding down the edge of the cliff. Marylin Cosmos slid across the ground and grabbed onto Demonis' arm."

"My father saved Lord Demonis' life that day." The students once again murmured their disapproval of Cable Demonis.

"Lord Demonis was once a good man, students," defended Savita. "Nevertheless, while my father was saving him, the flute's melody filled the sky with dragons. Lord Shade could see their defeat, but he knew, as well as everyone there, that this moment was their only opportunity to end the Dragon Wars. That's when Lord Radik Shade attacked Trisadez head on."

The students, enthralled by Savita's illusional theatrics, cheered for Lord Radik Shade.

"While on the attack, Radik raised his hand telekinetically summoning the Dragon's Flute from the warlock's grasp to his own. With the flute in his hand, he charged Trisadez fearlessly."

"The dragon's three mouths lit up with energy. Marlyn Cosmos aided Radik's attack by conjuring a blast of blinding light."

"The courageous Lord Radik Shade used his powers of telekinesis to leap into the air and land on the dragon's middle head. With both hands grasping his sword, he thrust his blade deep into the dragon's skull."

The class cheered as a hideous screech left the dragon's three heads. Trisadez fell backwards against the mountain. His heads shot blasts of lightning, ice, and fire into the mountain behind creating an avalanche.

Savita's illusion filled with dust, lava, and rocky debris.

"Sadly," continued Savita, "this avalanche not only buried Trisadez but also took the lives of Lord Radik Shade and my father, Marlyn Cosmos. It is their final resting place to this day."

Savita guided the focus of her story illusion to the aftermath of the avalanche. When the dust cleared, the warlock, Kaylitan, was found rummaging through the rubble searching frantically for the flute. Lord Drakus approached him.

Kaylitan reached for his wand.

Before he could grasp it, Lord Drakus swung his sword and decapitated the evil warlock.

All the dragons in Savita's illusion crumbled to dust.

"With the flute buried, the dragons scattered. One remained—one upon whom the Dragon's Flute had no effect."

Savita focused the illusion on Lords Drakus and Demonis who approached the last dragon. This dragon stood still on a nearby ledge observing their every move. With a swift leap, the enormous dragon landed before them.

"This dragon differed from most, students," explained Savita. "He had a dark grey belly with a unique shell of green and black scales, but it was the silver stripe down his back that caught the eye of Lord Drakus."

****

The Elvin library has this dragon recorded as a Silverback. According to their records the Silverback are the most intelligent and wise of all dragon kind. It is a rare species said to have inspired Lord Duren during the foundation of the Komalsh a thousand years ago. Since then, sightings of this esteemed dragon were scarce.

****

"Lords Demonis and Drakus were offered a ride to safety by the Silverback and to the sky they went." Savita's illusion blurred from focus. Then slowly the image transformed into the location of the Arkonian castle's front yard. Savita continued her history lesson.

"Once they landed inside the castle walls, they were confronted by a pregnant Lady Raine Shade and the Arkonian guard. Seeing two of the Komalsh accompanying the dragon placed everyone at ease. All but Lady Raine Shade who could feel the loss of her husband. The dragon sensed Raine's importance and introduced himself. His name was Stratos."

"Stratos foresaw Raine to be the next leader of the Komalsh and gave her a precious gift. We know that gift today as a magical book titled, *The Book of Dragons.* Written in this book were spells of great sorcery beyond imagination."

"Stratos also warns that the book has its own enchanted defence. You see, class, since this book possessed such great power, the ancient Silverbacks placed a spell on it preventing the reader from remembering its literary content. You could not remember to speak it, nor could you duplicate it in writing. Only with the original scripture could you use its ancient spells."

"After Lady Shade accepted this gift, Stratos leapt to the sky never to return."

"I was ten years old at the time, class," recalled Savita. "Raine Shade adopted me as her own and shortly after gave birth to her son, Nyte."

Savita ended the illusion leaving the students in the darkness of their own eyelids. One by one they opened their eyes.

Lady Dunlam rose from her squat. "This, students, brings us up to date on where we currently are in history. Remember, shortly after this, Lady Raine Shade separated, *The Book of Dragons,* into its fifteen chapters and then distributed those chapters equally among the remaining kingdoms. The purpose of course was to create peace. She felt that if each kingdom possessed a great chapter of power, it would deter war. This would be written historically in our records as the first attempt at a Drakonian unification. Thank you, Lady Cosmos, for your wonderful lesson."

Savita gave Elasia a gentle hug. "My time has run short, Lady Dunlam. I must be leaving now. Thank you so kindly for allowing me to help today's class. It felt good. Perhaps, it is something I will consider doing full time when I retire."

"Oh, my dear, it was our pleasure to have you…and as far as retirement is concerned, well…you have a long way to go for that. Enjoy the moment, Lady Cosmos, old age will be here soon enough."

Savita pulled back from the hug to offer a smile—one that was graciously returned by Lady Dunlam.

The students clapped their hands together in appreciation of their prestigious guest. Savita smiled in return and gave the students a short yet courteous bow. Humbled, she left.

Savita left the school's front entrance where Lord Bossel Dunlam waited anxiously. "Lady Cosmos," he greeted. "I must have a word with you."

"Of course, and please call me Savita. There are no reasons to use formalities."

"Yes, of course, Savita," answered Bossel with a smile and yet a trace of distress. "It's just…I've received…uh. Well, I will just get right to the point. I've received some disturbing news."

"What is it, Bossel?"

"I've been informed that Lord Minphis has been murdered. They say his body showed traces of mutilation. There were signs of torture."

"Lord Minphis!" repeated Savita who had heard nothing of this. "Why wasn't I informed?"

"I can only assume Lord Drakus wanted this to remain hidden for now."

"Who did you hear this from?" Savita was startled by the news. Her words came in rapid fire.

Bossel glanced around making sure they were alone. Then he explained. "I was in a state of meditation, Savita, when suddenly I was connected with the minds of the Lords investigating the murder scene."

"But how? And without their permission?"

"I don't know how, Savita. The visions were not of my control."

"What did you see, Bossel?"

"Apparently, his body was found near the northern side of Lake Lusetta somewhere between Mount Kabigatta and the Sykanian Kingdom."

Feeling distressed but needing to get the matter off his chest, Bossel continued. "Perhaps I may be growing a little paranoid...but, coincidence or not, he was one of the Komalsh who participated in our special mission—the assignment of hiding Lord Demonis' stone imprisonment a decade ago."

Savita rubbed her chin contemplating the possible scenarios involving her first assignment with skepticism. In a reassuring voice she delivered a logical antidote. "You are being paranoid, my dearest Bossel. Who other than Lord Siris would have known of Lord Demonis' stone imprisonment?"

Savita pulled her hood over her head as a light sprinkle of rain began to fall. "Need I remind you that Lord Siris lost his life to a swarm of Karnagins."

Unsatisfied with Savita's antidote Bossel revealed the truths behind his vision. Bossel's eyes shadowed in fear as he spoke. "Perhaps you are right, Savita, but there are two things that must be considered. One. There were no traces of Lord Siris' remains and two, there was a durenthium arrow lodged in Lord Minphis' skull. Its design is unique to one person…Fenka Rek."

Savita recalled the assassination of King Hexity. It was the only time she'd encountered Fenka Rek. It has been a decade since she has heard that name.

"It's quite possible, Savita, that the one who hired Fenka Rek to assassinate King Hexity at the peace conference a decade ago is the same one who has hired him to assassinate Lord Minphis today. I'm afraid someone is trying to locate Lord Demonis. Why else would Fenka Rek torture Lord Minphis other than to attain knowledge?" Bossel, acting as though a conspiracy was well at hand, continued his theory. "What if there was a connection between the fallen Komalsh and Fenka Rek's assassination? What if Lord Drakus was wrong?"

"Perhaps you're on to something, Bossel—something that should at least be mentioned to Lord Drakus. Yet, I hope for all our sakes you're wrong."

"Nevertheless," cautioned Bossel, "this should be investigated immediately, and you must tell Lord Drakus directly. Our telepathic ability to communicate has been compromised."

"Why compromised, Bossel?"

"Someone allowed me to see those thoughts at the murder scene. Someone wanted me to see yet they remain elusive. This person or thing shares our psychic ability, Savita."

Reassuringly, Savita said the words Bossel needed to hear. "I will see to it personally that Lord Drakus is informed."

Happy with the outcome, Bossel placed his arms around Savita and squeezed her like a grandparent. “Just be safe out there,” he warned. “No one can be trusted.” The light rain turned to a heavy downpour causing Bossel to retreat inside the school.

Savita hid under her hooded cloak protecting herself from the aggravated weather. The once crowded main street of Olemeeze appeared now to be nothing more then a ghost town as its citizens had run for cover. Savita walked through the vacant street of Olemeeze and headed toward the stables. There she rendezvoused with Nyte, Kelar and her unicorn Jinx.

Nyte and Kelar were already mounted on their horses and eager to go. Road trips were a much-needed break from the classroom.

“I can safely assume you two are anxious to leave this place?” Savita queried with an impish grin.

The two students nodded graciously as Savita mounted her unicorn.

“Then let us waste no time!”

Telekinetically, Savita opened the skookum barrier doors and the three rode off into a deluge of rain.

Chapter V
The Crossing.

By mid afternoon, the rains had surrendered to the summer sun's scorching rays. Lady Savita Cosmos, Nyte Shade and Kelar rode hard through a spacious and colourful rainforest.

The rainforest decor of flowered bushes, plants and ivy transformed the rocky ground into a living work of art. Native herbivores of all shapes and sizes roamed freely throughout the forest socializing in their circle of life. Large birds of prey to tiny birds of play shared the skies and trees above.

Alerted by the oncoming commotion of racing steeds, deer scattered along the path as two Olemeeze students raced by. Fueled by competition, Nyte Shade rode past his close friend, Kelar.

Now owning the lead, Nyte turned back to Kelar and threw him an arrogant smirk. Then, looking forward again, he noticed Savita and her unicorn Jinx were nowhere in sight.

"I really want a unicorn!" He grinned.

Ahead of the rivalling students, laid on its side was an old oak tree. Nyte maneuvered his horse clear through a pathway beneath it. While he was riding through its underside, Kelar directed his steed over the fallen tree and propelled past Nyte.

Kelar looked back to Nyte and arrogantly returned the smirk.

Nyte squinted his eyes. The race raged on.

Nyte veered to the left and rode up a hill hidden behind a thick colourful bush. Unaware of his whereabouts, Kelar raced down the open path. In an explosion of colourful bushes and scattering leaves, Nyte and his horse leaped ahead of Kelar and regained their lead.

“Nice!” smiled Kelar.

Nyte looked back to Kelar and could not resist the urge to deliver a second smirk with condescending arrogance.

Kelar squinted his eyes. Again, the race raged on.

Always competing, always trying to better one another, Nyte and Kelar were rivals and they lived for it.

Kelar spied a predator perched on a tree branch ready to pounce.

“A Raymer!”

****

The Raymer is a badger-like mammal native to Drakonia. Its dark green fur and black stripes act as a camouflage among the trees. With its sharp claws and teeth and with its patience and precision, this angry and fearless mammal made for a lethal Drakonian predator.

****

With deliberate movements and without haste, Kelar removed the bow from his saddle and shot off an arrow. The Raymer leapt down from the branch toward Nyte for the kill. Kelar’s arrow hissed by Nyte’s ear striking the Raymer’s forehead. The beast hit the ground dead.
Nyte turned back to Kelar and nodded his gratitude. Kelar nodded in return.

The two students raced up a steep, grassy hill where Savita stood patiently at its peak. On arrival they dismounted from their steeds and joined Savita.

The three gazed down the terrain of the steep hillside to a flat, grassy field below. Beyond that field flowed the raging Assaroe River, the first of two major rivers the travellers will cross before journey's end.

Savita pointed toward the barge crossing. "This is the quickest route to the other side…but something doesn't feel right."

"What troubles you, Savita?" worried Nyte.

"I sense remnants of spirits who have recently crossed," she softly spoke.

"You can sense dead people?" Nyte's voice trembled.

"I sure hope it's not the barge guys." There was worry in Kelar's voice. "I'm a horrible swimmer."

Savita leapt swiftly onto the back of her unicorn, Jinx. The joining of the two ignited a bright white glow and they vanished in a blinding flash.

Down at the barge crossing by the Assaroe River a similar flash of light appeared. As its blinding effect faded, both Savita and Jinx reappeared. The two students mounted their rides and rode toward Savita and the barge crossing.

"That was remarkable!" exclaimed Kelar. "I don't care how much we've read about unicorns—to actually see it teleport is amazing!"

Nyte, still rubbing the flash from his eyes agreed. "Yeah, but next time I don't think I'll stare right at it."

****

When the unicorns first arrived on Drakonia from Earth, they didn't possess the ability to teleport. But with the constant threat of Drakonian hunters, they fled for sanctuary in the Mystique Forest. With plenty of food and water and the protection of seclusion they never left the enchanted woods. The first generation of offspring born in the forest were influenced by its enchantment. Lord Duren gave credit to the water that streamed through the forest, for these unicorns were not only faster and smarter than their ancestors but they were born with the gift of teleportation.

****

The students arrived at the barge crossing and dismounted their horses. Nyte secured his ride and ran over to a small shack searching for Savita while Kelar eagerly headed toward the barge grasping the handle of his sword.

"Savita!" shouted Nyte. "Savita!" he called louder than before. Jinx waited outside the shack's doorway creating enough commotion to attract Nyte's attention. Jinx stared at Nyte…then at the doorway…then at Nyte… and again at the doorway.

"I get it, Jinx. Please stop doing that."

Then Jinx stared at Nyte…and then at the doorway.

"Oh boy," sighed Nyte.

Nyte entered the doorway of what appeared to be a dwelling built for the barge crew. It was a small wooden shack providing shelter for three adults uncomfortably. Its cabin-style doorway was noticeably crooked, and the windows looked uneven. The rooftop exposed a stone chimney that leaned to one side and its roof of cedar shingles was skewed and uneven. The place looked to have been built by a drunkard.

Hand on his sword's hilt, Nyte entered cautiously. Inside the cabin was a small wood stove. Beside it a skookum wood table and chairs. Tattered drapes covered the windows allowing in beads of light. The smell was unbearable.

Nyte pinched his nose to the decaying odour. He looked down to the floor where a beam of sunlight exposed a puddle of blood.

"Come over here," ordered Savita calmly yet firmly.

Stepping cautiously into the back room, Nyte walked toward her voice. Its enormous window let in enough sunlight to see the massacre. Blood was sprayed all along the walls and across the ceiling.

"What happened here?" demanded Nyte startled and confused.

Savita was kneeling beside a mutilated corpse in an effort to investigate. "As you can see, Nyte, this bridge crossing guard had his stomach and lungs eaten out."

Nyte inspected the corpse. "His body is still warm, Savita." Then he cringed.

"This can only mean the attacker is close by," answered Savita. There was a trace of fear in her voice. "What kind of predators inhabit this area, Nyte?"

Nyte shrugged his shoulders then stared into the corner where another corpse laid. Its only remains were two legs with hips that joined them.

Savita placed her hand on the back of Nyte's neck and spoke quietly so as not to alert the predator. "Nothing in these parts could possibly have done the damage you see here, Nyte. This is troublesome."

She surveyed the room with her eyes. "Where's the third person?"

"The third person?" stammered Nyte.

"Yes, Nyte. These barge crossing posts are always operated by three people. One for security purposes and two to run the crossing."

“So, where’s the third?” Nyte found himself choking on his words.

Kelar screamed and cursed. He was standing in the cabin’s back yard. Nyte and Savita ran out the back door unsheathing their swords. Ahead of them danced Kelar kicking around his left foot. “Take a gander at what I just stepped in!”

Kelar used his sword to scrape feces from his boot.

“That’s revolting!” he gagged.

Nyte sheathed his sword and laughed. “Why did you do that for?”

“It’s not funny, Nyte. This stuff reeks!” complained Kelar, “and look at the size of it!”

“Yeah, that’s one big pile of shit, alright.” teased Nyte.

Savita, still alert to potential danger, kept her sword drawn. She scanned the area again. Nothing. Unconvinced they were safe, she closed her eyes and searched again with her psychic gift.

Kelar, still wiping off his boot, took a second glance at a shiny object stuck within the feces. “Hey, I see a ring! There’s a ring in that big pile of shit.”

“Be silent!” hushed Savita. “I can feel the heartbeat of the Minotaur.”

“A mino what?” snapped Kelar.

“The Minotaur,” whispered Nyte.”

“What’s a Minotaur?” whispered Kelar.

Nyte pointed in the direction Savita was now facing. There stood the Minotaur.

“That’s a Minotaur,” answered Nyte.

The Minotaur emerged fifty feet away by the river’s edge. The nine-foot-tall half-human, half-bull held what looked to be the remains of the third barge attendant. Chunks of chewed flesh and blood stuck to his mouth and cheeks. He tossed the remainder of the corpse aside with one hand and stared at his new prey.

"Did I mention he has an addiction to human flesh," added Nyte while calmly unsheathing his sword.

Kelar drew his sword declaring, "No books are going to teach him what I'm about to do."

Kelar stepped forward flailing his weapon and attacked the Minotaur head on.

In hindsight, the idea to charge a bull lacked creativity.

The Minotaur ripped up the ground with his hooves. He snorted aggressively while lowering his head. With his mouth still dripping red from his former prey, the Minotaur returned Kelar's attack.

Savita stopped Nyte before he could follow. "Don't panic," assured the sorceress.

Using one of her many spells, she clapped her hands together and then thrusted them forward. A surge of visible vibrating energy shot into Kelar's body. His physical form exploded into its separate molecules while the Minotaur charged right through him. On the other side of the great beast, Kelar's body re-materialized and he staggered to the ground appearing rather discombobulated.

The beast, who cared not who it killed first, continued in the direction of its momentum. Nyte stepped backwards waiting for Savita to make a move. When she placed her sword back in its scabbard, Nyte looked toward her nervously.

"Uh…, Savita?"

The Minotaur was now travelling toward him at full momentum.

"UH, Sa-VI-ta!"

Pieces of the ground ripped into the air with every pounding stride.

"UH, SAVITA!"

Moments before impact, Savita telekinetically raised the beast into the air and tossed him into the river.

"That won't stop him!" panicked Nyte.

The Minotaur was now neck deep in the river fighting the current to get to shore. Savita began chanting a spell. "Cool chim lay frez cool chim. Cool chim lay frez cool chim." These words were echoing repeatedly from her mouth. She raised both her arms into the air.

The surrounding winds picked up speed and blew hard and strong. Her cloak fluttered erratically as if a sail were about to leave its mast. Her eyes glowed a bright blue. Then her chant screamed into the heavens.

The Minotaur was now up to his shoulders in the river slowly freeing himself from the raging current. Savita pointed her hands toward the river. Its molecules of water rapidly slowed to a halt as the Minotaur became imprisoned in ice. The wind died down as Savita gently lowered her arms.

Kelar rose from the ground brushing the grass from his apprentice robes. He joined Savita and Nyte on the frozen river. Looking down at the Minotaur frozen in time,

Kelar scratched his head, "You froze the river?"

"Sharp as a marble," humoured Nyte.

Kelar took offence and raised his blade pointing it at Nyte's face. Nyte slapped it down with his own sword pointing his finger in Kelar's face. "Careful, pal!"

"Ha, ha, Nyte bright," calmed Kelar. "I was only thinking maybe something a little stronger than ice would be appropriate."

The two students were interrupted by the horrific howl of the Minotaur struggling to escape. Kelar stood uneasy. "Well, do you want me to kill it?"

Savita gave Kelar a distasteful wince. "It is written in, *The Book of Malshidiel,* for the Komalsh to not only protect the castle and the Darkstar scroll but to defend the Earth creatures as well. One day, Kelar, they'll be our allies in the war against the Darkstar."

"Well, evidently our friend here wasn't informed," poked Kelar.

Savita let her distaste for Kelar's ignorance show up in her voice. "Do I need to recite all of your studies?"

"I know the story," rebounded Kelar. He was clearly agitated. "But how can this Darkstar, wherever it may be, threaten anyone while the very key that opens it is hidden safe in Castle Malshidiel? The scroll is well protected, Lady Cosmos, is it not?"

****

Kelar was one of many students who excelled in combat and survival. His skill was enough for certain of his teachers to turn a blind eye to his recent lack of attention to his book studies. This was becoming a more common practice at Olemeeze than traditionally acceptable and it was contaminating the ranks of the modern day Komalsh.

****

"Malshidiel had predicted the Darkstar's return Kelar," informed Savita. "It isn't an if. It's a when. It was also written that a special Drakonian will be born to this world—one with the ability to awaken Malshidiel from its slumber. Together they will unite allowing Malshidiel the ability to walk this world in our form. With the help of the Earth creatures, we will form an army and destroy the Darkstar once and for all."

"Which means what?" interrupted Kelar impatiently.

"Which means," spoke the suddenly agitated Savita, "if you would have paid more attention in school, you would know there is only one Minotaur. We must protect this creature for one day he will become a powerful ally."

Savita mounted her unicorn. Kelar approached her. "So that's why you stopped me from slaying this beast?"

"No, Kelar. I prevented the Minotaur from slaying you."

Kelar stewed in silence.

During the exchange between Savita and Kelar, Nyte walked closer to the Minotaur. He examined the ancient Earth creature with great curiosity. The Minotaur also hurled a curious look toward Nyte throwing Nyte off guard. Nyte slipped on the ice and landed next to the beast's face. The Minotaur's nostrils flared open inhaling Nyte's scent. With heightened reflexes Savita felt the Minotaur's breath and thrust her hand forward telekinetically pulling Nyte along the ice and out of harm's way.

"Did he smell you?" feared the sorceress running to his side.

"I don't know," startled Nyte.

"Did he smell you?" Savita's rage exploded with her asking for a second time.

"What does it matter?"

"He will never forget your scent Nyte. He will hunt you down. He'll never stop!"

"I'm sure he didn't," calmed Nyte.

Savita shook her head displeased. "Come now. We must leave before the ice melts."

Kelar also shook his head displeased. "So, we fear our allies. How comforting."

Savita dismissed his comment with distaste. She mounted her unicorn and led the two students across the frozen river. No words were exchanged.

Chapter VI
Kudos Nexus.

By mid afternoon, the wary travellers arrived at the Riegan River. The last few miles had been ridden through the Whispering Woods under the sun's scorching heat. After refilling their canteens and soaking their heads in the cold glacier-fed river, they mounted their steeds and followed Savita down stream.

"Excuse me, Savita," queried Nyte, "but isn't the next barge crossing up stream?"

"Yes, it is, but soon it will be nightfall and we'll need a place to rest."

"Where are we headed then?" asked Kelar.

"We're going to visit Kudos Nexus."

"Hey, I recognize that name. He's legendary!" Kelar was excited. "A powerful sorcerer and war hero during the Dragon Wars!"

Astonished by the remark, Savita spoke with emphasis. "So, you do read."

"A page or two," downsized Kelar.

"Well, you're correct. However, Kudos is retired now, and he doesn't share the eager ambitions he once had."

Savita's unicorn Jinx let out a hearty neigh.

"You're right, Jinx," surrendered Savita. "Who am I kidding? Kudos doesn't care about a damn thing anymore. He's been a hermit in these parts since the Dragon Wars ended. Nevertheless, he is wise and trustworthy. We can rest there for the night."

Savita and Jinx led the students downstream to Kadabra Creek, a vein of water forking off from the Riegan River. The old sorcerer's dwelling was nestled along that creek.

As the night sky glittered with stars, Savita and the students rode the final stretch toward the cottage of Kudos Nexus. On approach, the winds picked up and grew stronger by the second. The trees surrounding them danced violently about and, in the sky above, enchanted clouds swarmed together forming a child's face as if it were blowing out a candle. Its eyes squinted. Its cheeks puffed and the winds howled in the night.

"Are we there yet?" shouted Kelar, compensating for the howling winds.

Savita pointed ahead toward a shadowed cottage with a smoking chimney. Her arm struggling against the wind. The students stared toward the oddly shaped cottage. It was built in stone with carved spells and symbols engraved upon the walls for protection. Its roof was composed of large wooden shakes with no rhyme nor reason for shape or size. Vines and moss embraced its structure and the forest surrounding the cottage danced dangerously in the wind. The chimney released a tantalizing aroma of green coloured smoke even the winds could not filter away. Each inhale of its sweet aroma delivered increasing feelings of comfort to the three exhausted riders.

While dismounting from their rides, the unusual winds intensified. Savita, Nyte and Kelar struggled to maintain their balance.

Nyte stared into the wind. Using his hand to shield his eyes he could vaguely see the clouds shaped in an image resembling a large young face blowing as hard as it could.

"Savita!" shouted Nyte.

"What!"

"That cloud's really starting to creep me out!"

Savita turned to examine the unnatural cloud. Then she felt a familiar presence and instinctively turned back to see the home of Kudos Nexus emerge in her vision. There, exiting his dwelling was the old sorcerer himself.

****

Kudos Nexus was Drakonia's most famous sorcerer. He had long grey and black hair. His face was decorated with bushy grey eyebrows and a grey stubble. His nose was large and red from many years of the drink and his skin appeared a weathered golden brown. His age was unknown. Most just left it at old.

During the Dragon Wars, Kudos was a key factor in their defense while holding the rank of general for the Komalsh Elite. Over the years to follow he trained Drakonia's finest in the art of wizardry including his prize student, Savita Cosmos.

As of late though, he kept to himself—a jaded hermit and drunk. To him, society was noise. He liked it quiet.

****

While fighting to escape his home from the strong winds the old sorcerer raised his wooden staff and shouted angerly. "Hey! You, up there!"

The top of his wooden staff started to glow in an array of bright colours. "HEY, YOU!" screamed the sorcerer a second time.

The winds died down and the image in the cloud stared toward the upset sorcerer.

"Yeah, you! You stupid son of a bitch! How many bloody times do I have to tell you?"

The cloud's expression saddened, and the windstorm faded to a gentle breeze.

"Don't you blow on my house ever again, you stupid cloud! The nerve! Do you know who I am? well, do you?"

The cloud began to nod ever so slowly, and a grin of embarrassment crossed its face.

"Then get out of here. Damn it! Piss off!" Agitated the sorcerer.

Saddened by the order, the chastised cloud removed itself. The winds died down and nightfall became clear and starlit.

The sorcerer limped toward the tired travellers muttering to himself. "Bloody weather! I swear that grey cloud follows me around wherever I go!"

"I think you hurt it's feelings," remarked Savita wrapping her arms around the old sorcerer.

"Savita! It is so nice to see you, my child!" Kudos returned the hug with a big squeeze of affection.

"What happened to your long beard, Kudos?"

"I cut it off. I was sick of looking like a stereotyped wizard."

"And your robes? They are not white. They are grey."

"I just stopped washing them," chuckled the sorcerer.

"Kudos, this is Kelar and Nyte Shade."

Kudos stared at Nyte with delight. "I haven't seen you since you were knee high."

Nyte nodded reluctantly.

Savita smiled proudly. "Well, Nyte has been in the School of Olemeeze. Otherwise, he would know you better Kudos."

"This is true," smiled Kudos. "Well, Nyte, I knew your parents quite well. They were good people. You have good blood, son."

"Boys," interrupted Savita. "This is Kudos Nexus." The students exchanged handshakes with the sorcerer. "It's indeed a pleasure to meet you young gentlemen."

Kelar shook his hand with a disappointed expression.

"What's wrong with you?" noticed Kudos. "Well, speak son!"

Kelar hesitated before answering. "You are the great sorcerer and war hero of the Dragon Wars?"

"Well, "great" seems a little strong," answered Kudos.

"But you're so, …well, you're so old!"

"It happens," answered Kudos with an eye roll.

"I'm sorry, sir. With your storied history, I just had a different image of you," backtracked Kelar.

"That's all-right, son, I never knew you even existed." The sorcerer turned to the house and hollered aloud. "Frik, Frak! I need assistance! Chop, chop!"

Two three-foot-high lizard creatures exited the home strategically and cautiously. They had long pointy ears, sharp razor teeth and the devious yellow eyes of a mischievous predator.

"Frik, Frak. I would like you to escort their rides to the stable."

Frik and Frak obeyed their master by leading the two horses and Jinx to sanctuary.

"What are those, Kudos?" Kelar was most curious. Frik and Frak looked too creepy for words.

"Why, they're Earth critters known as gremlins. I created them myself," bragged the sorcerer. Kudos started scratching the back of his head. "For some unknown reason, they're the only creature Malshidiel left behind on Earth. Go figure?" shrugged Kudos. "Enough of this standing outside. Come into my dwelling and make yourselves at home."

Inside, the four sat in over-sized uncomfortable chairs placed before a stone fireplace. Its fire blazed green flames releasing a soothing aroma. The students melted into those uncomfortable chairs putting their weary bodies at ease.

"I spend a lot of time reading," reported Kudos. "One day I came across the gremlin conjuration in some old Earth literature I discovered at the Elvin castle's library."

Kudos turned to Savita with eyes widened.

"Mandrake! Part of the spell involves the mandrake plant! Do you believe that?"

Kudos Nexus grabbed a pipe from the table and looked about for a match. "Do you know how hard it was to find and retrieve a mandrake?" Kudos sat back into his chair. "Oh, I can tell you!" He recalled the memory by shaking his head.

"I thought mandrake was only used in love potions," commented Savita.

"That's what I thought, too! It's hard to believe that these are the product of mandrake." The old sorcerer pointed toward the incoming gremlins. Then smiled cheerfully as they served everyone tea.

"Impressive? Yes!" He continued. "But curious and sometimes mischievous little creatures. The two seem to have this uncontrollable desire to disassemble anything mechanical, especially Frak."

"How can you tell them apart?" asked Nyte.

"They both share similar shades of dark green skin. Frik, however, has black stripes on his back where Frak has black spots."

While the gremlin servants walked carefully back to the kitchen, Frak farted unexpectedly. The loud noise startled both gremlins who dropped their teapots and ran for cover.

"They are a peculiar creature, indeed." Kudos continued lighting his pipe.

After the light laughter subsided and the gremlins returned to clean their mess, Savita told Kudos of their eventful encounter earlier that day.

"We had a run in with the Minotaur today. I'm afraid he may have Nyte's scent."

"That's not good…not good at all," replied Kudos. "The Minotaur can be relentless. He is a very disturbed creature, indeed. If he caught your scent son, he won't forget you."

"I understand, sir. I've read about the Minotaur in school."

"You mean there's a book on that thing, too!" exclaimed Kelar.

"Have you ever read anything in school?" sneered Nyte.

"Enough to pass with the same grades as you," retaliated Kelar confidently. "But now that we're on the topic, where did this thing come from? I mean, if it's the only one in existence, how did it come to be?"

"Allow me to explain this Earth legend," volunteered Kudos. He lit a match, inhaled the skunk smelling herb from his pipe and then told the story to his tired audience.

"It was all started on Earth by a man named Minos from Crete who sought out the throne of that kingdom. Minos told the Cretans that any prayer he said would be answered by the gods."

"The gods?" questioned Nyte.

"Yes, their people mistook powerful entities for gods."

"Nevertheless, the Cretans challenged Minos by having him ask Poseidon, Lord of the Ocean, to send him a bull from out of the sea. Well, the whole kingdom came down to see this absurd request which even Minos did not believe. Minos prayed as hard as he could. He bargained that if the bull would come out of the ocean, he would sacrifice it in the glory of Poseidon. To the Cretans and Minos's astonishment, a white bull swam to shore. Minos was then made King."

Kudos offered his pipe to Savita who graciously declined. After inhaling another lung full of smoke, his eyelids grew heavy. He exhaled a smoke ring then continued the story.

"Unfortunately, Minos couldn't sacrifice the special white bull, so instead, he added it to his own herd and sacrificed an ordinary bull to Poseidon. The Ocean God was so infuriated by the broken promise that he put a spell on Pasiphae, the wife of Minos, to fall in love with the white bull. She loved the animal completely, but the bull would not return her love. So, she persuaded an inventor by the name of Daedalus; to build her an artificial cow so she could crouch within it and be sexually served by the bull." A disturbed look crossed Kelar's face.

"In time, she got pregnant," continued Kudos. "She gave birth to a monster with a calf's head and a human's body. It quickly developed into a full-grown male the Cretan's named Minotaur meaning the bull son of Minos."

"The King accepted this curse of Poseidon until one day the Minotaur developed the taste of human flesh."

"Daring not to kill the Minotaur and offend Poseidon again, Minos ordered Daedalus to construct a prison that would contain this beast. The prison he constructed was a Labyrinth, a maze of chambers and passages built partly above and beneath the ground where the Minotaur would never escape."

"So," spoke Kelar. "I'm guessing he escaped?"

"Correct, Kelar. After Malshidiel's gateways appeared, the Minotaur escaped and sought out the portholes seductive grasp. That is how the Minotaur came to be," concluded Kudos.

"That is about the sickest story I've ever heard. It's disgusting," snapped Kelar.

Kudos put his pipe down. "Like I said, I read a lot of books."

"Earth sounds so disturbing." Chortled Nyte.

"So, Lady Cosmos," asked Kelar changing the disturbing subject. "How do you two know each other?"

"Kudos is the teacher of all the greatest wizards and sorcerers of Drakonia," answered Savita proudly. "He taught my father before me."

With fond memories she smiled, "I've known Kudos since I was a child."

The old sorcerer smiled in return. "Savita was my brightest pupil you know. A blessing to teach."

"Speaking of sorcery," giggled Savita, "what's with the strange cloud outside?"

"One should never mix sorcery with alcohol," surrendered Kudos, "…a lesson I never seem to learn."

The green flames in the stone fireplace had died down to smouldering coals.

"Say, boys, how would you like to go out back to my garden?" Kudos pointed to a doorway at the back of the house. "Go grab me a bundle each of the sedavive plant. Our fire grows weak."

"What's a sedavive plant?" Kelar had never heard of such a thing.

"I'll show you," answered Nyte. "Follow me."

As instructed, the students left to Kudos' garden to fetch the plant he wanted. His garden was home to a variety of special plants. Some were colourful and exotic; others were green and ordinary. Some moved and wiggled about while others hissed and snarled. Some had a purpose for antidotes and cures. Others were grown for magical spells.

"That's the one we're looking for, Kelar. That's a sedavive plant." Nyte pointed to a three-foot-tall plant with large purple and green leaves. On top of it grew a single yellow flower. Nyte carefully picked off its purple leaves and handed them to Kelar. Before his eyes, the leaves dried and shrivelled.

"That's different," commented Kelar.

"Here, you try," suggested Nyte. "Take only the purple leaves. That's the colour they turn when they're ready to be used."

Kelar broke them off one at a time and watched them dry up in his hands. Then he reached for the yellow flower. Nyte let out a blood-curdling yell.

"Don't touch the flower!"

Alarmed, Kelar instantly sprang back. "Why not?"

"It will kill you dead on contact!"

"Now you tell me!" Kelar was shaking at the thought of having just had a near-death experience.

"I'm just fooling, buddy!" laughed Nyte. "But seriously, if you kill the yellow flower, the potency of the leaves dies with it…well at least until another one grows in its place."

"You freaked me out, Nyte!" scolded Kelar. "Yet, that was very clever!" He attempted a laugh, but it fell short. He was too shaken to laugh.

"The look on your face!" teased Nyte in return.

"I'll get you back," mumbled Kelar.

"What are these leaves used for anyway, Nyte?"

"Kudos is putting them in his fireplace. When inhaled, the green fumes act as a sedative relaxing your mind and body causing you to feel like you did when you were melting into that uncomfortable chair."

"Really, and here I thought it was the herbs from Kudos' pipe," replied Kelar biting into some rambutan fruit he picked from a nearby tree.

"Well, you could be right there, Kelar. I'm feeling kind of hungry, too."

****

As competitive as Nyte and Kelar were, they still shared a mutual respect. Both were at the top of their class in all aspects of the Komalsh training program. Their friendship was built around their successes.

****

A raspy squawk startled the two students. It came from inside Kudos' fenced yard. Quietly, they unsheathed their swords and crept toward the bush where the sound had originated from.

Another less threatening squawk left the bush.

"This doesn't sound dangerous, Kelar. Whatever it is sounds injured." Nyte placed his sword away and searched the bush. There, as expected, he found a wounded bird.

Hidden in the bush was a large bird with a two-foot wingspan. Its colours were white, orange, and yellow. It's long, curved beak was yellow and black streaks lined the feathers and around its eyes. It had large, sharp talons and the muscular build of a predator.

"That beak looks sharp Nyte. You'd better kill it before it bites you."

"That's your answer to everything, Kelar, isn't it?" taunted Nyte shaking his head.

"It's gotten me this far," retorted Kelar, not sure this was a matter to be taken lightly.

The two inspected the bird with wonder.

"Well, Nyte, you're the book worm. What kind of bird is it?"

"I don't have a clue." He removed his hooded cloak and carefully covered the bird's eyes before wrapping the bird. "It seems to be favouring its right shoulder. We should take it to Kudos."

Kelar shook his head in objection. "You're such a suck for animals. You're aware of this right?"

"I believe in karma," defended Nyte.

"What? Are you suggesting the bird will return this favour?" Kelar burst out into a fake laugh. "I think you've been sitting too close to Kudos!"

Inside, sitting next to the fire, Kudos mentioned news of a second assassination. Another Komalsh was found dead.

"I'm sorry, Savita. But it's true. First it was Lord Minphis who was tortured and murdered. Now Lord Tringle has met the same fate."

With an unsettled expression, Savita asked Kudos, "The weapons used…were they durenthium?"

"Yes, they were my dear. They were identified as the same used by the assassin known as Fenka Rek."

"Bossel was right after all," yielded Savita. "Somebody has hired Fenka Rek to locate Lord Demonis. He will torture and kill each Komalsh assigned to that mission."

Kudos nodded for a moment. He then calmly replied, "Or at least until one divulges his location."

Savita didn't share Kudos' calmness and reacted harshly to the sorcerer's statement. "That is highly improbable! The will and loyalty of the Komalsh are too strong!"

"You are right," surrendered Kudos. "It would be most difficult to acquire such information. However, this Fenka Rek uses methods even the worst find unorthodox. His moral compass differs from ours."

Kudos stoked the coals to his fire rekindling the last of the sedavive leaves for maximum effect. Savita stared deep into its resurrected flame listening to Kudos' words.

"Fenka Rek has been around for as long as recorded history. He is elusive. No one knows who or what he is, where his origins are or why he even exists."

Kudos inhaled a huge pull from his pipe. Then exhaled a large smoke triangle.

"However, there are greater evils at work here, Savita. Remember the peace talks a decade ago. Remember when Fenka Rek assassinated King Hexity?"

Savita recalled the night vividly.

"This secret King of Sykania stinks something fierce as well," continued Kudos. "Keep in mind, Savita, prior to Fenka's assassination of the former King of Sykania, his wife and two sons were also murdered—his royal bloodline terminated. Then, after a couple of years with the dead looking wizard, Malores, in charge, they inherited a new king—one voted by the people. Very unorthodox, indeed." Kudos inhaled from his pipe. Then blew out a smoke square.

"This new king, my dear, hasn't revealed himself in the years he has ruled. That kind of secrecy hides conspiracy." Kudos began rubbing his stubbly chin and appeared contemplative upon hearing his uttered words.

"The Sykanians are said to reveal this secret king at the upcoming peace conference," informed Savita.

She rose from the couch and paced about the room. With little more to go on Savita concluded, "I believe everything will unfold in time. For now, we need to contact Lord Drakus and have him place the remaining Komalsh under protection."

"A wise decision, Savita, and perhaps this new King of Sykania will shed light on the subject."

"We need to keep this quiet for now, Kudos."

"Indeed." Kudos took a pull from his pipe. The smoke he blew formed into a Celtic knot. "I sense our company has returned."

A creaking sound came from the back door. Nyte and Kelar, still arguing about karma, entered the room and showed Kudos their fascinating find.

"What species is this?" asked Nyte curiously.

"Why, my friend!" smiled Kudos in disbelief. "You have stumbled upon a rare bird, indeed!"

Savita, surprised as Kudos, answered for the sorcerer in astonishment. "Nyte! You've found a phoenix!"

"I thought the phoenix had darker colours."

"There are two different species of this special bird Nyte," answered Savita. "Please," she continued, "allow me to communicate with it."

Nyte handed her the injured bird. "It seems to be favouring it's right wing so be careful."

"I will, Nyte," reassured Savita with a smile.

The students watched in wonder as Savita performed a special Komalsh gift. Caressing the bird gently she began speaking to it. In the phoenix's mind, her words were telepathically translated into whistling and chirps the firebird understood. The phoenix whistled and chirped in return which telepathically translated in Savita's mind the words she could understand. Together they were happy for each other's company as they communicated back and forth.

"Your newfound friend is a female, Nyte, and her name is Blythe," answered Savita.

"Blythe is a pretty name," replied Nyte. "But what do you mean by friend?"

Savita answered with excitement. "You saved Blythe's life! The trauma of this experience has bonded her to you. In fact, you have a friend for life."

"Awe, Nyte's first friend," joked Kelar.

"You're a dork," retaliated Nyte.

"Nyte!" interrupted Kudos. "Take Blythe into my laboratory. I will put a splint on her wing."

"Frik! Frak!" hollered Kudos. "I need your assistance! Chop, chop!"

In a flash, the two resident gremlins pranced out from the kitchen.

"I want you both to escort Lady Cosmos and Kelar to their beds."

The two gremlins nodded their heads in a psychotic manner while drool dripped down their fang-filled smiles. Their eyes bulged and their ears made erratic circular motions. Their skinny arms hung limp at their sides as they simultaneously headed up the stairs enticing the guests to follow. Kelar was disturbed. Savita was entertained. When they entered the bedroom, Frik and Frak immediately started jumping on the beds thrilled with excitement. Savita found it amusing. Kelar didn't. Kelar grabbed a pillow and belted Frak off the bed to the floor. Frak cowered with fear as Kelar went to strike him again. Anger rushed through Savita as she pulled Kelar toward her and punched him in the jaw. Kelar hit the floor hard.

"Are you alright, Kelar?" asked Savita with a sprinkle of regret.

Kelar didn't respond. Frik and Frak hovered over Kelar curious if he were dead. They started to nudge him. Still there was no response. They gently kicked him. Still nothing. They started to kick him harder which escalated to jumping on him whilst laughing hysterically. Savita raised her hand and levitated the gremlins off Kelar carefully placing them onto his bed.

Savita knelt over the unconscious student and closed her eyes. With her psychic gift she reached out and felt his heartbeat, a steady healthy rhythm. "You'll be fine young one. However, for your rude behaviour you can sleep on the floor tonight."

Savita climbed into her bed and blew out the candle while delivering a warning. "Hate is the dictator of life, Kelar. This ignorance won't be welcomed inside the Mystique Forest."

The sorceress turned over and closed her eyes. "Good night," she whispered.

Down in the sorcerer's laboratory, Nyte held the injured phoenix while Kudos carefully placed a splint on her broken wing.

"Now, now, Blythe. This will be over soon," comforted Nyte.

A loud thump sound came from the ceiling above them where Kelar had fallen.

"What was that?" startled Nyte.

"Sounded like Savita's right hook," answered Kudos.

"Pardon me?" Nyte was confused by the remark.

"Never mind son."

"You know, Nyte, what defines a phoenix is their heart of virtue. You see, son, you have met your second most loyal friend of the animal kingdom."

"Second?"

"Why, of course, second. A Komalsh meets their closest friend inside the Mystique Forest. Once accepted by the forest, a unicorn will choose you. It will reveal itself from the woods and lead you through a safe passage to Castle Malshidiel. The steed will stand by your side until death. Nothing will be greater than that bond."

"They never mentioned how the Komalsh inherited their unicorns in school. The teachings of the forest were quite vague."

"Well, think of this as a cheat then," smiled Kudos.

"Anyway, Blythe is ready and on her way down the healing path which is more than I can say about my aching body. I'm exhausted, Nyte. Time for me to retire to my chambers." The sorcerer gave a yawn, stood, and stretched his arms high in the air.

"Good night, Kudos, and thank you."

"Think nothing of it, son."

The old sorcerer went to his chambers leaving Nyte and Blythe alone.

"You're going to be just fine, Blythe," reassured Nyte.

Blythe started to sing a soothing song harmonically sprinkled with tones so clear and poetically placed that the melodic tune brought goose bumps to Nyte's arms as he fell into the spirit of her song. When the melody ended, he picked her up gently and packed her off to the bedroom. Inside the room Nyte was startled by a snore coming from the floor. There lay Kelar with two drooling gremlins snuggled on either side. Perplexed as to why, but too tired to care, Nyte ignored him and placed Blythe gently onto a pillow. Then laying down next to her, he drifted off to sleep.

Lost in a realm of dreams and dreamscape, Nyte Shade found himself sitting at a table. He appeared to be in a tavern. He looked around a room that was filled with patrons. Next to him sat Kudos drinking down a pint of ale. Across the tavern floor stood Kelar. He was in pain favouring his right wrist. A fight broke out in the tavern. The room spun out of control. Nyte found himself laying on a floor. Beside him lay Kelar battered and beaten. Above them stood Kudos…protecting them from a gang of thugs.

A cage of bars wrapped around them. Nyte felt claustrophobic. Then everything faded to black.

As the golden sunrise peaked over the mountain, Nyte awoke to the communal songs of birds. He sat up from his bed blinded by the light entering from the sunlit window. Just a silhouette to his eyes, Savita stood there staring out into eternity. She'd been awake for some time. Beside Nyte silently slept the splintered phoenix in a deep recovering rest. On the floor slept Kelar accompanied by two snuggled gremlins.

"Good morning, Nyte." Savita spoke softly as she stared out the window.

"Good morning, Savita…is everything okay?"

"Everything is fine, son. There's no need for concern." She smiled at Nyte. "Instead, encourage good thoughts while you prepare yourself for the journey ahead."

Savita moved across the room to sit next to Nyte on the bed. She worried for him like any mother would.

"Soon you will challenge the Mystique Forest, Nyte. You must be prepared not only physically but mentally, too. The forest will crawl inside your mind. It will feed off your fear, anger, jealousy, hate…wherever you may hurt, Nyte, the forest will manipulate. You must be confident in who and what you are, my son. So please, keep your mind clear of my distractions."

"But I cannot feel clarity knowing you're in distress. You're my only family, Savita. I love you dearly."

Savita wrapped her arms around him. "I love you, too," she said with a sigh. "You are my son."

Nyte pulled away from her embrace. "Then I deserve to know, Savita."

****

At the age of sixteen, Savita adopted the two-year-old orphan, Nyte, after the passing of his mother. The years of raising him taught her one thing. Trust him.

****

"As you wish, Nyte," replied Savita. "Allow me to share my thoughts."

Savita stared deeply into his eyes. Telepathically she shared her memories of the Fenka Rek assassinations and her mission to hide Lord Demonis' stone imprisonment. Nyte rose and stood feeling overwhelmed by the secrets Savita shared. He now understood the gravity of her situation and could feel the weight on his own shoulders.

"These are my concerns," reminded Savita. "It's imperative you pass the forest and follow the Komalsh path. We need your help, Nyte."

Finding it hard to swallow, Nyte replied bravely. "I understand, Savita."

Kelar's eyes slowly opened. He groaned from a splitting migraine. On either side of him stood two gremlins staring at him weirdly. Their eyes bulged and drool clung from their fangs.

Kelar leapt up from the floor brushing his clothes off.

"What's wrong with those things!"

He wiped some slime from his neck. "They're so disgusting!" He cried out, "I'm not going to get warts, am I?"

"You'll be fine, Kelar." answered Nyte while carefully picking up the phoenix.

There was no doubt that Kelar was agitated. "What happened last night?" "Why did I wake up on the floor…with those…those things?"

"To much sedavive plant," answered Savita.

"Why is my jaw sore?" He gingerly moved his jaw from side to side to see if all his facial parts were still working.

Nyte carefully adjusted Blythe's wing for the trip downstairs.

"Still playing with that fire chicken." Kelar was in just the right mood to harass Nyte and poke fun at him. "I wonder what fire chicken tastes like?" he pestered. "Let me guess…a little karma flavoured."

"That was actually funny, Kelar," chuckled Nyte.

Kudos entered the room. “I don’t know how a phoenix tastes, but I do know how bacon and eggs taste. Come down to the kitchen. I’ve prepared breakfast!”

Kudos stomped down the stairs ahead of everyone. “Hurry! It’s getting cold…and afterwards I have a wonderful idea to share!”

A tantalizing aroma filled the kitchen as everyone seated themselves. Even the gremlins had a spot at Kudos’ table.

“Just dig in.” He cheerfully invited. “Don’t be shy there’s plenty!”

Kudos’ table was covered with platters of bacon and bowls of scrambled eggs. Each setting was accompanied by a plate and a pint of freshly squeezed rambutan juice—the Sorcerer’s favourite. Kudos had even prepared a meal for Blythe with orange and green worms the size of fingers wiggling frantically to escape the bowl.

“That’s disgusting! Why do I have to sit next to the fire chicken?” complained Kelar.

“Shut up and eat!” ordered Kudos while placing a full plate before him.

Kelar didn’t need to be told twice.

Kudos offered a plate of bacon to Savita who graciously declined. “After speaking with pigs, Kudos, I find it difficult to eat them.”

“Ah yes, I forgot. You prefer your vegetables,” apologised Kudos.

“Then what meat do you eat?” asked Kelar while enjoying his bacon.

“Fish and eggs mostly,” answered Savita. “I only eat what I can’t communicate with.”

“Are all Komalsh vegetarians?” Kelar was loathe to give up meat.

"Some choose not to eat any meat. Some eat only fish and eggs," answered Kudos. "But most believe in the circle of life and kill their food sacredly."

"It's a life choice, Kelar," added Savita. "One upon which the Komalsh religion has no policy."

"So, you choose not to eat meat…but bacon tastes so good!" Kelar pushed her for an answer.

"From what I've heard, so does human meat," defended Savita, "but I still wouldn't eat it."

Nyte removed the bacon from his plate. Kelar grabbed more.

Kudos waited until breakfast was finished to reveal his wonderful idea. After serving tea, he shared it.

"Savita, I did some thinking last night. I believe it would be wise for me to join you on your trip to the Arkonian castle."

"Are you sure your up for a long journey like this?" asked Savita respectfully but with notes of caution in her voice.

Kudos pounced. "I'm not that old! It's less than a couple days travel. I'm sure I'll survive."

"You're always welcome, Kudos." Savita responded with sincerity. "Why may I ask the sudden desire to return to the living?"

"I'd like to see this new King of Sykania in person. Perhaps it will shed more insight. I'd also like to participate in this peace conference. These are historical times for Drakonia."

"But I thought you were against political gatherings," jabbed Savita.

Kudos gave her his nasty eyes look. "I have lacked entertainment for many years, my dear. Perhaps the joke of politics will satisfy my needs."

"Well, to be honest Kudos, we could use your wisdom in these times. We are grateful to have you come along."

"What! We're not going to bring those two drool lizards, too, are we?" Kelar lashed out in distaste.

"The gremlins are staying," reassured Savita.

Kudos grabbed an apple from the table and threw it at Kelar's head.

"What's wrong, old man?" chuckled Kelar. "Apple too hard to chew?"

"You ever threaten or talk down to my gremlins again." Kudos shook his finger at Kelar with a chilling one-eyed glare that could turn smoke into stone.

"Or what!" chuckled Kelar, "you'll drool on me too?"

Another apple hit Kelar in the head. This time it was thrown by the gremlin, Frak. Frik joined in shortly after throwing apples at everyone.

After breakfast was finished and the apples were cleaned up, Savita, Kelar and Nyte mounted their rides and waited for Kudos. At the doorstep of his cottage, the sorcerer turned, dropped down on one knee, and hugging them, said farewell to his gremlin children. They'd never been left alone before.

"My two sons, from now until the time you are ready, I will prepare you to survive without me. When that day arrives, I will set you free to explore the world on your own."

The gremlins nodded with saddened eyes and lowered ears. They loved their adopted dad.

"Very well then," finished Kudos rising to his feet, "your first act of responsibility will be the upkeep of our home until my return. That means cleaning up after yourselves. I don't want to come back to a lunatic of a mess!"

The two gremlins teared up as they waved their goodbyes. Kudos mounted his white horse which he had jokingly named Hocus.

****

Hocus was an aging steed who was equally as stubborn as his master. As Kudos' steadfast mount and duelling partner, they fought bravely through countless wars. They loved many women and drank much wine together. Now neither of them can trust a fart.

****

With a jolt of energy, Kudos and Hocus galloped ahead of the others and led the way up the creek. Their destination, the Arkonian castle.

Chapter VII
Destiny.

Nyte Shade and Kelar arrived at the second barge crossing. Savita, who was already paying their barge fare, searched about. “Where’s Kudos, Nyte?”

“He’s back there somewhere. I think old Hocus wore himself out on the first straight stretch.”

“There he is,” pointed Kelar.

Down the hill came Kudos and Hocus slowly plugging along.

“Old people suck!” poked Kelar.

That “old person” fought the wars which gave you your freedom,” reminded Savita.

“I respect that, Lady Cosmos.” Kelar accepted her words of admonition and altered his tone. “It’s what he is today that concerns me. Just look at him. He drools more than his horse.”

“Did you miss me?” asked Kudos. “And, by the way, just for the record…we let you beat us. Isn’t that right, Hocus?”

Hocus nodded his head with a snort. Kudos dismounted and then stretched the clicks from his back. He stared at Kelar with a one-eyed glare. “Careful how you tread, son!”

“Or what?” said Kelar holding a smirk.

Kudos grabbed Kelar from his horse and pulled him to the ground hard. On one knee staring at his quarry eye to eye the sorcerer rasped, “You’ll be lucky to reach my age, young Kelar.”

Hocus nodded his head again and added a snort for good measure. Remounting his steed, Kudos took a big swig from his gourd. “Enough horse play…no offence, Hocus,” laughed the sorcerer. “Let’s board the barge and cross the Riegan River!”

****

The barge they boarded was 20 feet wide by 50 feet long. Attached to it was a two-inch-thick rope that pulled or loosened on either side of the river by enormous winding drums. These drums were powered by the river's current. The three crew members were shady-looking characters who took hygiene lightly. The one who seemed to be of greater importance had a thick scar running down the side of his shaved head. The smaller of the three wore an eye patch and favoured his left leg. The third and largest was the guard. His armour, stained in blood, could tell many stories of unpaid tolls.

****

"They must run into some pretty rough characters," Kudos thought.

As the barge began its voyage across the river, the four riders stood overlooking the bow. Other than themselves, only one other passenger was on board. It was an elderly woman sitting on a wagon pulled by a single scruffy-looking horse. She wore tattered robes with a hood that barely covered her full head of grey frizzled hair. Her nose was as pointy as her chin. Her movement still.
Nyte stared at her. She gave him the creeps. The older lady returned the stare. Nyte turned away to avoid the awkwardness. The old lady continued to stare.
The river's current picked up and the barge started to tremble. Nyte noticed an object fall from the lady's wagon. He walked over and picked it up. Oddly, it was a silver bull's horn. Nyte handed it back to her.

The eerie lady smiled revealing a full set of unusually sharp teeth. "Why, thank you, dear." She rasped.

"You are welcome, ma'am."

"I am a gypsy who travels from town to town selling trinkets and insight. My name is Jasmine."

"Hello, I'm Nyte."

The two exchanged handshakes. Her fragile grip was cold and dry.

"With your approval, Nyte, I would like to read your hand in payment for your kindness."

"Sure, I guess it couldn't hurt." The lady seemed nice enough and Nyte was curious as to what she might say. The gypsy grasped his palm and began to read. "It says here you will have two children with two different women…you ladies' man you," winked the gypsy.

"Wait a moment. How very peculiar." Jasmine, the gypsy woman, seemed mystified.

"What is it?" barked Nyte as fast as the words could leave his mouth.

"It's your lifeline, son. It ends here but then it starts again over there. Very peculiar indeed. It appears you are going to live a remarkably interesting life."

"Well, thanks anyway," and with that, Nyte pulled his hand away. His state of confusion knit his lips together. He thought to himself, "Should I believe her, or should I forget this ever happened?" He was leaning toward the latter.

"Hold on a moment, Nyte. I would like you to have this horn. It's special."

Nyte took the horn and looked it over carefully.

"What does it do?"

"Place the wide end to your lips then drink." Jasmine smiled revealing her sharp teeth.

Nyte did as he was told and to his delight the horn poured beer—a never-ending horn of cold, delicious beer.

"Thank you kindly!"

"You're welcome, Nyte. From what I've read on your hand, son, you'll need it." The gypsy woman smiled once again revealing her unusually sharp teeth.

A young girl's head peaked out from behind Jasmine. Hidden behind a wall of darkness shed by the carriage, her face became more visible the closer she moved into the light. Sunlight revealed a child no older than nine. She had long black and silver hair. Her skin was golden brown. It was her eyes that caught Nyte's attention for one was blue and the other green.

Jasmine carefully pushed the young girl back into hiding. "Well, safe travels, Nyte," attempting to usher him away.

"Safe travels to you, too, and thanks again." Nyte backed away cautiously. He returned to his horse and hid the horn within his saddle bag.

"Looking for a date to the peace conference, Nyte?" sniped Kelar.

"You're a funny guy," replied Nyte intensely.

"Yeah. I have my moments." Kelar could not resist any and every opportunity to throw jabs at Nyte.

"Will you two lay off each other? You are starting to drive me crazy." Savita was tired of the banter.

"Why, my dear," asked Kudos, "would you let them drive you crazy when you already know it's within walking distance!" laughed Kudos who drank from his gourd.

"Would you care for a pull, dear?"

Savita cringed from its smell and graciously declined.

After the barge landed at the dock, its ramp was lowered to the river's edge. Jasmine waved her farewell to Nyte while riding her wagon down the riverside. As she rode off, the little girl poked her head out the back and stared curiously at Nyte. Nyte smiled and waved to her. She returned the smile and waved back.

Then, Nyte followed Savita's lead into the lush forest.

The four riders travelled slowly through a rather hilly range of soapstone escarpments. It was a visually astonishing terrain molded by the winds of time. Beyond this range known as the Soapstone Hills, they galloped through the lifeless flat lands of Desolation Valley and by nightfall the weary travellers arrived at the rainforest surrounding Lake Aeron.

"There it is," slurred the inebriated Kudos. "Drakonia's largest lake!"

After setting up camp and starting a fire with Kudos' hooch, the four travelers sat down to a starlit dinner. As the night progressed and Kudos had long since passed out from the drink, Savita tested the students.

"Do you know where you are?"

Both students nodded and Kelar answered, "We're on the northwest corner of Lake Aeron. Roughly to the east of us is the Tarnian castle. Nyte's and my kingdom. To the south of us is the Thorenite castle where Nyte's friend, Terex, was born. And on the southern side of this lake is the Teasian castle where our teachers, Lord, and Lady Dunlam, were born."

"Excellent, Kelar, your sense of direction and geographical knowledge are strong attributes."

Nyte reached into his saddlebag and pulled out his magical horn. After taking a big drink, he handed it to Kelar.

"That old gal gave you this!" cheered Kelar.

"Let's only have one drink, Kelar. We need to be clear headed for tomorrow."

"That's a wise decision, Nyte." applauded Savita.

"Now, I'm off to bed. I suggest you follow in suit."

Exhausted, Savita nestled herself into a comfortable position and drifted off to sleep.

In the late hours of the evening, Nyte and Kelar were completely inebriated. Side by side, they talked throughout the night until, inevitably, the conversation trailed to the knot in each of their stomachs. The Mystique Forest lay ahead.

"We can do this, Kelar." Nyte was trying hard to be coherent. "Together, we'll succeed. We'll look out for each other."

"You promise, Nyte? We'll look out for each other?"

"Of course, Kelar. I love you, man!"

"You're not afraid?" Kelar's words came out garbled.

"Of course not!" Nyte tried his best to sound reassuring.

"I hope our schooling isn't important to the forest." Kelar's confidence was clearly in the tank.

"Why would you care? Your top of the class with me."

Kelar fell silent for a moment...then confided, "To be honest, Nyte, I cheated my way through class."

"You what!"

"I cheated! Before our teachers would grade my work, I'd sneak in and copy your answers."

"That does explain a lot—like why you didn't know what a Minotaur was."

Kelar's eyes started to blur moving in and out of focus. The world began to spin. He crawled to his blankets by the fire and closed his weary eyes. Nyte grabbed another blanket. He rolled it up and placed it under Kelar's head. Then laying down on his own, he stared into the star-clustered night sky.

"I am afraid...I'm very afraid," he whispered to himself while drifting off to sleep.

"Wake up, Nyte. It's time to go! Come on. Wake up!" repeated Savita jerking him back and forth.

Nyte slowly came to. "Where am I? Uh…never mind, don't answer that. It's all coming back now."

Kelar was already awake and vomiting by the lake.

"Is he going to be, okay?" Nyte asked with a strong note of worry in his voice.

"Okay?" shouted Kudos. "That little wimp bastard! You don't see me puking all over the place!"

"Bloody amateur!"

"Now everyone has to watch where they step, you little dork!"

Kudos drank from his canteen of potent hooch. He staggered into Nyte. "Hey, quit pushing!" accused Kudos.

The drunken sorcerer leaned against Hocus, his horse, for balance then started in with lecturing Nyte. "The liver is evil, son, and should be punished! Isn't that right, Day?"

"My name is Nyte, sir."

"I knew that. So…how do you feel, Day, who just became Nyte?"

"Never felt better sir. I'm not one for having hangovers."

"You're a good man, Nyte," nodded Kudos.

"Alright, everyone pull yourselves together and get ready to ride," ordered Savita impatiently.

"And that means you, too, Kudos," scowled the sorceress.

"Yes ma'am."

"Start drinking water."

"Wonderful idea, ma'am."

By nightfall, Savita, Kudos and the two students had passed through the Cheeno Mountains all the way through the Arkonian Forest to Repka Lake, the main water source of the Arkonian kingdom. Beyond that lake stood the Arkonian castle where the search for peace would continue.

Chapter VIII
The Door of Duren.

On the opposite side of Drakonia, the teacher, Lord Bossel Dunlam, and his group of graduating students arrived at the Kelasian ruins for their final historical lesson. They gathered before the old stone walls protecting the abandoned castle. Its only access, a large entryway formerly secured with thick wooden doors, had been ruptured inward a long time ago.

Lord Dunlam led his students through the splintered doorway and into the ghost Kingdom of Kelasia. Inside its walled barrier towered the Kelasian castle. Its once lightly shaded bricks were now scorched from dragon's breath. Its towers to the east now lay in ruins and the overgrowth of vines and unkept gardens served as proof of its abandonment for decades.

Behind the castle stood Drakonia's largest mountain. On the base of that mountain was the ancient Door of Duren named after the founding father of the Komalsh, Lord Mikel Duren. The students dismounted from their horses and gazed upon the creepy castle for all its horrific history.

Lord Dunlam ran his fingers through his unicorn's mane. "Shiraz, could you be so kind as to escort the student's horses to the stables?"

"I would be honoured," neighed the unicorn.

"Alright class, follow me inside." Lord Bossel Dunlam felt it an honour to lead his entourage.
Inside, the students searched the castle's interior full of lost memories. They wandered through rooms decorated with web-covered paintings and dusty statues. The musky odor of a forsaken past crept into their lungs.

Kris Tarius whispered to Arias Jackyle, "There's something very unsettling about this place."

"It's the smell of death and lost souls," whispered Arias in return.

"As you can see, class," continued Lord Dunlam, "the place was decorated with a dark goth-like atmosphere. This tells us the Kelasian King Tayta—Tayta being his only name, class, because of why?" inquired Bossel keeping the schooling alive.

Neasha Sentrix, who thrived on Drakonian history, answered unchallenged. "The Kelasians didn't believe in surnames. A last name would represent individual families where the Kelasians believed they were all one family—one family under one father, the creator of all life."

"However," explained Lord Dunlam, "after reading their historical records, we found that some Kelasians had visits by this god of theirs, a god who demanded sacrifice."

The class followed their teacher up a set of stairs leading to the library. In the library was a doorway that led outside to a large balcony. Out on the balcony, Bossel pointed to the dark scorch marks along its stone surface.

"These were once Kelasians. The marks are charcoal remains of citizens burnt from the fiery breath of dragons. King Tayta's people were slaughtered in the heat of battle."

"No pun intended!" interrupted Trayke Basa. "Ha, ha. Dragon's breath! Heat of the battle! Ha, ha!"

Bossel glared at Trayke.

Trayke felt his glare and stopped laughing awkwardly.

****

Trayke Basa was not only the pretty boy of the group but was also the class clown. He would tell you it was not by choice either; he would say he just couldn't help himself. Seeing the humour in everything was how his mind worked—an attribute making him popular among his friends…but not so popular among his teachers. In fact, he tends to find himself in quite the precarious situations at times.

****

Now, with the balcony silent from Trayke's unfortunate humour, Lord Dunlam continued. "Their whole population—men, women, and children—fought together to a bitter end. They would be the last kingdom destroyed by Kaylitan and the Dragon's Flute."

Lord Dunlam's face turned ashen. After a moment of silence and obviously shaken by what he was about to say, his shoulders drooped as he reached deep inside to report, "He committed genocide on his own people. A tragic loss, indeed."

Terex Gungnir stood at the back of the class. He felt more comfortable on a battlefield than in a classroom. Hesitantly, he raised his arm.

"What is it, Terex?" asked Lord Dunlam.

****

At times Terex Gungnir was known for getting frustrated when placed in a learning environment. Absorbing books was not his strong point. However, he never stopped trying. History was another class he struggled through. He passed every course by only a thread despite studying hard with the help of his friend, Nyte. Terex was more than a fighter. He was a warrior, who reflected an attitude of never giving up. He would learn more through life than he would in school, and he would continue to improve himself till the day he died.

****

"Yeah, so what you're saying is this Kaylitan guy was actually a Kelasian, right?"

"That is correct, Terex," answered Lord Dunlam encouragingly.

Terex smiled as he looked around to his classmates proudly. Then confusion overcame him, and he had to ask,

"Why would he destroy his own people?"

"The hardest road to return to is the road to sanity, Terex. Somewhere along the line something happened to Kaylitan…something snapped…and in the process he killed everyone he loved."

"Where did Kaylitan get the Dragon's Flute?" asked Kris Tarius whose deep-seeded desire to understand aroused his curiosity.

"No one knows how he came to have this enchanted instrument. Nor does anyone know of its origin. There are no records. We have come to assume it just came to be," confessed Lord Bossel Dunlam.

"Did Lord Cable Demonis go crazy, too?" asked Neasha Sentrix.

"Perhaps. I've known Cable since he was a child and now, he is nothing like the man he was. Truthfully, we don't know what changed him or Lord Cretes Siris. I do, however, find it mysterious how someone who has walked through the Mystique Forest unchallenged—someone whose mind had been opened to psychic gifts and vast knowledge of the Komalsh—would just turn renegade. Never has this happened in the history of our people…but these are not your present concerns. The history of this castle is."

"I have a question," announced Kris. "Why are we the only graduation class ever to spend the night here? Especially when the following day we challenge the Mystique Forest. It makes no sense, Lord Dunlam. We should be preparing for the forest if anything."

"Kris's right," defended Arias. "The history of this castle seems kind of pointless."

"This was the request of Lord Drakus," informed the teacher. "His uncanny ability to foretell the future deters me from questioning his motives."

With that, Bossel guided his class back into the library.

Inside there were old books covered in layers of dust and stacked on shelves reaching up into the vaulted ceilings. Dust-coated statues stood about the room and chandeliers draped in spider webs dangled from the ceiling. Sunlight peered through cracks in broken stained glass windows highlighting motes of dust dancing throughout the room and the musky smell of the Grim Reaper's breath was a simple reminder of the ghosts who lingered.

With more questions than answers, Kris Tarius and Arias Jackyle confronted their teacher.

"What is it, boys?" asked Lord Dunlam while admiring the sculpture of a dark angel. "Well, go on. I can feel your restless thoughts. However, it's up to you whether you share them or not. I would never enter your minds without permission. The Komalsh code forbids it."

The rest of the class gathered around Kris who always took a stand when it came to asking insightful questions.

"History books have mentioned Kaylitan as an apprentice."

"This is correct, Kris," replied Bossel.

"Then who was his teacher?"

"His teacher was a very powerful warlock named Kaleb."

"A warlock? Don't they practice witchcraft?" Terex was confused.

"You are correct," answered the teacher. "You see, all modern-day kingdoms have a wizard and apprentice for their majesties counsel. The Kelasians, however, had a darker impression on life. The reasons are explained here within this castle, students."

"Not all witchcraft is evil," shared Arias.

"This is correct," replied Bossel. "However, this particular group of Drakonians had no intentions of doing good with the craft. Which leads us to your assignment. You are to explore the castle and show me proof of their involvement with this dark power."

Eagerly the students paired up and began to explore the castle for clues. Bossel wandered downstairs to a large room at the back of the castle. There he knelt to the floor, closed his eyes, and left this realm to a meditated state of consciousness. He would allow the space for his students to search for clues that no longer exist. All knowledge pertaining to their assignment had been removed from the castle years ago. This assignment that he had just given to his students was never intended to be resolved. At Lord Drakus' request, they were to spend the night. The assignment was a ruse. Bossel never questioned why.

Trayke Basa and Terex Gungnir paired up to work together. During their rummaging through the castle, they found themselves in the Kelasian throne room. Terex unexpectedly sank into the late King's dusty throne now deteriorated with age. It was a failed attempt at trying to act like a king. Holding a long face, he slammed his fist down onto the throne's arm rest. "Reading frustrates me!" he scowled.

Trayke took a seat upon a wooden crate situated next to the throne. "I didn't think you could read."

"I'm too tired to inflict pain on you right now, Trayke."

"And I am too tired to receive pain, Terex." Trayke started investigating the closed crate. Using his dagger, he pried it open and gazed in disbelief.

"Don't get me wrong," continued Terex. "Reading is essential to learning. It's just that I'm getting fed up with all this learning. Really fed up! When are we going to fight? Where are the battles we trained for? Where is the bloodshed, dammit?"

"Yeah!" added Trayke. "Where is all the rum?"

"Yeah!" shouted Terex. "Where is all the...rum?"

Trayke removed two bottles of rum from the wooden crate that he had just pried open. With a sly grin, he handed one to Terex. "Here's the rum, buddy! They must have known we were coming!"

Terex held the bottle before him. He blew off the dust and used his teeth to remove the cork. Trayke, who was one step ahead, held his bottle high for a friendly cheer and sang after the two bottles collided, "Here's to you and here's to me. Forever friends we'll always be. But if we ever disagree, then the hell with you and here's to me!" They slammed back their bottles, wiped the spillage with their sleeves and after howling like wolves to the moon, they drank down another. The pattern continued for several rounds.

Elsewhere in the castle Neasha Sentrix and Kolos Dreken searched the Kelasian warlock's bedroom, a spacious room with an outer deck overlooking the southwest expanse of Drakonia's flat lands. Neasha searched the room's private library vigorously. For over an hour she scrolled through journals and books of Kybalion, Spagyrics and countless more volumes common to an alchemist's private library. Still, she found nothing. Kolos had given up long before and sat in a chair mumbling himself into a depression.

Flustered, Neasha laid down on the warlock's dusty bed and sulked at the impossible assignment. She stared out the window into the star filled night. "The time has passed by quickly," she thought.

Turning away from the window's view, she watched Kolos as he yawned and nodded off to sleep. Yawning herself, she laid her head back onto the pillow and stared up at the ceiling. On it was a painting of the Door of Duren. But this door was opened and inside were two red demonic eyes. Yawning uncontrollably, Neasha closed her eyes and dozed off to sleep.

Elsewhere in the castle Lord Bossel Dunlam, still cross-legged in a meditative state, had created a barrier of green psychic energy, which illuminated his body.
Kris Tarius and Arias Jackyle stood beside him.

"Where do you think he is right now?" asked Arias.

"He's in his mind," answered Kris."

"I know that." spoke Arias with a chuckle, "I meant, what place is his mind that keeps him in such a state of bliss? Just look at him smile."

"Only he can answer that Arias," explained Kris.

"He's in his own defined happiness. His place of meditation. Some of us may inherit this gift among many others. All Komalsh differ. Our strengths vary. I'm excited to find out what Komalsh gifts I have been bestowed.

"I am excited, too," answered Arias, "but I'm still a bit nervous. What if I fail, Kris? Am I truly ready?"
Kris drew out his sword and swung the blade sideways towards Arias' throat. Instinctively, Arias drew his sword and blocked the life-threatening blow. Eye to eye they connected. Kris held a confident look solid and fearless while Arias' expression showed shock and confusion. Kris lowered his blade.

"What the hell are you doing?"

"I'm answering your question, Arias. You see I placed you in a position of weakness and without thought you reacted. You didn't need answers; you didn't need education. You didn't need to be ready. All you needed was intuition. That intuition saved your life. That intuition wasn't taught nor was it trained. This is who you are, Arias. This is who we are."

Kris turned to an opened window and gazed out toward the stars. "Arias, my friend, I believe the Mystique Forest is all about who you are and what you are. If you trust yourself, the forest will trust you too."

Arias smiled and nodded. "You're probably right, my friend."

"Besides," continued Kris, "why else would Lord Drakus be pushing us through this? He must believe in us and if he does, then so should we."

"What about Terex and Trayke?" worried Arias.

"They're not the sharpest tools in the shed."

"Trayke, well, he'll drink the forest under the table and don't worry about Terex. He'll fight the Mystique Forest head on…and win."

"Ha, ha, you are probably right," relaxed Arias.

"I wonder how the others are doing. I wonder if they have found any clues?"

"Yeah, maybe we should go find them," suggested Arias. "We should get this assignment done before it's too late."

Arias set off into the castle.

"I'll catch up to you later," said Kris. "I'm going to go see the Door of Duren while we're here."

"Alright Kris, see you later."

After the two went their separated ways, Lord Dunlam released himself from his meditative state. He'd been listening to the students…some might say eavesdropping on them. The old teacher smiled while shaking his head in disbelief. "Perhaps Lord Drakus is right," he thought. "Individually they are weak, together they're strong."

Bossel rise to his feet and followed Kris outside. He kept his distance so as not to be seen.

In the throne room Terex and Trayke were deep into their bottles.

"This is some premium rum," smiled Trayke feeling rejuvenated from the morning's hangover.

"Hair of the dog, eh Trayke?" cheered Terex. "I wonder why it was never found?"

Terex looked around the room. Everything was left as it was that fatal night. Books were on shelves. Candle holders and furniture stood in the same place. A thick layer of dust and cobwebs formed the proof that nothing was out of place. The place appeared untouched since the night the dragons came.

Terex looked down at the freshly opened box of rum.

"Hey Trayke, I don't think we were supposed to touch that."

Trayke drank down a big swig and then held back the burning sensation in his throat by scrunching his face. After colour returned to his face, Trayke graded the rum.

"This is smooth!"

Terex shrugged off his moment of guilt and took a drink himself. After releasing his own painful expression from the rum's bite, he asked. "I wonder why this place hadn't been looted by thieves. It's totally unprotected." Standing at the doorway and hearing enough of the conversation to participate, Arias walked in and answered.

"This place is feared to be haunted, Terex. You see, with all the history of Kelasian witchcraft and their demise from the dragons, folks don't come near this place…and I don't blame them either. It's kind of creepy."

Arias sat next to his friends and glanced down at the open case of rum. "Let me guess. It was Trayke's nose that sniffed it out."

"Grab a bottle my friend. There's plenty to go around," goaded Trayke.

****

Arias Jackyle and Trayke Basa had a friendship like no other. Being children from two different cultures they'd first met at the school of Olemeeze and became close friends from the start. They were both considered odd among the children of their own kingdoms. Gifted with an elevated awareness. A higher level of consciousness which in time pushed Trayke into self-medicating with alcohol. Unlike Arias who maintained control, Trayke loved the booze.

Before any child enters the school of Olemeeze they must first accept a mind scan from a seasoned member of the Komalsh. In their case, it was Lord Drakus. In fact, all the graduating students who would challenge the Mystique Forest this year were, oddly enough, hand picked by Lord Drakus.

****

Arias sat with his friends and uncorked a bottle. Drinking a little more than normal, he found himself wearing the same scrunched face his friends had worn earlier.

Trayke laughed. "Smooth, isn't it?"

After a moment to compose himself, Arias continued, "As I was saying, there have been very few visits to this place. Historians mostly. People researching the Door of Duren which this castle was built around. On any occasion, only two Komalsh had ever spent the night. I cannot but wonder why Lord Drakus would request us to spend the night here. This isn't part of the Olemeeze school curriculum."

"Who were the other two Komalsh that spent the night here?" queried Trayke.

Arias drank some more. "What's that?"

"You said only two other Komalsh spent the night here. Who were they?"

"Well, that's what concerns me Trayke. The other two were Lords Cable Demonis and Cretes Siris."

"I'm sure there's a reason for this," added Terex confidently. "There's a method to their madness, Arias. I gave up on trying to understand." Terex took another swill of rum. "If you are curious, though, go ask Lord Dunlam again. Maybe this time you'll get a straight answer," he chuckled.

Arias drank another swig from his bottle and simply replied, "Nope…the rum is starting to go down easy."

The Kelasian castle was protected by fifty-foot-high stone walls. These walls were set into the towering mountain protecting the castle's back yard. Against the toe of that mountain, inside the castle walls, stood the ancient Door of Duren.

At the castle's front yard, its perimeter walls connected into the kingdom's only entrance. A thick wooden door lay in splinters from the final battle. It was said during the Kelasian kingdom's last stand that a single dragon stood at the gate blowing its fiery breath on all who tried to escape. This impenetrable fort was built to keep them safe and in an ironic twist of fate sealed their doom. These thoughts circulated in Kris' mind as he journeyed through the castle yard.

The castle's back yard was decorated with gazebos, stone statues and a fountain concealed by the overgrowth of vines and ivy.

"A beautiful place at one time," thought Kris while hiking toward the towering mountain.

****

The Kelasians were an advanced society. They invented many essential ways of living which modern kingdoms adopted today such as their aqueduct. The aqueduct was a complex set of drains using gravity and pressure allowing access to water for toilets and tubs throughout the castle. This included the ability to access hot water with the help of another invention they employed called heat vents. During the castle's construction, fist size exhaust holes were tunnelled through the stone walls. Heated from a furnace deep within the undergrounds of the castle, these tunnels channeled heat through the castle walls and floors keeping the castle at a respectable temperature. They also channeled from a water reservoir giving them hot water for bathing.

Another invention were their pillar lights. These pillar lights were specially angled mirrors surrounding the tops of six-foot stone pillars. On the tops of these bold pillars two feet in diameter were stone bowls to hold cloth, wood and oil used for slow burning. Once lit, the mirrors reflected and amplified the light.

****

Kris approached the towering mountain. Night had fallen across the land and vision became limited. In the darkness Kris overheard a twig snap. Cautiously he unsheathed his sword and turned toward it. Unable to see, Kris relied on his hearing. He heard a slight sigh exhale behind him. Kris turned and swung his sword. His blade skillfully blocked by another's.

"Who are you? Reveal yourself!" demanded Kris.

The sound of a footstep scraped beside him. Kris swung his sword again which too was easily blocked by his opponent.

A shadowed figure appeared before him delivering a blur of sword strikes. Kris blocked each one skillfully aside until his opponent's blade lifted his sword from his grip and tossed it through the darkness. Feeling the cold blade pressing against the side of his throat, Kris surrendered by raising his hands.

"You should see your face right now, Kris." The voice sounded familiar. "You look so silly."

Kris was confused. "Lord Dunlam?"

"Well at least your ears serve you well," answered Bossel lowering his sword.

Kris fought hard to breathe. "You scared the soul out of me!"

"Come, follow me, son. I'll show you what you're looking for."

Lord Dunlam grabbed a nearby torch. After locating Kris's sword, he went to the nearest pillar light and lit its top. Bossel continued to light each one as they headed toward the base of the mountain.

At the base of the mountain, they found an ancient stone stairway reaching high into the shadowed side of the mountain. The stairway was of Elvin design and built long before the Kelasian peoples ever existed. While lighting the stairway's pillar tops, Bossel led Kris up the ancient stairwell. "This leads to the Door of Duren, Kris."

The stairs led to a floor constructed of odd-shaped slabs of granite. Tall thick hedges decorated the perimeter and along the mountain's base stood the ancient Door of Duren. The door itself stood ten feet high and twelve feet wide. It was made of a polished durenthium metal, and it had clearly been designed by Elvin hands. Carved warnings of its trapped Nomayden prisoners were etched all around the door's perimeter partially hidden behind moss and cobwebs. On the right side of the door was an inset lever with ancient numbers around it with combination lock.

"Well, there it is," introduced Bossel.

Kris placed his hand on it. "It's so cold." He was not expecting the icy temperature while admiring its intricate design.

"Enjoy the wonders of a door, son. I'm going to return to my meditation."

Kris took the opportunity to ask Bossel the question he and Arias pondered earlier. "Where do you go Lord Dunlam? I mean…when you meditate."

"Well," stuttered Bossel. "If you really must know, I summon Mrs. Dunlam and we join minds. It's the place I'm happiest," grinned the old teacher.

Bossel patted Kris on the shoulder. "When I was your age, son, this door fascinated me in inexplicable ways I could not put into words. But I'm old now and it bores the shit out of me so goodnight, Kris."

The old teacher left to go back down the staircase.

****

Lord Duren, the first Knight of Malshidiel and founder of the Komalsh, was the one who led the way to defeating Drakonia's first real threat, the Nomaydens. These abrasive predators threatened the existence of all living creatures and were known to turn to cannibalism when all other options had been depleted. A humanoid predator species, that stood four feet high and weighed no more then 100 pounds, were pack hunters with black scaly skin and long pointy ears. They had cat-like eyes and razor-sharp, canine teeth. Their three-toed hands and feet held their long, sharp jagged claws—tools for carving the flesh from bones.

Thousands of these Drakonian predators were forced into the mountain's singular cave by Lord Duren's army. With the help of Elvin sorcery, the door was enchanted to imprison this threat indefinitely. Many had speculated the trapped Nomaydens fed on each other until only one remained—one who must surely have died of hunger a long time ago.

****

Kris was fascinated by this legend. The worst thing about these creatures was that the Komalsh were unable to read the minds of the Nomaydens. They couldn't communicate with them nor reason with them. They were nature's version of the perfect killing machine which no telepathic power could influence.

"Imagine that." Kris was flabbergasted at the thought.

"Lord Duren was given all this psychic power from the angel Malshidiel only to spend his whole life battling an enemy upon which it had little or no effect. He must have been innovative and exceptionally good with a sword. I admire that."

As Kris stood admiring the door, he noticed that the cobwebs around it were torn. In fact, the webs around the lever had also been separated.

"The door's been opened!" he concluded.

Kris stepped closer to the door and investigated its evidential tampering. "This is not good." He backed away cautiously and paused for a moment. Then his fear turned to curiosity.

****

Kris Tarius was a profound thinker and a strong student born with a deep-seated desire for truth and understanding. Ever since he was a child, he couldn't help but indulge his curiosity. If there was something he felt was misunderstood, he wouldn't stop until he understood it. When someone said it was impossible, he said it was improbable. As a child this character trait often got him into trouble. As he got older, it became a tool empowering him to excel in the educational programs at the School of Olemeeze.

****

Kris decided if he was going to feel right about the recent opening of the door, he'd have to understand it. He started searching the door for clues. During his investigation, the combination lock started to rotate and creek. Kris backed away slowly. Terror turned to adrenaline. After a moment of panic, he regained his senses and ran toward the hedge. There he hid with one hand on the hilt of his sword and both eyes on the Door of Duren.

Chapter IX
Kingdom of Peace.

Savita, Kudos, Nyte and Kelar rode across the draw bridge and into the Arkonian kingdom. The travellers were welcomed with open arms by nobles and villagers alike. While the Arkonian guards escorted their rides to the stable, they were greeted by two Kings. Cronos Sarius of Arkonia and Kalem Turek of Dosania.

"Welcome back to Arkonia, Lady Cosmos." King Sarius addressed Savita by her Komalsh title.

Savita smiled graciously and then gave the king a warm embrace. "It's always a pleasure to see you, your majesty."

During their embrace, King Turek politely nudged his way toward Savita. "How's my little girl doing?"

"Just fine, Kalem, and you?"

"I've conquered worse times. My condolences on the recent loss of your noble friends," uttered Turek with the deepest of sincerity. "It's a most unfortunate tragedy."

"We will get to the bottom of this, I assure you, my friend," promised Savita.

"That I do not doubt," replied King Turek. "So then, who are your guests?"

"You remember my adopted son, Nyte Shade.

"Yes indeed," smiled Turek.

"This is Kelar and of course you know Kudos Nexus," boasted Savita.

"Of course, we do," King Sarius' disappointment could not be contained beneath his angry scowl. "How could anyone forget the drunken sorcerer who cursed my prize horse!"

The King paused for a moment as he caught himself losing character. Instinctively, he controlled his sudden outburst and with a restrained sharpness in his tongue said,

"This drunk placed a spell on my horse, Sleipnir, causing him to speak fluently."

"I can explain that." defended Kudos. "You see, I was just trying to help you with that sick steed. He was dying! So, I used my magic." Kudos wiggled his fingers about. "Evidently it was the wrong spell, but hey! The horse got better, and besides, who doesn't want a talking horse?"

"The bloody thing hasn't shut up since the day you helped!" snapped King Sarius. "It wouldn't be so bad if he had something smart to say! But he's as sharp as a marble! The village idiot strikes up a more stimulating conversation!"

"Why don't you just put him down?" suggested Kelar.

"Who? The horse or the sorcerer?" snapped the King.

Kudos spoke in his own defence with confidence. "I was drunk, it seemed like the thing to do at the time."

King Sarius shook his head while trying to avoid Kudos' booze tainted breath. "Just stay away from me," he scowled.

King Sarius turned from the sorcerer and clapped his hands twice. Four elegant young women dressed in loose, white, silky robes came forward. Their transparent facial garments made it easy to acknowledge their beauty while their body language delicately sprinkled a touch of seduction no single young man could refuse.

"These young ladies will escort you to your quarters gentlemen," instructed King Sarius.

Without debate Nyte, Kelar, and Kudos followed their escorts respectfully.

"Are you not tired, Lady Cosmos?" The King of Arkonia was concerned.

"I must speak with Lord Drakus immediately, your majesty."

"Very well. Lord Drakus will be dining with me and my royal guests tonight." The King paused a moment. "Do tell, Lady Cosmos, do the Komalsh not have the ability to communicate by thought? Wouldn't that have been an easier solution?"

"Yes, we call it hailing and I've tried to get his attention, but he keeps blocking me," answered Savita.

"Then you must accompany me to our prestigious dinner, Lady Cosmos." King Sarius noted Savita's filthy face and well travelled Komalsh attire. "I tell you what, my warrior princess. There's still time for you to bathe and dress in more fashionable attire. Perhaps under all the soiling hides a beautiful lady."

"I'd forgotten what that feels like," surrendered Savita.

"An easy remedy my dear. Come with me and we'll prepare you for dinner," instructed the King.

****

Savita Cosmos, a powerful sorceress. Was acclaimed as the most powerful in Drakonia. She was also a prominent Komalsh who passed the test of passage through the Mystique Forest with little effort. Her parents had raised her with the proper manner and etiquette to mingle amongst royalty. Her Arkonian heritage gave her insight into literature and the fine arts. Gifted with a photographic memory and a love for reading, she absorbed knowledge quickly. A true warrior on the outside formed the armour of bravery and under that shell was a lady of nobility—a lady rarely seen these days. Having a bath and dressing up for a prestigious dinner tickled her pink.

****

The Arkonian dining room walls were decorated with priceless art and sculptures. Tables displayed colourful arrangements of flowers housed in blown glass vases. Golden suits of armour stood in every corner and in the centre of the room stood a thirty-foot-long dining table carved from a dark red cedar. Each table setting had silver-engraved cutlery, plates, and goblets. A bottle of Arkonia's finest wine accompanied every place setting.

As the festivities commenced, kings, queens and guests began arriving at a gradual pace. And as one might expect, the conversation and the laughter increased in volume as the attendees grew in number. Silver goblets of wine were raised and with each cheer, friends old and new drank to celebrate. This was, after all, the pre-peace-conference dinner hosted by the King of Arkonia. Camaraderie was the aim. No detail was overlooked.

Savita entered the room with grace and elegance. Her Komalsh lineage revealed a lady of nobility. The sorceress in her chose a black and red lace gown complementing her curves. Her silver jewelry glittered in the candlelit room. She was escorted to the head of the table where King Sarius and nobility rose to greet her. Beside King Sarius stood Lord Drakus and King Turek.

"Please, be seated!" spoke the King joyously. Musicians played flutes and stringed instruments quietly in the background while table servants delivered the dinner meal.

"Let the feast commence," shouted the proud King of Arkonia.

Savita, showing no appetite, sipped from her wine then rolled it around her goblet. "Excuse me, Lord Drakus."

"What troubles you, Lady Cosmos? I could feel it from the time you entered the room."

"The Fenka Rek murders my lord," answered Savita as she focused on the ripples in her wine. "My worry is for the ones who are at risk."

"I'm not worried," assured Lord Drakus biting into a leg of lamb.

Savita stood insulted. "It's quite clear my lord that something sinister is at work here. This cannot be excused as coincidence."

"I am quite aware of the current events, Lady Cosmos. You must trust me. In time, all will unfold."

"But, my lord, all who were appointed to hide Lord Demonis' statue are being hunted. Our people are being tortured then murdered!"

Drakus placed his finished lamb leg onto his plate. After wiping the remnants from his beard, he calmly replied, "I know what you are thinking, Lady Cosmos. Don't worry. I had Lady Dunlam removed from Olemeeze yesterday. She is now under the protection of Castle Malshidiel."

A sign of relief crossed Savita's face. "And what of Bossel?"

"He and the students are spending the night at the Kelasian ruins under my direction. Instead of interrupting their final class, I sent eight Komalsh under the command of Lady Sook to hide outside the castle for protection. Lord Dunlam will be fine, Savita. I assure you."

"Thank you, Lord Drakus. I should have never doubted your leadership in these times." Savita paused a moment. "But what of Lords Kloken and Pronyk?"

Lord Drakus delayed a moment as he glanced around their end of the table. Everyone in an ears reach was staring at him.

"Well…," said the eager King Sarius.

"Well, since you all seem genuinely concerned," spoke the hungry Lord Drakus, "Lord Kloken was located and placed under guard near Assaroe Falls. He then went home to the Fylosian kingdom on rest leave. Lord Pronyk, however, hasn't been located. I can't seem to hail him."

Drakus turned to his plate and continued to eat.

The table fell silent. Savita's appetite was beyond return.

On the western side of the Arkonian castle in their assigned quarters, Kudos, Nyte, Kelar and the four Arkonian girls were on the quest for inebriation. With the aide of Nyte's horn of bottomless beer and Kudos' home-made hooch the party was in full swing.

Although Nyte and Kelar stole the hearts of the girls, it was Kudos' character that kept the conversation alive. His charm and contagious laughter made for great company.

The girls danced around egging each other on. They drank and danced with flirtatious gestures.

"It doesn't get better than this!" howled Nyte falling off the end of the bed.

"Damn rights, it can get better!" shouted Kudos.

"Let's go to the Arkonian stomping grounds!"

"Yeah!" screeched the girls. "Let's go to the tavern!"

Trouble was brewing.

The royal dinner was at an end. Servants removed plates and cutlery while replacing empty bottles of wine. The stringed instruments continued to play softly in the background. The music seemed to muffle the garbled voices attempting to make conversation while becoming increasingly less sober. Drakonian royalty had a history of generosity in the imbibing department.

With a burning curiosity, Savita asked King Sarius, "Where is this new King of Sykania, your majesty?"

"He hasn't arrived yet my dear. He's scheduled to arrive tomorrow morning in time for the peace conference. Their wizard, Malores, assured me of his attendance."

"Who is he?" asked Savita.

"Nobody knows my dear. It's a secret kept behind their castle walls. You know what Sykanians are like." He winked. "They seldom interact with any other than their own."

"They're definitely not supporters of the peace conference," added Lord Drakus after drinking down his goblet.

"No, they are not, indeed," nodded the King.

"This wine is exquisite, King Sarius," complimented Drakus. "I would have to say the finest I've had."

"Thank you, Lord Drakus. We Arkonians take great pride in our wines and brandies."

"Have you tried Kudos' wine?" asked Savita. "Very unique, indeed."

"Yes, Lady Cosmos," added King Sarius with great distaste and acid in his words. "However unique and quality are placed on either side of the wine spectrum, I tell you that drunken sorcerer is not a favourite of mine! Not just the horse incident either, I might add. His whole being disgusts me. I feel enraged at the very sight of him!"

"Excuse me, Lord Drakus," interrupted King Turek hoping to deflate the vein protruding from King Sarius' forehead. "I was contemplating what you said earlier about your inability to communicate telepathically to Lord Pronyk. Is it possible he could be blocking you out?"

"Yes, indeed, but why would he?" question Lord Drakus.

King Turek leaped to his hypothesis. "We are unsure about anything to do with these assassinations Lord Drakus. A possible scenario could lead to Lord Pronyk as a suspect, or as an accomplice, if I may."

Lord Drakus downed another goblet of wine. Then wiped the spillage from his beard. "It is a possibility, King Turek, but highly unlikely. Lord Pronyk is a good man."

"So were Lords Cretes Siris and Cable Demonis." reminded Turek.

Drakus pondered a moment. "This is true, and in these strange times anything is possible. I assure you, however, no rock will be unturned. For now, my curiosity lies with this new King of Sykania."

Drakus waved his empty goblet to the servant as King Sarius rose from his seat and addressed his audience.

"Bring on the entertainment!" He clapped. A stream of men and women dressed in black satin clothing and masks representing different Earth creatures danced in synchronization around the table. The background music followed as the celebrations continued.

Well established in the tavern, Kelar and the girls seated themselves around the arm-wrestling table, a common event held in Arkonia as a source of entertainment and quick coin. Currently, Kelar was four wins in, and a large crowd had gathered around him. Their bets grew larger, the adrenaline grew stronger, and Kelar's ego grew out of control.

The escorting girls cheered Kelar on as he defeated a local farmer. Rising from the table, Kelar raised his fists in victory to the surrounding crowd.

"I am the reigning champion!" he cheered. The crowd booed in return.

At a table far from the taverns rowdy event sat Nyte and Kudos.

"What troubles you Nyte? You seem distant tonight."

Nyte stared around the tavern as though he'd seen a ghost. He refilled his pint with the horn he smuggled in and simply said, "Nothing at all."

Unhappy with his questions result, Kudos asked again. This time with a little more grit.

"What's the matter with you boy?"

Nyte stood silent and distant.

"Look at me!" ordered Kudos smacking Nyte on top of the head with his wooden staff.

"Ouch! What's wrong with you?" complained Nyte rubbing his head.

"I asked you a question. Your lack of effort needed a push."

"A push? You hit my head with a stick!"

"Details, details, always details with you. Just answer me the damn question!" Kudos leaned closer to Nyte and whispered humorously. "Don't make me turn you into a talking horse."

Nyte threw out a short burst of laughter. "What did you do to that horse, Kudos? How did a great sorcerer mess that one up?"

"Long story, now quit avoiding my question."

"It's nothing really."

"This nothing smells of something young Shade."

"It's just that, well…I have this secret."

"A secret? What kind of secret?"

"Well, it wouldn't be a secret if I told you," Replied Nyte.

Kudos bopped him on the head again with his wooden staff.

"Alright, alright, I'll tell you. Just stop doing that!"

"It's a deal!" replied the sorcerer.

"When I was younger, I would occasionally have dreams in my sleep."

"We all dream, Nyte."

"Yes, but mine sometimes come true. Like I foresee the future in short moments."

Kudos put his drink back on the table. "Interesting. Prophetic dreams you say? Please elaborate."

"As I've gotten older, they seem to be more frequent and longer. The only way I can silence them is with booze. It seems to calm the noise."

Kudos tilted his head back and downed the end of his pint. Then he stared at his young friend with great interest. "How detailed are these dreams?"

"Well, mostly just glimpses of an insignificant moment. However, the odd time, they're quite detailed." Nyte paused staring down at his drink. "Like the other night. I dreamt of this whole tavern and even parts of this conversation."

"What else, Nyte?" persisted Kudos.

"Well," chuckled Nyte, "the rest of the dream seems a little far fetched. My experiences after my dreams don't always come out the way I dreamt them. It's like my imagination took over and rearranged the coming events."

"Nor here or there, Nyte. Please explain your dream."

"Well, for some strange reason this whole tavern gets into a big brawl. The dream is a little blotchy but as I recall we all end up in jail."

"Jail!" repeated Kudos. "That does seem rather strange seeing that we are here as representatives in the peace conference."

"Yes, I guess your right," agreed Nyte.

"How many others know of this gift?"

"My closest friend, Kris Tarius, knows…and I'm pretty sure Savita knows, too, but nothing has ever been said."

"So, you've kept this a secret until now?"

"Yes, sir."

"Why tell me?" Wondered Kudos.

"I told you about it in the dream I had," replied Nyte.

"Interesting. Probably a wise choice to keep this a secret. Not everyone shares these kinds of gifts in a positive way. We should keep this to ourselves for now."

"I understand, Kudos."

"Do not fear your gift, Nyte, not by any means. To me, this sounds inherited from your parents."

Kudos paused in memory of Radik and Raine Shade. "I can see their faces like it was yesterday. I sure miss your parents, Nyte. Wonderful people they were."

Nyte paused as his intoxicated mind wandered. "You know, Kudos, I really wish I could meet my parents. I don't even know what my father looked like, and my mother's face is just a distant dream. Everyone who meets me seems to know who they were. Just the pressure alone to fill those boots…well, I find it overwhelming at times."

"You shouldn't worry too much, Nyte. I knew your parents quite well. They were genuine people. They never quit. Stayed true to their words and loved each other immensely."

Kudos lit his pipe.

Nyte stood silent. He had read all the history books on his parents but the things he wanted to know were only acquired intimately. He knew his father ended the Dragon Wars saving countless lives but what was he like to talk to? He knew his father was a great swordsman but what was his humour like? He knew his mother started the first peace conference but what was her favourite colour? He knew his mother inherited, *The Book of Dragons,* but what did her hair smell like? These were the questions to which he longed for answers.

"Your parents, Nyte, had many great and noble traits," continued Kudos, "traits which flow through your veins today. As for your dreams, perhaps that is something better explained by Lord Drakus."

Kudos contemplated a moment then asked, "After revealing your secret to me, was the rest of this conversation in your dream?"

"I don't think so."

"So, then my words may have altered the future."

"I don't follow." Nyte was drowning in confusion.

"You see, Nyte, time has been written. Well, most of it. There are forks along the road that decide a different fate. We all make choices which intertwine with all the people co-existing in this time frame. The unpredictability of the choices you make prevents any deep future insight or vision. But once those choices are decided, from that moment to the next fork in the road, the ability to foresee the near future becomes possible."

Drunken anger echoed through the tavern interrupting Kudos' train of thought.

"It appears Kelar has been quite successful over there. He's accumulated quite the audience. How about we mosey on over there and see what's going on."

As Kudos got up and left the table Nyte had a moment of clarity. He announced, "I do recall Kelar hurting his wrist."

Across the tavern Kelar was undefeated in arm wrestling. With a combination of large bets and quick wins he managed to attract a large crowd of drunken Arkonian farmers.

Although a good sport would say otherwise, losing is never truly accepted by anyone. But when it comes to a hard-working farmer and his money, the only way to keep people from growing bitter is to win it like a gentleman. It is important to show them great sportsmanship and to befriend the one you've competed with.

That was never Kelar's strong suit.

"I win again!" cheered Kelar while leaping up from the table. "In your face, farm boy!" He laughed while parading around the table. "I am the undefeated champion of Arkonia!" The student of Olemeeze primed with ego-building drink staggered through a crowd of irritated Arkonians. "Is there anyone here man enough to defeat me?" Kelar looked around at the restless crowd flexing his toned physique. He was unaware of the tension amassing in the room.

After his last competitor paid his losses bitterly, Kelar was confronted by a middle-aged man. He stood six feet high and weighed 240 pounds of toned physique. He had long black hair and his deeply set eyes were a cold, dark blue. Never losing eye contact, he volunteered, "I would love to partake in this local hand-holding event." The remark brought laughter from the onlookers.

"Excellent! How much are you willing to lose?" humoured Kelar holding out his hand to shake.

The stranger didn't return his friendly gesture.

"I tell you what, my presumptuous friend. I'll match you everything you've won tonight."

The stranger revealed a large leather bag of gold coins from his robes and observed Kelar smiling with greed.

"You're on, friend! What's your name?" asked Kelar.

The unknown man sat down positioning himself comfortably. Then he looked up into Kelar's eyes and casually replied, "Breton, Breton Korrigan. Captain of the Sykanian guard."

The crowds murmur fell silent. Some even ran for the exit.

"I'm Kelar, student of Olemeeze and soon to be a Komalsh."

"I never asked," replied Breton politely.

"Very well then, Captain Korrigan. Let's do this."

The two joined hands firmly and began to compete. From the get-go Kelar gave all he had. Breton held him back, never losing his smile. His cold blue eyes stared through Kelar's desperation. Moments passed and neither side gained the advantage.

"Time to go down." Breton threw his opponent a wry smile. With superior technique, the Sykanian captain went over the top and pulled Kelar down hard. In the process he broke the student's wrist. Kelar dropped to the floor in agonizing pain.

Captain Korrigan calmly rose from his seat. After grabbing his own bag of gold coins, he left toward the front doorway. Before leaving, he addressed the crowd of upset Arkonian farmers.

"To the workers of Arkonia who lost their fortunes to this petty example of a man. My winnings mean nothing to me. If you'd like your lost bets returned, I suggest you collect from him now."

Breton left the tavern. The tavern competitors surrounded Kelar.

"Yeah!" spoke the largest of them. "Let's collect on his friends, too!"

Right then and there Nyte's dream unfolded with uncanny accuracy and a major fracas broke out.

Outside the brawling tavern, Captain Breton Korrigan rendezvoused with a dead looking wizard dressed in purple robes. "Good evening, Malores. I have succeeded in my task."

Malores looked through the tavern doors and to his delight witnessed Nyte and Kelar in hand-to-hand combat with the Arkonian locals. "Well, well!" regaled the Sykanian wizard. "This ought to muddle the peace talks."

Malores grinned deviously. "You have done a great deed for your king and our people, captain."

"It was easier than anticipated, Malores." Breton felt his ego getting bigger, He was well pleased with his accomplishment. "What are my King's next instructions?"

Malores, still entertained with the tavern scuffle, answered, "You are to return to the mine site. Return to the Avila Mountain Range. There you will resume leadership. Their excavation efforts toward finding the Dragon's Flute have been nothing shy of a disappointment. You must influence advancement with all means necessary."

"Understood, Malores. I'll leave immediately."
Malores grabbed Breton's arm firmly. "We must find the flute, or all will be lost. Do you understand?"
Breton released the wizard's grip. "I will not fail my people." He mounted his horse and galloped into the night.

Malores crept back into a darkened alley as a half dozen Arkonian guards rushed by. Pleased by the results, he disappeared into the darkness.

In a synchronized fashion, the royal dinner's masked entertainers left the dining room accompanied by applause and cheering. King Sarius rose from his seat and held out his silver goblet of wine. "A toast to the flowers of Arkonia who have graced us with their entertainment this eve."

****

Arkonians take pride in their mastery of fine arts. They've become well renown in all Drakonia for dance, wine and art and have recently started a festival for the written arts.

****

A commotion broke out at the far end of the royal dining table. Guards were forced to intervene as a captain protected her queen.

Savita informed King Sarius quietly. "That is the Queen of the Sinasian kingdom your majesty, Queen Falyn Mordecia."

"Oh, yes, the sole child of Roche who ruled his kingdom for fifty years," replied Cronos Sarius nostalgically.

"That's right," recalled Lord Drakus. "They are a cursed peoples with a pheromone that strengthens the sexual urges of those who inhale it."

"As I recall, we had a little trouble with that during the last peace conference." King Sarius wanted to remain mindful and stay on top of any pitfalls that could impact negatively on the peace talks. "What seems to be the problem down there?" he hollered.

Guided by her Captain of the Guard and wizard, Queen Falyn Mordecia elegantly walked alongside the dining table and approached the King of Arkonia.

"I apologize, your majesty, but it seems King Rayden and company of the Fylosian kingdom are being influenced by our gift."

"I thought it was intended to be a curse?" Lord Drakus responded inquisitively.

"Indeed. Our people were enchanted by a dark witch. But to think of it as a curse would only surrender to the misery in which it was intended. We, the Sinasian people, have embraced this curse and accepted it as a gift." King Sarius disapproved. "Well, nevertheless, your blessing has caused quite the ruckus."

"I can hardly believe it took this long?" spoke Savita curiously.

Queen Falyn Mordecia smiled with dignity. "Yes, dear. Although we've embraced this blessing, our wizard, Orta Maynus, created a solution to our social issues." Falyn introduced the wizard with a hand gesture. "Orta has created a lotion which briefly covers the pheromone."

"I prefer being referred to as an alchemist, your majesty." Orta bowed with respect to King Sarius and company.

Queen Mordecia's Captain of the Guard intervened assertively, "My Queen, we haven't much time."

"Unusual for a woman to attain such a high honour as Captain of the Guard," noted Lord Drakus.

"Do you have a problem with a female captain?" She glared.

"Quite the opposite, really. We Komalsh have had many female leaders—my predecessor being one. Allow me to introduce myself. I am Lord Hirum Drakus." He held out his hand.

The captain stared coldly and after a moment Drakus' hand retreated.

"Oh, lighten up, dear," ordered Queen Falyn Mordecia.

The captain, still reluctant, held out her hand. "I am Captain Bianca Lesiah."

****

Bianca stood six feet tall with her 165 pounds of toned physique. Her high cheekbones accented her light grey eyes and short blonde hair. Jaded by society and life's mishaps, Bianca always held a rather cold facial expression but unlike most, her suffering empowered her. With great loss came her great drive for achievement…or was it revenge?

In her youth, she had disguised herself as a man while climbing the ranks among Sinasian knights. Upon reaching the top, she was honoured as Captain of the Guard by Queen Mordecia. It was then that she revealed her gender to all Sinasians by removing her upper wear exposing her breasts. A move Queen Mordecia proudly noted as the strongest expression ever displayed by a knight. A move, however, some men deemed an insult. They challenged Bianca only to lose their lives to her blood-stained sword. She was a warrior and not one to be taken lightly.

****

Hirum returned her handshake. "Do you dislike the Komalsh, Captain Lesiah?"

"Did you invade my mind to retrieve that information?" accused Lesiah.

"I had only assumed," replied Drakus. "Your response, however, already clarified it."

Captain Lesiah paused a moment. Then relaxed her guard. "You are right, Lord Drakus. I do not put my faith in the Komalsh, especially as ambassadors of peace policing a unified Drakonia. It's too much power to entrust to a group of people with your capabilities. Corruption is inevitable. Your history has proven that."

"Only two have fallen from the Komalsh path." reminded Drakus. "I assure you, Captain Lesiah, it won't happen again under my watch. The price is too high."

The captain nodded her head in respect to Lord Drakus. Even a smile tried to surface. "My Queen, we should leave before the potency of the lotion diminishes and I am forced to kill everyone in this room."

The captain's smile fully surfaced. The Queen concurred with the captain's fear of potentially ensuing mayhem. The captain then led her party to the exit.

Before leaving the dining room Captain Bianca Lesiah turned back and asked, "Tell me, Lord Drakus, what caused Cable Demonis and Cretes Siris to fall from their path?"

"I do not know," admitted Drakus.

"Then how do you prevent it from happening again?"

King Sarius rose from his seat. He spoke loudly so all could hear. "Cable and Cretes are the only renegades in a thousand-year history of the Komalsh. With their quick disposals long ago, there is nothing more to be feared. Brothers and sisters of Drakonia, peace is at hand and soon we'll have a unified Drakonia under one world order—one policed by the Komalsh. Tomorrow, my friends, is the beginning of a new era!" King Sarius raised his goblet of wine. "To Drakonia and the new world order."

Goblets were raised around the table. "To Drakonia and the new world order."

Queen Mordecia, without a drink, raised her hand and cheered with her fellow peers. Orta Maynus followed his majesty's gesture while Captain Lesiah showed a greater urgency in their safe removal.

All the guests were optimistic about tomorrow's treaty, all but King Dag Kaloun of the Drake kingdom. Irritated, he rises from the table and left the dining room. His Captain of the Guard, Mace Rasim, followed close behind while Sesh, his wizard, hesitated. He wanted the treaty. It would bring new knowledge to his extensive library, feeding his desire for a higher education. However, disobeying his king would lead to a beheading. So, he followed his majesty as any wise man would.

Savita watched as King Dag Kaloun's party left the dining room. Telepathically she hailed Lord Drakus.

"I can't stand that man!"

Drakus replied to her hail. "The Drake kingdom has the largest army in Drakonia. We will need their help so you better start liking him. Besides, I sense there's more to his story."

"What do you mean?"

"He suffers inside, Savita. The trauma in his life is influencing his irrational behavior."

"Well, more irrational than usual," jabbed Savita.

"We need a unified Drakonia, Lady Cosmos. King Kaloun and the Drake peoples are a big piece of that puzzle."

Savita nodded her head with a half smile. "As you wish, my lord. Perhaps you are right. Perhaps there is good in him."

"I know there is, Lady Cosmos."

****

Lord Hirum Drakus kept many secrets. All the truths he hid were revealed to him in his sleep through a rare Komalsh gift called prophetic dreams. With some of his dreams, Lord Drakus managed to use his insight to alter future realities from happening. But in the most part, the unpredictability of time was too unstable to alter.
Time is molded by an array of decisions made by all living creatures. Control was an illusion. Accepting this made life less complicated.

Lord Drakus had foreseen Savita's growing importance—an importance that secrets would no longer protect.

****

"Savita, there are far greater evils lurking in the shadows. As you are aware, our telepathic communication has been compromised. It is the reason I've been blocking your hails."

"Then why use it now, my lord?"

"Fenka Rek is not listening at this moment," answered Drakus.

Savita whitened in terror. "Fenka Rek shares our abilities? What is he?"

"More questions than answers, I'm afraid. However, Fenka Rek is not the true threat."

"Then who is? Who's behind this?"

"My dreams haven't revealed those answers, Savita. My intuition, however, points toward the new King of Sykania."

"But why search for Cable Demonis?"

"As you're aware, in the beginning Lord Duren gathered all the lost enchanted artifacts from Earth and hid them within the protection of Castle Malshidiel. This included the key scroll to unlocking the Darkstar. Whoever controls the castle would possess the power to conquer Drakonia. Lord Demonis could walk through the Mystique Forest unharmed."

"Lord Demonis is but one man," defended Savita. "Even without the protection of the forest, he couldn't possibly defeat the vast army of the Komalsh, especially on castle grounds."

Two Arkonian guards rushed into the dining room interrupting Savita and Drakus' psychic link.

"Your majesty!" spoke the taller of the two.

"Go on, what is it?" There was concern in King Sarius' voice.

"There has been a major disturbance at the tavern." The guard turned to Lord Drakus. "It involved two of your students and a very intoxicated sorcerer."

Chapter X
The Hounds of Hell.

Hidden behind the hedge, Kris Tarius watched as the Door of Duren's lock rotated. His heart pumped rapidly; his eyes widened. Kris firmly clenched the grip of his sword. The combination changed directions and started turning to its final click. With a loud clunk from the lock followed by a sharp clang, the door creaked open.

A light, chilly breeze left the cave and the smell of death followed. A burgundy cloaked figure walked out into the torch-lit night. A moonlit silhouette exposed a tattered cloak fitting snugly against a feminine frame.

With mechanical-like motion, her head turned to the left and appeared to stare into the darkness. She then turned slowly, looking forward as if to be searching for any threats.

Kris stepped closer to get a better look. The cloaked woman's head turned to the right and stared directly at him. A cold shiver ran down the startled student's spine. Slowly she extended her arm and with the snap of her fingers extinguished all the torches Lord Dunlam had lit earlier. Kris was once again blinded by darkness.

Quietly he gripped onto his sword's hilt and before he could unsheathe his blade, the cloaked women's decrepit face appeared inches before him. Kris froze in terror as the moonlight exposed her demonic features. She had long, deep red, greasy hair hanging freely from either side of her pointed ears. Her crusty, brownish cadaverous skin released a rotting flesh odour. The cloaked woman removed her hood revealing a sunken face with empty, soulless eyes engulfed in blackness. Dark mist permeated from her wretched skin. Suddenly, within the darkness of her stare there grew a bright silver light. Out of nowhere, a stormy gust of wind began tossing her hair violently, partially shrouding her face. Her diabolical eyes shone through her misty barrier; her long hair continued to whip about frantically as she spoke with a serpent's hiss. "Sleep!" Kris's eyes rolled to the back of his head. Then his body buckled to the ground as he became unconscious.

The burgundy cloaked woman knelt before him. Her face returned to her true beautiful Elvin form. She quickly cloaked her identity and remained invisible to unsuspecting eyes. Placing the palm of her rejuvenated hand on Kris's forehead, in her serpent's hiss, she commanded, "Forget what you've seen this eve."

As she returned to her feet, a roar of high-pitched screams escaped the open Door of Duren. The sounds grew louder and closer. Winds howled from the cave's entrance as a sinister smile stretched across the cloaked women's face.

"Do thy master's bidding."

The Arkonian prison was a cesspool of mildew and rats. The old brick walls and iron bars could tell a story that was decades old. The stench of urine and feces was as thick as a fall fog. Prisoners coughed, choked, and wheezed. Some moaned in pain with disease while others stood lifeless as though their very souls were stuck in limbo. The guards escorted the three tavern troublemakers down a long hallway. Prisoners reached through bars clawing and taunting them as they were ushered by. At the end of the hallway was the main holding cell—a large cell holding thirty prisoners uncomfortably. It was used to hold the arrested until sentenced by the Arkonian courts.

A guard opened the cell doors and the three numbed prisoners staggered in. Nyte fell into a corner. His eye was black, his lower lip swollen and knuckles bloody and bruised. Kelar, still supporting his broken wrist, dropped to the floor moaning in pain. Kudos, however, showed no facial signs from their recent brawl. After thanking the guards for their hospitality, he leaned against the cell door inebriated. "Now that was a party!"

Showing off his bloody knuckles to the other inmates, he announced, "I still got it!" Slapping his hands together with a loud clap he turned to the beat-up students.

"Ha, ha, wasn't this great! I haven't had this much fun in years! The booze, the women, a tavern brawl and now prison! I feel like I'm 50 again!"

"How!" shrieked Kelar stupefied. "Did you manage to get out of that tavern without a mark on your face?" Kudos raised his fists and started to shadow box. "Well, son, I may be old, but I still kick ass!"

Dancing around with pathetic knee-high kicks and angled Kung Fu-like chopping motions. Kudos showed Kelar he had no clue how to fight. He also made that apparent to the thugs huddled together in the far corner. Kudos caught eight of them staring deviously at the three newcomers.

"Hmm," said the leader of the gang. "Two broken boys and an old man who can't dance…easy prey."
The thugs approached the tavern troublemakers. Kudos backed up with his arms spread out to hide Nyte and Kelar behind him. Fear etched the wizard's face as he backed deeper into the corner.

The thugs fed from his fear like sharks to a pool of blood. Clutching their fists and grinding their teeth, they intimidated the old sorcerer. The prison thugs, AKA the Zidota brothers, started their attack. Kudos' timid expression of fear was then replaced by a devious grin.

Lord Drakus and Savita rushed into the prison. King Sarius and his guards followed shortly after gasping for breath.

"Where are they?" ordered Lord Drakus, enraged.
"There in the main holding cell awaiting their sentence," answered the cell guard.

A concerned expression stretched across the face of King Sarius, "but isn't that cell currently holding the Zidota boys?"

****

The Zidota boys were an eight-member gang of cutthroats and thieves led by the two Zidota brothers. They started off young as petty thieves who gradually escalated to a life of mayhem. Currently every local rape, theft or murder had been their calling card.

Recently, the eight of them were incarcerated by the Arkonian Captain of the Guard, Trent Ravit, who made it his personal vendetta after losing his four-year-old nephew to their ravaging hunger for murder. There they sat in the holding cell awaiting their trial and a guaranteed beheading—an event for which Trent and his family had front row seats.

****

The guards escorted them down the hallway to the holding cell.

"Are you okay Nyte?" called Savita.

Nyte laid in the corner of the cell inebriated and bloody. Kelar, white as snow, the paleness of his skin caused by the pain of his broken wrist, slowly fell into a state of unconscious. Kudos sat cross legged in the middle of the cell floor snoring in a deep sleep. Behind him piled on top of each other were eight dead Zidota boys.

"What happened here?" demanded the guard.

Kudos awoke and then made his way toward the cell entrance. The remaining prisoners huddled into a corner frantically staying out of the old man's way.

"He's an old man! He couldn't have! Could he?" astonished a guard.

Kudos grabbed onto the cell door bars. With a rasping voice and a noticeable slur to his speech, he delivered today's lesson. "Youth and agility, my friend, are no match for old age and sorcery."

Lord Drakus stood heated with anger. "What in the hell happened, Kudos?"

Kudos gripped the bars tightly to keep him upright while his legs wobbled. "Well, this pile of guys attacked us and I…"

"Not this, the tavern!" interrupted Drakus.

"Oh yeah, we got into some trouble there, too." His words were slurred.

"Do you think!" growled King Sarius.

Savita barged past everyone to make her way to the cell. Using her telekinesis, she opened the locked door and entered the prison cell. Showing little sympathy toward Kelar, she went directly to Nyte and examined him. "Why were you in the tavern, Nyte?"

"Especially during these crucial times," reminded the angered King.

"We were drunk!" replied Kudos. "It seemed like a fun thing to do at the time."

The King growled displeased. "Guards. See to it they are escorted to their rooms. I want no more problems, understood?"

"Yes, your majesty at once."

Lord Drakus leaned toward Kudos through the bars that kept him standing. "My old friend, no good can come from this."

Kudos leaned his face closer to Drakus. "Hirum, good has come of this. Nyte has shared a valuable secret. You should ask him about his dreams. It is especially important that you spend time with him before he faces the Mystique Forest."

Drakus listened intently knowing how wise Kudos is. They had been friends for many years.

"He has a hole inside of him, Hirum," continued the sorcerer. "He needs some parental guidance if you catch my drift."

"His mother?" replied Drakus understanding what Kudos implied.

"He needs to see the sword." Kudos' eyes widened. "It is especially important that he see's it before challenging the forest. The boy lacks his roots, Hirum. He has an unloved soul."

Savita overheard the conversation. Her eyes filled with tears she would never release. "I tried my hardest to raise him. I loved him like he was my own. Have I failed him, Kudos?"

"No, my dear, you have not." The old sorcerer knelt beside her and Nyte. He placed his hand on Savita's head and released a reassuring smile. "You did what no other could, my dear. Your love made him strong and healthy. What he lacks, only his parents could give. He lacks his roots. Normally, this wouldn't matter," explained Kudos aloud. "But Nyte is special. More so than any other Komalsh."

"Why is that?" King Sarius stared at the student bleeding all over the floor. "He doesn't look very special." Drakus cleared the King's confusion. "Nyte Shade's parents were both Komalsh. He is the offspring of two powerful leaders. This is exceedingly rare."

"Why is this rare? Don't you Komalsh get along?" Mocked King Sarius.

"Well," answered Drakus, "we can read the minds of others and can prevent others from reading our minds. This has its repercussions when engaged in something as complicated as love. You see, it's our hidden side that defines us, molds us, and protects us. To share that openly with another would be the ultimate test of love."

"Only to a soulmate," interrupted Savita smiling.

"But back to the point!" Kudos pounced out of boredom. "Nyte is showing the rarest ability the Komalsh possess. Prophetic dreams. Only Lord Drakus currently possesses this gift."

"It's our strongest psychic ability," revealed Drakus. "It defines who will lead the Komalsh."

"There is one thing different concerning Nyte, though," stated Kudos. "He is not a Komalsh yet, but he already possesses this gift."

"Interesting." King Sarius was amused. "But what does this all mean? Is he the one who will awaken Malshidiel? This chosen one, if I may?"

They all turned to Lord Drakus awaiting the answer. Even the frightened prisoners were filled with anticipation.

Lord Drakus shook his head. "Young Nyte Shade isn't the one to which, *The Book of Malshidiel,* refers. I've dreamt of greatness for Nyte's future. However, he is not the chosen one."

Savita knelt to Kelar and inspected his swollen wrist. "Sorry to interrupt but I'll need some materials to build a brace for Kelar's wrist. It's been fractured.

"This is unfortunate timing." Lord Drakus let out a huge and audible sigh. "Will they be fit enough for tomorrow's events?"

Savita shrugged. "Perhaps some sleep and a morning bath will make everything right as rain."

King Sarius chuckled. "I find your optimism to be quite entertaining. Nevertheless, we have a big day tomorrow. I suggest we all call it a night."

Savita held Nyte closely as she whispered in his ear, "I love you, Nyte. I will always love you. Don't you ever forget that my little man."

Nyte smiled, then surrendered to sleep.

As the burgundy cloaked woman stood over the unconscious Kris Tarius, screams from the opened Door of Duren echoed into the silent night. Small ghost-like shadow demons flew out the door in a frenzied swarm. Two separated from the colony and flew circles around the burgundy-cloaked witch leaving a trail of blackened mist. Hundreds more flew frantically toward the Kelasian castle. With vicious rage they entered through every crook and cranny of the castle's walls and swarmed its halls searching for souls.

Inside the Warlock's chambers, shadow demons swarmed the room. With predator-like instincts, they targeted Neasha Sentrix who slept peacefully on the Warlock's bed. With vicious fury, one separated from the colony and attacked her. Upon impact, the shadow demon absorbed through Neasha's face causing random black disfigurations all over her skin. In mere moments, it seeped into her brain leaving Neasha frozen and unable to respond. A second shadow demon separated from its colony and targeted Kolos Dreken who slept peacefully against the wall. It, too, absorbed into his face causing black skin disfigurations on impact. Kolos awoke abruptly in a frantic scream that echoed through the castle. Then his eyes closed, and he returned to sleep as though nothing had happened.

Outside the Door of Duren, the two shadow demons circling the burgundy-cloaked woman targeted the unconscious Kris Tarius but to their dismay, they were unable to enter his mind. Frustrated and lamenting with screeching rage, the shadow demons flew at eye level to the woman.

"Don't waste your time with this one," she rasped. "I placed a sleep spell on him. His mind is intoxicated. He is, therefore, unbreachable."

The shadow demons obeyed and flew toward the castle.

Outside the Kelasian castle, hidden within the forest, were eight Komalsh assigned by Lord Drakus to protect Lord Bossel Dunlam. Unaware of the student's current danger, they stood unseen, guarding the castle's perimeter.

The forest was dark and silent. Only the sounds of crickets off in the distance could be heard. That silence was suddenly severed by a pack of wild dogs howling at the harvest moon.

"What was that?" asked Lord Plake directing his question to the Komalsh commander, Lady Sook.

"They're just pack hounds, son. Stay focused on the task at hand. Fenka Rek could be anywhere."

Lord Plake was new to the Komalsh and struggled to manage his psychic gifts. Seeing the frustration in his eyes, Lady Sook decided on a new approach.

"Close your eyes, Lord Plake, and reach out to our unicorns."

The young Komalsh closed his eyes and reached out. "I can sense their beating hearts close by." He smiled.

"Excellent. Now close your eyes again. This time search deeper into the forest. Seek out the wild hounds." Lord Plake obeyed and reached out through the forest. He could sense the heart beats of birds and animals scattered throughout the forest. He reached out further until he located the pack of hounds. "I can feel them, Lady Sook! I feel their hearts beat!"

"As do I, Lord Plake. They're far away and pose no threat. So, try to stay focused on the task at hand, please."

Inside the castle hundreds of shadow demons swarmed the halls in a curtain of darkness. Lord Bossel Dunlam, oblivious to their presence, knelt within his psychic energy field of meditation. The shadow demons blackened the ceiling above then attacked the unsuspecting teacher. After several failed attempts to break his protective psychic barrier, the shadow demons retreated. Frustrated and fraught with frenzy, they fled the castle and headed toward the sound of howling dogs.

Deep inside the forest, thirteen pack hounds rummaged around for food. Above them the moon's light dimmed in darkness as a wave of shadows rolled over the hounds. One by one, the shadow demons targeted the dogs. Each hound dropped to the ground whimpering in agony. Unlike Kolos and Neasha, the hounds began to morph. Each one shook with seizures while deforming demonically. Painful howls escaped their lungs as they grew three times in size. Their fangs and claws extended inches in length. Their black hair solidified to a hard-protective armour. Now fully mutated, they rose from the ground and growled amongst each other—their eyes and teeth glowing in the darkness.

The largest of the hounds led the pack through the forest with uncanny speed and agility. Their clawed feet hurled patches of soil high into the air as they crashed through thick brush and wild terrain. The smell of human flesh guided them toward Lady Sook and her seven Komalsh.

Inside the castle, shadow demons stormed the throne room where Terex, Trayke and Arias slept beside three empty rum bottles. The demons circled the sleeping students and with a shadowed fury dove toward them. Moments after impact the three student hosts rejected their parasite demons. The shadow demons struggled to escape the students while screaming in excruciating pain. Then they evaporated into a black mist. The intoxicated students slept unperturbed.

Hidden in the forest, Lord Plake started to panic.

"What's wrong?" asked Lady Sook.

"Our unicorns…I no longer feel them?"

Lady Sook closed her eyes and reached out to their fallen unicorns. They lay lifeless on the forest floor in pools of their own blood.

"Oh no!" she gasped. "What's happening?"

The forest fell silent. Only the crickets could be heard. Then the crickets fell silent, too.

A cold shiver streamed down the necks of all eight Komalsh. Quickly they unsheathed their swords and formed a circle back-to-back. A twig snapped in the darkness.

Lord Plake turned toward it. "All I feel is darkness," he gasped.

With a quick pounce, a pack hound more than twice the weight of Lady Sook leapt out of the brush. Her sharp teeth clamped onto Lord Plake's head like a vice grip as she dragged him into the forest kicking and screaming. Hounds leaped out from all directions targeting the Komalsh. They snapped onto their heads and crushed them like grapes. They whipped their limp bodies around spraying blood around the forest. The screams of their victims ended sharply as they devoured their bodies alive. Lady Sook stood shocked. She was the only Komalsh standing. Her allies, her friends, were all dead.

"These are not pack hounds!" she panicked.

"I feel no heartbeats?"

"They're so big!"

"Somebody, anybody?"

Lady Sook gazed in terror at the blood and carnage, her sword drawn but never used. Everything happened so fast.

Twelve hounds surrounded her cautiously, their faces stained with red. Flesh dangled from their teeth.

"You're not pack hounds!" shouted Lady Sook.

"You're the hounds of hell!" She screamed as loud as she could while raising her sword.

Standing behind her was a hell hound far larger than the rest. He must have been a hundred pounds heavier and stood two feet higher. His fangs dripped with bloodied saliva. His breath smelt of unicorn flesh. Lady Sook was blinded to his presence, nor could she sense the ones who stood before her. Their hearts did not beat. They were the undead.

With a viscous snap, the larger hell hound bit off Lady Sook's head. Then crushed it down with his powerful jaws. Her headless body swung about aimlessly then staggered to the ground. She twitched about fiercely as blood sprayed from her severed neck. Then the hell hounds ripped her apart limb from limb.

Standing before the Door of Duren, the burgundy-cloaked woman's eyes pierced through the mist that engulfed her face. Her mouth opened wide and released a thunderous scream summoning her ghostly army.

The shadow demons responded by collecting into a spiraled storm above the castle. When all were present, they were vacuumed through the Door of Duren. The door closed shut and the night fell silent.

The woman walked off the castle grounds unnoticed. At the forest's edge she rendezvoused with the pack of hell hounds. The largest of the pack bowed before her. "The Komalsh are dead. What is my master's bidding?" His voice was surprisingly gentle.

The woman placed her hand on his forehead and scratched his ear affectionately. "Well done, Cerberus. For now, you must go into hiding. Only move in the shadow of night. Let no one know of your existence and kill all who do. Do you understand?"

"Yes, I understand Enchantress." He growled.

The burgundy cloaked women, the Enchantress, walked into the darkened forest. "You will be summoned when needed, Cerberus."

Her voice whispered into the night. And like her whisper, she too faded into the darkness.

Chapter XI
The Secret King of Sykania.

The following morning Savita Cosmos watched as the sun rose over the Arkonian kingdom. From her window, she bathed in its warm nurturing rays. Like most mornings, this was a peaceful time for her—a time she could organise her thoughts, meditate and mentally prepare for the day ahead.

From the window, she watched the early risers of Arkonia. Citizens gathered in the streets below setting up shops while children and their pets played in the streets.

"What a beautiful morning," She thought to herself, As the responsibilities of the day slowly came to light, Savita hailed Lord Hirum Drakus.

"Are you prepared, my lord?"

"As prepared as can be," replied Drakus. "You must deal with Nyte and Kelar, Lady Cosmos. I fear they're in rough shape."

"Should I just leave them out of today's events my lord?" inquired Savita.

"No, that won't be necessary. I feel their presence will pay off in the long run. Prepare them the best you can. I will meet you in King Sarius' chambers."

"Yes, Lord Drakus."

Nyte and Kelar were ill. They took turns vomiting into their buckets. Their bloodshot eyes and faces pale as snow were evidence of the previous lack of good judgement they had publicly displayed.

Both had promised never to drink again—Kelar more so. He favoured his splintered wrist.
Kudos, however, was dressed and ready for a brand-new day. With a cheerful disposition he left ahead of the others to get an early start.

"Boys!" shouted Savita entering the room. "It's time to clean up!"

Servants stripped the young men down and bathed them in separate brass tubs. They were given jugs of water and loaves of bread to help ease their hangovers. After dressing in clean clothes, they were presented to Lady Cosmos for inspection.

"You look…decent. How do you feel?" prodded Savita optimistically.

"I want to go to bed." Nyte's head hurt.

"I want to die!" whimpered Kelar.

"Oh, boy," surrendered Savita.

Inside the King's chambers, his majesty and Lord Drakus put the finishing touches on the peace conference accords.

"This could be the only solution for all the kingdoms votes King Sarius." Praised Drakus. "Thank you for your assistance.

"Anything to help the cause, my friend."

At the door, the King's Captain of the Guard, Trent Ravit entered the room. "Excuse me, your majesty."

"What is it, Captain?"

"Lady Cosmos and guests are in your waiting quarters."

"Let them in. This should be entertaining." King Sarius wrung his hands with a huge grin on his face.

The captain brought Savita and the two students before the King. He stared at them both for at least a full minute and then broke out into laughter.

Drakus, too, inspected the students but with a more optimistic approach. "Better than a kick in the balls I suppose. Where's Kudos?"

"He has already headed to the conference room," answered Nyte. "He said he wanted to get a good seat."

"I dislike that man," admitted King Sarius.

"We know, we know," sighed Drakus.

"Attention, everyone," announced Drakus. "Today we must be on our best behaviour. It's our job to convince the Kingdoms of Drakonia that I could take the lead as ambassador of peace to a unified Drakonia, one policed by the Komalsh. We know everyone wants this, but doubt clouds their better judgement. We must eliminate this doubt. We must prove our ability to lead Drakonia to a new world order of peace."

Lord Drakus led his Komalsh representatives down the hall toward the conference room. The dream of peace awaited.

As the sun rose over the Kelasian castle, Kris Tarius rose from the ground. He rubbed his eyes and brushed the dust from his green apprentice robes.

His memories of last night were vague. His mind was foggy, and his sense of balance was weakened. Before him, the closed Door of Duren was in plain view. He recalled coming here with Bossel to see it but nothing more. Unable to piece things together, Kris returned to the castle.

Inside the castle, Trayke Basa slowly rose from the floor. After clambering around the randomly tossed, empty rum bottles, he found a place to stand. "My head hurts," he moaned.

Terex rubbed his eye sockets deep. "Yeah, mine too."

"Would you guys keep it down!" complained Arias hidden under a pile of blankets on the bed.

"How did you get the bed?" Trayke was mystified.

"I was the last one standing, so I kicked you off and took it." snickered Arias.

"You're a jerk."

In a deep uncaring voice, Arias simply replied, "Yep."

Kolos staggered into the room almost knocking over a table.

"You look like shit," chuckled Terex.

"They must have found the cheap rum!" commented Trayke.

"You're not keeping it down, guys," reminded Arias as he snuggled under the blankets.

"I don't feel very well." The sickened Kolos was overcome with a gagging feeling."

"Where's Neasha?" wondered Terex.

"She's in the other room. She's not well, either." Kolos fell to the ground unbalanced.

Terex and Trayke quickly helped him to his feet.

"You need to lay down," ordered Terex.

Terex went over to Aria's bed. He lifted the mattress and dumped him to the floor.

Arias, under a heap of blankets on the floor, complained. "I'm starting to think you guys are incapable of keeping it down."

Trayke threw Kolos onto the mattress. Kolos wrapped his arms around his body and clenched his belly in pain.

"We'd better check on Neasha." Trayke was deeply concerned for her welfare. "Arias, stay here and keep an eye on Kolos. Terex and I will be right back."

"Yep." Spoke the pile of blankets.

When they arrived in the other room, Neasha was curled up in the fetal position hidden under a table. Lord Bossel Dunlam was standing nearby.

"Are you okay?" asked Bossel.

"My body hurts," gasped Neasha.

"Kolos is in the same condition, Lord Dunlam." informed Trayke.

"This is very unusual." Bossel examined her. "She has no fever or flu-like symptoms. Could it have been something you ate, Neasha?"

Neasha moved her head back and forth indicating no.

"Terex, take Neasha to the nearest bed. Perhaps more rest is all that's needed."

As the students came closer, Bossel smelled an odor of which he disapproved. "You two stink of booze!" he lashed.

Trayke was about to speak when Bossel stopped him with a single finger. "Uh, uh, uh, uh. I don't want to hear one word of it. You have two days to sober up before going into the Mystique Forest."

Bossel left the room disappointed. At the doorway he bumped into Kris who had just entered the castle—rubbing his head in confusion.

"Not you, too!" Disappointed, Bossel walked away.

"What did I miss?" questioned Kris.

Terex looked at Kris puzzled, "Where have you been?"

In the west wing of the Arkonian castle stood a conference room designated for the peace talks. It was furnished with a large octagonal table. Surrounding this table were thrones for each King and Queen flanked by smaller chairs for their respective wizards and captains. Prior to this peace conference only a wizard was required to attend with their majesty for council. However, after the assassination of King Hexity a decade ago, the Captain of the Guard was now a requirement for the proceedings.

All Drakonia's leaders were in attendance, all but the representatives of Sykania. At the head of the table sat Lord Hirum Drakus, Kudos Nexus and Lady Savita Cosmos. Behind them stood the battered and bruised Olemeeze graduates. Nyte's facial colour had returned. Despite some residual weakness, he wore a confident look apropos to the serious nature of these treaty talks. Kelar was pale and ill, his wrist held high to alleviate the swelling. This technique, according to his facial expression, wasn't working.

An usher entered the conference room and announced, "The King of Sykania has arrived."

The room mumbled in anticipation. The Sykanian wizard, Malores Barnett, entered the room. Following close behind him was the cloaked King of Sykania.

Lord Drakus rose cautiously from his seat. Both he and Savita's eyes lit up in astonishment as the new Sykanian king revealed himself. Savita's skin turned the same shade as Kelar's. Her stomach dropped. The room fell silent.

Breaking the absence of sound Lord Drakus spoke. "It's been a long-time, old friend."

The class gathered at the Kelasian castle's front yard—a class looking the worse for wear. There, Bossel proceeded with his final lecture.

"In two days, you start down the path of no return. First you will enter the Mystique Forest. The forest will challenge your mind and your spirit. No physical effort is required here. Yet, it can be the most exhausting experience you'll ever encounter."

"Like sitting in class," chuckled Trayke.

The class laughed. Bossel winced and then continued unperturbed. "Some may travel through the forest swiftly while others may take days. Some never find their way out while others perish quickly. The forest crawls into your mind and amplifies who you are. It feeds on guilt and lies. It sees your deepest secrets and forces you to confront them. This final test weeds out the weak, the deceitful and the rancorous. There is nowhere to hide, students, when the battle reaches deep within your very mind."

The class listened to their teacher's every word. Fear etched their faces.

"Once you've been accepted by the forest, a unicorn will choose you. This steed will become your ally for the entirety of your life."

"What do you mean choose me?" interrupted Trayke."

Bossel paused—exhibiting painful frustration in response to the second interruption. Trayke was the only student who could test his patience.

Bossel glared at Trayke and with an angered voice explained, "The unicorns that were born in the forest possess many special gifts—one is the ability to find a Komalsh they can tolerate. In your case, Mr. Trayke Basa, it will most likely be a docile delinquent donkey! Now quit interrupting me, you little bastard, or I will go over there and beat you with the dull side of my sword!"

Trayke crept behind Arias. He was afraid.

The class gave Bossel a moment to relax the vein protruding from his forehead. It was something only Trayke could inflame.

"Now then," continued Bossel after collecting himself, "once you and your unicorn unite, the steed will guide you through safe passage to Castle Malshidiel."

"What gives us our psychic abilities?" asked Kris Tarius. "It's never been mentioned in class."

Bossel closed his eyes. "If I told you, son…you'd never attempt it."

"That's not really giving me that forest-fresh feeling, teach." Spoke Trayke while lighting his pipe.

"Trayke? I wasn't aware you smoked?" Bossel was baffled.

"Only when I drink, sir," replied Trayke.

Bossel's vein protruded.

After collecting himself once again, the teacher finished his speech. "So, once you've acquired your Komalsh abilities, you'll become almost invincible."

"Almost?" questioned Terex.

"We can all still die, students. If a major organ like your brain or heart are ruptured. Then death is inevitable."

"What about decapitation?" teased Terex.

"Yes Terex, unfortunately that is the leading cause of our deaths," answered Bossel in the gravest of tones.

"What about your skin?" asked Trayke smoking his pipe.

"Skin?" squinted Bossel wrinkling his nose.

"Yeah, isn't skin an organ?"

"He's right," agreed Arias. "Skin is an organ."

"Shut up, the three of you!" Bossel was irritated by their apparent light-hearted banter. "Just understand, students, everything you learned at Olemeeze will aide your journey ahead."

"Now then," a flustered Bossel continued, "Neasha, Kolos. How are you two feeling?"

"Surprisingly well," replied Neasha in high spirits.

"Yeah, me too." followed Kolos. "It must have been something we ate."

"Very well then, students. Everyone, mount up. We have a two-day journey ahead. Our destination, the Mystique Forest."

At the Arkonian castle everyone stood in awe as the King of Sykania revealed himself.

"Yes, it's been too long, Lord Drakus."

Savita gasped. "Lord Siris!"

"That's King Siris to you, peasant!" cackled Cretes.

King Cretes Siris leapt up onto the octagon table. Using his telekinesis, he summoned the gourd from Kudos' hand to his own. After taking a drink, Siris cringed. "You always knew how to wake up, old man!"

Siris laughed his distinguished cackle, then stood before Lord Drakus. Swords were drawn around the table pointing toward Siris.

"Swords at a peace conference?" questioned King Siris. "I am not carrying a weapon." Siris held his robes open revealing his words to be true. "I didn't even bring my Captain of the Guard."

"He was at the tavern last night!" volunteered Kudos. "What are you up to?" demanded the sorcerer. Siris hurled the gourd at Kudos. Kudos caught it with ease.

"Mind your own business, drunk!" Siris turned to his captive audience and made his demands. "I'm here for one reason and one reason only." He pointed his finger toward Drakus. "To declare war on the Komalsh."

The room erupted with mumbled confusion.

"We will fight you on the Field of Blood, Lord Drakus. You and whoever stands in our way of destroying you. Do I make myself clear?" roared Siris to his silent audience.

Drakus leaped onto the table, "Or we can settle this here and spare the lives of countless others."

"No blood should spill on the table of peace, Lord Drakus," smiled Siris stepping down from the table. "I'll send you a messenger holding a blank letter, Lord Drakus. On receiving this letter, I will expect the Komalsh to challenge us the following sunrise before our castle on the Field of Blood. If you do not show, we will hunt down and slaughter every Drakonian in our path. Their blood will be on your hands, Lord Drakus."

Siris cackled as he and Malores left the conference room, his laughter echoing down the hallway. The room fell silent. That silence was broken as Kelar erupted with vomit all over the floor.

"Amateur!" shouted Kudos.

"Order. I want order!" demanded King Sarius.

"You!" The King pointed to Kudos. "I want him removed now!"

The guards ushered Kudos to the exit by the scruff of his grey robes. Being difficult the whole way out, Kudos apologized profusely to the King. "Look, I'm sorry about that damn horse!"

Then he was gone.

"There was nothing gained in having Kudos escorted out," advised Savita politely.

"No dear. But it sure felt good." King Sarius heaved a huge sigh and then exhaled audibly.

Nyte helped Kelar clean himself up. "So much for peace," he uttered under his breath.

"What do you say to this!" shouted King Dag Kaloun of the Drake kingdom.

Savita cringed. "Here it starts."

"You know what I see, my fellow Drakonians. I see a conflict among the Komalsh. How could we appoint their leader as ambassador of peace when they themselves are in civil war?"

The Tarnian King Ses Thel disagreed with King Kaloun's shallow view. "You fail to see the gravity of the situation King Kaloun. The Sykanians under Siris' rule will not stop after conquering the Komalsh. Their tyranny will spread across Drakonia. This should be taken as a threat to us all!"

King Turek of Dosania took the stand. "Their army is vast and powerful. Without unity, our kingdoms will fall."

"This is our battle," intervened Drakus. "One I have foreseen."

"You don't say," snarled King Dag Kaloun. "I found it quite entertaining watching you try and end it while standing atop our table of peace!"

"Answer me, Lord Drakus!" glared King Kaloun. "Do your actions reflect the qualities of an ambassador for peace?"

Drakus looked around the octagon table to the anxious kings and queens of Drakonia. They sat silent as if frozen in time. How could talks of peace invite war on Drakonians? Who would lead them through the challenges they now needed to face? Drakus directed his eyes toward King Sarius who nodded in return. The two had written a contingency plan regarding the ambassador role in the accords. It was now time to reveal it.

"I have a proposal for all kingdoms," answered Drakus. "If the Komalsh undo the wrongs of today—if we destroy the Sykanian threat and bring order to Drakonia, would you all surrender your chapters to the Book of Dragons? Would you allow the Komalsh to police a unified Drakonia as written in the peace accords? Would you appoint Lady Savita Cosmos the title as ambassador of peace for a unified Drakonia?

"Me?" Savita was startled at hearing her name.

"Yes, Lady Cosmos. It's evident I couldn't possibly gain the trust of this table. But you are the sorceress of light. You are trusted by all."

King Sarius rises from the table. "All in favour of Lord Drakus' proposal, please rise."

One by one Drakonian royalty stood up around the table. They smiled to Savita with regained hope. Only one remained seated.

King Dag Kaloun sat in anger, denying the potential Sykanian holocaust. Hesitantly, he rose from his seat and surrendered. "Return our chapter of the Book of Dragons…if I must, then I must…but you…" pointing to Drakus, "…must kill Lord Siris. You! You must return his chapter as well and show it to us all! Only then will my kingdom return to this table! Only then will we surrender our chapter and only then will we negotiate peace!"

Lord Drakus waited to let the full weight of the bargaining words settle on all those present. He then bowed slightly telegraphing his agreement to follow and said, "Agreed."

The leaders of the Kingdoms applauded with approval and cheer filled the room. The journey toward peace took its largest step in over a decade.

Lord Drakus sat quiet. He had prophetic dreams of this outcome. He stared at all the happy leaders. Even King Kaloun had a partial smile.

Savita glowed as he remembered. It was a peaceful part of his dream. But it wasn't the end of his dream. His face showed signs of terror. But only for a moment.

"If you'll excuse us." Lord Drakus was cordial, but he was in no mood for pleasantries. "We have a war to prepare for."

Leaving the stables, Lord Drakus, and his unicorn Mythra headed toward the Arkonian kingdom's front gate. Riding close behind was Lady Savita Cosmos, Nyte Shade, Kelar and the sorcerer, Kudos Nexus.

While leaving the Arkonian kingdom they passed the farthest stable from the castle. Inside lived a lone horse. These were the quarters of the King's prize horse, Sleipnir. The horse said goodbye and hello to everyone coming and going. When he recognized Kudos, the horse shouted with excitement.

"Hey, Kudos! Remember me? I haven't seen you in a long time! We have so much to talk about! Want to go riding? Do you! I like riding! I could ride for days! Of course, I would need a water break. Do you like water? I think water is great! Where are you going, Kudos?"

Kudos left quietly while hiding his head beneath his hood.

"Hey stable boy! You got a new shovel! I love shovels! What's your favourite colour, stable boy? I'm colour blind so I really don't have one myself. Hey, look! A squirrel! A squirrel!"

The stable boy broke down in tears and pleaded for Sleipnir to shut up, but the horse could not.

"That's right, Kudos," waved the Arkonian King.

"Just keep on going, you drunk son of a bitch!"

"Will someone please shut that damn horse up!"

Chapter XII
In the Shadow of Shade.

After a long day of riding, Lord Drakus and company arrived at Lake Aeron. After setting up camp, they dined quietly under a starlit canvas. At dinner's end Kelar and Nyte, who were battered and bruised, retired to bed early while Drakus, Savita and Kudos sat up around the campfire.

Kudos tossed a bundle of sedavive leaves onto the fire producing a green smoke. "King Siris! Well, I didn't see that coming!"

"Nor did I, Kudos," spoke Drakus defeated. "My dreams have been vague and distorted as of late. I fear they may have been suppressed by a higher power."

"Do you believe Fenka Rek is responsible for suppressing your dreams, my lord?"

"I don't know, Savita. Whoever or whatever it is, it's elusive."

Kudos drank from his gourd. "It's clear now that King Siris and Fenka Rek are searching for Lord Demonis. This trio will rain havoc on Drakonia."

"After receiving the blank letter from King Siris' messenger, I will lead the Komalsh into battle and end this Sykanian threat forever!" Drakus gritted his teeth as he spoke then drank from Kudos' gourd.

"Why a blank letter?" inquired Kudos.

"Excuse me?"

"He'd spoken of summoning the Komalsh to war with a blank letter. I don't understand this?"

"When we were allies, Cretes Siris would always say actions speak louder than words."

Kudos stretched his aging body. "Well, I'm unfamiliar with that kind of crazy but I do respect his devotion to it."

Kudos yawned and then stretched the kinks from his back. "Time for rest, I suppose."

"Yes, it's getting late," agreed Savita.

Drakus stared into the fading green flames. He inhaled its medicinal fumes. "One moment, Savita."

"Yes, my lord."

"Tomorrow, Nyte will ride with me. I have a special gift for him, one that will ensure his safe passage through the Mystique Forest."

"A wise decision, Hirum," nodded Kudos.

"As you wish, my lord. Good night." Worried, Savita crawled into her blankets.

Sound asleep, Nyte wandered in the realm of dreams and dreamscape. His prophetic visions blazed with pain and anguish. Then unconditional love warmed his soul like the gentle heat of embers in the hearth. His eyes wept as a woman appeared from brightness. The angel stared deep into his eyes restoring lost childhood memories. She infused him with love.

"Mother?"

"Son."

Then everything faded to black…

"Wake up, Nyte. It's time to leave!" nudged Kelar.

Nyte woke up rubbing his dampened eyes.

"What's wrong, Nyte? Do you miss your fire chicken?" taunted Kelar.

"Do you miss your gremlin cuddles?" retaliated Nyte.

Kelar cringed. "Those things are hideous!"

Kudos threw Drakus' gourd and hit Kelar in the head.

"Ouch! What the hell man!" cursed Kelar.

"You leave my gremlins alone!" warned Kudos.

"Why did you throw my gourde?" snarled Drakus.

"Well, I wasn't going to throw mine." Kudos felt justified in his choice. "It could've exploded!"

"Are you okay Nyte?" Worried Savita.

"I'm fine. I just had a vivid dream."

"Maybe you could share that dream with me sometime?" encouraged Drakus.

Nyte hesitated and then replied, "Sure, why not."

"It's okay everyone, my head's fine. Thanks for asking," announced Kelar sarcastically.

"That's too bad," taunted Kudos. "Perhaps I should've thrown my gourd."

"Hey Nyte, we'll be escorting Kudos home," explained Savita. "Lord Drakus has requested for you to ride with him."

"But what about the Mystique Forest?"

"Don't worry, son, we won't miss it," laughed Drakus. "We're just going to take a different path. There's something I'd like you to see."

Nyte reluctantly agreed, "Yeah, okay,"

Kudos placed his hand on Nyte's shoulder. "All will be fine, young Shade. It has been a pleasure to meet you again, all grown up." The sorcerer spoke with pride.

"Thank you for saving our hides in that jail, Kudos."

"Think nothing of it, Nyte. In fact, thank you for the greatest night I've had in years," giggled the sorcerer.

"Until we meet again, young Shade."

Kudos struggled to get onto his horse, Hocus.

"Take care of Blythe for me," reminded Nyte.

Kudos nodded gracefully, "But, of course."

"Oh, and here Kudos, you can have this." Nyte handed him the horn of bottomless beer.

"Why thank you, son!"

Savita gave Nyte a hug. "We'll see you at the Mystique Forest, little man. Safe travels." She kissed him on the forehead.

"Safe travels, Savita."

Savita, Kudos and Kelar mounted their rides and headed toward Kudos' home. Nyte watched as they rode off into the woods. Then he mounted his horse and followed Lord Hirum Drakus.

Lord Hirum Drakus and Nyte Shade rode along the south side of Lake Maximus. By mid afternoon they had arrived above the raging Assaroe falls. During their travels, not a word had been exchanged. Now riding at a slower pace, Nyte expected Lord Drakus to speak in riddles inevitably leading to a moral lesson. But Drakus rode slowly and remained silent.

Nyte noticed a sheathed sword strapped to the back of Drakus' unicorn, Mythra. It was of Komalsh design with a distinctive purple hilt. Nyte vaguely recognized it, then shrugged it off as coincidence.

Feeling uncomfortable with the silence Nyte asked. "I have a question, Lord Drakus."

"I was wondering when you'd start," moaned Drakus.

"If psychic power comes from the mind, why do Komalsh use their hands to make objects move?"

Drakus smirked. "That's very observant, Nyte. The answer is simple. Although our minds have been opened, many of us can't let go of our physical being. We still feel the need to use our hands when, really, we don't even need our bodies. It's just a comfort zone, I suppose. Some things are hard to let go of."

"Okay." Nyte accepted the explanation. "Another thing I found confusing is if we're supposed to protect the Earth creatures, why don't we just stuff them all in Castle Malshidiel? Isn't that where they'd be protected? Wouldn't that be safer than allowing creatures like the Minotaur to roam freely?"

Drakus shook his head with a chuckle. "Not all these creatures realize their importance to Malshidiel. The Elves, unicorns, Kobolds, and a few others are aware, but most Earth creatures have predator instincts making them difficult to reason with. For example, try to bunk a Gnome with a basilisk."

Nyte laughed. "I suppose a dragon and a Centaur sharing a meal wouldn't go over well either.

Okay, okay." repeated Nyte. "I get it."

After a short burst of laughter, the awkward silence returned. Curious, Lord Drakus broke that silence. "I hear you've been experiencing prophetic dreams. Can you tell me what you saw last night?"

Nyte's heartbeat raced. "I saw death, a lot of it. In the Field of Blood, Lord Drakus. It's a massacre for both sides. The ground is stained in red. The sky filled with smoke."

"I'd like you to keep that a secret between us for now, Nyte."

"Yes, Lord Drakus," promised Nyte.

"What else did you see?" persisted Drakus.

"It was very strange; I was talking to my mother." Nyte paused as he recalled the dream vividly. "She told me to come to you."

Lord Drakus stood humbled. "Nyte, your mother was a dear friend to me. I was with her the day she sacrificed her life."

Nyte bit down onto his lip. He was never told how she died. Why she died. No one seemed to know anything. Even her body was never recovered, leaving Nyte and Savita with an empty grave and shallow hearts.

"How did my mother die?" This was the first time in his life when he was able to even raise the question. The words left his mouth without warning.

"A secret that will reveal itself in time," assured Drakus.

The two rode to the top of the Assaroe Falls to a place overlooking the vast lands protected by the Fylosian kingdom under King Will Rayden. The falls fed a peaceful countryside fuelled by the mighty Assaroe River, the largest river in Drakonia.

After setting up camp, the two sat on the mountain's ledge. They gazed across a panoramic view reaching as far as the eye could see. It was a vast area of fertile lands illuminated like a painting by a red setting sun.

"Nyte, in the history of our people, you are the only one to be conceived by two Komalsh leaders. Thus, you have evidently inherited a special gift we call prophetic dreams."

"Kudos told you?" mumbled Nyte.

"He and I go way back, Nyte. But he wasn't the first to reveal your secret. I, too, possess this gift and within my dreams, I foresaw your growing importance."

"My importance?" fumbled Nyte.

"Yes, Nyte. You possess the Komalsh's most powerful gift, one handed down to you by your parents."

"So, what does this all mean?" Nyte was drowned in confusion.

"For now, let's set aside the questions about your future." Drakus spoke calmly to not raise any alarm.

"Instead, I'd like to discuss your past."

"What about my past?"

"You have lived in the shadow of great parents you'll never know nor understand. Savita's done the best she could raising you. However, I fear without your parents to guide your way, you have fallen short without their love to inspire you."

Nyte stared toward the falling sun. "I wish I knew my parents."

"The Mystique Forest will feed from that Nyte." Warned Drakus.

Drakus could see the ongoing battle fought behind Nyte's blue eyes. This was a gentle man who laughed plenty and made others around him feel better. But behind his wall of smiles crept sadness. Drakus saw the young man's depression slowly consuming him. He felt a shadow of emptiness eclipsing his heart. Nyte was a candle burning on both ends. Drakus felt his pain.

Drakus pointed to a struggling tree. "You see that oak tree over there, Nyte?"

The tree leaned over a cliff with its short roots revealed on one side. It was a young tree struggling to survive.

"In some circumstances, the oak tree will grow too fast for its roots to keep up. Inevitably, the tree will fall. The only solution to this problem is by cutting off the top of the tree. This allows the roots the time to catch up."

Drakus walked over to his unicorn, Mythra. He unsheathed the purple handled sword that Nyte had noticed earlier.

"There's a special bond between parents and their offspring. Before your mother crossed over, she placed a special spell on her sword. She then handed it to me and made me promise that I would pass it on to you. This is that sword." Lord Drakus raised the sword upright. "Please kneel before me, Nyte Shade, son of Raine."

Nyte complied while bowing his head.

"Today, son, we trim the top of your tree." Drakus stabbed the sword deep into the ground before the kneeling student.

Nyte placed both hands on the hilt. Dusk settled across the land. Stars appeared. Then a flash of blinding light burst from the blade.

When Nyte's vision returned, he found himself standing in a forest. He was surrounded by colourful bushes and towering old growth trees. Green vines with red thorns embraced the trees seeming to hold the forest together.

Awed by its visual beauty and astonishing fragrances, Nyte explored deeper into the forest.

Along his path he confronted a cloaked woman. Unafraid, Nyte approached her.

"Hello, my son." She spoke in a most gentle voice. Nyte's mind wrestled with the possibility that his heart told the truth. "Mother?"

"Yes, son." She smiled.

"It can't be?" Nyte froze. Was this real?

"I am merely the reflection of my soul placed within this sword, Nyte—a gift only you can open."

She held out her hand and caressed Nyte's cheek. Her touch felt so soft, so real. "You look so much like your father." She gasped holding back her tears. Then her smile returned as she spoke the words Nyte longed to hear. "I love you so much, Nyte."

A tear escaped Nyte's eye. "I love you, too, mother." The two embraced for what felt like eternity. Nyte could feel the warmth of her skin…the pounding of her heart…the movement of her breathing chest and a scent he had long ago remembered—a repressed memory revived. She felt so real.

"I'm sorry I left you, Nyte. But I had no choice. You are my world and I'm so proud of who you've become." Nyte held her tight…tuned in to her every word.

"The day I left you in Savita's arms crushed my heart."

"I remember. You said you'd love me forever."

"I'm so sorry, son. All I wanted was to watch you grow. Live a normal life. But that wasn't in my design, nor is it in yours."

"Our design," probed Nyte, "is to avoid love?"

"No son, not at all. Being loved is vital. It feeds us strength and power. It gives us our will to survive. The time I had with your father was the best part of my life. It was so awfully short, but everybody dies, Nyte. Not everybody truly lives. My family gave me a life worth living. Don't ever be afraid to love, son."

Nyte stood confused. He had promised himself never to get close to anyone. He vowed he could never bear to hear again those words his mother spoke so long ago: "I will love you forever."

He hated those words. Nothing lasts forever. His family was proof of that.

"Is there anything you'd like to know, Nyte?"

"What's your favourite colour, mother?"

"The same as on the hilt of my sword." giggled Raine at the simplicity of his question.

Nyte giggled, too. "Okay, I had always wondered why you named me Nyte? No other shares that name."

Raine smiled and blushed. "I gave birth to you over there." She pointed to an open patch of soft grass where the nightshade plant grew wild around. "It is why I chose this place for this very day. The best day of my life, son. The day you came into this world and gave it meaning."
Nyte dropped to his knees while fighting off his tears. Raine followed him down clutching him close.

"Nyte, hear my words. You do not walk in the shadow of Shade. You are the Shade who creates the shadow. Know who you are and embrace it with all your love. Become what you were born to be."

"What am I supposed to be?" teared Nyte.

"A legend, my son."

The two smiled into each others glazed eyes. "I am no legend mother." Nyte was adamant. His words were curt and firm.

"You will be."

Fog swirled around them forming images of angels and demons reminding Nyte of the question burning inside him.

"How did you die, mother?"

"I don't remember dying."

"What?"

"The sun is rising, son; our time here comes to an end."

"Wait, mother?"

"I will always be looking over your shoulder, my beautiful child. I will love you forever."

Nyte held his mother close. She held him equally. The fog grew thicker. Their embrace grew weaker. Then her scent faded, and everything brightened into a white void. From that void whispered his mother's voice, "Tell Savita I thank her for raising my son."

Nyte awoke on his knees still grasping the sword's purple hilt. His eyes and cheeks glazed with tears and his heartbeat rapid. It was now morning, and the sunrise was behind him.

Nyte's blurred vision slowly came to focus. He noticed the silhouette of a figure kneeling before him. It was Lord Drakus.

"There's something wrong with your eyes, Nyte, they're leaking all over the place."

"Lord Drakus?" Nyte struggled to regain his senses.

"That's right, son." Lord Drakus helped Nyte to his feet. "How do you feel?"

"I feel as though a load has been lifted from my shoulders." Nyte was surprised by his response.

"That sword belongs to you now, Nyte. It's a graduation gift from your mother. I, too, now feel complete for my last order from Lady Raine Shade has finally been resolved."

"Graduation gift? But I haven't passed the Mystique Forest yet."

"You will now, Nyte," assured Drakus while rubbing his belly. "I'm hungry. Let's go catch some breakfast."

Nyte grasped his new sword firmly. Its handle was purple, his mother's favourite colour. He swung it around with elegance and grace and then held the blade upright. Staring into its reflective durenthium blade, he saw his mother staring back. She smiled and winked.

"Thank you, mother."

A warm gentle breeze dried his tears, and a new Nyte Shade was born.

Far away in the lower corner of Mount Kabigatta, two others had spent the night awake. In a log cabin tucked away on a mountain's ridge, the helpless Lord Pronyk laid strapped to a blood-stained table.

His mouth was gagged to muffle his screams. His eyelids were removed to prevent him from sleep and rods were inserted throughout his body like a voodoo pin doll.

The windowless room made it impossible to gauge time. Just one small lantern illuminated the darkened cabin. Lord Pronyk had been here a week without food or rest. He lay on the verge of insanity. Meditation was his only defence.

A cloaked man removed the gag from Lord Pronyk's mouth then seated himself into a dark corner. "Where is the location of Lord Demonis?" he calmly rasped.

"I don't know…I swear…I don't know!" pleaded the once proud Komalsh lord.

“I smell your lies,” rasped the cloaked man while lighting his pipe. He blew smoke across the lonely lantern’s light. “Your friends have died by my hands.” The cloaked man refilled his pipe. “I’m referring to the Komalsh who aided you in hiding Lord Demonis’ stoned imprisonment.”

“I don’t know what you’re talking about!” Pronyk was near tears. He wanted to cry. Perhaps crying would numb his pain.

The cloaked man lit a match and took another pull from his pipe. The match light vaguely revealed his identity. As legend has written, the very sight of his face was a premature death sentence.

“Do you know who I am?” The prestigious assassin spoke as he rose from his seat.

“No! Who are you?” he whimpered.

“I’m Fenka Rek!” Grabbing a hammer from the table he shattered Pronyk’s left kneecap. Pronyk screamed in agony—an agony Fenka Rek found intoxicating.

“You have a weak mind, Lord Pronyk…one I’ll soon break.” Fenka Rek stared into his fear-filled eyes. A devious grin stretched across his face. “Even your own thoughts betray you,” he rasped.

Pronyk endured a moment of clarity. He noticed his weapons on the table behind Fenka Rek. Using his psychic gift, he unsheathed his dagger slowly then telekinetically tossed it toward the back of Fenka Rek’s head. On impact the dagger shattered like glass.

“What is real?” asked Fenka Rek. “Do you believe the table you’re bleeding over is? It seems solid…but then again, are you real?”

“I’m real!” whimpered Pronyk.

Fenka Rek extended his hand and made a fist. In response, Pronyk’s soul stood up from his body. It gazed around in confusion.

“This is who you really are.”

Pronyk's soul looked down at his body. Angered at the very sight of himself, the psychotic soul clawed away at his mortal body. Pronyk's sharp screams echoed outside the cabin. Fenka Rek returned to his chair and relit his pipe. Lord Pronyk never gave up. With a mere thought his soul returned to his body. He concentrated hard on his healing ability and telekinetically pushed the rods from his body. His opened wounds mended quickly, and his pain diminished.

"I am a Komalsh. You cannot break me!"
Pronyk telekinetically summoned his sword from the table. He swung it around and decapitated Fenka Rek still sitting in his seat. The assassin's head rolled along the floor and his body fell limp to the ground.

"Do you even know what's real anymore?" whispered Fenka Rek's voice as though it was emanating from all four walls of the dimly lit cabin.

Lord Pronyk awoke still strapped to the table. Rods still pierced his body. Fenka Rek blew smoke across the lonely lantern's light. He rose from his chair and whispered into Pronyk's ear, "Do you ever wonder why you cannot communicate telepathically to the others?"

Pronyk stood baffled at his truth. He tried for days without success.

"I'm blocking your thoughts like I control your reality. I'm far more powerful than you could possibly imagine." Fenka Rek proceeded to walk around the table.

"The Komalsh are weak. Soon, like yourself, they will all die."

"I'm not afraid of the afterlife," proclaimed Pronyk.

"And I am not afraid to send you there," replied Fenka Rek. "In fact, I'm going to send your whole family there."

Terror swept across Pronyk's lidless eyes.

"I tell you what," offered Fenka Rek. "Share with me the location of Cable Demonis and in return I'll spare the lives of your family."

"Now tell me, where is Cable Demonis?"

Beside the Assaroe Falls, Lord Drakus stood over an open flame cooking the trout they'd caught. Nyte, still shaken from his spiritual encounter, asked him, "What was my father like?"

"Your father was a noble and brave man. Arguably the greatest of all Komalsh leaders."

"I thought Lord Duren was?" Nyte was confused.

"Lord Duren was the first. We know little about him. History written in ancient text tells of a great fire in Castle Malshidiel. Most of the history books from that era were destroyed."

"Your father, however, was my friend. A wise and encouraging leader. He was a true reflection of the Komalsh and a loving husband to your mother. The hardest thing I ever did was return to Raine with the news of his passing. A sad day indeed." Drakus' facial expressions sobered as he recalled the memories that had dimmed over time.

"How did my mother die?" asked Nyte.

Fenka Rek felt exhilarated. He whistled while strolling around his prisoner's table. Dragging behind him a rusty, dull axe he asked once again, "Where is the location of Lord Demonis?"

"I do not know!" repeated the distressed Lord Pronyk.

Fenka Rek raised his axe and swung down hard. The rusty dull blade went halfway into Pronyk's left ankle. He swung again. This time the instrument struck a new blow and made it two-thirds of the way through his limb. Screams echoed off the cabin walls. Fenka Rek swung down a third time pushing the rusty axe straight through his bone and into the wooden table. Pronyk's dismembered foot fell to the floor. Lord Pronyk screamed himself unconscious.

Fenka Rek wiped the blood splatter from his face. He pulled the axe out of the table and rested it on his shoulder. With a simple thought he telepathically forced Pronyk to awaken from his unconsciousness. Fenka Rek hovered over him staring coldly into his eyes. "I will keep removing limbs until none remain. Then I cut off your head and kill your family. Or you can end this senseless violence by simply answering my question. Then, perhaps, I will even spare your life."

Pronyk lay there weakened from his healing power's draining attempt to recover. "Please stop. I don't know, I don't know what you're even talking about!" With a powerful swing Fenka Rek chopped off his right hand. Pronyk raised his right arm now freed from his shackle. His pinky finger dangled from his wrist. He gained enough awareness to pull his severed ankle free from its shackle. "Get away from me!" he screamed while holding out his wounded limbs.

Fenka Rek swung his axe and chopped off Pronyk's handless arm at the elbow. He climbed up onto the table and rested his axe blade on Pronyk's throat. "Where hides Lord Demonis?"

Pronyk nodded off unconsciousness from the amount of blood lost. His body lay limp on the table. Once again, Fenka Rek recovered his vitals telepathically. "Tell me or I will chop your children into pieces," threatened the assassin. "That's right. I know where they are, and I'll bring you their heads to prove it!"

Lord Pronyk was broken. He himself was prepared to die. But the thought of his children's massacre was unbearable. Defeated he let down his psychic guard and allowed Fenka Rek to read his thoughts.

Fenka Rek reached into the opened doors of Pronyk's mind. Traveling through memories he located the whereabouts of Lord Cable Demonis, his stone imprisonment hidden on the highest peak of Mount Maximus within a limestone cave.

Fenka Rek closed his eyes and hailed Lord Drakus. "Listen, listen to the cry of a coward."

Fenka Rek raised the dull rusty axe over his head. His shadow on the wall from the lonely lantern amplified his size. Fenka Rek then repeatedly chopped at Pronyk's face. Pronyk's screams were hailed to Lord Drakus as Fenka Rek intended, screams that ended in a sudden silence.

Stepping down from the table Fenka Rek tossed his bloodied axe to the floor. He sat back in his chair and grabbed a nearby rag to wipe the blood splatter from his face. The assassin savoured the aftermath adrenaline as it slowly dwindled down. He lit his pipe and blew smoke across the lonely lantern's light. Taking a moment to compose himself, he rose from his chair and stared into the wall mirror. Fenka Rek wore a dark charcoal-shaded light armour with a black hoody. He grabbed his black, horned helmet shaped like a skull with fangs along the jawbone protector, from the table and placed it over his head. With his identity now concealed he whistled a joyous song while leaving the cabin.

Fenka Rek mounted his undead horse, Apocalypse, and rode toward the rising sun.

"What's wrong?" Nyte sensed something but could not place it.

"It's nothing," replied Drakus holding his head in pain from Fenka Rek's telepathic message. "Just a headache son. No need to concern yourself. Finish your breakfast. We must leave soon."

"But I asked you how my mother died?"

"I'll reveal everything you need to know in time, Nyte. For now, we must get moving. The Mystique Forest awaits you."

Nyte nodded reluctantly.

Chapter XIII
The Strength that Bines.

After leaving the abandoned Kelasian castle, Lord Dunlam and his students spent the night near the Assaroe River barge crossing. At the break of dawn, Lord Dunlam sat cross-legged on the ground in his usual meditation posture. Connected with his wife Elasia, they embraced each other's energy.

"Bossel." whispered Elasia.

"Yes, dear."

"I can sense someone staring at you. You must awaken."

"I was trying to ignore him my love," admitted Bossel. Elasia smiled at her husband's unwillingness to separate from their psychic bond. "I will see you in person tonight, Bossel."

"Oh, alright, I'll see you tonight, love."

Bossel's green field of psychic energy collapsed and before him stood Kris Tarius.

"Well Kris, what is it?" asked Bossel, displeased.

"My parents are fishing close to here."

"I thought your family was Tarnian, Kris?"

"We are sir. My family fishes this river when the salmon run. I would like to see them before challenging the forest."

"As you wish, Kris. Just rendezvous with us at the Mystique Forest," instructed Bossel.

"Thank you, sir."

Kris mounted his horse and left to visit his parents.

Nyte Shade and Lord Drakus rode past the Fylosian kingdom through a forest of old growth trees surrounded by thick green brush. They had chosen to ride the path most travelled.

"Hold up," ordered Drakus staring off into the forest.

"What is it?" whispered Nyte.

"Look closely," pointed Drakus.

There in the bush stood a human-like figure. He appeared injured and whimpering in pain.

"He needs our help." Nyte headed toward the injured man.

Drakus grabbed the reins of his horse. "That is no man, Nyte. It's a Mimic."

Drakus dismounted from his unicorn and held out his hand. He telekinetically raised the creature from the bush and suspended him for Nyte to see.

****

The Mimic is a human size predator native to Drakonia—a cold-blooded reptile which stood on two feet and ran on all fours. It possessed the ability to take a close resemblance to its prey. It mimics not only in features but also in sounds, an evolutionary gift to lure its prey. Hence, the name Mimic. They were armed with sharp claws and fangs that release a mild nerve toxin to disable their prey. They fear fire and aren't known to attack larger numbers. Like wolves, they hunt in packs and have been found to weigh up to 200 pounds.

****

"Interesting creatures." Nyte studied the Mimic suspended before him.

Drakus placed it down carefully. The Mimic raised its arms to look big while growling and snapping viciously. Outnumbered, it cowered on all fours and ran into the woods. Others like it growled around the forest hidden to the eye.

"Sounds like they're here in large numbers," noted Drakus. "A good time to be on our way."

Kris Tarius rode up river to a small village along the west side of the Assaroe River. Fisherman were mending nets while their wives and children cleaned up after a community breakfast. Kris tied his horse to a tree and searched for his family.

"Son!" hollered a short, stocky grey-haired man.

"Father!"

The old man approached him and gave his son a big bear hug. After a quick greeting, his father guided Kris to their small cabin overlooking the river. There in the doorway stood his mother. Excitedly, she ran to her son and embraced him in the way only a mother could.

"I missed you so much, Kris." Tears were streaming down her cheeks as she spoke.

"Me too, mother."

"For gosh sakes, Joyce, let our young man breathe!" defended his father.

"Settle down, Sieg! My boy's home and anything you have to say doesn't count!"

"We're both so happy to see you, Kris. Tell us, how's Olemeeze treating you?"

"Very well, dad. I challenge the Mystique Forest tomorrow."

His father wore a proud smile. "We heard, son. I always wanted to be a Komalsh. But I wasn't even accepted into the school let alone that Mystique Forest! Guess I was destined to be a stinky old fisherman. But you, son, you did it! I'm so proud!"

"We both are, Kris!" echoed his mother caressing her husband's arm.

"Come on, boy!" invited his dad proudly. "Come have a sit with me."

The two sat on rocking chairs overlooking the Assaroe River. They sat quietly taking in the sound of the streaming water.

"Dad."

"Yes, son."

"I want to thank you for raising me to become the man I am."

His father smiled while lighting his pipe.

"But I also want you to know that if I had to change…if I had to choose to be someone else…I would want to be just like you."

His father's throat swelled. His eyes fought off a tear. No more words were said. None were needed. The two sat there with equal admiration for one another—both relaxing to the soothing sound of a flowing river. This was a simple life. One worth living.

Kris needed this. He needed a break from the complicated world that surrounded him. What better place could he be and what better company could he be with.

A woman dressed in a tattered dress approached them from the river. Kris rose from his chair with delight. It was Bella Flora.

****

Kris grew up with Bella in the Kingdom of Tarnia. As kids they were inseparable. Kris had cherished every moment with her. They were best of friends, but he had to leave her when he was chosen to attend the School of Olemeeze. They would see each other every time Kris came home to visit but his focus then was always on his studies.

Today, however, he felt something different. He was nervous and exited at the same time. She looked so beautiful, so confident. He stood speechless.

****

"Hi Kris."

"Hello, Bella! What are you doing here?"

"My father left farming to fish with Sieg. With mother passing, I thought I would tag along with him. That way I can make sure he stays out of trouble." She laughed uncomfortably. "So, I hear you are to challenge the Mystique Forest. That is so impressive. I'm very exited for you." She tried to smile to cover her worry.

"Thank you, Bella, and you don't need to worry. I'll be fine," reassured Kris with a smile. "What have you been up too?"

Bella raised both arms revealing her tattered dress. "Father says soon the fish will be plentiful and I will get a new dress." Bella giggled, "but I think I will just hide the coins for the cold season when food is short. Father never thinks ahead."

Bella grabbed Kris's hand. She hazed directly into his eyes. "I'm incredibly happy, Kris. I love life, especially when you're in it." She blushed.

Exiting a cabin across the meadow, Bella's father hollered out for her. Then noticing Kris, he made a waving gesture with a hearty smile.

"I must go, Kris. Perhaps you can visit me when you've become a Komalsh?"

Kris smiled from ear to ear. "I will. You can count on it."

Bella reached into her pocket and revealed a silk handkerchief she had made. "Keep this for luck."

"Thank you. I will cherish it always."

"See you later, Mr. and Mrs. Tarius."

"Goodbye, love," they replied in sync.

Bella left as gracefully as she arrived. She turned back to see if Kris was still watching her, then smiled and ran to her father.

"She looks so beautiful," Kris told his father.

"She is a good woman, Kris. She would make a fine wife."

"You two would make lovely children!" added his mother.

"I don't have the time for fatherhood. I will become a knight of Malshidiel soon."

"I don't care who you're the knight of. You better make me a grandmother!"

"In time, Joyce!" defended Sieg.

"My visit here is short. I must be leaving. I just wanted to see you two before challenging the forest." Said Kris nervously.

His mother held him tight. "You'll do fine, my son. I believe in you."

"Thanks, mother."

Sieg escorted Kris to his horse. After mounting his ride, he asked his father, "Do you have any last words of advice for me?"

“Well, son, the first rain drop to hit your head is an act of god. The second is your own damn fault!”
Kris laughed for a moment…then paused into what became a nervous silence.

Sieg grabbed the reins and spoke, “I bet you’re pretty nervous about the Mystique Forest.”

“I’m scared, dad.”

“You’ll do fine, Kris. We all believe in you.”

“I’m going to make you proud, father.”

“You already have, son.”

Kris rode off toward the Mystique Forest, his visit had gained him the strength needed to move forward.
A tear rolled down the cheek of his father’s weathered face as he watched Kris ride away. Under his breath, he said these words: “I’m so very proud of you, son.”

Bella ran to her home and collapsed into her dad’s lap crying. “I didn’t want him to know how scared I was, dad!” As she turned her eyes to the window, she whimpered, “Please come back Kris. Please!”

“Now, now dear. Kris will be alright.” He stroked Bella’s long hair and used his soothing voice to ease his daughter’s fears. “It was wise of you not to show weakness. I mean it dear. Kris could use all the strength he can get. You are a good friend to him.”

“I want to be more than a friend, father. I love him dearly.”

Her father smiled and held her close. “You always have Bella. You always have.”

By nightfall Lord Drakus and Nyte Shade arrived at the Mystique Forest. There under the starlit sky, campfires were lit, tents were set, and dinner was being served to the students and Elvin teachers of Olemeeze.

Savita greeted the two incoming riders. Lord Drakus, who was more concerned for dinner, headed straight toward the teacher's fire where he was welcomed with dinner and mead.

"Are you okay, Nyte?"

"Yes, Savita, I am," he replied peacefully.

"I was worried for you, Nyte. Did you see your mother?"

"Yes, I did."

Savita looked saddened. "I hope you feel better now, Nyte."

"I do Savita, much so."

"You understand, Nyte, that I could never replace your mother. But I did the best I could."

Nyte could see Savita's turmoil beating herself up inside.

"Savita."

"Yes?"

"Read my thoughts. Read what my mother wished you to hear."

With permission given, Savita did. Within Nyte's memories she saw Lady Raine Shade smiling to her as she whispered, *"Tell Savita thank you for raising my son."*

Savita's heart dropped. Holding Nyte closer, she wept. "All I ever wanted was to spare you the pain I endured through the loss of my own parents. Your mother raised me through difficult times, allowing me to become who I am today by allowing me to feel loved. When she asked me to take care of you, I felt the time had come where I could repay her. I loved you like you were my own, but I never felt like I could ever replace what was taken from you."

"Savita, I, too, need to thank you. I never realized how much you sacrificed for me. I always took it for granted. On the ride here I thought about all you've done and the memories we've shared. You are the most amazing person. I love you, Savita. Thank you for being…my mother."

Nyte squeezed her tight. Then arm in arm, they wandered over to the camp for dinner.

Later that evening, Kris Tarius arrived at the Mystique Forest. His handkerchief gift from Bella wrapped around his knuckles.

"Did you see your parents?" asked Bossel intercepting his arrival.

"Yes, I did, sir."

"You are glowing tonight, Kris. Did you fall in love while you were away?"

"Excuse me? No, no! I don't…I mean of course not. She's just a friend!"

"Who is?"

"Never mind!" He felt flustered.

"Master Tarius, there's nothing wrong with love."

"I am a warrior sir; I have no time for something as insignificant as love."

"Love is what a warrior fights for, son. Without it, you're just a killer."

Kris smelled the handkerchief. Bella's fragrance emanated from its silky texture. "She makes me feel weak, sir."

"I believe you are mistaking weakness for strength, Kris."

"I suppose."

"Nevertheless, you must be hungry and tired. There's dinner waiting for you. Rest up, Kris. You have a big day tomorrow."

Kris wandered through the crowd of students and Elvin teachers. There were fire pits scattered about attracting different crowds. Tents were set up along the Mystique Forest's edge and off in the darkness a lonely fire burned. Recognizing Nyte sitting there staring deep into its flames, Kris wandered over and sat beside him. On his lap was a sword.

"Nice sword, Nyte. Where'd you get it?"

Nyte turned to Kris white as snow. "My mother gave it to me."

"Wow, are you okay, Nyte?" Kris was shocked. "I can't imagine how overwhelmed you must be!"

"I've never felt this good in my life, Kris! Through this sword, I met my mother."

"What was that like?" Kris was sincerely curious.

"Her favorite colour is purple…but never mind me, Bossel mentioned you went to visit your parents. How are they doing?" Nyte deflected the question and set up a detour in the conversation.

"They're just fine, Nyte. Happy and content as usual."

"Geez, I haven't seen that look in awhile." Nyte grinned.

"What look?"

"That look!" He pointed at Kris' face. "The one that says you spent time with Bella Flora."

Kris giggled. "Yeah, I saw her." He smiled in fond memory.

"Did you finally tell her how you feel about her?"

"No, not yet Nyte. But I will. Right after I pass the Mystique Forest."

Kris pulled out a gold ring. "I'm going to marry her, my friend. As soon as I become a Komalsh."

Nyte punched him in the shoulder. "It's about time!"

****

Nyte Shade and Kris Tarius, both from the Kingdom of Tarnia, were first introduced as babies. In fact, other than their parents, they were the first people they ever met. This had entitled them to introduce one another as their oldest friend.

They had, however, been separated on multiple occasions by Lady Savita Cosmos who, during Komalsh missions, had entrusted Nyte with Ayesha Gungnir, mother of Terex, where Nyte would be protected within the walls of the Thorenite castle. During those times, Kelar and Bella Flora, also Tarnian, started chumming with Kris.
Even after being separated as children, which to them seemed like years, Nyte and Kris would reunite like they'd never parted. Best friends for life. Once enrolled together in the school of Olemeeze, the two grew up together and were now inseparable.

****

Kris stared into the dark depths of the Mystique Forest. "Are you ready for this, Nyte?"

"As ready as I'll ever be."

"What happened to your face?" Kris hadn't noticed the evidence before. "The black eye and swollen lip are something new. Did you forget how to throw a punch?" he chuckled.

"Kelar, Kudos and I got into a fight at the Arkonian tavern."

"Weren't you supposed to represent us at the peace conference?"

"Yeah, things got complicated," sighed Nyte.

"You don't say!" laughed Kris. "I suppose Kelar was responsible for your…complication?"

"His ego has created many…complications, over the years," recalled Nyte.

“Yeah, I remember,” chuckled Kris. “He’s been complicated ever since he first arrived in Tarnia.”

The two drifted off into silence while gazing into the dark and eerie Mystique Forest.

“Your dreams…,” asked Kris, “did they foresee tomorrow’s results?”

“Sorry, my oldest friend, they haven’t.”

Before Kudos and Lord Drakus were introduced to Nyte’s ability to foresee the future, Kris was the only one with whom he shared this secret. He made Kris promise to never say a word. That was a secret Kris would take to his grave.

“What does Lord Drakus think of your dreams?”

“He believes my gift to be inherited from my parents who were powerful Komalsh leaders.” Nyte stared off into the forest still holding his precious sword.

“You are a leader, Nyte. You always have been.” reminded Kris.

“I’m only as strong as the friends who surround me, Kris.” Nyte rose to his feet. “Why didn’t you propose to Bella earlier? She’s a great person.”

Kris stared back into the Mystique Forest. “If I fail the forest tomorrow, Nyte, I wouldn’t want her to know how much I cared. I couldn’t let her go through life as a widow.”

Nyte placed his hand on Kris’s shoulder. “Well then, I look forward to your wedding. Now go get some rest old friend, you’ll need it for tomorrow night’s celebration.”

“Brothers for life,” smiled Kris.

“Brothers for life.” Nyte smiled in return.

Nyte left Kris and wandered over to another fire. Surrounding it were Kelar, Kolos and Neasha.

Neasha snuggled up to Kelar, her skin pale and clammy. Kolos too looked ill as he bundled himself deep within his blanket. Nyte placed his hand on Neasha's forehead. She had no fever or flu-like symptoms. Yet she looked in rough shape.

Kelar too looked pale and clammy.

"I don't feel well, Nyte," reported Kelar. "It seemed like the closer I got to here, the sicker I became."

"It's just your wrist my friend. You need to keep it elevated," instructed Nyte.

"It's something different than that, Nyte. Something doesn't feel right about this place." Kelar was clearly worried. Something was off.

"You probably just have the willies…a case of the yips," assured Nyte. "Get some rest my friend, you'll feel better in the morning."

"Okay, buddy. Night, Nyte," teased Kelar.

Nyte rolled his eyes and turned to leave.

"Wait, Nyte, hold on."

"Yeah."

"I just wanted to say good luck for tomorrow and thanks for being a good friend."

Nyte nodded and smiled. "Good night, Kelar. Brothers for life."

"Brothers for life," echoed Kelar.

Nyte left to take a place at the next fire where Arias, Trayke and Terex seemed to be distancing themselves from their teachers.

"How's everyone feeling tonight?" asked Nyte.

"Actually, I'm kind of excited about it, Nyte." Terex had a hard time hiding his exhilaration. He was wide eyed and pumped with adrenaline.

Trayke sipped on a large bottle of rum he had scooped from the Kelasian castle. "I'm not afraid." His slurring of his words, however, spoke volumes.

“I thought you were hung over today?” Nyte’s sarcasm did not go unnoticed despite Trayke’s less than sober state.

“How did you know that?” Trayke replied in his stupor.

“Because you are hungover everyday, Trayke.” Laughter surrounded the fire.

“Ah well, hair of the dog!” Trayke chimed back at the friendly banter.

“Yeah!” cheered Arias. “We’re drinking away the willies!”

“The willies? I have butterflies in my belly the size of dragons!” Terex was pumped with adrenaline.

“Now they’re drunken dragonflies,” laughed Trayke.

“To drunken dragonflies!” cheered the three students.

“Try not to get too drunk, boys.” warned Nyte. “I’m off to bed.”

“Night, Nyte!” cheered his friends.

“That never gets old,” mumbled Nyte while returning to his tent.

Under the starlit sky, Nyte lay on his back gazing into its infinite wonder. The brightest stars were like destination points on an enchanted map—the moon’s mass magnifying its dominance.

Nyte’s eyelids grew heavy. He held his mother’s sword close.

“I am not afraid,” he whispered to the forest. Then slowly he drifted off to sleep.

Hours had passed when Nyte awoke. He got up from the ground and looked around. Everyone was gone. There were no tents, firepits, horses or unicorns. He looked to where he’d slept, his blankets no longer there. The once lush green Mystique Forest was now a barren wasteland of withered trees.

Nyte explored the forest's edge when he heard his name whispered from its darkened depths.

"Nyte Shade."

Nyte followed the whisper cautiously. The further he walked into the forest, the thicker the fog rolled in. Nyte approached a large oak tree. Its top was severed. Shadow demons flew around it like a cyclone of frantic bats. Then, appearing from behind the tree, a cloaked knight stood with his sword drawn. Nyte approached him while unsheathing his mother's sword.

The dark knight lowered his hood. It was Kelar. He wore the look of hate and rage. Two other dark knights emerged from the rolling fog. He recognized Kolos and Neasha who both shared the same angered expression. The three knights ran toward Nyte swinging their swords downward. Nyte raised his mother's sword and a burst of light flashed from her blade. The three dark knights exploded into a stormy mist of shadow demons.

The severed oak tree awoke from its slumber. Its roots burst from beneath the soil grabbing onto Nyte's legs. He swung his mother's sword severing himself free of their grasp. The tree collapsed into a roll of mist. Nyte was now lost inside a barrier of thick fog.

A phoenix appeared through the haze. It was Blythe, from Kudos' garden. Circling the bemused student, she burst into flames to help guide him through the fog toward the safety of the forest's edge.

At the forest's edge, the thick rolling fog dissipated, and the barren forest returned to its lush fertile form. The air smelled sweet, and the breeze felt gentle. The sun shone brightly and warm while Drakonian wildlife roamed peacefully. Nyte noticed another cloaked knight—one hidden under Komalsh robes. The whispering winds claimed the stranger to be Malshidiel's chosen one.

"With my body, Malshidiel will walk this realm and united we shall destroy the Darkstar."

"Who are you?" Nyte approached.

"I am the hidden knight," whispered the wind.

"The who?"

"Nyte, its time to wake up! Nyte, its time to wake up!"

"Wait, what's your name?"

"It's time to wake up, Nyte!" shouted Kris. "Come on man!" Kris shook Nyte till he woke.

"Where am I?"

"The Mystique Forest, oldest friend. Everyone is waiting for us."

"It's time!" shouted Lord Drakus in the biggest voice he could put forth.

"Line up students!" ordered Lord Bossel Dunlam. Lord Drakus stood before Savita and the students. On either side of him were Lord and Lady Dunlam. Also arriving earlier that morning were two of the Komalsh Elite, Lady Tuza and Lord Jamala, who stood off to the side.

In the background, the Elvin teachers took down the tent village and prepared for their journey back to Olemeeze. Their job here was done.

"Students," addressed Drakus, "the Mystique Forest awaits you. Remember all you've learned. Everything you've ever studied will aide for this very moment. Lord and Lady Dunlam, Lady Cosmos and I will enter the forest first. We will be waiting for you on the other side."

Lord Drakus paced before the students. "There are three outcomes to the forest. One, you pass and in a timely manner, you arrive at Castle Malshidiel."

"Two, you fail peacefully…and this is where the forest will return you."

"And three," paused Drakus, "the forest deems you a threat and kills you."

The student's stomachs dropped. Their hard swallows revealed their response.

"If deemed a threat and you do manage to escape the forest's fate, these two Komalsh have been appointed to execute you." Drakus raised his hand directing their attention to Lord Jamala and Lady Tuza.

"Understand, students, the forest protects Castle Malshidiel from any threat. Lord Jamala and Lady Tuza are just a precaution for few have ever escaped. Since our school of Olemeeze's curriculum was designed to screen out possible failures or threatening ones, the forest deeming you a threat is highly unlikely. The Elves and the Komalsh took many precautions when designing your education. You are the graduates of such precautions. We will see you on the other side."

Lord Drakus followed by Lord and Lady Dunlam disappeared on their unicorns into the forest.

Savita gave Nyte a reassuring smile. She placed her hand on his cheek and spoke proudly. "See you on the other side, son."

Savita mounted her unicorn, Jinx, then galloped into the forest and vanished.

The students stood stone cold silent. Each one staring fearfully into the Mystique Forest.

Neasha wrapped her arms around Kelar and squeezed him tight. "I love you!"

"I love you, too," he replied.

Her eyes widened. This was the first time Kelar returned those words. Neasha smiled with joy in her heart as a tear rolled down her cheek.

"Let's do this!" shouted Terex pumped with adrenaline.

Nyte looked over to Kris. "I'll see you on the other side, old friend."

Kris returned the smile. "See you there, old friend."

Nyte Shade's confidence was strengthened by his mother's words. Her graduation gift allayed any doubts of failure. Still, he was not sure he was prepared for the unknown and the Mystique Forest was riddled with the unknown.

Kris Tarius held tightly onto the silk handkerchief he had received from Bella. Determination to return to her empowered him. He smiled ear to ear as he and Nyte ran toward the Mystique Forest.

Trayke Basa, holding onto an empty bottle of rum, took a step forward and tripped over a rock. Clumsily clambering back to his feet, he threw his empty bottle of rum high into the air and charged toward the forest.

Terex Gungnir squeezed his fists flexing his toned physique. His jaw clenched; his eyes became slits as his face prepared for battle. He charged toward the forest with powerful strides screaming a deep battle cry.

Arias Jackyle jogged hesitantly behind conflicted on whether this was a good idea or not. Then shaking off his doubt, he lowered his head and sprinted toward the forest.

Kelar and Neasha Sentrix kissed each other softly. They winked to one another and then ran together holding hands.

Kolos Dreken was suddenly struck in the head by an empty bottle of rum falling from the sky. He dropped to the ground hard. Rising from the tall grass, he wiped the blood from his forehead and trailed last toward the forest.

While the students ran in full stride, green vines with red venomous thorns reached out from the trees in the Mystique Forest. Each one targeted a different student. They wrapped them in a cocoon of vines and pierced their venomous thorns deep within their flesh. With quick snaps, they dragged each student deep into the dark depths of the forest.

The forest's edge was now silent. Only Lady Tuza and Lord Jamala remained. Quietly, they stood on guard waiting patiently and prepared to kill any who escaped the forest deemed a threat. But these two Komalsh weren't anticipating anything. No one escapes the Mystique Forest.

****

Into the depths of their uncharted minds, the students would face their final test—one which will define them for the rest of their lives.

****

Chapter XIV
Inside the Mystique Forest.

Nyte Shade's eyes slowly opened. He found himself laying on his back staring up into the trees. The forest around him was silent. His friends were nowhere to be seen. Cautiously, he rose to his feet.

The forest was littered with old growth trees towering to the heavens. Green brush decorated the forest floor and bright coloured flowers illuminated the shadows. The trees were wrapped by green vines armed with red thorns dripping a clear venom. Alive they slithered slowly about guiding their movements by feel.

Nyte walked deeper into the forest. He felt safe and unafraid. Despite the terrors he expected, the further he journeyed the more relaxed he became.

Arriving at a grassy meadow sided by a small stream, Nyte started recognizing his surroundings. Even the fragrances triggered his memory. He approached a patch of grass where the nightshade plant grew wild around. "I was born here," he whispered to himself.

"Mother!" shouted Nyte, "Mother!" turning his face and shouting in a different direction.

"Yes, my son," whispered the soft breeze.

"The Mystique Forest is my birthplace…isn't it?"

"Yes, Nyte. A strong reason you differ from the rest of our kind. You were raised and nourished here until you were two. Then Savita took you to Tarnia."

"I feel no fear," reported Nyte.

"Nor should you," spoke the soft breeze. "The forest accepted you from birth."

"Where are you, mother?" Nyte turned all directions searching the forest.

"The reflection of my soul is in the sword. With the help of the forest, I can speak through your dream."

"I'm dreaming?" Nyte was mystified.

"You have been since you entered the forest. That is why you appear to be alone."

The breeze picked up to a heavy gust. "NYTE SHADE!" It howled. His mother's sheathed sword exploded with a flash. His surroundings spun into a cyclone of clouds and his veins burned as the vines venom filtered through his mind.

Everything fell silent. Nyte stood in an empty void of darkness.

From the darkness his mother appeared dressed in white Komalsh robes. "You must return your father's sword to the forest," instructed Lady Raine Shade.

"How would I retrieve it, mother? It's buried with the Dragons Flute under a mountain of rock."

"The sword will find you, my son."

Nyte started to feel an excruciating pain as the venom hit its final stage. His vision blurred and his veins burned.

"What's happening to me?"

"Wake up, Nyte…wake up!" roared the wind.

Nyte awoke in a cocoon of green vines with their red thorns imbedded deep throughout his body. He could feel his blood dripping from each thorn's painful puncture. Hanging captive from a tree, he struggled to break free. The vine felt his struggle and gently released him to the ground. Nyte lay weakened from the venomous invasion. Collecting himself and rising to his knees, he felt empowered with energy. His mind opened as the venom became one with his blood stream. Nyte rose to his feet. His thorn wounds and black eye from the tavern's fight healed instantly. His body and mind were connected spiritually to nature and the lifeforce of the vegetation surrounding him.

The forest pulsated with energy. Nyte's heightened senses became difficult to control. The venom burned through his veins. His body felt toxic. His stomach was nauseous. Nyte closed his eyes trying desperately to regain focus. Slowly he reopened them. He felt a calm in his thoughts…a balance in his soul. He felt powerful. Coming to his senses, he looked around. As he became aware of his surroundings he announced aloud, "I'm inside the Mystique Forest."

Above him his friends hung from trees cocooned in the same green vines with red thorns…each one secreting blood and venom. Each one was trapped in a dreamworld of their own design.

"Mother! Where did you go?"

The forest stood silent.

Nyte journeyed down a path through the forest of towering trees and mythical landscape. Unicorns galloped in the distance. Pixies and fairies flew carelessly but with curiosity to their new arrival. Brownies on nearby branches watched quietly while nymphs sang a delightful song enhancing the beauty of their natural surroundings. The forest itself seemed alive as green vines with red thorns slithered thinly over the forest floor.

At the end of Nyte's wander, he came across a flowing stream. Drinking from it stood a storm grey unicorn with a black tail and mane. He approached the steed cautiously.

"It's okay, Nyte, I don't bite. My name is Loki."

"You know my name?" Nyte was taken aback."Yes sir. The forest told me all about you. It helps us unicorns decide which Komalsh we will choose."

"So, you've chosen me, Loki?"

"I'd be honoured to join you, Nyte." The steed bowed as he spoke.

"Okay." Nyte stood speechless.

"Come, Lord Shade. Allow me to take you to Castle Malshidiel."

Nyte mounted the saddleless steed and together they rode for the very first time.

Nyte would recover quickly from the venom's unpleasurable side effects. On the way to the castle, he felt enlightened while bathing in his own psychic energy. His mind reached through the forest feeling the heartbeats of all its creatures. Even the trees and plant life seemed to breathe.

"In time you'll gain control of all your thoughts." reassured Loki. "This is a passing stage."

"You're aware of how I'm feeling?"

"Of course. Our souls are connected by the forest." answered Loki.

"I can feel your soul, Loki." Nyte was already feeling a sense of connection.

"And I can feel yours," Loki said with pride.

"I can't believe I'm talking to a unicorn!" Nyte wondered if he should be pinching himself.

"You now have the ability to communicate with most creatures," informed Loki. "It is one of many gifts granted to the Komalsh."

"I'm a Komalsh." Nyte felt humbled as he let the reality of his words sink in.

"Indeed, you are, Lord Shade." Loki had chosen well.

****

The two became acquainted fast. Their friendship molded by the universe. Ironically enough, Loki and Nyte were both born in the Mystique Forest around the same time. What they didn't remember was that they had met once before.

****

Nyte and Loki left the forest where Lord Drakus and company awaited their arrival. Beyond them was the most breathtaking castle Nyte ever laid eyes on, Castle Malshidiel.

Nyte would be one of two Drakonians ever to walk through the Mystique Forest unchallenged. There was no conflict within him, only peace. The forest accepted him from birth and because of this, he was the first to exit. The only other one who ever passed unchallenged was Lord Mikel Duren, the Komalsh's founding father.

Kris Tarius awoke standing inside the Mystique Forest. He recalled the vines reaching toward him but was foggy about the events that followed. His fellow students were nowhere to be seen and Bella's silk handkerchief was gone.

Kris explored cautiously through the old growth forest. Its towering trees were constricted by green vines with red protruding thorns. These vines connected the treetops together in a webbed umbrella protecting the forest floor from the sun's hot summer rays. The air felt refreshing enveloped in its sweet morning mist and heavy dew.

Along his hike, the vines slithered about forming a tunneled pathway with their red thorns dripping a clear venom. Kris pulled his hood over his head and journeyed down the tunneled path. At the tunnels end, he arrived at an open field. On the right of the field stood five cloaked Komalsh. On the left he saw his beloved Bella.

One of the Komalsh stepped forward lowering his hood. Kris recognized his friend, Nyte.

"Come join us, my oldest friend."

Bella whimpered to Kris. "Please don't do this. I need you. Our family needs you!"

"The Komalsh need you, Lord Tarius. I need you." persisted Nyte.

"Don't you love us?" pleaded Bella embracing her pregnant belly.

Kris approached Bella. His heart ached for her. He wrapped his arms around her in a loving embrace. Then releasing her, he looked back to see Nyte.

Nyte Shade and the other Komalsh were now laying on the ground in pools of blood. Kris ran to Nyte who gasped his dying breathe.

"Why did you leave us, old friend?"

"I'm sorry, Nyte, I'm so sorry," bellowed Kris.

Nyte Shade closed his eyes and exhaled his dying breath.

Bella screamed in agony. "Kris! Come back!"

Kris turned to her. She lay on a bed of straw, old and grey. Her skin was wrinkled, her lips dry.

"I waited for you, my love." She whispered as she moved toward the realm of eternal sleep.

Kris collapsed his face into her neck as he cried the tears of a broken man. Then Bella's body evaporated into the morning mist.

The choices he had were difficult. The conflict of juggling two worlds or the simplicity of choosing one. But Kris wasn't about simplicity. If he understood the problem, he could find its solution. It seemed no matter which direction he chose, certain death would occur. But death is inevitable. The trick is how to make the most out of life. Talking to himself inside his head, he thought, "What was my fathers last words of wisdom again? Oh, yeah…the first drop of rain to hit your head is an act of God. The second is your own damn fault. Live and learn."

Immediately, Kris had the gut feeling he was no longer alone. He looked around cautiously. In the cold crisp silence of the misty forest a branch snapped. Kris followed the sound leading to a shadowed figure. The stranger approached Kris while lowering his hood. There before him stood an old man with a long grey beard. He was clothed in Komalsh light armour weathered by time. His gentle smile placed Kris at ease. The old man unsheathed his sword and with two hands offered it to Kris. It was a durenthium sword made in the same design used by the Komalsh.

****

The Komalsh choice of weapon was a sword with a long blade curved slightly upward towards the point. A sharp serrated edge was fashioned halfway down from the top of the blade to the hilt. However, the sword handed to Kris had been slightly altered. Halfway down his blade and before the serrated edge was a thumbnail-sized hole shaped like a diamond.

Every Komalsh designs their own hilt. The colours and material used give the weapon a distinctive look complementing the Komalsh who owns it. Oddly enough, this durenthium sword's hilt reflected Kris to a tee.

****

"It's my gift to you, Kris Tarius."

"How do you know my name?"

The old man placed his hand on Kris's shoulder and smiled his wrinkles away. "I know you more then you know yourself."

"Thank you for the sword," said Kris as his eyes took in the workmanship with admiration.

"You are most welcome."

"Once you leave this forest, Kris, you will embark on an amazing journey through life. Always remember to keep your friends and family close to your heart and enjoy every moment as if it were your last."

The old man leaned up against a tree and slowly slid his back down against the trunk. "Tell Bella I love her," he whispered while handing Kris a tattered silk handkerchief. The old man lowered his head and slipped away into the Spirit World.

The silk handkerchief was like the one Bella had given him. But this one was old and tattered. As Kris tried to draw the man's face from his memory banks, he realized they shared an uncanny resemblance. Staring back to the handkerchief he excluded the improbable and accepted the facts. Kris just witnessed his own death.

With his new sword he dug a hole and placed his older self carefully into the grave. He wrapped the handkerchief around the dead man's knuckles and buried him. Using his student sword as a tombstone, he closed his eyes and gave his older self a moment of silence and reflection.

When Kris's eyes re-opened, he found himself wrapped in green vines with red thorns punctured throughout his body. His veins burned as the venom filtered through his mind. Dangling from a tree, he struggled to break free from his cocoon. The vine felt the struggle and carefully released Kris to the ground. There he lay sickened from the venom's invasion.

Moments later Kris slowly rose from the ground feeling empowered. His mind opened as the venom became one with his bloodstream. The wounds Kris had incurred from the thorns healed before his eyes and in his hand was a durenthium sword.

Kris' body and mind had connected spiritually to the nature and lifeforce that surrounded him. The forest pulsated with energy. His heightened senses became difficult to control. The venom burned through his veins. His body felt toxic. His stomach felt nauseous. He closed his eyes and pictured his beautiful Bella Flora standing before him smiling.

Kris' mind calmed. His pain faded. When he reopened his eyes, he gazed around in silence only to find the silence interrupted by the sounds of an excited unicorn. Behind him stood a steed on his hind legs thrusting his fronts high into the air. With a powerful strut, he galloped toward Kris stopping abruptly.

"Hello, Kris Tarius." The unicorn continued, "Allow me to introduce myself. My name is Dusty."

****

Dusty was a solid black unicorn with light grey tail and mane. He's bold, brave and enjoys combat with honour. Dusty is known to have a soft heart for the weaker species, or as he'd prefer, the little guy. Dusty despised ignorance, bullies, and the illusion of one's power. If you didn't have a purpose in making the world a better place, then you had no purpose in the better world.

****

"I've chosen you, Kris Tarius, to follow your lead and am honoured in doing so." With that, the unicorn bowed as only a unicorn can.

"Thank you, Dusty. However, I may need your help in the leading end of things. I fear I may be conflicted."

"Then together we'll find resolution," assured the steed.

A green shaded vine with red thorns rose from the ground handing Kris Bella's silk handkerchief.

The forest accepted Kris. The unicorn chose him. Dusty led them out of the forest and after a distance Kris would lay eyes on Castle Malshidiel for the first time. Nyte and his unicorn, Loki, intercepted Kris and Dusty.

"So, my oldest friend, when's the wedding?" Nyte gently teased.

"I suppose I should start practicing my proposal." Responded Kris.

"I'd be honoured to be the best man." Nyte said as he beamed with pride.

"You always have been." Kris replied with a smile.

"Come, my brother, Lord Drakus awaits."

Arias Jackyle ran straight toward the Mystique Forest with his head held down. A green vine with red thorns wrapped around his body and dragged him into the darkness of the forest. Arias slipped off into the depths of his unconscious mind. There he found himself surrounded by old growth trees and colourful exotic plant life. He was all alone.

"HELLO!" he hollered. "CAN ANYONE HEAR ME?" Arias waited for a reply, but the forest remained silent and still. That stillness was disturbed by an enormous constrictor snake slowly slithering across his path.

Arias stood still. His heartbeat rapid. The snake stretched 30 feet long and was four feet in diameter. Its colours, like the forest vegetation, were thick rings of red, yellow, and black wrapping around its body. The head was shaped like a python with a dislocating jaw enabling it to swallow its prey whole.

Quietly, so as not to make the snake aware of his whereabouts, Arias slipped away through the forest muttering to himself in disappointment. "Smart one, Arias. Shouting your head off in a reptile infested forest. Stupid, stupid!"

Arias' silent escape away from the snake brought him to a rocky hillside wrapped in vines. At its base stood a cave.

He entered the cave leading to a hollowed interior of stalagmites and stalactites. Among them Arias recognized a black shiny metal imbedded in a large stalagmite. After inspecting it and to his astonishment recognized the tip of a large deposit of durenthium. Arias used his dagger to pry away the excess stone surrounding the indestructible metal. After a strenuous workout he mined enough stone to release a generous portion of durenthium. Removing his cloak, he wrapped the precious alloy and turned to leave. There before him stood the enormous snake. Arias stood deathly still. The snake used its forked tongue to probe Arias' body. It worked its way up from his feet until reaching eye contact.

Arias remained deathly still. The snake's tongue gently touched his face. Sensing no fear, it pulled its head back and stared deep into Arias' eyes.

"If this snake snaps at me, I will cram this durenthium down it's throat," plotted Arias in thought.

The snake coiled and raised its head as if to stand and with a calm hissing voice it asked, "You're not stealing my durenthium are you?"

"Excellent! Diplomacy." Arias' mind was racing. He answered, "I wasn't aware that it belonged to anyone." The snake squinted with a look of painful discomfort and then returned to probing Arias' face. "I am the protector of this forest," it angrily jeered with a raspy hiss, "and all it's belongings."

Arias noticed a red thorn lodged between the scales on its neck. It looked like a venomous thorn from the vines he saw earlier.

"Are you willing to part with this?" Arias hoped the snake would entertain a barter. "I could offer you a trade." The snake paused in contemplation. Still aggravated by the thorn but tempted with curiosity, it hissed, "What did you have in mind?"

"I can remove that thorn in exchange for the durenthium and safe passage," offered Arias.

The snake pondered the deal then reluctantly lowered its neck revealing the thorn. Arias had the opportunity to kill the snake while it bowed into a position of weakness. But he couldn't bring himself to do so. He had the opportunity to make a peaceful resolution. So, Arias grabbed the thorn gently and pulled it out fast.

The snake sprang up capturing Arias' eyes once again—its tongue tickling his chin. With a soft serpent's hiss, it congratulated him. "The forest has accepted you. Wake up, Arias Jackyle, wake up."

Arias awoke struggling with the cocoon of vines enveloping him. Feeling his struggle, the vines released him gently to the ground. Arias' veins burned as the vine's venom filtered through his mind. He lay there sickened from the venom's invasion.

After a few moments, Arias rose from the ground. He removed the last of the thorns from his body. Each thorn puncture healed instantaneously. His mind started to open as the venom became one with his bloodstream. The forest pulsated with energy. Arias' senses gained extraordinary perception. His body and mind connected spiritually to the nature and the lifeforce that surrounded him.

His heightened senses became difficult to control. The venom burned through his veins. His body felt toxic—his stomach nauseous. He closed his eyes to simplify his thoughts. When his eyes reopened, Arias could feel the heartbeats of all the life surrounding him. Then he felt a peaceful presence behind and turned to greet it.

"Very well done," spoke a brown unicorn with black tail and mane. "I'm known as the peace maker among my kind. My name is Shiloh." With that, the unicorn bowed. "It was a wise decision to choose diplomacy over violence, Arias. Exceedingly rare does negotiation have a place in this cold world. But when revealed, it truly is the difference in creating a better one. I would be honoured to ride with you."

Arias held a permanent grin. His mind was desperately trying to keep up. The thought of a unicorn talking and knowing his name held a distant priority to the venom's mind opening effect. Collecting himself the best he could, he replied to the unicorn, "Okay, how about we get out of here."

"I know the way," assured Shiloh.

Arias grabbed his cloak. Wrapped inside it was the durenthium he remembered having hid there in his dream. He stood dumfounded. "Did I pull this out of my dream?"

"It's not uncommon, I assure you, Lord Jackyle."

"What about the snake in my dream?"

"In this forest you'll find dreams and reality to be the same," answered Shiloh.

"Wow, that's deep. I'm still trying to catch up here. My mind is going so fast."

"It will take a bit for your mind to calm, Lord Jackyle."

"Please just call me Arias. All my friends do."

"Arias it is," replied Shiloh with dignity.

Arias mounted his new friend and together they road out of the forest. There before them stood the most spectacular castle Arias had ever seen, Castle Malshidiel.

****

Terex Gungnir was no pushover. At six foot two, 220 pounds, he was renowned at the school of Olemeeze as the strongest and most skilled fighter. He didn't have the finesse with a sword like the others but made up for it with strength and stamina. No one beat him at an arm wrestle let alone hand-to-hand combat.

He was also the only student ever to be accepted by the school of Olemeeze from his birthplace, the Thorenite kingdom. This accomplishment made him a celebrity to his people.

****

Terex ran toward the Mystique Forest with his fists clenched. "Bring it on!" he roared.

Green vines with red thorns reached from the forest and pulled him in violently. Everything went dark.

Terex awoke sitting against an old growth tree. The forest was dark and quiet without even the song of a bird or the chirp of a cricket. Even his friends seemed to have vanished.

"I'm alone?" When the words came out, he wasn't sure if he was making a statement or asking a question. Terex got up from the tree and followed a moonlit path into a fog-layered forest. He navigated through dead trees and brush. At the path's end stood an eerie graveyard on an open field of darkness. Lit torches were scattered about illuminating the area while spirits flew around undisturbed by Terex's presence.

A murder of crows gathered around a tombstone staring at Terex in silent stillness. Enticed by their lure, he approached the grave. Written on the tombstone it said: Ayesha Gungnir. Rest in Peace.

Terex dropped to one knee mourning the loss of his mother. "I'm sorry I wasn't there, mother. I'm so sorry."

While he knelt in mourning, the dead began to rise from their graves and gather around the grieving Terex. Shoulder to shoulder, they moved toward the unsuspecting student.

His mother's corpse sprang from her grave and reached for Terex. "My beautiful son," she rasped as the words scraped through her voice box.

"Mother?" Terex exclaimed, taken aback by the sound of her voice.

He stood startled as the circle of zombies reached toward him. They grabbed his arms and forced him to his knees. His mother's corpse approached him tearfully. "You abandoned me, Terex. You left me to die by the hands of your brother!"

"He said you died from sickness." Terex was baffled by her accusation.

"I did, son. I died from the sickness of your brother. He's disturbed, Terex. He smothered my face and took my breath from me."

The zombified Ayesha placed her decayed hands upon Terex's cheeks. She gazed deep into his eyes inducing a hypnotic illusion.

Terex was now standing in the corner of his mother's room. A stranger stood over his mother while she lay in her bed. He was suffocating her with a pillow. Her body thrashed fiercely about until she no longer had the breath to fight. The stranger rose from her dead body and faced Terex. It was his brother Traybiss. A psychotic grin appeared on his face.

****

Traybiss was Terex's older brother. His size made the muscular Terex seem tiny. He stood over six foot six with 275 pounds of pure muscle. He gave the impression he was always a little on edge—some would even say crazy. Traybiss, like his brother Terex, was built for war. While Terex was at Olemeeze studying to become a Komalsh, Traybiss was said to have stood by his mother's side while she passed away from the flu. But none of this was true.

Their father, while fishing with his son Traybiss, had drowned years prior. When interviewed by Thorenite authorities, Traybiss was exonerated regarding any foul play and his father's death was ruled accidental.
But Terex thought differently. He saw the darkness in his brother at a young age. As children Terex witnessed Traybiss killing small animals and performing cruel actions toward himself and others. When Terex mentioned his brother's abnormal behavior he was merely dismissed as an imaginative child. The day Traybiss returned home alone from the fishing trip, Terex noticed deep scratch marks on his arms—a sign of struggle that eluded the authorities.
Traybiss had been declined entry to the School of Olemeeze. This fostered jealousy toward his brother and hatred toward the Komalsh. The jealousy turned to hate—a hate that gave Traybiss' self justification for his journey down the road of insanity. It was a road with only one direction. One fate.

****

Traybiss lashed at Terex who punched him to the ground hard. Traybiss shook it off with a smile and slowly rose to his feet.

"Why did you do this, Traybiss? How could you kill our mother?" Terex's fists clenched as he spoke.

"She was weak. They both were, brother," he scowled.

"You killed our parents!" Terex grabbed his brother by the throat and pulled him to the ground. Traybiss tried to laugh as Terex squeezed his fingers deep into his throat. Then everything melted like wax.

Terex escaped the illusion still gazing into his zombified mother's hypnotic eyes. He pushed her to the ground then turned to greet the zombies that surrounded him. With a devilish grin, he unsheathed his sword. Terex slashed, hacked, and chopped the zombies around him until only he and his undead mother remained.

Terex approached her. She leaped violently toward him and with a swift swing of his sword Terex decapitated his zombified mother. Turning in all directions he screamed for his brother to reveal himself. But the night stood silent. Terex knelt before his mother's tombstone. He placed his hand upon the cold stone slab. Closing his eyes, he swore his oath. "I will avenge you mother…father. Traybiss will die!"

Terex left the graveyard and made his way back through the darkened forest. The murder of crows followed. Inside the forest, Terex approached a shallow pond. He stared deep into his rippled reflection. Lost in a moment of thought his reflection started to smile.

Terex did not. He moved closer to the pond when a hand burst through the water and pulled him under. Terex was trapped struggling for air. The water's surface became an impenetrable barrier. Remaining calm he felt around the surface barrier for a weakness. Terex found a thinned area in the barrier and pushed his fingers through it. Getting a grip on either side, he ripped the barrier open and pushed his body through it. On the other side stood his mother and father as he remembered. Arm in arm, they smiled proudly.

"Congratulations, son, you passed!" declared his mother with a huge smile.

The pond behind him burst up into a giant wave and crashed down on him like a wall of darkness. Terex's eyes slowly opened. He found himself dangling from a tree wrapped in a cocoon of vines. Momentarily sickened by the venom's invasion, his veins burned as the vine's venom filtered through his mind. His healing ability, stronger than most, ejected the thorns from his body while still trapped in his cocooned restraint. With a claustrophobic rage, Terex stretched out his arms and legs ripping through the vine's grip. He fell to the ground hard severely fracturing his arm on impact.

Terex stood up from the ground. His broken arm reset and then healed instantaneously. His wounds from the thorns disappeared without a trace. His senses were enhanced as the venom became one with his bloodstream. Terex's body and mind connected spiritually to the nature and lifeforce that surrounded him. The forest pulsated with energy.

Terex's heightened senses became difficult to control. The venom burned through his veins. His body felt toxic. His stomach was nauseous. But his healing ability was too potent for the venom's poison. His body and mind healed instantly.

"I feel powerful!" roared Terex with his fists gripped for war.

"You are powerful," spoke a deep voice.

Terex turned to the pleasant energy he felt behind him. There stood the largest unicorn he'd ever seen.

"Allow me to introduce myself," said the unicorn. "I'm known as the warrior to my kind. My name is Chaos and I have chosen you, Terex Gungnir, for one reason. You're a warrior just like me!"

Terex gave a thumbs up to the unicorn and responded, "If you ride with me, we ride for war!"

"Only death can stop us!" affirmed Chaos in return.

****

Chaos was a solid black unicorn with a white diamond patch on his nose. He was larger than most—a muscular steed with a warrior's heart. He is fearless and cunning. The Mystique Forest named him Chaos and chaos is where he felt most comfortable. He is the shining light amidst the darkness of war. Chaos brought order.

****

"I have to admit, Chaos. After seeing unicorns, I was getting kind of worried," admitted Terex.

"What do you mean?"

"Well, they all seemed scrawny and weak to me. No offence but until now I had no pride in riding a unicorn into battle."

"I get it," replied Chaos. "I feel the same toward you, Komalsh. Do I really want some peacemaker on my back? They're just going to get stained in blood."

"I know, right!" laughed Terex. "I was worried I'd get my fluffy little unicorn dirty."

"Ha! I hate those unicorns!" snarled Chaos. "I don't know whether to protect them or put them out of their misery!"

"I feel the same way about most people." Terex spoke as empathetically as he could to his new ally.

The two left the forest walking side by side. They shared war stories and battles fought. Their friendship was gradually being sewn together by their acts of heroism and a brotherly bonding from mayhem's malice. They saw themselves as the Lords of war.

When they arrived at the forest's edge, Terex looked upon Castle Malshidiel for the very first time.

"Unbelievable!" he spoke with amazement.

"It truly is," agreed Chaos. "Welcome to your new home, Lord Gungnir."

Trayke Basa threw his empty bottle of rum over his head and staggered toward the Mystique Forest. On route he tripped over a rock and fell. Gathering himself to his feet, he watched as his fellow students were being snatched by vines and dragged into the forest. Fueled by second thoughts, Trayke turned to run away when a vine grabbed his ankle and dragged him into the forest kicking and screaming. As he abruptly drifted from sight, there was nothing but silence.

Trayke appeared in a forest surrounded by old growth trees and colourful exotic plant life. He smiled from ear to ear as he encountered the sweet-smelling pollen. He then frowned after realizing he was all alone.

"Where did everybody go!?" shouted Trayke at the top of his lungs.

A silent moment passed before a reply shouted from the forest, "Come find us, we're having fun!"

Trayke smiled his goofy grin, "Okay!"

Trayke ran deeper into the forest searching for the ones who were having fun. He ran around a tree and hit a low branch clotheslining himself to the ground. Returning to his feet Trayke tripped over a rock and slid down a muddy ravine. At the bottom, he submerged into a slimy swamp. Disgusted, he swam to the edge and crawled out. "I'm not having fun," he mumbled while wiping swamp slime from his face. Trayke sat down on a log to catch his breath. He cried out, "Where is everybody?"

Moments later the forest replied, "We're hiding from you!"

Trayke's goofy smile turned to a dumbfounded look. "But why?" he asked.

A meaner voice replied from the forest, "Because nobody likes you!"

Then the whole forest broke out into laughter.

"That sounded close!" thought Trayke rising back to his feet. He took five steps forward then dropped down a steep cliff.

Parallel to that cliff stood a tree. On the way down Trayke managed to hit every branch before splashing into another swamp. Struggling frantically to reach shore, he crawled up onto the water's edge. Gasping for air he once again wiped his face clean of the swamp slime. "What the hell was that all about?" cursed Trayke.

A moment later another lower voice answered from deep within the forest, "That was the ugly tree and you hit every branch!"

Another roar of laughter exploded from the forest. Trayke s traightened his clothes and brushed his hair with his hands. With his chin held high, he carried on down a path ignoring the heckling forest. That's when it occurred to Trayke that the laughter was coming from the trees. Their branches swayed about on a windless day pointing toward Trayke whilst laughing uncontrollably.

"This is no fun at all," mumbled the student.

Out of the corner of Trayke's eye, he saw a shadow run behind a tree. Curious, he walked over to investigate. There behind it hid the spirit of a young girl. Startled, she ran out from behind the tree and away from the laughing forest. Trayke followed the spirit to an open grassy meadow. There she turned back to greet Trayke. She stood unafraid and confident. With a friendly wink she vanished into an explosion of stars expanding into the cosmos. Trayke stopped and stared into its infinite wonder. As the universe presented itself, a tear ran down his cheek while he witnessed human and animal spirits alike being pulled into its infinite beauty. After the last spirit was absorbed into the cosmos, it collapsed into nothingness and all that remained was the grassy meadow.

In the middle of that grassy meadow stood an oddly shaped tree. It was much shorter than the others. Its branches were barren, and its roots were exposed along the surface of the soil. Curious, Trayke approached the tree and to his surprise noticed the surface blink. He moved in closer and to his disgust discovered it was covered in eyeballs. Trayke stood before the tree dumfounded and disgusted.

The tree stared back at him. Trayke held out his hand and the tree's eyes focused on it. He moved his hand back and forth. The eyes followed. He jumped over to the left. The eyes on the tree followed to their right. Trayke jumped to the right. The eyes followed to their left. He leaped back and forth repeatedly. The eyes frantically tried to keep up as its branches shook with delight.

Trayke stopped. He was out of breath. The tree quietly stared.

Leaning on his knees, Trayke giggled his silly laugh. "I get it!" he said pointing to the eye-covered tree. With one hand on his hip and the other now rubbing his chin, he pondered, "Somehow a hidden test is at play here."

Trayke turned around to the other trees of the forest. "What does this mean?" he shouted.

A moment passed and there was only silence. The eye-covered tree more so.

Trayke walked to the backside of the tree and discovered it had no eyes. Only half the tree was covered. So, he took the liberty to pester it. Trayke went behind the tree and to the left side waved his hand around. All the eyes looked over to the left as far as they could reach. Trayke switched to the right side and waved his hand around. The eyes looked over to the right side as far as they could reach. Trayke switched back and forth as the tree desperately tried to keep up. Angered, the tree's eyes looked straight forward, and a huge branch slapped down squishing Trayke like a bug.

"Ouch, that hurt!" cried the student struggling to his feet. "Okay then. How about this?" Trayke stood in front of the tree and stared into its eyes. "Let's see who blinks first."

Every eye on the tree stared back into Trayke's. Fifteen seconds had gone by and Trayke was starting to lose it. He made nasty facial expressions to prevent him from the losing blink. Sweat dripped down his forehead, his eyes struggled to stay open. On the verge of defeat, Trayke raised his hands over his head and yelled, "Boo!"

Every eye on the tree blinked.

"Ha, I win!" shouted Trayke.

The tree's eyes squinted in disgust toward the cheating student.

"It was fair!" defended Trayke. "Oh, come on now. Do you want a rematch?"

With a startled twitch, the tree's eyes focused on something behind Trayke. Instincts flaring, he turned around while unsheathing his sword. There stood the oddest-looking unicorn he had ever seen. He had larger than normal ears and a white hide covered in grey patches. His tail and mane blended into his hide like camouflage gone wrong. His cockeyed jaw allowed his oversized tongue to droop freely to one side and his lazy left eye appeared to be stuck gazing in a different direction from his right.

Trayke gasped as he uncontrollably blurted out, "You are the strangest...anything, I have ever set my eyes on." Trayke glanced back to the tree who stared back at him. Turning back to the unicorn, Trayke corrected himself, "You are the second strangest thing I have ever set my eyes on."

The unicorn took offence. "Well at least you don't see me talking to a tree!"

Trayke looked back to the tree. The tree looked back to Trayke and crossed all its eyes at him.

"I was up on that hill over there watching you dance around that tree like a moron. I thought to myself, "Oh my goodness! One of the villages must have lost their idiot! I had to come down to see what you were up too…what are you up too?"

"I'm trying to find my way to Castle Malshidiel," answered Trayke.

"So, you thought asking a tree covered in eyes would be helpful?" Chuckled the unicorn.

"Well, not exactly…"

"Oh, please tell me." The unicorn could hardly contain his amusement. "Did you honestly think the tree was going to answer you? Ha! You're killing me!" chortled the steed as it rolled on its side in laughter. "They are eyeballs, not mouths!" At this point the steed broke into full-blown laughter.

Trayke stood there unimpressed.

"Do you even see an ear on that tree? It doesn't even have a clue what you're saying! Ah ha, ha, ha!"

The tree stood there with a vacant look.

"Wow!" giggled the unicorn. "I'm starting to feel those mushrooms."

"Mushrooms?" Trayke and the tree's eyes lit up.

"Yeah, magic mushrooms!" The unicorn leaped up. "I'll show you where they are!"

The tree's branches shook about with excitement.

"Would you like some?" asked Trayke to the tree. The tree trembled with apparent delight.

"All right then. I'll be right back."

Trayke followed the unicorn into the woods. They wound up at an open patch of unicorn feces decorated with brightly coloured mushrooms the size of a fist.

"See! They are all over the place!" Given his altered state, the unicorn was especially excited about this.

"Wow, they're huge!" exclaimed Trayke gathering as many as his cloak could bundle.

"They taste funny."

"Not as funny as they feel," rebutted the unicorn.

Trayke absolutely loved the unicorn's humour and realized a proper introduction had never occurred.

"What's your name, by the way?"

"My name is Charley. Get it? Charley horse."

"Ha! That's funny…but you look more like a Jack to me," stated Trayke.

"A Jack?" Charley didn't know what that meant.

"Yeah, like as in Jack ass!"

"Ha! I see what you did there! Good one, Trayke!"

"Hey, wait a minute." Surprised Trayke. "How did you know my name?"

"Well, you've got to know these things when you're a unicorn, you know," replied the steed.

"Good to know, good to know. Hey, I always wondered what the unicorn's horn was for…what's it for?"

"That's a random question," replied Charley.

"It's the mushrooms. I'm starting to feel funny already."

"Told you so!" laughed the unicorn, "but to answer your question, Trayke, it's a weapon!" Charley started jumping around like a puppy wanting to play. "See that stump over there?"

"I do."

"Watch this!" Charley held his head down and charged the stump. At impact he missed the target and tumbled into the bush.

"You missed, Charley."

"I know, right! It's my damned lazy eye. I see three of everything!" Charley was clearly flustered.

"Try and aim for the middle one," suggested Trayke. Charley took his advice and charged the stump again. This time hitting the target.

"Good job, Charley!"

"Thanks, buddy!" Charley struggled to get his horn free from the stump. "Hey, can you give me a hand over here?"

"Ah, man. That's heartbreaking," sighed Trayke. After Charley was freed from the stump, the two returned to the tree of sight, a name they jovially came up with on their journey back.

"Oh, glorious tree of sight. We have brought you offerings of shit flowers," joked Trayke—a description inspired by the psilocybin mushrooms.

"Wait a moment. How is the tree supposed to eat them, Trayke?" asked Charley.

"I'm not sure. But man am I ever high!"

"Yeah, I started to peak again when I was stuck in that stump," reported Charley.

"The potency must have something to do with the forest," concluded Trayke, "or perhaps that they're grown in unicorn poop." Trayke started to formulate the origins of the mushrooms enhanced potency when a humorous thought crossed his mind. "Wait a moment!" He laughed pointing to Charley. "You're eating mushrooms from your own shit!"

Charley broke into an uncontrolled laughter. "That's so gross!"

The tree of sight started to shake its branches as it stared at the mushrooms with hunger.

"Hold on a moment." Trayke struggled to regroup his thoughts. "I need to focus here. I must figure out this test so I can get to Castle Malshidiel."

"What test are you referring to?" asked Charley with fully dilated pupils.

"There must be a test here to prove my worth so I can become a Komalsh. Then a unicorn will choose me and lead me to the castle."

Charley stood confused. "Where are we going to find a unicorn, Trayke?"

Trayke burst out into laughter.

"Aren't you forgetting something?" spoke the tree of sight.

Trayke and Charley stared at the tree in disbelief. The tree stared toward the mushrooms.

"Well, that's strange." Mystified Charley. "A tree that can talk."

"The forest is full of them," sighed Trayke. "They're not nice either."

Trayke dumped the mushrooms at the base of the tree. The tree revealed a large mouth and swallowed them whole. "Thank you Trayke." It burped. "And by the way, yelling boo is, in fact, cheating."

"I'm sorry," replied Trayke. "I just hate losing."

"Apology accepted and congratulations, Trayke Basa! The forest accepted you shortly after you witnessed the spirit. You've only remained here because you haven't realized you're dreaming enough to waken you."

"I'm dreaming?" Trayke looked to Charley who nodded in return.

The trees mouth opened wide and Trayke's eyes closed as his body fell limp into its own void.

Trayke awoke in a cocoon of vines which gently released him to the ground. He lay there on his back sickened by the venom's invasion. His veins burned as the vine's venom filtered through his mind. His body felt toxic—his stomach nauseous.

Trayke's heightened senses started to empower him. His thorn wounds healed instantly. His body and mind connected spiritually to the nature and lifeforce that surrounded him. The forest pulsated with energy.
Still laying on the ground, Trayke slowly opened his eyes. Standing over him stood the oddest-looking unicorn he'd ever laid eyes on. His big droopy tongue dropped onto Trayke's forehead.

"Let me guess…you're Charley."

"I was wondering when you'd wake up, Trayke. I entered your dream to see if I could help. Man, are your dreams messed up!"

Trayke stood up from the ground. "I feel so…so sober!"

"Get used to it," replied Charley.

"What do you mean?" Answered Trayke.

"Your enhanced ability to heal will prevent you from ever getting drunk." answered Charley.

"No bloody way!"

"Way, man. Way," nodded the steed.

"So, does this mean you're the unicorn who chose me to be your Komalsh rider?"

"Until the day you die, Trayke."

“What happens if you die first?” asked Trayke.

“Well then I guess you’re walking everywhere,” chuckled Charley.

Charley led Trayke out of the Mystique Forest where they gazed upon the magnificence of Castle Malshidiel. It was there that Lord Drakus, and his teachers awaited them.

Kelar ran toward the Mystique Forest holding Neasha Sentrix’s hand while Kolos Dreken trailed close behind. On approach to the Mystique Forest green vines reached out and pulled them in aggressively.

Inside, the forest was dark, and rain poured down hard. Lightning lit up the sky and thunder raged with vengeance. Kelar’s eyes slowly opened. Neasha was no longer with him. His splint was missing, and his wrist was no longer broken. Slowly he rose from the ground staring into the storm-filled skies. Anxiety bubbled through his veins. Cautiously, he trekked forward to explore the darkened forest more deeply.

Along the path, nearby trees awoke from their silent slumber swatting Kelar viciously with their branches. Kelar unsheathed his sword and struck them down while forcing his way through.

Escaping the swatting trees, Kelar wandered out into an open field. The thunder, lightning and heavy rainfall faded into a starlit night. Its moistened air released a musky odor and the winters cold revealed his breath. In the middle of the field stood a cloaked figure. Kelar approached the stranger. Each step closer the sky turned brighter, the air was drier and the heat more inviting. The stranger turned around and before Kelar stood Lord Drakus.

“Kelar, there is an evil shadow demon hiding within you,” he warned while pointing to a shallow pond.

Kelar walked over to the pond and stared into its murky waters. His rippled reflection appeared with a shadow demon shimmering across his face. Kelar pulled away in terror. "What was that?"

"You were left on the doorstep of a Tarnian family's home, Kelar. They raised you from a young child. What happened before that day is a mystery stored deep within your mind—a mind guarded by a dormant demon."

Lord Drakus unsheathed his sword. "The forest deems you a threat, Kelar…you must die!"

The shadow demon shimmered across Kelar's face with rage. Empowered by the spirit, he unsheathed his sword and swung down onto Drakus' blade. The powerful blow forced Drakus down onto one knee. With great fury, Kelar swung his blade around and decapitated Lord Drakus. His head rolled to Kelar's feet and stared back up at him. "You failed." Rasped the severed head.

Kelar backed away from the head in horror. Around him children's voices whispered through the forest chanting his name. They grew louder and angrier as eyeless children dressed in white robes appeared from the shadows of the forest. Their arms were raised and pointed slightly forward guiding their blinded steps as their empty eye sockets shed tears of blood.

The head of Drakus now took the form of a unicorn's and before Kelar stood the body with its front legs thrusting into the air. The children's chants grew louder as the decapitated unicorn galloped through the horde of eyeless children.

Kelar followed behind the headless steed. Swinging his sword, he lopped off the hands and fingers of children who reached toward him. Thunder, lightning, and rain exploded with fury as Kelar ran back through the swatting trees in a desperate attempt to escape.

The headless unicorn ran through the forest and leaped off the edge of a cliff.

Kelar slid to a stop before the ledge. With the eyeless children trailing close behind, he jumped off into the darkness. At the end of his fall, Kelar landed in a pond of dark water. The children stood along the cliff's edge still chanting his name.

The pond was red and littered with human limbs. Kelar waded through it and toward its swampy shore. Screams of terror echoed across the water. Crawling to shore, Kelar staggered toward the violent screams. There layed Neasha Sentrix tied down by green vines with red thorns imbedded throughout her body. On top of her sat a gnome sewing her eyelid's shut.

Kelar ran toward her calling her name, "Neasha!" The gnome instantly cast a spell forcing a shadow demon to shimmer across Neasha's face. She screamed violently in discomfort.

Kelar ran up to the gnome and kicked it. On impact the gnome shattered like ceramic. On the ground the cracked remnants of its face frowned in failure. "You have failed, Neasha Sentrix."

Kelar removed his dagger and cut Neasha free from the vines. He removed the thorns embedded in her body and guided her to her feet.

Frantically, Neasha clawed at her stitched-up eyes. "I can't see." Her words were laced in panic.

Eyeless children walked out from the lake—their white robes stained in blood. Raising their arms, they walked toward them chanting Kelar's name.

"There's no time for that, Neasha. We must run!" Kelar threw her over his shoulder and ran through the forest. "I don't know how to get out of here!" His fear had him running aimlessly.

"I can't see!" Neasha cried still clawing at her eyes.

"It's okay, I'll protect us!" promised Kelar.

Another shriek of terror echoed through the forest. Kelar ran toward it with Neasha over his shoulder. The screams came from Kolos Dreken who stood over a woman's body stabbing her repeatedly with his dagger. He screamed with rage while pulverizing her chest. A shadow demon shimmered across his blood-splattered face revealing the malice in his eyes.

Beside him another body lay dead. He, too, had been mutilated by Kolos's dagger.

"I hate you, mother!" screamed Kolos. He raised his dagger into the air and thrust one last blow to her forehead leaving his blade lodged in her skull. Kolos rose from the ground gasping for air.

The rain poured down hard. Thunder and lightning collided.

The other corpse slowly rose from the ground. His chest cavity revealed the damage made by the dagger. Kolos backed away in fear. "Father? I already killed you!"

"What the hell!" Terrified, Kolos froze.

Kelar swung his sword around and decapitated Kolos's father. "We don't have time for this!"

"What direction do we go?" Panicked, Kolos couldn't decide.

The winds grew angry as the headless unicorn galloped toward them. Eyeless children appeared all around chanting for Kelar's demise.

"What the hell is going on?" screamed Kolos.

"We've failed the forest!" cried Neasha. "It's trying to kill us!"

"Neasha's right," surrendered Kelar. "We've failed."

Outside the Mystique Forest under the clear blue-sky Lord Jamala, Lady Tuza and their unicorns, Flash and Spirit, waited patiently for any students the forest deemed a threat. Off in the distance, a blizzard of dust and the drumming sound of pounding hooves approached them.

"Do you feel that?" questioned Lady Tuza. "It's Lord Siris."

Over the ridge, 40 Sykanian Knights rode up to the Mystique Forest led by King Siris and his wizard, Malores Barnett. They formed a line before the two Komalsh.
King Siris dismounted from his steed and approached Lord Jamala and Lady Tuza. To fight the Sykanians would be a fair match for the two Komalsh. To fight King Cretes Siris would be suicide. Even now at the age of 40, he was still the greatest swordsman of all Drakonia.

King Siris approached Tuza and Jamala with sword in hand. "Join me or die," he calmly offered.
"We choose death!" answered Lord Jamala.

The two Komalsh unsheathed their swords and attacked. With two blocks and two swings from his own blade King Siris slit the throat of Lady Tuza and stabbed his sword through Lord Jamala's heart.

Lord Jamala dropped to the ground dead. Lady Tuza lay weakened. She applied pressure to her neck while gasping for air. Her slit throat started to mend. King Siris placed the end of his blade on her temple and pressed it through her skull.

****

Both unicorns lowered their heads and returned to the dark depths of the Mystique Forest. With their Komalsh riders now having passed on to the spirit world, their purpose here was over. They would live out the rest of their lives hidden within the forest's protection. The loss of their dearest friends would be mourned inside the forest's enchanted realm.

****

Siris wiped the blood from his durenthium blade. "Malores, wait here till I return."

"As you wish, your majesty." The wizard would be obedient.

Using his Komalsh abilities, King Siris searched the Mystique Forest for Kelar's heartbeat. After locating him, he ran into the woods.

Inside the Mystique Forest, the rains poured down hard. Lightning bolts flashed across the sky as Kelar swung his sword around slashing three eyeless children across their faces.

"My father keeps getting up!" Kolos was still in a panic.

Kelar ran at Kolos' headless father and booted him back down to the ground.

"What the hell is that?" pointed Kolos to a forty-foot-long constrictor snake slithering toward them. It had black, yellow, and red stripes with a dislocating jaw to devour its prey.

"I can't see anything!" The frightened Neasha was still clawing at her stitched eyes.

With a sharp snap the snake bit off Kolos' pointing arm. Kolos stared at the stub of what was left of his arm in silent shock. Blood sprayed from his severed limb in palpitating spurts. His zombified mother and headless father tackled him to the ground as he screamed in pain from his mortal wound.

Kelar swung his sword around decapitating another eyeless child. Returning to Kolos, he kicked him free from his zombified parents. A green vine reached from above and wrapped around Kelar's neck. Its powerful squeeze pushed red venomous thorns deep into his throat. Kelar dropped Neasha to the ground while gasping for air.

Neasha reached for her dagger and sliced her eye lids open. Blood poured down her face. She ran to Kelar's side and cut the vine from around his neck ripping his throat free of its thorns.

"Get up Kelar! Get up!"

King Siris ran through the forest following Kelar's heartbeat beacon. He approached an old growth tree holding an enormous cocoon of vines. The forest had taken the three students and combined their cocoons, interconnecting their dreamscape prisons. King Siris raised his hands and telekinetically pulled on the web of vines. With great psychic force, he ripped the vines apart pulling their wrapped bodies safely to the ground. Siris left the forest with three cocoons hovering close behind.

While they were leaving the Mystique Forest, a unicorn stood in the distance watching Cretes Siris' every move. Siris felt the unicorn and stared in return. They were close friends at one time. Before his defection they rode together following the Komalsh code. When Siris changed his unicorn, Aelianus, banished himself into the Mystique Forest. They haven't seen each other since.

A shadow demon shimmered across Siris' face yielding a quick glimpse as to what changed him. Aelianus now understood his defection and galloped away never to return.

King Siris made his way out of the forest where Malores and his 40 Sykanian Knights awaited patiently. He telekinetically lowered the cocooned students gently to the ground.

Inside the forest's illusion, Neasha fended off the onslaught of chanting children. Kelar, fallen to his knees, grasped his infected neck trying to breathe and Kolos lay powerless from blood loss.

Eyeless children by the hundreds surrounded the failed students. The headless unicorn galloped through the children toward them. The snake crept up behind Neasha slowly opening its mouth.

"Get up, Kelar! Get up!" she cried.

Lord Drakus stood inside the forest's edge awaiting the students who passed. With him stood Savita, Bossel and Elasia Dunlam.

Lord Drakus' second in command, Lord Soren Kyros, approached the group from the castle grounds.

****

Lord Soren Kyros was a respected man among the Komalsh. Both courageous and wise, he stood six-foot one inch tall and weighed in at 190 pounds. His passion for knowledge and discovery made him a fan favourite of the Elvin elders who were a key factor in the educational programs of Olemeeze since the rise of Lord Duren.

Currently, with the help of the elves, he built the most advanced ship ever to sail Drakonian waters. Lord Kyros' true passion was the sea. He respected and understood the power of the ocean making him qualified, by Elvin standards, to be second in command for this ship's mission of exploration—a position he eagerly accepted. The ship was scheduled to set sail in the next couple days.

****

"I don't know why we wait Hirum," urged Bossel. "If those undisciplined students do pass, it will take them days to find their way here."

"Now, now Bossel," defended Lord Kyros using his hand to gesture the need for calm. "They will be here shortly, you'll see."

"Lord Kyros is right," agreed Drakus. "The student is only as smart as his teacher. I have faith in your ability to teach, Bossel."

Bossel rolled his eyes.

"Look!" pointed Savita excitedly.

Nyte Shade and his unicorn Loki exited the forest first. He smiled with a nod to Lord Drakus who eagerly returned it. After dismounting from his unicorn, Savita wrapped her arms around him. "I knew you'd make it, son."

"Here comes another!" cheered Kyros.

Next to arrive was Kris Tarius and his unicorn, Dusty. Nyte wrapped his arm around him. "When's the wedding, old friend?"

Arias Jackyle and his unicorn, Shiloh, appeared from the forest followed by Terex Gungnir and Chaos.

"Congratulations!" announced Lord Hirum Drakus. "You've all passed."

The graduates looked to each other saddened by their total count. A large lump filled the back of Arias' throat. He clenched his jaw tightly. "Trayke, you bastard. Come on, man. Where are you?"

A loud noise rustled around the forests edge. Then out rode the ugliest unicorn any of them had ever seen. Riding it was Trayke Basa.

"A match made in heaven!" chuckled Bossel. Trayke dismounted from his unicorn. His mind was unravelling psychic thought he couldn't process quickly enough.

Arias gave him a big hug unaware of his friend's psychic struggle. "You made it buddy!"

Logs and rocks started to float behind Trayke. His unicorn, Charley, also began to rise. Arias' legs started to feel light as he held on to Trayke for more reasons than a hug.

"Relax your mind, Lord Basa!" instructed Bossel.

Trayke felt proud as to how his teacher addressed him. "Lord Basa." He was now a Komalsh. Trayke closed his eyes and regrouped his thoughts. Then everything that floated lowered gently to the ground.

"What happened to you in the forest?" Arias was concerned.

"Well, I made a tree blink…but never mind that. Did you know we can't get drunk?"

"What do you mean we can't get drunk?"

"I'm not sure how I could word that any better." explained Trayke.

"It's true," answered Kris. "Our healing abilities prevent us from it."

"What did you mean when you said you made a tree blink?" asked Terex.

"There was this tree covered in eyes and I beat it in a staring contest," clarified Trayke.

"Did you cheat?" asked Nyte skeptically.

"Of course! But I apologised and gave it some magic mushrooms."

Everyone fell silent.

"It's true," defended Charley breaking the awkward silence. "I ate some, too!"

The vein in Bossel's forehead swelled. "What in Malshidiel is going on here!" He addressed Lord Drakus. "None of these students should have passed! Has the forest gone mad?"

"No Bossel," calmed Drakus. "The forest understands that a different breed of warrior is needed for the times to come."

Drakus smiled at the graduates of Olemeeze. They released an aura of unconditional love not seen in previous generations. Their friendship was their strength and their simplicity grounded them. Bossel, however, remained unconvinced.

Lord Kyros patted Drakus on the back shaking his head with a chuckle, "A different breed, indeed."

Outside the Mystique Forest, King Siris telekinetically released the three failed students from their vined cocoons. There they lay as prisoners in a hypnopompic paralysis. Kelar grasped his infected neck struggling for air. His thorn wounds oozed infection.

"You have to help him!" pleaded Neasha.

King Siris grabbed Kelar by the collar and pulled him up to greet his eyes. "Listen to me or you will die!" He warned. "This is all an illusion, Kelar. None of this is real."

Kelar's eyes widened. "An illusion?" he gasped.

"Yes Kelar," nodded Siris with calming intentions.

Kelar stood up on his own. His thorn wounds vanished. His pain diminished. Neasha, too, listened and her slit eye lids returned to normal. The two students knelt beside Kolos whose arm reappeared. He wiggled his fingers in disbelief.

"The forest doesn't kill you," explained Siris. "It merely convinces your mind to."

The Sykanian wizard, Malores, approached the students offering them a small vial each. "Drink this. It will counter the poisonous toxins in your blood stream."
The students drank down its contents eagerly.

"Those thorn wounds, however, will take time," said Malores after examining them.

Aware of Siris' peaceful intentions, Kelar still dwelled in the shadow of doubt. "What do you want of us?"

"I want the three of you to join me and my war against the Komalsh. In exchange I will give you the psychic ability you have failed to achieve."

The three students hesitatingly exchanged looks.

"Or…you can wait here for the Komalsh to kill you. The choice is yours." Said Siris in the simplest form.

Kelar stared at the corpses of Lady Tuza and Lord Jamala. The Komalsh left to kill them. Reluctantly he accepted Siris' offer.

Neasha and Kolos followed in suite.

"Malores. Gather those vines. We need to extract the venom."

"As you wish, your majesty."

Siris revealed the Book of Malshidiel, the original text he'd stolen from Savita ten years ago. With his mind, he instructed it to open at the chapter of his choice.

"Careful, Malores. The vine's venom is highly toxic but within those toxins are the answers to psychic enlightenment. We need to extract that from the venom if we are to give our new allies their Komalsh abilities."

"Excuse me, your majesty, but even with the toxins removed, the venom still can cause insanity, even death," alerted Malores.

"Correct wizard. Only a disciplined mind could embrace it."

"You assume their training in Olemeeze was enough to prepare them?" queried Malores.

"I'm sure of it," answered Siris coldly. "If not, then they are no use to us anyway."

Kolos and Neasha stripped the two dead Komalsh of their clothes and weapons. They dressed and armed themselves and were entranced by their Komalsh appearances.

Kelar stared off into the forest. He favoured his splinted wrist and squirmed uncomfortably from his thorn wounds.

"I failed," he felt sickened in disbelief.

From the inside of the Mystique Forest Nyte stared back in return and called out, "Where are you Kelar?"

In the depths of depression and despair Kelar hung his head, "Goodbye, Nyte."

Chapter XV
The Young Lords.

Lord Drakus led the young Lords through the grounds of Castle Malshidiel. Its legendary dreamscape surroundings were pleasant to the eyes and nose. The colourful gardens flourished. The soapstone walkways and gazebos were carved with detailed perfection and the Earth creature populace reflected peace and tranquility, sharing smiles of acceptance and gratitude toward the new arrivals. A creek flowed from the Mystique Forest through the castle's yard feeding a small lake. On the other side of the lake its waters released into the vast bottomless ravine protecting the castle from the restless ocean. In that lake mermaids swam to shore flirting with the young arrivals. A startled griffin awoke from its nap on a grassy field and flew over Castle Malshidiel.

The castle itself, of gothic design, was perched on a narrow ledge overlooking the ocean. Dividing the castle from the sea was a bottomless ravine endlessly devouring the ocean's salty waters.

"Welcome to your new home," smiled Lord Kyros holding out his hand to Nyte Shade. "It's a genuine pleasure to meet you, son. I'm a true fan of your father's work."

Nyte shook his hand in return. "And what work would that be?"

"It was under his leadership that the first exploration voyages of Drakonia's surrounding islands took place. His passion for knowledge guided the way to who I've become. Lord Radik Shade was a great man."

Nyte was humbled. "Thank you, Lord Kyros."
Kyros hailed Nyte telepathically. "I see his greatness in you, too, Lord Shade."

"I can hear your thoughts," hailed Nyte telepathically in return.

"And I can hear yours."

"Oh, Lord Kyros!" Savita was filled with joy to be able to join in. "I wanted to be the first to speak telepathically to Nyte."

Nyte and Kyros laughed out loud.

"What's so funny?" asked Terex.

"Can you hear my thoughts, Terex?" Nyte sent the question telepathically.

"Well, Nyte. What's so funny?" Terex had no way of knowing what was going on beyond his ears.

"Terex hasn't developed his telepathic ability yet," hailed Savita.

"When will he?" hailed Kris Tarius now realizing he could.

"We're all different Kris," answered Kyros. "Some of us inherit certain gifts faster than others."

"I guess its an inside joke." Terex was not impressed.

"An inside joke, indeed!" laughed Kris in thought.

"Hey! I can hear your thoughts!" Suddenly and without announcement, Terex telepathically had two-way communication. "Hey, I can speak without words too!"

Arias and Trayke also began to hear the psychic conversation. Each young Lord was amazed with their new-found ability.

"Remember, students, thoughts can only be read when permission is granted." Bossel expressed this condition out loud.

"We're no longer students," reminded Arias.

"You'll always be students to us," smiled Lady Dunlam. "Now, Bossel dear."

"Yes, my love."

"Why don't we escort the young Lord's unicorns to the leather shop. We will get them fitted with saddles for our new Lords."

"Of course, my dear. Then maybe we can go for a walk along the creek?" Bossel sent an exaggerated wink to his audience of new Lords.

"I would enjoy that," said Elasia as she blushed.

"Lord Drakus," said Kyros. "If I may be excused as well. I have a voyage to prepare for."

"Understood, my friend. I'll see you at the departure party."

"What are they talking about, Savita?" asked Nyte.

"Lord Kyros and the Elvish hierarchy have assembled a special crew to set sail across the vast White Sea. It's meant to be an exploration voyage of uncharted waters."

"What's so interesting about a vast ocean?" inquired Terex.

"The Elves and I believe there are undiscovered lands in the far reaches of the ocean," volunteered Lord Kyros. "The only way to prove this theory is to sail beyond the White Sea."

"So, you're sailing the sea to find land?" Terex could not see the big picture.

"Essentially," said Kyros with an ever so slight hint of arrogance.

"Allow me to explain," intervened Drakus. "Lord Duren made a list of enchanted Earth artifacts he failed to find during his first mission. We believe they could be out there somewhere. So, our mission is to discover new land and search for these missing artifacts."

"We are to complete Lord Duren's first mission," confirmed Kyros, "a mission that started over a thousand years ago."

"What an epic adventure!" The mere thought of the mission excited Nyte.

"Epic, indeed!" agreed Lord Kyros. "Now then, I must be off. Farewell young Lords and congratulations once again on becoming Komalsh."

"Young Lords," commanded Drakus, "it's time to go inside the castle. Follow me."

King Siris and his Sykanian Knights escorted the failed students to an unrevealed destination two days west of the Mystique Forest. Kelar and Neasha were given a horse to share while Kolos rode solo.

Neasha held Kelar close, her nerves still shaken from the forest. Kelar cradled his splintered arm. His skin was white as snow. Their futures now felt uncertain, darkened like a sky of falling arrows. All hope diminished as they rode silently among the Sykanians.

Siris broke that silence. "Kelar."

"Yes, King Siris."

"Do you understand why I left the Komalsh?"

"No, sir, can't say that I do," answered Kelar defeated.

"Too many rules, son. Too much of what you can and cannot do. I'm a King now. I make the rules and, trust me, the Sykanian people are happy. Right boys!" urged Siris. The Sykanian Knights cheered their king in return.

"The Komalsh have the power to change this world," explained Siris, "yet they sit back and do nothing."

"Well," informed Kolos, "the Komalsh are trying to negotiate peace with the kingdoms of Drakonia. Once that is established the Komalsh will be able to unite Drakonia." Siris laughed rudely. "They've been trying to do that since as long as I can remember. Trust me, it won't work. The only way to establish world order is by dominating it. One leader to rule all. There too many religions and too many points of view. Only we, my friends, can teach Drakonian people of the one true god. Only then will there be peace."

"You're right," agreed Kelar. "The Drake kingdom alone will prevent peace. I saw it at the last peace talks."

"I'm from the Drake kingdom," prompted Kolos.

"Yes, Kelar." Siris ignored Kolos' insulting demeanor. "That is why we must conquer all kingdoms. We must eliminate any debate and force order upon Drakonia."

"What religion are you proposing to use?" inquired Neasha skeptically. "The one true god?"

"The Komalsh religion, my dear. After reading the original text we believe the Komalsh have translated it wrong. They are in fact protecting the one who will destroy us all."

"Are you suggesting Malshidiel is the Darkstar?" Kelar wanted to know.

"There is so much to teach you." Siris smiled. "But first we must unteach you."

Outside the entrance of Castle Malshidiel, Lord Drakus continued his tour announcing with pride, "Within this castle lies a collection of the most powerful and enchanted items ever created. When the Earth creatures first arrived a thousand years ago, these precious items were scattered across Drakonia. As requested by the Mystique Forest, Lord Duren's first mission was to gather these enchanted items and protect them within these very walls. From spell books to special swords, magic mirrors to enchanted wands as well as stones and staffs. It's all here." The young Lords entered through the castle's doorway. The main room stretched as high as it did wide. Stone carved staircases scaled the inner walls reaching the floors above. Hallways stretched as far as the eye could see. Stone statues of fallen heroes stood against walls decorated in Elvin paintings. Large dark crystal chandeliers with candled light illuminated a mystically decorated atmosphere. What they saw was a combination of peace and war décor with a gothic edge.

"As Komalsh, it is our duty to prevent these enchanted treasures from falling into the wrong hands." commanded Drakus.

Trayke snickered uncontrollably.

"What is so amusing, Lord Basa?" queried Drakus.

Trayke stopped snickering and tensed up. It was one thing to get under Bossel's skin, but annoying Lord Drakus would be unwise.

"Well?" Drakus pushed.

"Well…it's just…I can't see the danger in leaving something like this in the wrong hands." A white goose waddled by Trayke. He picked it up and displayed it to the others.

"Be careful with that goose," warned Drakus.

The goose started to panic and laid a golden egg.

"Shit!" screeched Trayke dropping the bird. "Gold just fell out of her ass!"

Nyte picked up the egg and examined it. It was a solid gold egg.

"It's okay, Nyte, you can keep it." Drakus was feeling particularly benevolent toward his top graduate.

Nyte slipped the gold egg into his robe. The frightened goose laid two more eggs, then waddled off down the hall. Nyte shrugged his shoulders and pocketed the other two.

"Trayke is correct," agreed Drakus. "Some of our treasures are far less dangerous than others. However, in the wrong hands even that goose could create problems."

"Those golden eggs could support an army," suggested Terex militantly.

"Or cause one person to kill another out of greed." simplified Drakus.

Nyte Shade recalled his incident with the Minotaur. "I imagine the creatures Malshidiel brought from Earth could cause some problems, too."

"Indeed, Lord Shade. When the Earth creatures first arrived here, Lord Duren faced many issues with Drakonians fearing these refugees," instructed Drakus. "As we're aware, fear often leads to violence, and this is the reason why Lord Duren and the Elves appointed the Komalsh guardians of the Earth creatures."

"What about the scroll, Lord Drakus?" asked Kris. "Isn't protecting that our prime directive?"

"Indeed, it is Lord Tarius. That started back on Earth where the Elvin elders protected both the sphere's imprisonment of dark energy called the Darkstar and a secret key scroll possessing the ability to release its dark energy. After losing the Darkstar to Baelin, Malshidiel brought them to Drakonia, and the burden of the scroll was placed on Lord Duren and his Komalsh.

"I don't understand, Lord Drakus." Arias was not following. "If the Darkstar is the prison for such great evil, then why bother creating a scroll key to release it?"

"I'll answer this one my lord," volunteered Savita. "All detaining spells require a retaining counter spell. A door cannot be locked without a key."

"Then why not just destroy the key?" suggested Kris.

"Doing that will open the doorway," explained Savita. "The spell on the scroll does just that. It destroys itself to unlock its doorway."

"Nevertheless, the scroll is hidden within this castle," informed Drakus. "We are its guardians."

"Do we know where the Darkstar is?" inquired Nyte.

"After Baelin reclaimed the Darkstar from the Elvin guardians on Earth," explained Drakus, "Malshidiel arrived to recover the scroll and save the Mythicals from Baelin's ruthless army. Malshidiel brought them here to Drakonia as a haven for its Earth creatures and a hiding place for the key scroll. Unfortunately, Baelin grew wise to the angel's plan and tossed the Darkstar through one of Malshidiel's portholes. The Darkstar was last seen embedding itself into the back of a red dragon while passing through to Drakonia. So, to answer your question, Lord Shade, all we know is the Darkstar is somewhere in Drakonia."

"Why would Baelin toss the Darkstar through the porthole?" asked Terex.

"He's using it as a homing beacon to Drakonia. Baelin knows where we are."

"Why did Malshidiel bring the Earth creatures to Drakonia?" Trayke was confused as to why it was important to bring people to a place of potential danger.

"Their importance will reveal itself when the Darkstar returns," answered Drakus.

"But aren't we preventing that to begin with by protecting the key scroll in this castle?" Once again, Terex was needing help to dissolve his confusion.

"The ancient prophecy speaks of Baelin's return and the Darkstar's awakening. It's not an "if", it's a "when". That is why we abide by the Komalsh code and order young Lords to protect us from the Darkstar's corruption." Lord Drakus led the group up a staircase to the centre floor. A pleasant aroma from the kitchen stole the young Lord's attention. Before entering the dining room, Drakus stopped his tour.

"Before meeting the castle's cook, I need to warn you he's not human, well…only humanish. A little hard on the eyes if I may. We keep him wrapped in robes as requested by all our Komalsh."

"He's a little strange, too!" added Savita humorously. Then yawning she excused herself. "I grow tired and will head to my room now. Congratulations on your graduation young Lords. I'm so proud of you all."

"Good night, Lady Cosmos."

The young Lords entered the dining room—a spacious room furnished with long rectangular tables spaced perfectly in rows. Each table was occupied by Komalsh of all ages and genders eating their meals under the gentle murmuring of conversation.

Nyte rubbed his eyes and yawned. Contagiously, it spread through the group. They had a long day, and an early night was foreseeable.

"Welcome, young masters!" hollered a happy voice walking from the kitchen.

Lord Drakus approached the cook and placed his arm around him. "Young Lords, this is the castle's cook. His name is Twiggins."

****

Twiggins was a six-foot-tall skeleton wrapped in red robes. His eyeballs protruded from their sockets and although he had no cheeks nor tongue his ability to speak was articulate. His peculiarly soft bone structure gave him the ability to form any expression he felt, which most often was joy and happiness. Twiggins took pride in spreading cheer to all who surrounded him. His high pitch cackle often echoed down the castle hallways bringing smiles to those who heard. He shared a calm disposition and was always willing to listen to those who needed to speak. Twiggins was also an amazing cook.

****

The young Lords stood awkwardly silent before Twiggins. His soft skeletal facial structure molded into a big smile hoping to ease the tension. This only made things worse.

"You will get used to our cook's good looks soon enough," assured Drakus to his unconvinced audience.

"Come, gentlemen!" invited Twiggins. "Please be seated. I have prepared a flavoursome soup!"

The young Lords, hungry as they were, accepted the uncanny chef and sat down to the dinner table. Twiggins scurried about topping off drinks and refilling bowls. He took pride in nourishing the Komalsh. To Twiggins all who stayed in this castle were considered family.

"That was delicious!" said Terex with a note of surprise after swallowing down his second bowl.
The others concurred with tired appraisal.

"Thank you, kindly." The chef bowed humbly.
Arias leaned back in his chair. "So Twiggies, are you all bones under that robe?"

"Not just bones!" shrieked Twiggins while yarding his robe open. "See, I have guts too!"

The young Lords jolted back in horror. Hidden behind Twiggins' robe was all the insides you'd expect in a human body. His lungs were breathing, his heartbeat pounding behind his rib cage and a full set of intestines that seemed to hold into place.

"Shit man!" Cringed Trayke. "We just ate!"

Lord Drakus quickly helped the obscure cook put his robe back on.

"Excuse me?" Twiggins was confused about what Trayke said. "You all look the same on the inside."

"You'll have to excuse Twiggins," apologized Drakus. "He's been in this castle since the beginning. He doesn't get out much." Drakus began to make circle motions with his index finger around his temple. "He's not all there, if you know what I mean."

"Fine then," snarled Twiggins. "But I'd like to remind you all that beauty is on the inside."

"I'm not seeing it," protested Trayke quietly to the others.

"Perhaps you should keep your beauty covered up from now on," suggested Drakus.

The young Lords started feeling the draining effects from their adventurous day—something both Drakus and Twiggins anticipated.

"You'll have to excuse us, Twiggins," announced Drakus. "It seems our young Lords here are starting to feel the venom's hangover. I shall escort them to their quarters before I'm forced to pack them."

"How exciting!" grinned Twiggins with an expression that would frighten a child. "The soup I prepared will help them rest."

"Thank you kindly, Twiggins." Nyte smiled. He was ready to retire. "It was a pleasure to make your acquaintance." Nyte held out his hand and shook Twiggins boney fingers. He stared into the obscure space where Twiggins' eyes should be. They were there but different. They were spooky yet somehow gentle, safe, loving, and wise.

"I knew your mother and father Nyte. The Shade family have my upmost respect." Twiggins rendered a nostalgic smile.

"How did you know I was a Shade?" queried Nyte.

A wider smile stretched across the skeleton's face and his eyes softened. "You have your mother's eyes and your father's nose."

Nyte smiled with pride.

"Don't let the cook fool you," interrupted Drakus. "I told him before you got here."

"Why can't I ever get the opportunity to be mystical?" protested Twiggins wiggling his fingers about.

"You are mystical enough, bone head," quipped Drakus. "Now then, gentlemen, follow me to your chambers."

The young Lords thanked the eerie cook and followed Lord Drakus out of the dining room. The last to leave were Trayke Basa and Kris Tarius. Trayke, who left a partial bowl of soup uneaten, thanked the cook.

"For what?" complained Twiggins. "You barely ate! Are you dying or something?"

"What do you mean?" asked Trayke.

"Just look at you! I've got more meat on my bones!"

"You're a skeleton."

"I was being sarcastic," said Twiggins.

Trayke patted his stomach. "I'm fit as a fiddle."

"Fit? If you were any skinnier, you'd fall through your asshole and hang yourself!"

Kris broke out into laughter. "He's right you know."

Trayke rolled his eyes. "You stay out of this, Kris!" He then pointed his finger at Twiggins and said, "And you, I happened to train extremely hard for this body."

"You stink like rum," noted Twiggins.

"He's right Trayke. You do stink like rum," agreed Kris.

"Weren't you supposed to stay out of this?" reminded Trayke.

Twiggins leapt onto the table and summoned the ears of all the Komalsh who dined. "Now listen up! You are what you eat! You eat nothing, you become nothing! So, nobody leaves my kitchen without finishing their plate!"

The Komalsh around the room covered their eyes in awkward disgust as Twiggins robe swayed open revealing his guts.

"Get off the table, Twiggins!" shouted a Komalsh from across the room.

Collectively, other Komalsh joined in at booing Twiggins down from the table.

"Put your bloody robe back on!"

"That's disgusting!"

"What's wrong with you, Twiggins?"

Kris looked at Trayke—then looked at his bowl. Trayke looked down to his bowl. "Alright, alright, but I'd like to inform you that I ate a healthy serving of mushrooms already today!"

The cook's head shook while he leapt down from the table. "Tsk, tsk. I can tell I'm going to have a real bone to pick with you, Trayke…wait a tick, that was funny! Do you get it? Do you??"

Twiggins broke out into a witch's cackle. "A BONE TO PICK!!!"

His high pitch laughter filled the room and rolled down every corridor of the castle.

"Its funny because I'm a skeleton!" Twiggins loved making fun of himself even if it made others uncomfortable.

Outside the dining room, Lord Drakus and the others looked back. Contagiously, they all giggled as the loud cackle coming from Twiggins echoed down the hallway.

"That's one messed up laugh," chuckled Terex.

"That's Twiggins," said Drakus. "You'll get used to it."

"What is this, Lord Drakus?" asked Arias pointing to a small table decorated with a single hand-size cube of black glass.

Drakus placed himself between it and the three Lords. "This is a gateway to the Hidden Night. If touched by your skin, it will absorb and imprison you inside the crystal cube. The only way to escape the Hidden Night is by someone on the outside guiding you out. If the person imprisoned doesn't trust the voice, the cube will not release them. Trust is the key to opening the Hidden Night.

Arias, Nyte and Terex's eyes filled with wonder at its shiny black glass. It was as though the cube itself was asking them to touch it.

"No one touches the Hidden Night. That is the law." Drakus continued down the hall.

Avoiding the Hidden Night's temptation, the young Lords followed.

Trayke finished the last of his soup. "Are you two happy now?"

Twiggins, pleased at Trayke's efforts, escorted the tired Lords to the doorway. "Sleep, sleep. Rest is good for the mind. A rested mind is good for the soul."

"Thank you," acknowledged Kris.

"You're most welcome, Lord Tarius."

****

Twiggins had taken care of Castle Malshidiel for over a thousand years and has fed every Komalsh to ever call it home. He also remembered each lord on a first name basis.

Not only did he nourish their bodies but was also known to nourish their minds through spirituality. Twiggins was a great listener and a wise speaker. Although he was a strange creature with a peculiar demeaner his methods of spreading love and joy seemed to be contagious to those around him. He was the castle's chef and the castle's butler.

****

Trayke and Kris went down the hallway to catch up with the others. Trayke staggered from exhaustion and leaned up against a table displaying a black glass cube.

"What's this?" Trayke gazed upon the cube.

Kris studied it closely, then turned to Trayke. "It's a glass cube."

“I know that, jerk off!”

“Then why did you ask?”

“I meant what is it?” Trayke gazed deep into its alluring temptation.

Kris went down on one knee also mesmerized by its energy. “Maybe we should touch it,” he suggested. Then squeezing his eyes shut Kris shook off its temptation. Trayke, however, couldn’t resist. Mesmerized by its allure, he reached out his hand to touch it.

Drakus, Nyte, Terex and Arias ran down the hall toward them.

“Don’t touch the cube!” warned Drakus.

Trayke stopped for a brief second. Then he touched it anyway. In an instant his body turned into smoke, and he was vacuumed into the black glass cube. It dropped to the ground like an anvil.

“I said don’t touch it!” Drakus was visibly shaken.

“What the hell happened to him?” wondered Kris. “It looked like the cube just sucked him in!”

“Ha, we always knew Trayke sucked!” Arias was amused.

“That’s the funniest thing I ever heard.” chuckled Terex.

“So, now what do we do?” Nyte needed a plan.

“Someone will need to guide him out using their voice,” answered Drakus.

“Wouldn’t it be easier if we just left him in there?” chuckled Arias.

Terex laughed. “We should at least shake the cube and see if it rattles.”

“It doesn’t work that way.” Drakus was serious. He wanted to diffuse the humour.

Nyte Shade looked deep into the cube. He closed his eyes to avoid the temptation it released.

“Just focus on Trayke’s heartbeat,” instructed Drakus.

After a moment to focus, Nyte locked onto Trayke's heartbeat and whispered, "Do you hear my voice?"

"Nyte? Is that you?" echoed Trayke from inside the glass cube.

"Yes, Trayke, just follow my voice." Nyte hummed a familiar song—one they were both fond of as kids. Trayke followed his voice to a doorway inside the cube. The Hidden Night released smoke which slowly reformed back into Trayke.

"That felt freaky weird!" Trayke shivered from head to toe.

"You had to touch it didn't you?" Nyte chastised Trayke for acting without exercising any caution.

"Enough shenanigans!" ordered Drakus. "It's time to get you to your rooms."

Drakus led the young Lords down a long hallway with no doors or windows. At the end of the hallway, he stopped.

The new Lords stood tired and confused.

"I think we took a wrong turn," said Trayke.

"Be patient," calmed Drakus.

Before their eyes, the castle's hallway walls transformed into a liquid state and began molding into five separate doorways leading into five different rooms. After taking form, the stone resolidified.

"Choose your rooms and get some sleep," commanded Drakus. "I'll see you in the morning."

"What just happened?" While Kris was amazed, his question was followed by an uncontrollable yawn.

"The castle reforms to accommodate its Lords. It's always nice to see rooms appear rather than disappear," answered Drakus returning down the hallway.

The five new Lords exchanged tiresome looks. They nodded happily amongst each other. They had passed the Mystique Forest. They were now Lords of the Komalsh—a graduation short lived as they were too tired to celebrate. The young Lords dispersed to their rooms and closed the doors behind them.

Lord Drakus returned to his quarters—the same room used by all his predecessors. A room placed on the highest peak of the castle. He wandered out onto his balcony overlooking the White Sea. There stood his niece, Milita, watching the vast ocean being devoured by the bottomless ravine.

"You look so much like your mother." He complimented.

Milita smiled. "You always say that."

****

Milita Drakus had long red hair cascading down to the small of her back and captivating light green eyes. Her dark skin was soft like silk. Her beauty reflected her soul. She stood five foot nine and weighed 130 pounds. As an intelligent young woman at 16 years of age, she had already graduated the Olemeeze curriculum. Homeschooled in Castle Malshidiel, her grades were among the highest in Komalsh history and her combat training excelled under Lord Drakus' teachings. Her love for animals and nature was counterbalanced by her anger toward God's plan—a plan that took her parents away at a young age leaving her conflicted about the Komalsh religion.

****

"You haven't been sleeping very well, Uncle Hirum. What troubles you?"

"Just the everyday life of a leader, Mili, nothing to be concerned with."

Milita wasn't naive but she let this one slide and Drakus was thankful for that. As a rule, when Milita wanted answers, she usually got results.

"Fair enough," she replied staring out into the vanishing ocean. "I was just thinking about my parents and those spineless cowards who took their lives. I want to find them, uncle. I want to make them pay!" Milita was exasperated with her feelings of powerlessness.

Drakus put his arm around her. "When I arrived at their wagon, it was too late. They were gone and so were your parents. Fortunately, I found you, just a baby wrapped in blankets. Your mother had hidden you inside the wagon. She was a remarkable woman, my sister."

Milita stewed in silence. She'd heard that story too often.

"That was a long time ago, Mili. If those people are still alive, the odds of finding them are very slim."

"I'll find them, uncle."

"You must focus on today, my dear. You have a bigger destiny—one that can't be compromised on something as dark as revenge."

"Yes, you still believe me to be the chosen one." Milita's gaze froze with confusion. "I feel so much hate and conflict. How could I be the one Malshidiel had chosen to wake? Why would it want my unsettled soul to walk in this world?" She stared back into the violent ocean. "And why all the secrecy about it? I've been hiding in this castle for ten years. I'm going crazy, Uncle Hirum!"

Drakus leaned up against the stone railing. Directing his eyes up into the starlit sky he spoke. "When you were six years old, a miracle happened, Mili. We were walking along the Mystique Forest's edge when a vine reached out and pulled you in." Drakus paused remembering how scared he was. "You should have died. I searched the forest from top to bottom, but I couldn't find you. Later that day you found me. You passed through the Mystique Forest riding your unicorn, Stormy. That day you became the youngest Komalsh ever to possess our psychic gift. Too young you were to walk freely among others without it. Even among us Komalsh, you were a troublesome child. Your psychic ability caused a lot of fuss." Drakus couldn't help but chuckle as he recalled some of her damaging mishaps. "If it weren't for Twiggins' supervision, I fear none of us would have survived."

A laugh half escaped Milita's mouth. "I love Twiggins. He's always there for me." Her fondness for him was obvious.

"I swear that's why Malshidiel put him in this castle." Drakus smiled as he spoke the words.

"Yeah," smiled Milita in return. "He never left my side."

"Remember that time, Mili, when those mermaids were picking on you. You got so mad you levitated them out of the lake and floated them over this bottomless ravine?"

"Yes, I do." She recalled the event with feelings of guilt.

"It was Twiggins who talked you into releasing them back into the lake. You could have hurt them."

"I always get so angry," admitted Milita.

"That's why we kept you safe within the castle grounds all these years. Most people in the outside world would have feared you. They weren't ready to understand your importance."

"It's the same reason why the Komalsh keep their distance, isn't it, Uncle? We possess the ability to help the world, yet we don't."

"The world fears us, Mili. We were created to protect the Darkstar's scroll and the immigrated Earth creatures. Lord Duren realised this when the Komalsh first formed. He found out the hard way that it was safer for us to do our job if we were to avoid the politics and religions of Drakonia."

"So why the peace talks? Why now intervene?"

"The time has come to be diverse, Mili. The Darkstar is awakening and with it Malshidiel. Your destiny has arrived. I've dreamt it."

The two paused in silence listening to the powerful sound of water falling into the bottomless depths of the ravine. Drakus removed a talisman from around his neck. "This has been handed down from each Komalsh leader since the day Lord Duren first received it. It is the symbol of our religion and the key to Malshidiel's hidden chambers."

Milita's eyes widened.

****

The pentacle star was the symbol warn by all Komalsh. Each of the star points represented an element. Matter, energy, water, air, and the upper more dominant point representing the universe. Each point pierced through the radius of a circle that surrounded the star. That circle represented life and inside the circle was the spirit world. This pendant signified the Komalsh religion.

****

"We've held this key for over a thousand years anticipating the arrival of the chosen one: You. You, Milita, are that one. The Darkstar has awoken earlier than anticipated. Its darkness shadowing Drakonia and the gateway to Baelin's arrival grows stronger every day. That gateway is blocked by sorcery using Lady Raine Shade's spiritual energy."

"Lady Raine Shade? I thought she died?"

"It's complicated," sighed her uncle.

Drakus twisted the talisman separating it into two halves. Taking a durenthium chain from his pocket he turned one of the talisman halves into a necklace then offered it to Milita. "In time the other half of the talisman will find you," assured her uncle.

Milita accepted the burden and placed it around her neck. "Where does Malshidiel sleep?"

Drakus gazed back to the stars. "That too will find you. For now, you must pack your things."

"My things?"

"Yes, Mili, tomorrow you will travel to the Elvin castle. There you will prepare for the times to come." Drakus smiled into Milita's light green eyes. "As far as avenging your parents, that too may find you."

Milita held her uncle tight. Tears rolled down her cheeks. She loved him like no other.

"I'm afraid, Uncle."

"Me, too!" He laughed. "Those poor Elvin elders are in for a real treat!"

Milita lovingly punched her uncle in the shoulder. She wiped the tears from her cheeks and smiled brightly. "I'm not that bad!"

"You are the brightest star in the darkest sky, my niece."

Milita held him close.

"You should get some rest, Mili. You have a big day tomorrow."

Milita kissed him on the cheek and went to the door. On her way out she stopped to ask her uncle, "Are the new Lords what you expected?"

Drakus smiled, "Far more than I could've ever anticipated."

Milita smiled in return. "Good night, Uncle Hirum."

"Good night, Mili."

Milita returned to her room.

While the castle slept Milita escaped from her window like she'd done many times before. After scaling down the castle wall, she swiftly leapt to the ground. Maneuvering through the shadows, Milita avoided the few who wandered sleepless. Unseen she entered the Mystique Forest and ran through the darkness.

Guided by her psychic insight, Milita leapt over obstacles and maneuvered through brush and trees. Spotting her favourite old growth tree, she jumped a quarter of the way up the enormous trunk and quickly climbed to its highest reaches. There Milita stepped out onto a giant branch overlooking the forest top. From there she could see beyond the woods and out into the forbidden lands of Drakonia. This was a calming place for her. A place she hid when she wanted to be alone.

Stretching her arms out like wings, Milita inhaled a big breath then fell backwards surrendering to the fall. While free falling to the ground, she faced the star-lit sky unafraid. The tree's branches reached out and cushioned her descent until the bottom branch carefully lowered her to the ground.

"Sneaking out again, Mili?" asked her unicorn waiting at the bottom of the tree.

"Stormy!"

"One of these days that tree will let you hit the ground," she warned.

"I'll heal," said Milita, unconcerned.

"You'll still feel pain!" cringed Stormy.

"You worry too much, Stormy. Besides, the tree likes me." Milita placed her hand on the tree and felt its life force.

Thrilled with life she mounted her steed. "Come, Stormy, let's ride to the outer perimeter and take a peek."

"Lord Drakus forbids this, Mili!"

"All the more reason to, Stormy!"

"As you wish." Her unicorn adored her and found it hard to do anything but obey her wishes.

The two rode fast through the Mystique Forest until reaching its outer perimeter. There they slowed to a trot allowing Milita to enjoy the forbidden fruit of the forests outer edge.

"How did you know I was sneaking out tonight, Stormy?"

"We grew up together, Mili. I know when my bestie gets antsy."

"If I never snuck out, Stormy, I'd have gone bonkers! Thanks for always being there for me."

"That's just what friends do, Mili. Wait! What's this? Look ahead Mili!" alerted Stormy galloping toward it.

"Oh no!" Milita dismounted leaping to the ground. She knelt before the naked bodies of Lord Jamala and Lady Tuza. "I just talked to them both this morning." Her heart was saddened.

"Who could have done this?" wondered Stormy.
"These kills are precise, Stormy. Whoever did this not only trained in Komalsh combat but excelled at it."

"How can you be sure, Mili?"

"Look. Lady Tuza's throat was slit and there's a blade puncture in her head. I'm guessing that the slit throat was to immobilize her enough to kill Lord Jamala. Then the footprints and the blade puncture indicate the assailant killed her last. These were Komalsh, Stormy. Whoever did this was skilled."

"Look over here, Stormy. There are horse tracks everywhere. Must be over 40 at least. This suggests an army of knights."

"So, who do you believe to be this master swordsman?" asked Stormy.

"I think it's obvious. King Siris is stirring the pot. What's interesting, though, is why strip them of their clothes and weapons?"

"Come on, Milita, we should leave before we're noticed," warned Stormy.

"Yeah, you're right, Stormy. The Komalsh will find their bodies. There's no more we can do at this point." Milita mounted Stormy and the two rode back into the Mystique Forest.

While making their way back through the Mystique Forest, Milita stewed in curiosity. "I need to know what happened, Stormy."

"Perhaps, the forest can tell you." suggested her steed slowing to a stop.

"Good idea, Stormy, I'll ask."

Milita closed her eyes and opened her mind to the forests will. There she stood in a subconscious realm, a place between dreams and reality. Inside appeared a large snake with yellow, red, and black stripes. His body erect before her while his tongue tickled her face.

"Why did you summon me, Lady Drakus?" It softly hissed.

"I need to know what happened here today?"

"The students Kelar, Kolos Dreken and Neasha Sentrix failed, and the forest deemed them as threats to Malshidiel."

"Three threats in the same class? There hasn't been that many in the history of the Komalsh. That seems rather unusual."

"Unusual and disturbing for they also escaped the forest," reported the serpent in a heightened volume of hisses.

"How did this happen?" persisted Milita.

"I sensed demonic shadows hibernating within the weaker two. However, the one they call Kelar had something far darker—a darkness I wish never to endure again."

"How did they escape?"

"Cretes Siris intervened."

"And what of Lord Jamala and Lady Tuza? Who killed them?"

"They died by the blade of Cretes Siris. The failed students now ride with him."

Milita felt disturbed. Her stomach knotted. "Thank you for your time, Naga."

"My pleasure, Lady Drakus." With that, the serpent left.

Milita opened her eyes. The trees of the forest whispered in the wind telling her of the dangers to come. She was the chosen one and her uncle was right. The Darkstar grows stronger every day.

"Take me home, Stormy."

While Milita and Stormy snuck out of the forest and back toward the castle, Lord Drakus observed them from his bedroom balcony. He smiled, shook his head, then went back to bed relieved she was safe…again.

Milita crept into her bedroom like she had done many times before. Crawling into bed she closed her eyes and processed her eventful day. Gripping the talisman around her neck she started to cry. Her tears soon turned into a flurry of thoughts that buried her deep in sleep.

In her dreams an old memory resurfaced. The moment she handed Nyte the ring of smiles. They were only children. Milita smiled while she slept.

Lord Drakus lay on his bed staring into the ceiling. He was unable to hail Lord Jamala or Lady Tuza telepathically. The facts were few, yet his gut convinced him they were dead. As he drifted off to sleep, his prophetic dreams would whisper their truth revealing the misfortunes of the day and the challenges yet to come.

At the far end of the castle the new Lords had long since fallen asleep. Nyte Shade, who had fallen into the realm of dreams and dreamscapes, saw images rushing through his mind. His mother requesting his father's sword. His friends old and new. Out from the shadows appeared Kelar. He grabbed onto Nyte and tried dragging him down into the shadows. Thunder and lightning embraced the skies and the surrounding Mystique Forest burst into flames. An evil spirit shimmered across Kelar's face. Then everything went dark and silent.

In the darkness rose a five-pointed star talisman floating weightless. Behind it stood a beautiful dark-skinned woman with long red hair. She smiled softly, and in a child's voice, spoke, "Love lasts forever, silly."

Nyte smiled while he slept. Then everything faded to black.

Chapter XVI
Psychic Enlightenment.

Under a starlit sky in the late hours of the evening, King Siris and his Sykanian Knights arrived on the sandy beach of the White Sea. Like a finely tuned machine, the Sykanian soldiers set up tents and collected wood for fire. Neasha sat on the beach staring out into the powerful waves. A moonlit path shimmered in wave-like motion along the water's surface. After a long day's ride, the salty air felt revitalizing to her wary mind. Slightly agitated due to her wounds from the thorns, she pulled the hood of her Komalsh cloak over her head.

Kelar sat down next to her. He held her affectionately. "Are you okay, Neasha?"

"What's going to happen to us, Kelar?" She was deeply worried.

"I don't know. But whatever happens, we will face it together."

"I love you, Kelar." She whimpered.

Even though he grimaced in pain from his broken wrist, Kelar turned Neasha to meet his lips. "I love you too."

Neasha pulled back. "Do you believe King Siris…that Malshidiel is the Darkstar?"

"At this point survival is all that matters. We are outcasts to Malshidiel. We either stay with the safety of the Sykanians or we take our chances alone. Either way, the Komalsh are going to try to kill us."

"I think we should run away, Kelar. Just the two of us. We can start a new life." Neasha was serious.

"When the chance arrives, we will. For now, lets see where this road takes us," insisted Kelar.

Kolos joined the two nestled on the beach. "King Siris has asked me to retrieve you two. He's asked us to join him at his fire."

Kelar ran his fingers through Neasha's hair. "Lord Siris may be our only hope," he whispered.

"Don't you mean King Siris," Neasha had caught the difference in the reference. "What Komalsh would ever desire to be a king?"

"One who understands how to bring peace to Drakonia," answered Kelar.

"Well, are you two coming or do I have to entertain the king myself?" persisted Kolos oblivious to their conversation.

Kelar, Kolos and Neasha joined the King at his fire. The pit was surrounded by Sykanian guards cooking pheasant over an open flame. Beside Siris quietly sat his wizard, Malores, carefully stripping down the vines gathered from the Mystique Forest. Together they sat around the fire sharing good food, wine and to the three newcomers' amazement, even a few laughs. Cretes Siris was an entertaining man. His laughter was even somewhat contagious.

Kelar watched him closely. "Here is the greatest swordsman of all the Komalsh," he thought, "a true leader of men with the hope for peace." He turned his eyes to look at Neasha. She was laughing at Siris' jokes and stories. Kolos, too, seemed entertained by the King's warm personality. Even the dead looking wizard had a couple of jokes to share. This Sykanian family had welcomed them with open arms. Kelar felt humbled. Yet his throbbing wrist reminded him of his despair.

"That looks uncomfortable," observed Siris.

"It throbs." Kelar grimaced.

"Excuse me, your majesty," interrupted a Sykanian soldier. "Fenka Rek has arrived."

"Well, show him to me!" ordered Siris. "You are going to love this guy, Kelar. He's a real piece of work!"

The King rose from his seat as a dark armoured knight, hidden behind a horned helmet, appeared before them with his undead horse by his side.

****

Fenka Rek stood five nine and weighed 205 pounds—his identity was concealed by a black horned helmet. This helmet was shaped like a skull with devil's horns and fangs along the jawbone protector. He wore dark charcoal-coloured light armour wearing no symbols of kingdom, cult, or religion. He was armed with a two-handed sword and a bow with arrows strapped to his back. Hidden on his wrists and the toes of his boots were stiletto like blades and a whip hung from his belt. His light armour was scratched and dented from many failed attempts on his life. Fenka Rek was a warrior, an assassin, a killer. His legacy spanned a thousand years.

****

Fenka Rek nodded to Kelar. A grin formed behind his partially covered mouth. Then he turned to address the king.

Kelar studied the image before him closely but was unable to recognize any facial features through Fenka Rek's skull shaped helmet. He observed the prestigious assassin's light armour. It was designed for agility. He also noticed Fenka Rek wore no cloak or cape. Those garments would be awkward in battle. His weapons were made of durenthium.

"Who was he?"

Fenka Rek's undead horse, Apocalypse, was partially armoured as well, hiding its hideous decaying body but not its odor.

Few had ever been this close to the infamous demon knight. Fenka Rek was known for bringing a death sentence to those he visited—his devotion seemingly dedicated to the Grim Reaper. While some deemed him a myth, those who had encountered him were too dead to discredit it.

"I've located Cable Demonis," reported Fenka Rek.

"Excellent!" replied King Siris nodding to his guard.

The guard held out a bag of gold coins. His arm trembled with fear.

Fenka Rek snatched it from him. Startled, the guard fell to the ground backwards struggling to regain his footing. The prestigious assassin placed his reward in the saddle bags of his undead steed.

"Aren't you going to count it?" pressed Siris.

"I trust you wouldn't cross me," rasped the demon knight.

His undead horse, Apocalypse, stared at Siris. The steed's darkened eyes elicited fear. He raised his upper lip revealing his sharp dripping fangs then snapped at Siris with a deep growl. Siris showed no reaction toward the horse.

"You have your coins," scowled Siris. "Now tell me, where is Cable Demonis?"

"You'll find him in the limestone cave at the peak of Mount Maximas," answered Fenka Rek.

"Excellent," replied the smiling Siris. "Would you care for something to eat or drink?"

Without a response Fenka Rek mounted Apocalypse and disappeared into the night.

"He's not very social, is he?" Siris seemed annoyed but first things first. "Hey Malores."

"Yes, your majesty," answered the wizard while continuing to carefully drain venom from the vines.

"We'll start our journey up Mount Maximus at sunrise. Soon Lord Demonis will be free."

"I'll scroll through the maps, sire. I'll find us the quickest rout," promised the wizard.

Siris looked at Kelar's splintered wrist. "You're no good to us like that, son. Malores, how are you making out with those vines?"

"One moment, sire." Malores drained the last vine into a bowl then stirred while reading through, *The Book of Malshidiel*. Satisfied with the results he placed the bowl before Siris. "It is done your majesty."

"Excellent work, wizard. Kelar, Neasha, Kolos. It's time! Come, drink from this bowl, and open your minds to psychic enlightenment. Who wants to go first?"

Kolos lamented, "But we failed the Mystique Forest!"

"It's not the forest that prepares you, Kolos. It's the training at Olemeeze," assured Siris.

Neasha added, "Yes, but if our minds aren't prepared, ingesting the venom could lead us to insanity, even death! Are you sure this is a good idea?"

"To be honest, I don't really know what will happen," admitted Siris while scratching his head, "But I can tell you this." The King's tone turned ruthless. "You are good as dead if you don't!"

Kelar knew Siris was right. Without psychic enlightenment they were no match against the Komalsh. How could he possibly protect Neasha? Kelar took the wooden bowl from Siris. Both Neasha and Kolos watched fearfully. Kelar stared at Siris who smiled with anticipation. Then he placed the bowl to his lips and drank.

Kelar passed the bowl to Neasha. Reluctantly, she drank from the bowl, too. Handing the bowl to Kolos she wiped the spillage from her lips. "It tastes awful." She grimaced.

Kolos waited a moment to see if his friends would instantly die. But nothing happened.

"Well, go on!" urged Siris.

Kolos then drank from the bowl, too.

Siris and his Sykanians stared silently awaiting.

"I feel tired," yawned Neasha.

The other two concurred.

"Well then, I told you everything would be okay!" shouted King Siris to his crowd of Sykanians. "However, I am a bit curious." The King turned to his wizard, Malores. "What would happen to someone who wasn't trained at the school of Olemeeze?"

Malores shrugged his shoulders. "I don't know, sire."

The King surveyed his Sykanian audience. "Well, I guess there's only one way to find out. I need a volunteer, preferably one nobody likes."

An awkward fear spread through the Sykanian knights.

"Anyone? Come on now, choose or I will." Siris was so calm.

Three Sykanians dragged a soldier to the fire kicking and screaming in confusion. They threw him before Siris' feet.

"Hello there! What's your name?" asked Siris pleasantly.

As he stood, he stuttered, "My, my, my name is Randall, your majesty."

"Well, that's a nice name." nodded Siris.

The Sykanians gathered around all nodding with their king. "How would you like to have psychic abilities beyond your wildest imagination?"

Randall, a small lanky man, was warming up to the idea. He stared around at the anxious crowd then back to his king. "I would like that very much, your majesty." Kolos handed him the wooden bowl.

"All you have to do is drink." Spoke Siris with a sinister smile.

Randall took the wooden bowl and drank from it. His audience stood silent awaiting the outcome.

"That's awful!" He grimaced while returning the bowl to Siris. Slurring his words, he said, "I don't feel very well."

Randall backed away clumsily. "I don't feel very well," he repeated. Randall staggered unbalanced. He leaned against a large boulder gripping onto its pointed top. Blood started to seep from his nose. A surge of pain shot through his skull. He started screaming at the top of his lungs while grasping his head. White foam filled his mouth followed by a spray of puke across the front row Sykanians. Randall released his head and dug his fingertips into the boulder so intensely his fingernails snapped off. His eyeballs swelled outward, and blood poured from his ears. Randall's panicking screams rose sharper and higher. His knees wobbled as he steadied himself against the boulder. Neasha tried to hide her face tucking it into Kelar's neck, but nothing could deafen Randall's high pitch screams.

Kolos cringed. Kelar and the crowd of Sykanian Knights were silenced in disgust while Siris gazed with curious delight.

Randall held himself up from the boulder. With an intense rage fueled by adrenalin, he started smashing his forehead into the boulders jagged top. Blow after blow he hit harder and faster until the final lethal blow crushed his skull. Randall's body fell limp over the boulder and then slid lifeless to the ground. Everyone was silenced in disgust.

"Did you see that!" Siris was stimulated by what played out before him. "That was so intense! Wow! How he dug his nails off and that whole face smashing thing!" Siris gasped. "Have you ever seen anything like that, Malores?"

"No, your majesty. I can't say that I have." The wizard was disgusted.

"Do you want to see it again?" Siris loved the adrenalin.

All the knights started backing away.

"What?" shouted Siris. "We got to do it one more time!"

A Sykanian knight grabbed Randall's body and dragged him down to the beach. There he noticed a lone man walking toward them. "Your majesty!" he warned. "There's an intruder approaching."

Staggering down the beach, a wary old drunken traveller led by lantern light approached King Siris' fire. "What's all the yahooing about?" he slurred.

"Hey there!" greeted Siris. "You thirsty for some wine?"

The old man looked to his empty bottle. Unable to refuse a free drink, he approached the fire and introduced himself. "Hello, my name is Farley."

"Welcome Farley! Come join us! Allow me to introduce myself. I am King Cretes Siris, at your service."

"A king! Wow, that must be fun!"

"Yes, it has its moments. Would you care for a drink?" Siris handed him the wooden bowl.

Farley smiled a toothless grin. "Would I!" Then hesitated when noticing his audience staring at him quietly. "Are…they, okay?" he asked.

"Don't worry about them, Farley. They don't get out much."

Farley nodded it off then took the bowl. "Why are we drinking wine from a bowl?"

"It's the latest trend. Everyone's doing it," assured Siris.

"You don't say." Farley blanketly accepted the explanation.

"Oh yes, you have to be up on the latest trends when you're a king, you know."

Farley raised the wooden bowl to his quiet Sykanian audience and uttered a toast, “To getting out!”

“To getting out!” replied the Sykanians.

Farley tilted his head back and drank the bowl empty. His audience stood silent while awaiting the outcome.

Siris’ eyes widened with anticipation. Neasha covered her mouth. Kolos cringed. Kelar squinted. Malores yawned with boredom.

The old man licked his lips clean while looking around to the silent crowd. “This wine’s awful!” cried Farley.

Everyone stood quiet awaiting Farley’s demise. This made Farley uncomfortable. “What’s wrong with you people?” He turned to Siris, “This wine tastes like shit!”

“What does shit taste like?” laughed Siris.

The old man laughed back. “Ah, you got me there! But seriously…got anything good to drink?”

Kelar started to feel drowsy. He noticed Kolos and Neasha were feeling the same. He took Neasha by the hand and Kolos by the arm laying them next to the fire. He wrapped a blanket over him, and Neasha and they held each other close. Their eyes grew heavy as they surrendered to the venomous sleep.

“Well! How do you feel?” asked Siris anxiously.

“Well, I do feel kind of sleepy,” replied Farley.

Siris was enraged. “Well, this sucks!” shaking his head. He fumed, “I can’t believe you are one of us!”

“One of what?” wondered Farley.

“A lord of psychic enlightenment, like me, like all the Komalsh!”

Farley pointed his finger at Siris and looked around to the other Sykanians. “I want whatever he’s drinking.”

Siris kicked a pot of stew out from the fire and stomped away to his tent with a tantrum.

“What’s eating him?” asked Farley.

"Your majesty," shouted Malores, "what should we do with the old man?"

"Who are you calling old, pasty face!" Farley was in no mood to be ignored.

"Pasty face?" The wizard sought clarification. Frustrated, Siris answered, "We'll have to keep him!"

"Will you feed me?" asked Farley.

"Keep him sire?" Malores had no idea what that meant.

Siris raised his arms in the air. "Well, we can't just leave a powerful old person wondering endlessly about now, can we? Think of the trouble he'd get into." Siris pointed his finger at Farley. "This is a real downer! We could have been cheering on this asshole while he smashed his head in. Instead, we have a powerful geriatric drooling jerk to feed! Somebody hang a bell around his neck so we don't lose him!"

Siris stormed off to his tent. Malores grabbed a large cow bell and wrapped a length of fabric around Farley's neck from which to hang it. Farley liked it. Then Malores helped him move closer to the fire where he drifted off to sleep.

All through the night Kelar faded in and out of consciousness, his body layered in sweat. In the dark hours of the morning, his eyes opened. At first his vision was blurred. Then slowly Neasha's face came into focus. Kelar smiled at her. He stared past her and saw Farley standing by the forest's edge waving at the bush.

"What's he doing?" thought Kelar weakened from the venom.

Beside the bush Kelar saw another person waving back to Farley. "Who is that?"

The person by the bush looked around the tented village. When the coast was clear of wandering guards, it called out to the old man using Siris' voice.

"Want a drink?" It reached out to Farley.
Farley reached out in return.

The person by the bush went down on four legs and snatched Farley's hand. Ferociously it dragged him into the woods. Five others like it appeared from the woods savagely biting into his flesh. Sharp screams escaped Farley's lungs as he was torn apart limb from limb. The commotion alerted Siris' guards who defended the camp from the attacking Mimics. The deceitful predators dragged Farley deep into the forest. Loud screams and cow bell sounds echoed through the woods while the predators savagely feasted.

Siris ran from his tent with his sword unsheathed. "Malores! What happened?"

"Mimics, your majesty! They've taken Farley!"

"Oh…that's it?" Siris put his sword away. "What a mess! Who would a thought a little old man like that could hold so much blood?"

Off in the woods a loud cow bell rang incessantly.

"What's that sound, Malores?"

"That would be the cow bell, sire."

"You put one around his neck?" Siris smiled and then chortled.

"Well, you did ask, sire."

"I was just kidding around, Malores." chuckled the King.

"My apologies, your majesty."

"No worries, wizard."

The bell sound got louder as Farley's body was being ripped back and forth.

"I do hope it ends soon, Malores." yawned Siris. "It'll be hard to sleep with that bell going off all night." Then after one final loud clang, the bell stopped. The night was now silent. Only the crickets could be heard.

"Well then, that's that. Perhaps you should drag those three to my tent, Malores." He gestured to Kelar, Neasha and Kolos.

"As you wish, sire." The wizard bowed to Siris before attending to his next task.

Siris returned to his tent. He crawled inside his bed and snuggled in for a good night's rest.

Chapter XVII
Utopia.

As the sun dawned on Castle Malshidiel, its morning rays peeked over the Mystique Forest and peered through the window of Nyte's chambers. The salty smell of ocean mist rejuvenated the new Lord's rested mind as he awoke to the soothing sound of ocean waves tumbling into the bottomless ravine. Outside his window, Earth creatures worked the castle yard. Some farmed; some fished while others catered to its upkeep.

Outside the Mystique Forest's protective perimeter, a creek branched off from the Assaroe River and flowed through the enchanted forest. Once through the forest, the creek continued through the gardened paradise of Utopia and fed into a large lake. On the outer side of that lake, its fresh waters released into the bottomless ravine. Like the Mystique Forest, the ravine was Castle Malshidiel's protection from the outside world.

Inside Nyte's mind Savita hailed, "Are you awake Nyte?"

"Yes, I am," he replied in thought.

"Knock, Knock." She spoke in thought. A moment later two knocks followed from his bedroom door. Instinctively, Nyte closed his eyes and telekinetically opened the door.

Savita entered his room. "Your abilities grow stronger, Nyte. How do you feel?"

"I feel like my mind has become my teacher. If that makes any sense?"

"More than you know, Nyte. As your mind expands it also adapts and guides you through your psychic evolution. Soon you'll be wondering why you felt the need to close your eyes to open that door."

Savita opened a large wardrobe in his room. "Inside are your new Komalsh robes and light armour. You won't be needing the armour. However, your robes are now essential to being in our ranks. Wear them with pride, Nyte. You've earned it."

"I will."

"Breakfast is being served as well. Unfortunately, my attendance has been requested elsewhere. Therefore, I will not be joining you. I'm merely here to say good morning."

"Good morning, Savita."

"I'm so proud of you, Nyte!" Savita's animated excitement seemed so out of character.

"I know Savita. I'm proud too." Nyte gave the biggest grin he could muster.

"I'm running behind, son. I must get going. Enjoy your day!"

"I'll see you later Savita."

Nyte dressed in his Komalsh robes and left his room. Waiting just outside his door, dressed in their own new Komalsh robes, were his friends Kris Tarius, Arias Jackyle and Terex Gungnir. All were complimenting each other with sarcastic appraisal.

Impatiently awaiting Trayke, Arias knocked on his room door. "Hurry up, man. Its time to eat!"

The door opened and Trayke stood flustered. "I can't get that damn goose out of my room!"

Arias looked at the foot of Trayke's bed. There slept the golden egg-laying goose. "You've only been a Komalsh for one night and you're already fighting worldly issues." Arias could not refuse the opportunity to tease.

"Forget the chicken. Let's go eat." The hole in Terex's stomach was eating away at him.

"She's a goose, not a chicken," reminded Trayke.

"Oh, that's right, you're the chicken," countered Terex.

"Why is the goose in your bed?" asked Arias.

"Couldn't you have kicked her off or something?"

"She's really mean," answered Trayke.

"You really are a chicken!" laughed Terex.

"Maybe the goose and Trayke are sweet on each other!" Kris did not want to be left out of the banter. Trayke was becoming more and more flustered with the rhetoric. "What's wrong with you guys? That goose snores really loud. It's hard to sleep!"

"Sounds like the honeymoon's over!" laughed Nyte. The new Lords broke out into laughter at the expense of their good friend.

"Alright, alright, let's just go eat." To Trayke there was no other choice but to surrender to the harassment.

The five new Lords followed the tantalising aromas of the kitchen to a dining room packed full of hungry Komalsh. Gnomes were assisting Twiggins as he catered to an overcrowded dining room.

The young Lords made their way down the centre isle. They were greeted by all within a handshake's reach.

"Welcome to the family!" shouted a table of Komalsh raising their goblets.

The surrounding Komalsh brothers and sisters raised their goblets high and joined the cheer. A warm feeling of family spread through the young Lords as they seated themselves to an empty table.

Twiggins greeted them. "Good morning, young Lords! Do you know what the best thing about mornings is?"

"No, Twiggins, I really can't answer that." Yawned Trayke.

"Breakfast! The most important meal of the day!" The gnomes served plates of scrambled eggs and an assorted variety of fruits and bread.

"Eat up. There's plenty more!" Twiggins was beaming with pride. "Most important meal of the day!" He repeated while heading to another table.

"Twiggies sure likes his mornings," yawned Arias.

"I don't trust anyone who's that happy this early," yawned Kris.

"He's a well-spoken, walking skeleton. What's not to trust?" Nyte's contribution was sprinkled with sarcasm.

As the new Lords enjoyed their breakfast, Terex asked the question that burned inside each of them. "What do you suppose happened to Kelar, Kolos and Neasha?"

"They failed," answered Nyte coldly.

"Then what became of them?" persisted Terex.

"I'm sure they are fine," answered Kris.

"Can you pass the salt?" interrupted Trayke reaching out his hand. The saltshaker momentarily vibrated then slid across the table and into Trayke's hand.

"Never mind."

"Did you do that purposely?" asked Terex, "like with your mind?"

"I guess so. It just sort of came naturally." Trayke explained what just happened the best he could.

Terex focused on the saltshaker. He reached out his hand and squinted his eyes. The saltshaker started to vibrate then it snapped out of Trayke's hand and moved toward Terex's head. With supernatural reflexes, Twiggins snatched it out of the air.

"Good catch!" clapped Trayke. "Good catch!"

"Way to go, Twiggies!" applauded Arias.

Terex felt embarrassed. "I'm sorry, he said. "Perhaps I need a little more practice."

Twiggins placed the saltshaker on the table. "Not practice you need, no, no. Just time is all. That's all. Your soul is still mapping an unlocked mind. The two-need time…just time."

“So, what you’re saying is I’m adapting and soon will have better control?” Terex had a way with seeking clarification.

“No, no. Control is an illusion. Nobody in the universe has that. You will understand when you see. It is what it is and that’s all that it will be,” riddled Twiggins leaving it for the Lords to figure it out.

Lord Drakus entered the room and sat at the head of their table. A gnome served him breakfast while Twiggins poured juice. “As soon as we’re done here, I’ll show you around Utopia.”

“Utopia?” Trayke had never heard of Utopia.

“Yes, Lord Basa, Utopia is the name of our village,” answered Drakus.

A saltshaker flew across the table and hit Trayke in the forehead.

“What’s wrong with you?” Trayke cursed out loud while holding his forehead.

“I’m sorry.” Terex may have apologized using his words, but everyone could hear his snicker.

King Siris and his Sykanian Knights arrived at the toe of Mount Maximas, Drakonia’s highest peak. A treacherous mountainside of narrow roadways leads through a labyrinth of jagged terrain. This mountain housed Earth’s most dangerous fugitives since the dawn of their arrival. In single file the Sykanians ascended the mountain following the instructions on Malores’ map.

Kelar, Neasha and Kolos had been developing their psychic abilities at an unusually fast pace. Their thorn wounds had healed without a trace, and they were already communicating by thought.

“The old man was eaten by Mimics!” hailed Kelar telepathically.

"I hate those things!" answered Kolos in thought. "They ate my dog!"

"Nobody likes them, Kolos." hailed Neasha. "Nor did we like that stupid dog!"

"Ouch!" Kolos took the comment as an insult.

Siris could sense their telepathic chatter. Pleased by their quick adaptation to the venom's gift he interrupted their hidden conversation aloud. "How's the wrist Kelar?"

Kelar removed the splint Savita made for him at the Arkonian prison. His wrist had completely mended.

"You are pretty much immortal now, son, minus penetration of the heart or brain or my personal favourite, separating the two by decapitation." He grinned in fond memory then added, "You will heal from everything else."

"We know, King Siris. We've studied to become Komalsh our whole lives," reminded Kelar bitterly.

"The Komalsh banished you, Kelar. They'd rather you were dead. They fear how powerful you'll become. They fear the shadow spirit within you."

Kelar recalled the shadow spirit reflection from the pond inside the Mystique Forest. "Where did it come from King Siris?"

"I can tell you that Kolos and Neasha were joined by this blessing while they slept at the Kelasian castle. Lord Demonis and I as well. You, however, Kelar remain a mystery to me."

"I don't find that comforting."

"It is to me," said Siris. "It was your shadow spirit that allowed me to find you three. A powerful presence lay dormant inside you, son. I believe you to be the one who will destroy Malshidiel…the chosen one."

"You still haven't answered the question," persisted Neasha. "Where did they come from?"

"A gift from the universe, Neasha. Since my bonding with this spirit, I have gained an insight and strength far greater than the Komalsh religion had to offer. I understand Malshidiel to be the Darkstar, and I understand it can only be defeated with the help of the shadow spirits."
Kelar, recalling his episode in the Mystique Forest, confessed. "Lord Drakus referred to it as a shadow demon…not spirit."

"The Komalsh religion has blinded him to the truth Kelar," explained Siris.

"I'm confused," added Kolos. "We've been taught our whole lives that Malshidiel is our guardian."

"Propaganda, Kolos. It's how our world is controlled. Don't worry, my young Lords. Soon your dormant spirits will awaken. Then you will understand, as I do, the only truth there is."

After breakfast was finished, Drakus led the young Lords through the castle's front gates and out into the village of Utopia. Several stone-built cottages sat nestled among a flowered landscape. The village cottages and buildings were connected by a maze of soapstone pathways. There were gazebos scattered about and three separate stone bridges crossed the creek. At the mouth of the creek stood a wooden water wheel supplying the castle's aqueducts. On the other side of the creek, farmlands held fruit trees and vegetable gardens. Beyond the vast lake near the edge of the crevasse stood barns for milk cows and coops for chickens. Earth creatures who volunteered their services to the castle roamed freely about pursuing their duties.

Fauns, beings who possesses the legs, tail, and ears of a deer with the body and face appearing close to human like, were scattered about tending to the vast gardens.

Nymphs, who could fit in the palm of your hand, flew carelessly around the fruit trees and hedges enhancing their beauty and health.

Gnomes played an important role as they tended to firewood and castle maintenance.

Kobolds, too, inhibited the castle. These little people, who lived to extremely old ages, cleaned the castle, and tended to the cows, chickens and vegetable gardens. Everything and everyone had a purpose at Castle Malshidiel, a meritocratic society of peace and harmony sheltered from the outside world.

"Welcome to Utopia," announced Lord Drakus with a smile.

Drakus led the new Lords to a dull yet skookum building with a smoking chimney that never quit. "This is where our Komalsh armour and weaponry are made." Spoke Drakus proudly while opening the front door.

Inside they were greeted by two dwarves, a metal smith named Burlok and his apprentice, Grundy.

"Welcome." Growled Grundy.

"You don't look too welcoming," Trayke fired back.

"Don't mind him," assured Drakus. "Grundy always looks that way."

"Welcome to my shop!" Burlok greeted the visitors with the cheerful disposition that his apprentice didn't share. He approached his guests while wiping his hands with a rag. "How can I assist you this fine day, Lord Drakus?"

"We have new Komalsh, Burlok. We'll need swords for each of them." Drakus' pride was self-evident.

"I already have one," reminded Kris.

"What do you mean you already have one?" challenged Burlok with intrigue.

Kris unsheathed the sword he received in the Mystique Forest and handed it to Burlok.

After examining the sword, he understood. "The wonders of the Mystique Forest never cease to amaze. Wouldn't you agree, Lord Drakus?"

"Yes, indeed. This one I don't even want to attempt wrapping my mind around." This was new to Drakus. Burlok wheeled the sword around. "We definitely made it. Funny though, I don't recall doing so. May I ask where you got it?"

"It was a gift from an old man in the Mystique Forest. I believe him to be the older version of me," offered Kris.

"What do you think, Grundy?" Burlok invited his opinion to the conversation.

"I try not to boss. Thinking irritates me," grumbled Grundy.

"Everything irritates you. I mean do you remember making this sword. It's practically new!"
Grundy growled, "No, boss, this is strange indeed."

"Look here, Grundy. This is unusual." Burlok pointed to the blade. "There's a diamond-shaped hole the size of a thumbnail through the blade. What do you suppose that's for?"

"That's very strange, boss." Grundy continued to grumble.

"It's not the strangest thing I've encountered," added Burlok recalling unexplainable moments near the Mystique Forest. "Remember that time it snowed here in the middle of summer. Couldn't believe my eyes!"

"Yes, I recall." Drakus was not happy about recalling how his niece, Milita, was the root cause to that mishap.

"Nevertheless, you're not needed here Kris."

"I, too, have a sword, Burlok," said Nyte.

"Well, I recognize that sword!" smiled Burlok. "I made that one for a special Komalsh indeed! You must be Raine's son."

"Yes, I'm Nyte Shade."

Burlok bowed before him. "I was a close friend to your parents. As a matter of fact, I recall the day they named you. You were just a lump in your mother's belly at the time!" The old dwarf lit up as he smiled over his fond memories. "Nicest people I ever met." Burlok tapped his finger on the pommel of Nyte's holstered sword. "This is a special blade, son. Wield her with honour, Lord Shade."

"I will, Burlok. It was a pleasure to meet you."

"Likewise, and remember, son, I'm here to answer any questions you may have. Don't be a stranger." He smiled with an exaggerated wink.

As Nyte Shade and Kris Tarius left to explore Utopia, Burlok and Grundy assembled the remaining young Lords.

"Well then, newcomers," announced Burlok. "The swords we make here will be individual to each of you. These weapons will define you as the Komalsh you'll become."

"Grundy!" yelled Burlok.

"I'm right beside you, boss," gritted Grundy.

"Prepare the dragon's breath!"

"Yes, boss."

Burlok paced before the young Lords like a drill Sergeant. Holding his hands behind his back, he gave his introductory speech.

"No two swords are the same. We keep to the code of Komalsh design. However, like yourselves, each are special in their own way. The main alloy used is the strongest in all Drakonia. It is a rare metal only found in the caves of the Mystique Forest. We call it durenthium after its founder Lord Duren. Only dragon's breath can reach the temperatures needed to melt the durenthium and with these hands I'll create the sword which will truly define you as Komalsh."

"Follow me!" The old dwarf led the group through a doorway into a high-ceilinged shop. Inside the shop were large anvils and assorted hammers displayed around a work bench. Beside the bench was a forge strong enough to withstand the heat of melted durenthium. Beside that stood a quench tank filled with oil and a slack tub with water—both liquids provided by the Mystique Forest.

Grundy led a young dragon through the outside doors toward the forge.

"Don't be alarmed by this dragon," reassured Burlok. "She's harmless. Her mother was killed by dragon slayers. I took her in and raised her from a hatchling. Her name is Ashes," chuckled the dwarf. "She was named after a few mishaps."

Ashes followed Grundy like a happy puppy. She loved helping and thought the world of the two dwarves. "Wait here," growled Grundy to the dragon.

Ashes was pleased to obey and showed her love by licking his face.

"Your breath stinks," grumbled Grundy.

Ashes hiccupped and out came a burst of flames singeing Grundy's unkept beard.

"Well, that pretty much sums up my day," growled Grundy patting out the flames.

Burlok placed some durenthium into the forge. Then he continued his lecture. "When raw durenthium is mined, it is a shiny black. Once brought to melting point, it transforms into a dark silver."

Burlok wiped his hands clean from the unpolished durenthium. "Now then, lets get started!" He smiled eagerly. "We have plenty of durenthium for everyone."

"Yeah, I already have some," said Arias.

"What do you mean you already have some?" growled Grundy unconvinced.

"I do, look. I found it in the Mystique Forest. I helped a snake in a dream and to make a long story short, I received durenthium out of the deal." Arias ever so calmly shared his story.

"I thought you said only dwarves could find durenthium?" growled Grundy through his singed beard.

"If it can snow in the summer, my apprentice, then anything's possible."

"I hate that story." grumbled Grundy.

"You hate everything!" reminded Burlok cheerfully. Drakus headed to the exit. "I'm needed elsewhere. Good day, my friends."

"Good day, Lord Drakus." The Metalsmith ushered him out with respect and then turned to direct his attention to his first project. "Arias! Bring me your durenthium. It's time to get busy!"

Outside the Metalsmith's doorway, Savita intercepted Nyte and Kris. "Hey, little man. I'm going away now on a special assignment. I'll be gone for quite some time."

"Be safe out there, Savita." Nyte hated to see her go. He would worry for her safety.

"I will. Do you two like your new home?" Both Nyte and Kris smiled in astonishment. "Yes, we do. Utopia is just what it is." They both agreed.

"Good. I will see you when I return." Savita kissed Nyte on the forehead then addressed Kris. "Goodbye, Lord Tarius."

"Goodbye, Lady Cosmos." Kris was flattered with all the formalities.

Kris and Nyte explored the wonders of Utopia. Its flower décor was pleasant to the eyes and the fragrances were sweet to the nose. The soapstone pathways were spacious and wide, connecting the village dwellings like a maze. Fellow Komalsh and Earth creatures alike wandered about performing their daily routines greeting the new Lords as they walked by. Kris and Nyte followed a path toward the creek and crossed the stone bridge nearest to the lake. Halfway across they leaned over the railing and looked about silently, absorbing the wonders of Utopia.

In that silence, Nyte confessed. "I feel guilty about Kelar and the others, Kris. Should we have done more?"

"What more could we have done, Nyte? We passed, they failed. It is what it is. I'm just thankful we made it." Kris looked out into the cow pastures. Short red bearded Kobolds were herding cattle into barns for milking. "I think we need to focus on the now, Nyte. We are Komalsh! Just look at this place…it's surreal."

Nyte stared down the creek's current toward the mouth of the lake where a large wooden water wheel stood. "I do agree, Kris. Its like living in a dream."

"Speaking of dreams, look over there, Nyte!" Kris pointed toward the lake. "Mermaids!"

The two jogged down the stone path toward the lake's beach.

****

As students of Olemeeze, they studied all Earth creatures (Mythicals) including these aquatic beauties. However, few Drakonians had ever actually seen a mermaid in person.

****

The mermaids swam to shore greeting the young Lords. Flirtatiously, they waved. The young Lords stood on the beach and waved in return. When the mermaids swam into clear view, both Kris and Nyte slowly stopped waving and their expressions of excitement dimmed. The schoolbooks they studied portrayed mermaids as beautiful women. These must have been prepared by a drunken artist with an exaggerated imagination, for the human part of these creatures shared little likenesses with those images.

Kris was most disappointed by what he saw. "It's not how I imagined, Nyte."

Nyte concurred. "Yeah, their human part doesn't look very human, does it?"

****

The mermaid's fish tails were an amazing assortment of rainbow reflective scales with wide fins. Their human half, however, was not as romantic as fantasized. Their blue scaly skin was coarse to the touch. They had enlarged gills on either side of their throats. Their eyes, like those of a cod fish, showed no romance and their lake-slimed hair was nothing you'd want to run your fingers through.

****

Nyte smiled pleasantly. "Good morning, ladies!"

"Good morning!" They giggled.

"What are you lovely ladies up to today?" added Kris accepting his disappointment.

The six mermaids swam in close together giggling nervously. "We're gathering fish for Twiggins," answered one flirtatiously biting off a trout's head.

Another of the mermaids blurted out, “We aren’t supposed to eat them!” Being shy but suddenly more outspoken than anticipated, the mermaid hid behind the others bashfully.

“What are your names?” asked Kris.

“You wouldn’t be able to pronounce them,” spoke the shy one still hiding behind the others.

“You’re cute!” giggled the fish biter whose smile revealed a mouth full of long transparent fangs.

“Alright, alright! Enough flirting with the help.” shouted Twiggins walking knee high into the water. “Well, ladies, where’s todays catch?”

The mermaids each revealed a net full of live trout.

“Nicely done! Hey, wait a moment…this one has no head.”

The guilty mermaid looked downward with her arms crossed behind her back.

“No worries, dear. There’s plenty here to go around. Thank you, my fair ladies, for all the fish. I will cook them tonight!” Twiggins joyously made his words sound like a song.

“You’ll ruin them!” spoke the shyest one poking her head out from behind the others.

“The Komalsh aren’t fond of eating their fish alive,” explained Twiggins.

The mermaids looked to each other and giggled.

“That’s weird,” spoke the shyest.

With that, the mermaids swam off into the lake waving to the young Lords singing, “Bye boys!” as they flirtatiously vanished into its depths.

Milita Drakus stood on her uncle’s balcony. From a distance she could see Twiggins down at the lake conversing with two Komalsh she didn’t recognize.

"Good morning, Mili," smiled Drakus stepping out onto the balcony. "Did you sleep well?"

"I did sleep well, uncle."

"Are you packed for the trip? Where are your things, Mili?"

"My things are down in my chambers." She was not happy. She was content to stay.

"Is there something bothering you, Mili?"

"I don't want to leave you, uncle. I'm afraid I'll never see you again!"

Hirum held his niece close. "I love you dearly, Mili. I assure you everything will be fine." He released his grip and stared into her soft green eyes. "Now go on and grab your things."

Lady Savita Cosmos stepped out onto the balcony. "Good morning, Mili!" Her smile grew as she spoke.

"Savita! Good morning! Are you coming with me?"

"Of course, Mili. I will be your guardian. Come now. Let's gather your things."

Savita followed Mili to her chambers where they prepared her things for the travels ahead.

"Is that everything?" asked Savita staring at one little bag.

"I guess so." Mili shrugged. She wasn't sure. She had no experience with such an undertaking.

Savita sat down next to her. "Now, now, my dear everything will be fine. I will not leave your side, Mili. Just the two of us in a castle filled with overly educated, boring elves."

Militа giggled. "Yeah. However, I am looking forward to their library."

"The largest in all Drakonia," added Savita.

"I heard they even have books from Earth!"

"Yes, they do," answered Savita.

"You've been there?"

"Yes, Mili, during my sorcery apprenticeship under Kudos Nexus all my literary studies were done at the Elvin library."

"You've lived an interesting life."

"I've lived a boring one, Mili." Downplayed the sorceress who'd spent most of her childhood studying and training.

Milita changed the subject abruptly. "I saw two of the new Lords from uncle's balcony this morning."

"Wow, Mili. Your mind is all over the place today!" Mili smiled. "Are they cute? I couldn't tell from that distance."

"Milita Drakus!" Savita was not going to play into being a matchmaker. "You have other priorities for now. Stay focused."

"I'm a woman now and I have needs." She bit her bottom lip. "I'd love to meet that special someone."

"I'm sure you will eventually, Mili."

"Why didn't you ever marry, Savita?"

"Never met the right person, I suppose."

"Have you ever been with anyone? You know, with someone special."

Savita smiled.

"You have!" Mili smiled in return. "Who?"

"There have been a couple, you little brat. But the Komalsh and my adopted son have swayed me away from that kind of commitment."

"How old is your son?"

"He'd be a year older than you, so seventeen."

"What does he do? Is he handsome?" She pushed.

"Milita!"

Mili persisted. "I would love to meet him."

Lord Drakus entered her room and interrupted the conversation. "I'm sure you'll meet him one day, Mili. Now come, ladies. Pegasus has arrived."

"Pegasus? I thought we were riding?" said Mili.

"Flying is the quickest and safest passage, my dear," explained her uncle.

"What about Stormy?" asked Mili.

"I've made arrangements with Twiggins to tend to your unicorn while you were away. Now come. Pegasus awaits you on the balcony."

****

Pegasus was a white winged horse who was one of two offspring to Medusa. After Perseus beheaded Medusa, the winged horse sprang fully developed from her headless body.

His journey through life had offered many adventures with a rider named Bellerophon. Together they rid the terrorized Lycian communities of a chimaera—a fire breathing monster with a lion's head, goat's body, and a serpent's tail. They would also defeat the Amazons, fierce female warriors who terrorized the coastline of Syria. Bellerophon would then fly Pegasus to Olympus to take his place among the gods. In the process he lost his life to Zeus who took Pegasus for his own using him to carry his thunderbolts. Shortly after arriving on Drakonia, Pegasus became an ally of Lord Duren and the Komalsh. For over a thousand years, he too awaited Malshidiel's return.

Although this flying horse would take lengths to avoid human contact, including most Komalsh, Pegasus took a shining to Savita ever since the day they were introduced by the sorcerer Kudos Nexus.

****

While Savita loaded Pegasus with their gear, Lord Drakus said his farewells to Milita. "The elves will guide you through your times to come. Please accept their wisdom, Mili."

"Alright Uncle, but I hate leaving you."

"Milita, promise me you won't get into any trouble while you're there."

"Yes, Uncle." She smiled with an air of obedience.

"Milita!" Drakus could tell she was insincere.

"Alright, I promise!" She spoke with a struggle. "You promise me Stormy will be okay!"

"I promise. Goodbye, Mili. I love you." Lord Drakus held her tight. Tighter than he'd ever held her before.

"Goodbye, Uncle Hirum." Milita could not hold back her tears.

Savita mounted Pegasus. She extended her hand down to Mili who pulled herself up onto the winged horse. With a smile Milita waved down to her uncle and he up to her. "I'll make you proud!"

"I already am, Mili. I always will be." Her uncle waved as they departed.

With a swift leap the winged horse flew off into the sunny sky.

On the grounds of Utopia by the lakes shore, Kris Tarius gazed into the sky. "You won't believe this, Nyte. They even have flying horses!"

"Pegasus!" exclaimed Nyte.

Kris was impressed. "This place is amazing! I've never seen so many Earth creatures in one area."

While Nyte watched the winged horse fly, he focused on the rider and felt her heartbeat. "Savita?"

Another heartbeat appeared behind her. Nyte focused closely onto it. "Who's that?"

Nyte grasped the ring of smiles on the chain that hung from his neck. "I recognize her…"

Up in the castle tower a knock echoed from Lord Drakus' door. Behind it stood Lord Dunlam. His face appeared weathered with sadness.

"What is it, Bossel?"

"Lady Tuza and Lord Jamala are dead, my lord. Their bodies were found just outside the Mystique Forest perimeter. The surrounding foot and hoof prints indicated a small army of about 40. The prints next to their bodies, however, indicated they lost in a sword fight against only one opponent. The bodies were then stripped of their clothes and weapons."

Drakus rubbed his chin. "What of the failed students?"

"All three are missing, my lord." Bossel's expression broadened. "A war is brewing, Hiram, and I believe Cretes Siris to be stirring it."

"Understood, Bossel. Prepare an evening memorial for the deceased. I will prepare a speech."

"As you wish, my lord."

Drakus closed his door, then leaned against it. "The war has already begun, my friend."

Chapter XVIII
The Charm of Dosania.

By late afternoon, Pegasus and his two passengers had flown a great distance. To avoid the Sykanian kingdom, they travelled over the Avila Mountain Range toward the Western Sea. This treacherous range of jagged mountain separated a rainforest known as Jirasab from the rest of Drakonia. Jirasab was the dragon homeland.

"Isn't this the Avila Mountain Range?"

"It's okay," assured Savita. "We're on the safe side."

"Safer side," mumbled Mili.

Savita squeezed her hand. "It's okay, Mili. Dragons normally stay in the protection of Jirasab…usually."

Pegasus soared above the Avila Mountain Range. Behind them the White Sea faded in the distance. Below them were the jagged peaks of the mountains and ahead an uncertain future.

Suddenly, a terrible screeching sound ripped through the air. Savita pointed toward a crevasse on a flattened mountain top where a thick net tangled over a rock hung down into the dark depths of the crevasse. "Over there Pegasus!"

Savita landed the winged horse and dismounted. Cautiously, she approached the crevasse when another roar escaped its depths followed by a burst of flames.

"What's the netting for?" queried Mili.

"It's a dragon trap," whispered Savita.

"But it's so small," remarked Mili.

"It's designed for younglings. Wait here, Mili. I'll be right back." Savita leaned over the crevasse and looked down into the darkness. A deep growl rumbled below.

"Be careful!" whispered Mili.

Savita scaled down the netting. The further she descended, the darker it became. Now completely submerged in darkness she could see two glowing eyes peering from the depths below. A deep rumbled growl filled the darkness followed by a burst of flames engulfing the crevasse walls. With the aide of the light emanating from the flames, Savita saw a rare full-grown Silverback dragon. It was hung upside down with its wing tangled in the netting. Then the flames diminished, and the crevasse returned to darkness.

"A Silverback dragon!" Savita was astonished.

"What did you expect? A mermaid, perhaps?" The dragon replied with a trace of sarcasm.

"I'm here to help you. I'm a Komalsh. Are you okay?"

"Oh, just wonderful…and you?" Sarcastically replied the depressed dragon dangling from the netting.

"I'm going to cut you free," cautioned Savita.

"I suggest you untangle my wing first. I'd rather not fall to my death."

"It's too dark to see. I'm going to use a spell. Would you please close your eyes for a moment? I don't want to blind you."

"Are you claiming to be a Komalsh and a sorceress?" The dragon was intrigued but obediently closed his eyes.

"What a dull childhood you must have had."

Savita raised her hands above her head and with her palms pointed upward she concentrated. Her body began emanating a blue aura followed by a bright blue flash. The energy released became absorbed into the surrounding inanimate objects. Vision was temporally restored.
Savita climbed down the illuminated netting to the dragon's tangled wing. Using her dagger, she started to cut the netting around it.

Mili stood staring into the crevasse. "What was that blue flash about, Pegasus?"

Before Pegasus could reply, the hairs on Milita's neck stood up. She felt the presence of others and turned to greet them. A gang of dragon slayers emerged from the rock face.

"Who are you and what could you possibly be doing to our trap?" Milita assumed this to be the voice of their leader—a voice that sounded annoyed.

"I am Lady Drakus of the Komalsh."

The leader cringed while shaking his head. "Well, that's no good, no good at all. You see, we don't care too much for your kind. Your bleeding-heart religion is bad for our way of life. Allow me to offer a proper introduction. I am Monty, leader of this fine dragon slaying family."
Milita gently caressed the hilt of her sword. "I cannot allow you to slaughter innocent younglings. Surrender now and no harm will come to you."

The dragon slayers found humour in her words.

"Innocent?" laughed Monty. "They're vicious predators!"

The largest of the slayers rested a club on his shoulder. He stepped closer to Milita and looked down at her. "I have a family to feed!"

"Yes, and so do dragons." Mili stood firm. "There are more honourable ways to make a living."

"I suppose you're right," grinned Monty. "However, nothing else pays quite as well. Isn't that right, boys?"

A cheer spread through the rowdy slayers.

"I see you have a winged horse," said Monty. "I'm sure there's a good market for one of those, too!"

The dragon slayers drew out their weapons.

Monty issued a threat: "Surrender the winged horse or die. This is a one-time offer, princess."

Lady Drakus unsheathed her sword. "Nobody calls me, princess!"

The larger dragon slayer wheeled his club high and smashed down at Milita with all his strength. Mili casually stepped to the side and watched the club crush the ground. Using her sword, she twisted her blade around the club and tossed it down the crevasse. With seemingly unnatural speed and strength Milita thrusted her sword through his stomach lifting him into the air. The dragon slayer screamed in agony as she tossed him down into the crevasse. Milita stood in a combat stance as the remaining twelve dragon slayers moved to attack.

Meanwhile, down the crevasse …

"Almost through the net," assured Savita. "Just a little bit more."

A club fell from above and grazed the dragon's head. He shouted out, "What are you doing up there, Savita?"

"What is she doing up there?" asked Savita to herself. A large man came falling, disappearing into the dark depths of the crevasse.

"I hope that wasn't anyone you knew," said the dragon.

Savita looked up and telepathically hailed Milita. "What's going on up there!"

"I'm a little busy at the moment!" replied Milita thrusting her sword through the chest of a dragon slayer.

Savita finished cutting through the last bit of tangled netting and freed the dragon's wing. She scaled up the net to a ledge in the rock. Stowing her dagger, she unsheathed her sword and cut the main rope holding the trap. The dragon disappeared into the darkness.

Savita felt the danger above and leaped to the top of the crevasse with her sword drawn. There stood Mili and Pegasus surrounded by twelve dead dragon slayers.

Savita put her sword away. "I can see why Lord Drakus locked you up in a castle all those years."
Mili rolled her eyes. "They weren't interested in diplomacy, Savita. Isn't that right, Pegasus?"
Pegasus nodded his head in agreement.

With an explosion of dust, a Silverback dragon emerged from the crevasse. Its wings were spread wide, and its roar fierce as he gracefully landed before them. Understanding the unpredictability of dragons, Savita stood between Mili and the predator. Even Pegasus took a combat stance.

The dragon stared down at them. His expression turned peaceful. "Thank you for your assistance."

"You're welcome," replied Savita.

"Allow me to introduce myself. My name is Stratos," spoke the dragon.

Savita's eyes widened. "You are legendary!"

"I believe the appropriate reply to an introduction would be sharing one's name," informed the dragon.

"Sorry." She knew she had embarrassed herself. "I'm Lady Savita Cosmos. This is Lady Milita Drakus and, of course, you know Pegasus."

"I see, and who are your lazy friends?" gestured Stratos to the dead.

"What happened, Mili?" Savita asked.

"It was self defence, I swear!" defended Mili.

"Yes, it appears you self defenced all over the place," added Stratos with a trace of sarcasm.

Mili stared at the ground. "It wasn't my fault."

"I'm not angry with you," assured Savita. "I trust your better judgment. I'm just upset. I should've never left you alone."

"I can take care of myself." Mili spoke with confidence.

I concur with Lady Drakus," intervened Stratos. "Perhaps, Lady Cosmos, you should consider protecting everyone else instead."

"I know you can take care of yourself, Mili." calmed Savita. "I just don't know how I'm to explain this to Lord Drakus."

Stratos needed to excuse himself and be on his way. "Well, as thrilled as I am to the outcome of your quandary, I have more pressing matters to attend. Thank you once again, Lady Savita Cosmos."

"Wait! How did a legendary dragon like yourself get caught in a youngling trap?" Milita was curious.

"Well, I've been covering this whole mountainside as of late," answered Stratos, "purposely setting off these traps in the hope of protecting our young. Evidently, I got clumsy with this one."

Stratos leaned his head down to Savita's eye level. "Can you explain why you keep referring to me as…legendary?"

Savita felt star struck. "You were the one who gave Lady Shade, *The Book of Dragons*, were you not?"

"The same," answered Stratos.

"That makes you legendary to us. And that was the last time you were seen."

"Yes, a sad day that was for Lady Shade," recalled Stratos. "She had lost her husband during that final dragon war. If it weren't for the bravery of Lord Shade and the Komalsh, the tyranny of the Dragon's Flute would have ravaged Drakonia."

"Yes, it was a tragic loss of life." Savita would forever remember the day her parents died.

"How is Lady Shade?" asked Stratos.

"She passed away," answered Savita.

"My uncle says she's still alive. Actually, he just said it was complicated," revealed Mili.

Savita's stomach dropped. "Then where is she, Mili?"

"I don't know. He just said it was complicated," repeated Milita. "I'm not sure I understand all the secrecy."

Stratos was not expecting this. "A complication, indeed. Who is your uncle, Milita?"

"Lord Hirum Drakus is," she bragged.

"Interesting. It was he and Lord Demonis whom I returned to Lady Shade that day."

"Once again, why you're a legend," reminded Milita.

Stratos spread his wings for flight. "Again, thank you, Lady Savita Cosmos. Perhaps the day will come when I can repay your good deed. Until then, I bid you farewell." With a powerful leap Stratos flew off into the cloudy skies.

Savita watched Stratos disappear into the clouds. Distressed she telepathically hailed Lord Drakus.

"Does Lady Raine Shade still live?"

Moments passed but Drakus did not reply.

Without hope for resolution, Savita focused on the job at hand. They mounted Pegasus and flew toward Dosania, the birthplace of Milita and the Drakus bloodline.

Pegasus flew safely past the Avila Mountain Range and headed north along the western coastline. Before nightfall they arrived at Castle Dosania.

After unpacking the winged horse, Savita kissed his nose. "See you in the morning, Pegasus." Then the winged horse flew off to the safety of a nearby mountain top. King Kalem Turek and his son, Prince Adonis, waited for Pegasus to leave before greeting their guests. The Dosanians lived by the Komalsh religion and with it the education and respect of all Earth creatures. The shyness of Pegasus was taught to them as children. Always give the winged horse space.

"Welcome to Dosania, Lady Cosmos," greeted King Turek. "Lord Drakus has informed us of Milita's growing importance. It's a great honour to assist the Komalsh during these historical times."

"We are grateful for your hospitality, King Turek." Savita smiled fondly to the king. She'd known him since she was a child.

Turek gave Savita a big hug. "Enough with the formalities, Savita. I miss you so much my dear!"

"I miss you, too, Kalem."

King Turek welcomed Milita. "My you have grown, child! I remember Adonis, my son, and you playing together when you were no higher than my knee."

Adonis apologized to Milita. "I'm sorry for my father. He doesn't realize how embarrassing he is."

"That is quite fine," giggled Mili.

"Allow me to welcome you home Milita. You must be famished. Please follow me. I'll show you to a good meal and, if interested, some good old Dosanian festivities." Adonis offered his charming smile.

Milita blushed. "I'd like that very much!"

The king joined the conversation. "Go have a good time, Mili. You've been cooped up in Castle Malshidiel for far too long. Isn't that right, Savita?"

"Yes, I suppose it couldn't hurt," agreed Savita reluctantly.

"As for you, Savita." Turek wrapped his arm around her, "You and I have much catching up to do!"

Outside the castle walls were dark and dreary from a heavy downpour of rain. Inside the King's living room, Savita nestled warm and dry on an enormous couch enjoying the luxuries of royalty. Across from her sat King Turek drinking mead from his golden chalice. They spent the evening catching up with each other's lives and recalled fond memories. When the logs in the fireplace burnt down to embers a memory of Savita's resurfaced—the night she lost, *The Book of Malshidiel*, to Cretes Siris a decade ago. Savita had promised to return it. It was a promise she never kept.

"Siris must still have the book." Savita proclaimed.

"I would suspect so, Savita," agreed Turek. "With him back from the dead you may still have a chance to reclaim it."

"I will reclaim it." She vowed.

"What of Milita Drakus?" Turek took an abrupt detour. "Is she the one to awaken Malshidiel?"

"Lord Drakus believes her to be," answered Savita as though she read it from a book.

"What do you believe?"

"I don't know. She's filled with so much anger toward God and the religions who worship. I feel she may be too conflicted to awaken an angel sent by God. It seems contradictory."

King Turek drank down his mead. He wiped the spillage from his beard, then shared his pearls of wisdom. "The many different religions have divided the people of Drakonia, Savita. There is only one God, yet they discriminate and kill one another. I don't blame Milita for feeling conflicted."

"Yes, I agree. However, our Komalsh teachings differ from the ones who commonly follow versions of Earth's religious text. For one, our belief is of God being the universe that awaits our return as opposed to one with rules determining who will go to heaven and who will burn in hell. It's atrocious to think the great creator of life would have no mercy on his creations."

"Atrocious as it may be," defended the king, "it still exists. The many translations of one book through different eyes has created Drakonia's many different religions. Milita understands this through what she's learned. But keep in mind she lost her parents at a young age. A heart broken by God's plan is not an easy mend."

"But she has read Malshidiel's teachings. She understands our souls are nurtured within these bodies to embrace and learn all life's experiences. They are meant to take with us when we pass on and become one with the universe. We don't believe in heaven or hell, and we understand God is an infinite energy that has little influence during our stay in the realm of time. Everything that happens to us is the result of the universal connection of all living creatures whose decisions weave the fabric of life. Life is holistic. The death of her parents was tragic, yes. But she is a victim of circumstance not God. God doesn't create the life you live. You live the life you create in the boundaries of a world you cannot control."

"Sometimes it takes more than reading scripture to accept it, Savita. The lessons we learn here can take a lifetime to accept. My people have followed the Komalsh religion since the beginning of Dosania. But it's one thing to believe it and yet another to live it."

"I know, but in Milita's eyes, life would seem to be unfair."

"I understand her confusion when such atrocities of violence are bestowed on God's disciples. She is young yet, Savita. She just needs time to come to grips with it."

"I do understand how she feels," admitted Savita. "When my parents died, I felt a part of me die with them. I had always hoped they could hear me when I spoke to them and when I said I loved them, I could almost hear them whisper it back to me. I felt empty and alone. If it weren't for the friendship of Lady Raine Shade, I don't know what I'd done."

"Perhaps you should do the same for Milita," suggested King Turek.

"I see your point. However, Mili has a rage far darker than I ever did. Lord Drakus believes only the Elves counsel can help her."

"She will still need a friend, Savita."

After dinner, Prince Adonis gave Milita the royal tour of the castle. Sheltered for a decade under the safety of Castle Malshidiel, Milita felt like a stranger within the community, architecture and even decor of her Dosanian birthplace. Things are very different here. She had been born into a fellowship of dark-skinned peoples who followed the Komalsh religion. Milita always felt a longing for her heritage while living in the multi-cultural Komalsh society of Utopia. It was a longing that brought an enormous smile to her face as she toured through the castle. Milita was enthralled with the beauty that surrounded her. Its interior decorated with pillars and statures of angels and peaceful creatures. The ceilings were covered in artwork telling the stories of famous Dosanians. Milita also took a shining to the prince. He was charming and sensitive with a soothing voice that melted her heart.

"This place is beautiful, Prince Adonis."

"Please, just call me Adonis." He begged. "And thank you for complementing our castle, Milita. We Dosanians take pride in our surroundings. A clean peaceful environment encourages a positive lifestyle."

"It certainly does." Milita's heart was warmed. Her face glowed.

"Outside our protected walls can be a dangerous cycle of depression. Inside our walls we have only peace and tranquility."

"I remember little of my childhood," admitted Milita. "In some ways I feel like a stranger to this place."

"You are born of Dosania, Milita. We are your roots. If you ever decide to leave the Komalsh, our doors here will always be open," assured the prince.

Adonis led Milita to her room. "This was the room where you and your parents lived, Milita. Other than its upkeep, nothing has been moved or changed."

Milita's eyes watered. But she wouldn't release a tear.

"Inside the wardrobe, you'll find your mother's ballroom dresses." The prince charmed her with his smile.

"I would so much like to be your date for tonight's ballroom dance."

"A dance?" Milita knew nothing about a dance. The moment felt awkward.

"Yes, the Komalsh do know how to dance, do they not?"

"Well, yes, the Komalsh are educated in all the fine arts. It defines us as civilized. It's just I, well, I…have never been asked on a date before."

"Never? But you are so beautiful and vibrant." Adonis gently grasped her hand and kissed it. "Would you, Milita Drakus, allow me to escort you to the ball?"

"I'd love to!" She blurted uncontrollably. In fact, her words did not match his question.

"I'm delighted," smiled the prince. "I will see you shortly."

"See you soon, Adonis." Mili entered her room and closed the door. Inside she leaned against it giving a muffled cheer. "He's so cute!

Across the room stood her mother's wardrobe. Beside that was a tub filled with hot soapy water. Milita searched through her mother's dresses. After choosing what to wear she stripped out of her Komalsh robes and light armour and sank into the tub.

Savita stared out the king's window, watching the downpour of rain channel through the streets.

"Kalem," Savita started anxiously. "Milita mentioned that Lady Raine Shade wasn't dead. Lord Drakus said nothing more than that it was complicated."

“Then where would she be?” King Kalem Turek appeared honestly shocked at the news.

“So, you know nothing of this?” interrogated Savita.

“I’m afraid not, my dear. This comes as a complete surprise to me as well.”

“Perhaps it’s better we keep this our secret for now, Kalem. I don’t want Nyte to find out. Not until I can validate its truth.”

“Have you asked Lord Drakus?” wondered Turek.

“I haven’t been able to reach him. Telepathic communication has been compromised since the Fenka Rek murders. He won’t respond to my hails.”

“Then perhaps the Elvin elders could shed some light” suggested King Turek.

“Perhaps. I think I’ll go wander the castle, your majesty. I need to settle down if I’m to get any sleep.”

“Have a good night, Lady Cosmos. As always, your secret is safe with me.”

After bathing, Mili put on the dress she chose and admired herself in front of a tall mirror. She glowed with excitement at the beauty of her mother’s dress. While looking into the mirror she noticed a painting on the wall behind her. It was a portrait of her departed parents. She turned to admire its intricate detail. They were posing with their wedding rings. Her father’s ring was shaped like a quarter moon, her mother’s, like the sun. Milita remembered Uncle Hirum explaining why they chose those rings. *“A perfect balance, Mili, where one is in constant chase of the other and both believed to be the chaser.”* Milita’s eyes teared.

In the corner of the room was a small bed. It was hers as a child. She pictured her mother reading bedtime stories to her. Her mother was a loving woman. She was a member of the court and sister to Lord Drakus. Milita pictured her father painting that very portrait. He was a famous artist, his work praised by Dosanian critics as a beacon of peace. He was a kind humane man. A loving father and husband. We were a happy family. Until the tragic day their lives were taken. Milita saddened. She wouldn't cry. Her parents' murderers didn't deserve her tears. They only deserved her cold blade. She will find them, and she will gut them. Milita reached for her sword and swung it around. Even in a dress she wheeled her blade with the finesse of a warrior.

A sudden knock came from her door. Milita replaced her scowl with a smile then answered the door. Outside stood Prince Adonis in his ballroom suit.

"You look beautiful, Milita!"

"Thank you, Adonis, so do you…or I mean, you look handsome." She corrected nervously.

Adonis noticed Milita's sword in her hand. "It's a ballroom, Milita…not a battlefield." He held out his elbow and charmed her with a smile.

Milita placed her sword against the wall and reached for Adonis's inviting arm. The prince escorted her to the ballroom.

When entering the ballroom Milita was astonished by the beauty of its décor. The dance floor was made of polished marble. There were elegantly crafted tables placed around the dance floor accompanied by beautifully dressed men and women. Paintings decorated the walls and sculptures were on display. Against the back wall stood a stage reserved for a stringed band which played the most melodic music Milita had ever heard.

An usher stepped forward raising a red flag. Around the room, guards took notice and raised their red flags signaling silence. The music stopped and all the ballroom patrons stood at attention.

"Ladies and gentlemen, it is my great pleasure to announce the arrival of Prince Adonis and Lady Drakus." The crowd applauded the couple with smiles and cheers. The prince waved his hand in return while displaying his perfect smile and announcing, "Let the festivities continue."

The music continued and the party resumed. Adonis led Milita to his royal table where the most prestigious of Dosanian nobles sat. After brief introductions by the prince, they sat in their respective places. Beside Milita sat a beautiful young woman who, too, adored the prince. Keeping with pleasantries, Milita reached out her hand while introducing herself.

"Hello, I'm Mili."

The woman stared coldly at Milita. After eyeing her up, she raised her hand and returned the gesture. "I'm Myrrha."

Milita didn't need her psychic abilities to know how Myrrha felt toward her. Her cold shoulder brought discomfort to an already awkward moment. This was quite evident to the others who sat at their table too. Unwilling to ruin the evening, Milita ignored her unpleasant vibes.
"Would you care for some wine?" offered a servant while successfully extinguishing the awkward moment.
"I would love some!" Milita welcomed the moment.
After the servant filled her goblet, Milita grabbed it with both hands and drank it down fast.

"That was delicious. Could I have another?"

Amused by her behavior the servant refilled her goblet. "Perhaps, my lady, you should enjoy it but slower."

"Oh, yes." Milita blushed. "Sorry, I'm a little nervous," she confided. "Don't be alarmed though. I can't get drunk. It's a Komalsh thing."

Myrrha rolled her eyes. "Barbarian." She lashed out while leaving to the dance floor.

Milita glared back while reaching for her sword. Then remembered she didn't bring it.

"What a bitch!" Milita quietly cursed Myrrha under her breath.

"That she is, my lady," agreed the servant.

Mili giggled with embarrassment. "You weren't supposed to hear that!"

The servant winked an exaggerated wink and lowered his voice saying, "I've forgotten already, my lady."

"What is your name?" asked Milita.

"I am Tobias, my lady." He bowed.

"Well, Tobias, I'm glad one person in this room knows how much I dislike that woman."

"I am delighted to be that person, my lady."

"Milita. Would you care to dance?" The prince held out his hand.

"Okay!" She looked into his eyes and smiled. Taking her hand, the prince led her on to the ballroom floor. Nervously, Milita followed his lead trying carefully not to step on his feet.

"You seem nervous, Milita. Please, try to relax and, perhaps, you'll enjoy yourself more," suggested Adonis. Milita fell prisoner to the prince's soothing voice and felt captivated by his soft brown eyes. Melting into his arms, she smiled blissfully.

"That's better." The prince returned her smile. "Your green eyes are so unique, Milita. Your red hair like silk. Your smell intoxicating." The prince held her closer.

"I adore you, Milita."

Mili fell for the moment allowing her warrior heart to be completely defenceless. She adored the prince. She even contemplated love.

Across the dance floor, Myrrha glared at her. Infuriated she guided her dance partner toward Milita and the prince.

While serving wine Tobias watched as the two dance couples came closer together. "Oh no!" he gasped.

As the dance couples collided, Myrrha extended her leg and tripped the love-struck Milita to the ground. As she sprawled on the dance floor, the prince knelt beside her. "Are you okay, Milita!"

The music came to a grinding stop. The Ballroom patrons gathered around mumbling in audible murmurs. Myrrha hovered over Milita with a sinister smile. Then she backed away slowly as Tobias pushed his way through to help the prince return her to her feet.

Enraged Mili approached Myrrha hastily. Then realizing all eyes were watching, she regained her poise "I'm sorry, Myrrha. I must have tripped over your fat ankle."

"Fat ankle? My ankles aren't fat!"

"Excuse me!" interrupted the prince before things could escalate. "No harm was done. Shall we sit down for some wine, Milita?" The prince offered her his arm and escorted Milita back to the table. The music continued and the dance resumed.

Tobias refilled Milita's goblet. "Do not let her ruin you're evening, my lady. She is a troublesome character if I may."

"Troublesome? I'd like to punch her out!" stewed Mili.

"As inviting as that would be, my lady, I'd strongly suggest a more civil approach." Tobias appealed to her for reason in her response.

"I'll show her civil," grumbled Mili.

When the song ended, Myrrha returned from the dance floor and sat next to Milita. There the two exchanged dirty looks. The prince, who was occupied with entertaining others at the table, seemed oblivious to the tension escalating by the two ladies.

"Where did you find that dress, my dear?" Myrrha did not hide her offensive tone. "I believe it went out of fashion during the dark ages." She snickered while enticing others to join her.

"It was my mother's."

"Indeed," scoffed Myrrha. "And those green eyes of yours. So unfortunate for people who live life burdened with deformities. You must have a difficult time facing a mirror."

Milita stood speechless and saddened as others joined Myrrha's condescending comments with laughter.

"If I may, my ladies." Tobias had remained near Milita and jumped in attempting to neutralize the mockery. "Dosanians are a brown-eyed dominant peoples. However, green eyes, as rare as they are, shouldn't be considered a deformity but rather a uniqueness. A powerful trait when one judges art, is it not?"

"Shouldn't you be serving drinks," snarled Myrrha. "Imagine that…a servant claiming to know anything about art!" Myrrha and her friends laughed in Tobias' face.

Tobias' eyes moistened. "But of course, my lady. I'm sorry to have intruded."

"Just don't let it happen again!" ordered Myrrha while holding out her empty goblet. "It appears you can barely do the job you are meant to do!"

"My apologies." Tobias adopted a cowering stance while refilling her wine.

“You see my dress?” Myrrha made certain all at the table could hear her. “Crafted by the finest seamstress in our kingdom. Daddy paid handsomely for it.” Myrrha stood and turned around gracefully to exhibit its white beauty. “Perhaps, I will give it to you, Milita…when it’s out of fashion, of course.” She giggled a sly giggle.

Milita was enraged. She pictured punching Myrrha in the lips…several times. But knew the outcome would only aide Myrrha’s plot to steal the prince’s hand. So instead, she waited for opportunity. That opportunity soon arrived when Myrrha placed the goblet toward her lips. Milita telekinetically tilted the goblet prematurely causing red wine to spill down the front of her beautiful white dress. Myrrha panicked in embarrassment. “You did this, didn’t you, Milita!” She pointed with accusation.

Mili shrugged her shoulders.

“You are just jealous of me!” whimpered Myrrha with dry tears.

“Perhaps you’re just losing your motor skills.” suggested Mili. “I read once that it was typical for people with enlarged ankles.”

“Yes, my lady, I’ve read that, too,” defended Tobias.

“I’ve not heard such a thing.” Prince Adonis’ attention was diverted when he saw the wine spill.

“My ankles are not fat!” shouted Myrrha attracting a crowd. “This was you Milita!”

Mili used her psychic gift again forcing Myrrha to slap herself. The crowd stared at Myrrha in confusion. Myrrha stood dumfounded. Then Mili did it again twice more while repeating in a mocking tone. “Quit slapping yourself, quit slapping yourself.”

“It appears your enlarged ankles are giving you quite a beating.” Tobias couldn’t resist weighing in.

Speaking directly to Prince Adonis, she delivered her threat. “I want that servant imprisoned now or you will hear from my father!”

Then she slapped herself again.

"Are you feeling, okay?" asked the prince.

"I am just fine!" she bellowed. Then she slapped herself again.

Tobias's eyes dampened with sadness were now replaced with joy.

"Put that man in prison now!" cried Myrrha.

"Make it so," ordered Adonis to the guards.

Milita raised her hand and telekinetically unsheathed a guard's sword into her hand. Standing in front of Tobias, she held the sword out for combat.

"I will not let you arrest him!" she threatened.

The music once again came to a grinding halt. The room once again mumbled with murmurs. The guards backed away and the prince stood confused.

Milita could feel the intensity of the room. All eyes were on her while wearing a long dress with a sword drawn…at a ballroom dance…not good.

She could never get comfortable with the dress. But the sword felt right. She looked around to take note of the beautiful people. They were all afraid. Milita had disrupted their peace and tranquility. Or was it that she had just disrupted the illusion that the Dosanians surrounded themselves with.

Milita didn't belong here. Milita didn't know where she belonged.

Lady Savita Cosmos stood at the ballroom entrance. She had witnessed it all. Mili could feel her psychic stare. Her disappointment. Savita turned and left the ballroom. She was too tired to deal with anything.

Adonis took Milita by the hand and led her away from the crowd. She tossed the guard's sword to the ground. "I'm so sorry to ruin your evening, Adonis. I just couldn't let that woman get away with this. Tobias is innocent."

"That is quite fine, Milita, and for the record, Myrrha has many issues. However, fat ankles aren't one of them." The prince smiled as he tried to make light of a matter that had grown too intense.

Milita laughed as she found peace with the prince's words. "I had a wonderful time, Adonis. I really did. Thank you!"

"The pleasure was mine." Adonis kissed her hand sending goosebumps up her arm. "I would be honoured if we could pursue another date. Perhaps, when you've finished your stay at the Elvin castle."

"I would love to, Adonis." She blushed.

Milita watched the guards arrest Tobias. "What is to become of him?"

"The servant? Well," whispered Adonis in secrecy, "he will become my personal assistant. No punishment will happen."

"Your personal assistant?"

"Yes. I've observed his actions of late. He's a cunning and educated man who's not afraid to be outspoken. You have no idea how refreshing that is for me," answered the prince.

"What of Myrrha. Won't she expect punishment?"

"When her new dress arrives, she will have long forgotten Tobias."

"She sounds like a shallow person."

"She means well," defended the prince.

"I suppose it's time I retired to my room, Adonis. I leave tomorrow before sunrise."

"I suppose so." smiled Adonis. "Thank you for a lovely evening, Milita. I look forward to your return."

"Me, too, Adonis. Good night."

"Good night, Milita, and welcome home."

Chapter XVIIII
Faith.

In the early morning hour behind the walls of Castle Malshidiel, Lord Nyte Shade had tumbled down that rabbit's hole of dreams and dreamscape. There he stood on a farmer's field beneath a blood-stained sky. The air was polluted with ash and smoke. A white two-story home appeared engulfed in flames. A woman's scream echoed through the night.

Nyte ran toward the burning home. A woman knelt before it. Her eyes teared with grief and despair. Kneeling beside her he asked, "Are you okay?"

In her arms she held a child burned to a crisp. Its corpse crumbled into ashes and slipped through her fingers like sand through an hourglass. She bellowed the tears of a broken-hearted mother.

Cretes Siris walked out from the burning house. He raised a prosthetic wooden leg high into the air and smacked Nyte across the head.

Nyte dropped to the ground hard. He felt warm blood oozing down his face as Siris raised the wooden leg for the final lethal blow. He smiled at Nyte while speaking with a child's voice.

"Without faith…" a baby wept.

"Without destiny…" a tiger roared.

"Lord Nyte Shade, you will die!"

Siris collapsed to the ground in ash.

The house behind him exploded into flames. Its fire spread rapidly incinerating the kneeling woman. Its flames shrouded Nyte's body and burned his flesh.

"Find the house of faith!" screamed the flames of fury. "Find the house of faith!"

Nyte awoke leaping from his bed. His sheets were smoldering in smoke. His skin was hot to the touch. He submerged himself in a tub of yesterday's bath water. Then rose gasping for air. Steam emanated from his body. His heartbeat was rapid. The dream…the nightmare was over.

King Siris and his Sykanian Knights travelled a narrow barren road along the edge of Mount Maximus. They arrived at a fork in the road. The path to the left went inside the hills and up through the mountain. The path to the right hugged the mountain's outer ridge. King Siris waited impatiently for further instructions as Malores fumbled through his maps.

"Enough sight-seeing, Malores. This mountain won't climb itself!" Siris never hesitated to display his irritation.

"One moment sire." spoke the wizard fumbling through his handbag. "There we go. This map will guide us through the mountain passage."

"That bag looks like a purse, Malores!" pestered Siris.

"It's a handbag, sire." confirmed Malores.

"Hey, boys, check out Malores' purse."

The Sykanian Knights broke out into laughter.

Malores winced. "Really, sire?"

"Settle down, wizard. I'm just raising morale," chuckled the King. "Now tell me what your map says."

"According to this map, the shortest route would be the path to the left."

"Excellent, Malores. Lead the way!"

The wizard led the Sykanians through a winding maze of switchbacks scaling a jagged and barren mountainside. Kelar and Neasha, still sharing a horse, rode quietly, staying close to Siris.

"Have you noticed your inability to communicate with animals?" asked Siris.

"Yes," confessed Neasha. "I've tried to communicate with this horse several times without success. Why is that?"

"Neasha, that is a gift the Mystique Forest offers—that and a unicorn companion. Without passing the forest, you will receive neither."

Kelar's curiosity compelled him to learn from Siris. "I have been wanting to ask what happened to your unicorn?"

"Well, son, the day I left the Komalsh was the day the shadow spirit awoke and in a single moment I lost the ability to communicate with my unicorn. I tried hard to reconnect but there was nothing. We were best friends for years, Kelar. Until that day, when I looked into his eyes, all I saw was the mind of an animal. The morning after when I awoke, he was gone."

"What was his name?" asked Neasha.

"Funny thing is I can't remember."

Neasha held Kelar closer. "Is there anything else we should be aware of?"

"Well, we do need to get Kelar a durenthium sword. Your new speed and strength will shatter an average blade."

"How will I find one?" asked Kelar.

"The same way I found one for Neasha and Kolos. In the hands of a dead Komalsh."

After cooling down in the tub, Nyte dressed into his Komalsh robes and headed to the dining room. The others had already started their day.

Nyte sat down at the table and ate his breakfast quietly. His skin was still warm to the touch and the nightmare fresh in his thoughts. He looked around the table to see if anyone noticed his peculiar behavior. But the Komalsh who gathered were more interested in their breakfast. Nyte returned to eating when a soft whisper spoke his name.

"Nyte."

He looked around the table again. Everyone was eating oblivious to what Nyte heard. Shrugging it off as a figment of his imagination, Nyte returned to his breakfast when his name was spoken again. This time sounding loud and clear.

"Nyte!"

Startled, Nyte jumped up from his seat and looked around the table. Everyone was still eating their breakfast unperturbed. He looked around to the other tables, yet nothing was out of the ordinary.

The voice whispered Nyte's name again ending with a sharp T.

Twiggins came over and removed Nyte's unfinished plate—something he'd normally never do.

"Do you hear that, Twiggins?" asked the startled Lord.

"It's not my name it calls," answered the uncanny skeleton returning to the kitchen.

The sharp whisper lured Nyte from the dining room and down the hallway. He could see the castle walls fluctuate with energy. Nyte placed his hand on the stone wall. Its fluctuating energy illuminated his hand up to his elbow. It was a strange feeling as though his arm was submerged in water, only dry and warm. The energy gently guided him down the hallway toward a large stone stairway leading under the castle. One by one, the steps twitched with the same energy.

At the bottom of the stairway was a large doorway leading into a candle-lit room. Inside were statues of past Komalsh leaders. The energy from the stairs travelled across the floor and was absorbed into two separate statues.

At a closer look, Nyte recognized the statues to be likenesses of his parents, Radik and Raine. He stood awed by their features.

"They were great leaders, Lord Shade," spoke Drakus standing in the shadows.

"I couldn't feel your heartbeat?" said Nyte.

"I didn't want you to," answered Drakus. "A gift you should learn."

"Yes, Lord Drakus."

"Did you hear the whispers, Lord Shade?"

"Yes. They led me down here."

"Malshidiel is reaching out to you, son. Come, follow me." Drakus led Nyte to the back of the room. A single large window overlooked the ocean waterfalling into the bottomless ravine.

"What does Malshidiel want with me?"

Drakus pointed to a dark corner of the room. There stood two large durenthium doors with carvings of archangels engraved on their surface. Drakus removed the talisman from around his neck and showed it to Nyte. Its shape resembled the Komalsh five-pointed star encased in a circle. Each point poking through the circle represented an element. But this was only half of the talisman. Nyte noticed where the two durenthium doors closed together was engraved an inset with the same symbol as the talisman would be if it were whole.

"Where's the other half of the talisman, Lord Drakus?" inquired Nyte.

"It's in a safe place for now, Lord Shade," he said assuredly. "When the two halves of the talisman are united and placed properly on this door. It will act as a key to awakening Malshidiel from his slumber."

Nyte took a closer look at the doors. On the outer sides of the middle hinges of both doors were inserts shaped to hold the half talismans. An engraved line travelled from either side crossing the doors to the middle inset which took the shape of the whole talisman.

"I can only assume the middle inset is where the key goes. That is my best guess," said Drakus.

"Are you sure you're not suppose to put the separated halves on either side?" wondered Nyte.

"That's quite possible," agreed Drakus. "The only instruction about how it worked burned in the great fire during the Lord Duren era."

"Where is the Scroll Key to unlocking the Darkstar?" asked Nyte.

Drakus pointed to the wall beside Malshidiel's chambers. Telekinetically he opened a hidden doorway. There on display was a four-foot-long gold cannister holding the key scroll inside.

Nyte stared at it with amazement, then in terror. Drakus handed Nyte the half talisman. "I need you to hold this for me."

"Why me?" hesitated Nyte.

"Malshidiel has whispered, and it is your name he calls. You must protect this talisman with your life. It has many seekers, Lord Shade. You would be wise to keep it hidden. Allow no other to know of its existence until the chosen one seeks it out. Then you will guide her here to Malshidiel's chambers so she can awaken the angel. The two will take form as one allowing Malshidiel to walk among us. They'll lead us to war against the Darkstar."

"The chosen one has arrived?" Nyte was in a state of disbelief…even a little stunned. "Her? who is she?"

"That secret will reveal itself in time," answered Drakus.

Nyte stared at the talisman. His curiosity made him ask, “When it’s all said and done, what will become of her, the chosen one?”

“After Malshidiel completes it’s mission, the angel will return to the afterlife and the chosen one will follow,” answered Drakus.

Nyte placed the half talisman around his neck and hid it within his robes. “Lord Drakus, what if Malshidiel doesn’t succeed?”

“If the Darkstar proves victorious. The demons will rise, and mankind will be enslaved. The fabric of our reality will intertwine with the afterlife and time will cease to exist. Eternal slavery under demonic law.”

“How will I find the chosen one?”

“She holds the other half of the talisman. Its cosmic energy will guide you together…but if that fails then just look for trouble. I’m sure you’ll find her there.” Drakus voice grew weaker as he related the least desirable of the two outcomes.

Travelling slowly up a narrow trail, King Siris and his Sykanian Knights struggled through a barren passage of loose rock and debris.

“Do you have just the one purse, Malores, or do you have others to match your shoes?” cackled Siris.
The Sykanian Knights laughed at their wizard.

“Just the one, sire,” surrendered Malores.

As they approached the peak of the path, it leveled off to a field of tall grass. At the far end of the field the path continued back up the mountain. Beside that path nestled a large cave.

The grassy field around them was littered with skulls and bones. Some old and dry while others were still covered in decaying flesh. Its foul odour lured vultures and diseased rodents to a welcoming meal. King Siris led them through the carnage. The welcomed breeze thinned the smell of rot and decay.

"This field is a feeding ground for more than just scavengers," warned Siris.

At a stone's throw distance from the cave, Siris halted his Sykanian troops.

"What is it, sire?" Malores worried for his king's concern.

"The heartbeat I feel ahead of us, Malores, is not a friendly one."

"I don't suppose it has anything to do with the carnage surrounding us?"

"That's what I like about you, wizard. Nothing gets by you!" Siris spoke sarcastically.

A mist cleared revealing a withered, blue-skinned witch sitting atop a pile of human bones in front of the cave. Her face was hidden behind long, black, greasy hair with only one widened eye peering through knotted strands. She sat upon her throne of bones gnawing on a human foot. Upon seeing her, Siris announced, "Her name is Black Annis. This is the closest you'll want to get."

Malores reached for his wand. "She is a dark creature, sire, chased up these hills long ago by villagers who lost their children to her hunger."

"What are you going to do, Malores? Poke her with your wand?" Siris hooted spreading more laughter throughout his knights. "You're better off hitting her with your purse!" laughed Siris even harder.

The Sykanian Knights all burst into laughter.

"Why do I even bother?" mumbled Malores.

"She doesn't look very threatening," commented Kolos.

"Don't be fooled," warned Siris. "Black Annis is a dangerous witch. The only reason we still live is due to her confusion of what's real and what's not. Her mind is her prison, and her sight is poor."

Malores lowered his wand. "Then how do you suggest we get by her, your majesty?"

"Are there any archers among us?" asked Siris.

"I'm an archer, sire." volunteered a young knight.

"Wonderful!" praised Siris. "I want you to shoot an arrow right through her eye."

"Yes, sire." The archer stepped forward. He drew back his bowstring and released an arrow at Black Annis' head.

The arrow missed.

"I guess I should have asked if there were any good archers here." King Siris was clearly disappointed.

"Sorry, sire."

The archer pulled back the bowstring and took a more careful aim. Confident with his shot, he released the bowstring and his arrow sailed right toward Black Annis' head. With unnatural speed, the witch snatched the arrow from out of the air inches from her eye. She placed it under her nostrils and inhaled the archer's scent. Her single piercing eye stared directly at him.

"Do you have a contingency plan, sire?" Malores was having misgivings.

"I've dealt with Black Annis before, Malores."

"We know nothing of her, King Siris." Neasha was clearly irritated by Siris' actions. "No one has ever confronted her and lived. We don't even know how she subdues her victims. Other than a hunger for flesh she's a complete mystery to the Olemeeze library!"

"Then let us introduce ourselves, follow me!" ordered Siris courageously.

They galloped toward the blue witch halting just before her. Black Annis dropped the foot she was chewing on and greeted everyone with her widened eye—the archer more so.

The archer felt nervous. "She won't stop staring at me, sire."

Siris smiled sadistically. "The moment she caught your scent was the moment you became real to her."

Telekinetically, Siris lifted the archer from his horse and tossed him to the feet of Black Annis. The archer stumbled to his feet and unsheathed his sword.

Black Annis stared at him with her one widened eye. She smiled peacefully behind her long black hair.

The archer lowered his sword. He stood captivated by her one eye. Blood started to seep from his ears then his nose and within moments the archer collapsed to the ground dead. Black Annis rose from her throne of bones. She grabbed the archer by the foot and dragged him into the cave.

"What just happened?" Malores was dumbfounded. "Why didn't she kill us?"

"I guess archer tastes better," laughed Siris.

"You sacrificed him so we could pass, didn't you?" applauded Kelar.

"Absolutely! Black Annis is a powerful witch. But she only kills what she eats. You saw how scrawny she is. That archer will last her all week!"

"Neasha!" ordered Siris coldly. "Take the archer's horse. Let's get moving."

King Siris led his knights past the cave and up the mountain path. Lord Demonis' stone imprisonment was close. Siris could feel it.

Lord Drakus and Nyte stood by Malshidiel's chambers admiring the key scroll. It was inside a shiny four-foot-long gold cannister. The scroll itself was made from papyrus and written on it was the spell to releasing its demon captives.

"Why is it so shiny, Lord Drakus?" wondered Nyte.

"Wouldn't it be easier to hide if it were, I don't know, not so shiny?"

"I always wondered that myself, Lord Shade."

The two laughed together. Nyte thought highly of Lord Drakus. He was smart, wise, and treated everyone with respect. In return he was respected by all. Nyte understood why his mother passed down the mantle of leadership to him. He was a well-rounded leader. A good man.

Recalling his haunting dream, Nyte told Drakus of how he awoke smothered in heat.

"You have a powerful gift, Lord Shade. It is growing in intensity more so now as the venom runs through your veins." explained Drakus.

"These dreams are far more vivid than before. I could feel the flames burning my skin. The pain was so real…could I die in my dreams?"

"No, you can't. It's still just a dream. But the message, however, is insightful. A glimpse into a possible future. Heed this dream as a warning and seek out these images to understand their truth."

"Where would I possibly start?"

"Just get on your unicorn, son, and ride. Your future will always find you."

"It still would be nice to know where I'm going, Lord Drakus."

"Life's a journey, son, not a destination. Just get on your unicorn and ride."

"Yes, Lord Drakus." Nyte still was not sure of how to proceed.

In the last couple of days Terex, Trayke, and Arias learned the fine art of sword making. With the help of Burlok, Grundy, and Ashes the dragon, they were all now armed with a Komalsh sword and dagger.

Arias, having left over durenthium, constructed himself an authentic X shaped boomerang. It's design not only offered him a weapon but a multi-purpose tool as well. Lord Arias Jackyle prided himself on his creativity.
Terex unsheathed his sword and slapped the boomerang out of Arias' hand.

"Ouch! What's wrong with you?" cursed Arias.

"I just don't understand why you made that paper weight." Terex questioned the usefulness of such an item.

"This is a tool." Arias picked it back up.

"We are knights, not carpenters," reminded Terex.

"It's a weapon as well," defended Arias.

"Well, you go into battle with that little thing and see how far you get," poked Terex.

"He's right," agreed Trayke. "It's awfully small."

"Size doesn't matter," answered Arias.

"I'm sure you say that to all the girls," joked Terex. Then he wheeled out his sword before Arias. Intimidating, isn't it?" Terex winked.

"I have to go with Terex on this one, Arias." agreed Trayke. "Far more intimidating."

Nyte Shade and his unicorn, Loki, bolted from the castle stable passing his friends and disappearing into the Mystique Forest.

"Where do you suppose he's going?" wondered Trayke.

"I don't know?" giggled Terex. "Maybe Arias' boomerang scared him away."

After leaving the Mystique Forest, Nyte and Loki journeyed along the outside of the bottomless ravine toward the White Sea's shoreline. From there they travelled east along its sandy coastline. The heat from the morning sun forecast a hot day to come.

Ocean waves lapped the shoreline cooling the air with salty mist as Loki's powerful strides ripped through the sand. Nonstop, for miles they rode up the coastline and by early afternoon arrived where the Assaroe River filled the salty sea. There they stopped to appreciate the ocean waves as they slowly sculpted the sandy shoreline.

"I love the smell of the ocean breeze." shared Loki.

"Yeah, me too." Nyte felt soothed by Loki's words. Loki caught a sudden scent of smoke. Startled, he looked around. "Do you smell that, Nyte?"

"Smell what?"

"Smoke! Fires are bad during the summer!"

Nyte searched the field behind them. "Over there, Loki, I see smoke!"

The two rode inland up a gravel road and then across a farmer's field. In the middle of the field stood a white, two-storey home engulfed in flames. Surrounding the house, local farmers armed with buckets of water tried desperately to gain control of the blaze.

"The house of faith!" gasped Nyte. "Just like my dream foretold. Get us there quickly, Loki!"

Loki galloped toward the burning house. While in full stride his horn started to glow.

"What are you doing, Loki?"

The white glow engulfed their bodies. Nyte started to scream and in a blinding, bright, white flash the two vanished.

A women stood outside the front yard of her burning home. She dropped to her knees shedding tears of terror. Her husband held his beloved wife desperately trying to restrain her. “You can’t go in there! You will surely die!” he pleaded.

The wife struggled and cried till her body fell limp with exhaustion. “My baby!” She cried. “Oh god, help my baby!”

More local farmers arrived in wagons carrying buckets, shovels, and axes. The community fought the blaze courageously.

“Please help my baby!” she cried. “Please God, not our baby!” The wife collapsed into her husband’s arms.

“Oh God, please, please, not my baby!”

A bright white flash appeared before them and from it emerged Nyte and Loki.

“My baby is in there! Please help my baby!” She begged.

Nyte stared at the burning house. He stood breathless with the resemblance from his dream. Without further delay, he jumped down from Loki and removed his hooded cloak. After submerging the cloak in a barrel of water he put it back over his shoulders and ran toward the house. Nyte kicked down the front door and entered the burning house.

Inside the smoke was too thick to see. Flames engulfed the walls, and the heat was unbearable. Nyte used his psychic gift and located a heartbeat coming from the far room. He ran toward it through the smoke and flames. There Nyte located the baby girl. She was crying in her crib. He wrapped her with his dampened cloak and carried toward the front doorway. Before escaping the house, a large support beam broke loose and pinned Nyte to the floor. His spine snapped on impact paralyzing him from the waist down. Trapped under the beam, Nyte's skin burned from the intense heat. He wrapped the baby tight in his cloak as the entire room burst into flames.

Outside, the house was engulfed in flames. The fire fighting farmers backed away surrendering to defeat. There was nothing more that could be done but watch as it burned to the ground. Loki started to worry.

Inside the burning house, Nyte's back had already healed. His skin regenerated faster than the heat could burn. But the little girl protected in his wet cloak was short of time. Nyte tried desperately to free himself from the support beam but couldn't get it to budge. Taking a moment to collect his panicked thoughts Nyte closed his eyes and used his psychic gift. He levitated the beam off him and tossed it to the side.

The smoke in the room was now too thick to breathe. The walls lit up with flames. The ceiling started to crack and fall. Then a bright white flash blinded him.

Outside the mother and father gazed in horror as they watched their house collapse into a pile of burning debris.

"MY BABY!" She screamed in defeat.

Her husband's eyes swelled from tears of despair. "No, no, please God, no."

A bright white flash exploded before them and Nyte and Loki appeared. Nyte carefully climbed down and unravelled his smoking cloak. Inside nestled a perfectly healthy baby girl.

The mother, blinded by tears, held her baby close. "My baby!" She cooed and rocked as she held her baby tight to her chest.

The father wrapped his arms around them both promising repeatedly that he'd never let go.

"My baby, oh my baby." She wept tears of joy.

Nyte and Loki helped the farmers contain the spreading flames. After a couple of hours of hard work, they managed to save a barn, two cows and rescue a complicated cat from a tree. Afterwards, the community gathered and prepared a barn style feast celebrating the heroes of the day. Loki, too, had a place at their table where he was adored by all the children.

The mother and her baby girl sat next to Nyte. "My name is Lindy. This is my husband, Eli. Thank you. We are forever in your debt."

"My name is Nyte, and this is Loki."

Loki nodded with a snort and the children all laughed.

Eli shook Nyte's hand. "God bless you."

Lindy handed the baby to Nyte who reluctantly accepted her. He wasn't comfortable holding such a small child.

"Don't be afraid," smiled Lindy. "She's just a little person. Her name is Faith."

****

"Without faith, without destiny, Lord Nyte Shade will die!" recalled Nyte from his dream.

****

Nyte stared into her eyes, they sparkled with curiosity. "It appears I have found Faith," he whispered to the child. Faith smiled in return while squeezing the end of his nose.

Eli handed Nyte a plate of dinner while Lindy took Faith back into her arms.

"I couldn't help notice your chest emblem, Nyte." said Eli. "The five-pointed star inside a circle. You are a Lord of the Komalsh."

"Yes, I'm known as Lord Shade."

"Then why would you help us? Don't get me wrong. I'm forever grateful for what you've done, but the Komalsh aren't known to help anyone."

"The Komalsh have sworn an oath to protect Castle Malshidiel," explained Nyte. "In the past that oath had been compromised when helping others. That's why we keep to ourselves."

"Then, why today? Why us?"

"It was the right thing to do, and no rules should ever prevent anyone from doing the right thing," answered Nyte.

"Then there's still hope in this world," smiled Eli.

"And Faith," added Lindy while kissing her baby.

"What will you do now that your home is gone?" asked Nyte.

"We will make do, all we really need is each other." smiled Lindy.

The farmers and their families gathered around the table. An elder spoke on their behalf. "We, as a community, will donate our available funds and skills to rebuild your home. I, myself, don't have much for gold, but I do have carpentry skills," offered the elder.

Everyone reached into their pockets revealing all they could spare and placed it on the table. Cheer spread through the barn as a small pile of coins accumulated.

Nyte removed a golden egg from his robes and placed it on the table. The barn fell silent as a tomb as everyone stopped to gasp at the glittering wonder.

"This could build an entire town!" Eli was taken aback. While he ogled the gift with delight, he did not believe he deserved it. "But…but we cannot accept this."

Nyte rose from the table—his dinner finished. "The golden egg is yours to do with as you choose."

"It's okay!" assured Lindy. "We just need to be responsible with this blessing."

"Alright then," agreed Eli. "First, we build a home. Then we build a water reservoir to help protect all our homes from fires. The remainder will be spread throughout our community!"

The townspeople celebrated. Music was played and wine poured. The barn party was just getting started. As the celebrations went into full swing Nyte and Loki tried to wander away unnoticed.

Eli ran after him. "Are you leaving?"

"Yes, we are. I'm uncomfortable with goodbyes. I thought we'd just slip away."

"Well then, thank you, for saving my baby girl. If you ever need anything, just ask. That goes for you, too, Loki." Eli patted the unicorn. "One day, somehow, I will repay you. I promise."

Nyte mounted Loki. He noticed Lindy standing by the barn. Faith was in her arms. She waved to them and made gestures of gratitude.

Nyte waved in return.

"We will pray for you, Lord Shade." Eli knew he would forever remember this day.

"Thank you."

Loki lifted his front legs into the air in excitement and haste, and then galloped down the riverside back toward the White Sea.

As the sun disappeared behind the ocean horizon and the moon began to appear in a clouded night sky, Nyte and Loki galloped in bouts of darkness down the sandy beach. Nyte closed his eyes and listened to the crashing waves. He focused on Loki's hooves tearing up the sand and the winds whistling down the coastline. Nyte reached out further with his psychic gift. He felt the heartbeats of birds flying through trees and animals roaming the forest. Ahead of them, an alarmed deer darted into the forest. In the ocean, he felt a pod of whales crashing through waves. His psychic abilities expanded exponentially "I can feel everything, Loki!"

It was in that moment, Nyte's level of consciousness reached a higher plateau and in the distant ocean he heard the whales speak.

"I cannot begin to explain the connection I'm having, Loki."

"I understand, Nyte. We unicorns are born with it. Are you hearing the whale's message?"

"Yes, I am Loki. They communicate with more than sounds and their message spreads love."

"Yes, Nyte, they reach out to all who listen. It is unfortunate most don't hear their calls."

"Most people can't listen," said Nyte.

"Most people won't listen," explained Loki.

Loki slowed to a stop along the beach. Under the star-lit sky they could hear the towering waves rolling over the sandy shore. In the distance they could hear the songs sung by whales spreading messages of endearment.

"Hey, Nyte."

"Yes, Loki."

"I just wanted you to know how impressed with you I am. You risked your life to save that child."

"Thank you, Loki, but I'd have survived. My body heals quick remember."

"True, your body would heal. The trauma of a child dying in your arms, however, is one that you'd have to live with the rest of your life."

"I'd rather live with that, Loki, than to live a life knowing I could have made a difference and never doing a damn thing about it."

"The Komalsh forbid us to help people," reminded Loki. "Malshidiel is our priority."

"That didn't stop you from helping me save Faith." reminded Nyte.

"Indeed," admitted Loki. "Like you mentioned to Eli, it was the right thing to do. I suppose I should get used to bending the rules if I'm to ride with you."

"Something tells me that won't be a difficult task for you, Loki. Besides, the threat of the Darkstar is upon us. The rules will need to change."

"Change is good, Nyte. I'm here with you until the end."

Nyte scratched Loki's ear as they listened to the songs of whales.

"Friends for life, Loki."

"Friends for life, Nyte."

The two returned to the Mystique Forest and back to Castle Malshidiel.

****

A friendship between a Komalsh and their unicorn is sacred—a bond like no other in the universe. A unicorn can feel the spirit within all living creatures, allowing them an insight into deciding which Komalsh they choose to devote themselves to. In time that friendship invokes a powerful connection of trust and love and, inevitably, becomes their most powerful gift. Today Nyte and Loki started down that road to friendship.

****

In the late eve, King Siris and his Sykanian Knights reached their destination atop mount Maximas.

"According to Fenka Rek, Lord Demonis' stone imprisonment hides deep within that limestone cave." Malores pointed to the spot.

"Knights! Dismount and set up camp!" ordered King Siris. "Kelar, Neasha, Kolos, and you, Malores, follow me."

Siris grabbed a lit torch and headed into the cave. Inside, the phosphorescence from limestone deposits illuminated the cave walls. The other end of the cave opened to a large domed area. At the top of the dome was an opening looking out into the starlit sky. All along it's walls were berry stained drawings from a tribe long lost. The ancient artwork depicted hunters and wars fought. There was also a peculiar drawing of a disc shaped object landing from the heavens.

Siris could feel Demonis reaching out to him. He walked into a darkened corner of the cave and reached out his torch. The flame's light shimmered off the stone statue of Lord Cable Demonis.

"At long last, my friend. Soon you'll be free." Siris smiled. "Malores, reverse the spell and release our friend."

"Yes, sire." Malores grabbed, *The Book of Malshidiel*, from his handbag. He scrolled through the chapters searching for the Gorgon Spell, the one Savita used on Demonis a decade ago.

"I've located the spell, sire."

"Proceed, wizard," ordered Siris.

Malores began chanting the spell backwards as instructed by the book.

"Grana, fausohl, mestra, Alla."

"Grana, fausohl, mestra, Alla."

The statue of Cable Demonis started exuding a red aura. Malores continued chanting the spell and the statue's aura burst into a blue flame. The stone surrounding him crumbled into a pile of blue burning debris. Lord Cable Demonis was now released from his stone imprisonment. Weakened from hibernation, he dropped to his knees gasping for air.

Siris kneeled beside him and asked, "Cable, can you hear my voice?"

Demonis nodded weakly. He handed Siris the scroll of music for the Dragon's Flute, the one he'd stolen a decade ago. Demonis smiled devilishly, then collapsed to the ground.

"He needs to rest, sire," warned the wizard.

Siris and Malores helped Demonis to a blanket laid out by Neasha. She covered him with another to keep him warm. Kolos started a fire while Kelar lit torches around the cave's perimeter.

Siris watched over Demonis. After ten years of stone imprisonment, Cable showed no sign of aging.

"Rest, my friend. Replenish your strength. Soon we will finish what we started a decade ago."

Chapter XX
The Dragon's Flute.

That evening Savita, Mili and Pegasus arrived at the Elvin castle, an enormous structure seven times the size of an ordinary castle. Its unique gothic design, like Castle Malshidiel, was alien to Drakonian culture.

The castle stood on a barren mountain ridge overlooking the Western Sea, its towering structure could be seen for miles around. It had two separate drawbridge entrances, one on either side over deep ravines. The powerful river Triton channelled through those ravines draining into the Western Sea.

Pegasus landed within the safety of the castle walls where three Elvin elders waited patiently for their arrival.

"Lady Cosmos, we've been expecting you." The high priest smiled to see she had arrived.

"Good evening," she bowed. "I've brought Lady Milita Drakus."

"Hello, Lady Drakus. I am Nym, the high priest. To my right is Respen and to my left, Eldrin."

Eldrin approached Pegasus and wrapped her arms around him. Pegasus nuzzled her face in return.

"It's good to see you, Pegasus." Eldrin so adored him.

****

Eldrin was an elderly Elvin woman with a contagious smile. Her free spirit was often frowned upon by her conservative peers.

Respen, the castle librarian, showed little emotion. He was an over-educated Elvin who, for the most part, was stuffy and boring.

****

The high priest, Nym, empathised with Milita. "I have mixed emotions of excitement and fear toward the task that burdens you, Lady Drakus. I can't imagine how you must feel."

"I feel terrified by the unknown," admitted Milita.

"To fear something is to not understand it," assured Nym. "Knowledge is your greatest ally."

"Then I look forward to your counsel, Nym."

"The Darkstar grows stronger by the day, Lady Drakus. Malshidiel's time is upon us. Are you ready?"

"When do we start?" answered Mili confidently.

"We will begin at sunrise." Nym smiled with reassuring hope.

Eldrin placed her hand on Milita's shoulder.

"Everything will be right as rain. Come with me, Lady Drakus. I'm sure a hot bath and some sedative tea will help tonight's rest."

Milita followed. She missed her uncle already.

Early the next morning in the limestone cave on Mount Maximus, Lord Demonis woke for the first time in ten years. As his blurred vision slowly came into focus, he stared through the opening at the top of the cave. He watched the dark sky brighten into morning light. His memory was vague, and confusion swept his mind as he struggled to process all that had happened. Demonis' cluster of thoughts were suddenly interrupted by an obnoxious snore. There beside him lay a decrepit looking wizard. Angered by the noise, Demonis kicked Malores out of his bedding and stood up aggressively.

"Who are you?" he demanded.

"Oh shit!" The wizard stumbled to his feet. Panicked, he called out, "King Siris!" He called a second time. "King Siris." Malores knelt before Demonis. "I'm the Sykanian wizard, Malores Barnett. I freed you, my lord." His voice trembled with anxiety.

"Don't worry about him, Cable," spoke Siris still laying in his bed. "You've been in a stone prison for a decade. We have much to catch up on my friend." Demonis smiled a devilish grin. "Did I hear him address you as…King Siris?"

Siris got up and tossed his crown to Demonis.

"You've done well Cretes." Demonis was impressed.

Then he glared at the wizard still on his knees. "What's with the purse?"

At the break of dawn, Milita started her training. She was to stay at the Elvin castle for months in preparation for the merging of an angel. The Elvin elders had divided her days among them in three sessions with each covering a different focus.

Eldrin led her morning classes through a release of spiritual meditation. Her meditations were a mindful practice of connection to the universe going deeper than herself. It seemed paradoxical to Milita until Eldrin explained how the path to the universe passes through honest self-reflection. Cross legged in a cocoon of telekinetic energy; she probed deep into her psyche. Afterward, she would release her pent-up aggression by jogging the castle's perimeter through a course of jagged terrain and ocean shore obstacles.

In the afternoons, Milita would spend hours in the Elvin library with Respen. They read and reviewed countless amounts of ancient text regarding the Darkstar, Malshidiel and the history of their existence.

Her evenings were spent with Nym where he'd guide her through techniques in psychic enlightenment. He wanted her to focus her rage and transform it into a useful tool. This would help her to be disciplined in mind and soul. It didn't take the Elvin high priest, Nym, long to recognize Milita's rage. She fed on vengeance toward those who took her parents lives.

****

When Milita was a young child she and Lord Drakus were walking along the outer edge of the Mystique Forest when a green vine with red thorns pulled her in. Milita became a Komalsh, inheriting psychic powers her undeveloped mind couldn't comprehend. To protect herself from the pain caused by the loss of her parents, Milita built an emotional psychic barrier preventing anyone from getting close to her. She also manifested an anger toward the one she called God which blinded her with grief and sorrow. Milita never realized the pain she was in. To her it had become the norm.

Lord Drakus understood this, and worried revenge would consume her. So, he reached out to the elves for counsel.

****

Nym recognized her conflict early. He also recognized just how powerful her psychic connection was. This was an unstable balance of power and emotion. Nym feared her. He feared failing her.

King Siris and his Sykanian Knights returned to the path down Mount Maximus. Demonis took Neasha's horse (the one that formerly belonged to the deceased archer), and Neasha once again rode with Kelar. Neither of the two minded.

They passed the cave of Black Annis who sat on her throne of bones gnawing at the archer's decapitated head. All the way down the mountainside, they travelled until reaching the toe of the mountain. From there they headed toward the Avila Mountain Range, a multi-day journey which gave Siris the time needed to update Demonis on his lost decade.

King Siris and his Sykanians journeyed up the Avila Mountain Range to a mining camp overseen by Breton Korrigan, the Sykanian Captain of the Guard. His Sykanian slaves hammered away at the rock in search of the Dragon's Flute.

****

During the final Dragon War, Lord Radik Shade defeated the dragon, Trisadez. In the process, the three headed dragon's blasts of fire, ice, and lightning hit the mountain side burying them and the flute in rubble and lava.

At the start of the mining project to recover the Dragon's Flute, Siris used his telekinesis to remove all the loose debris only to uncover a tomb of igneous rock. Discouraged, he decreed slavery among the poor class of Sykanian citizens and forced them to work breaking rock day in day out. The Dragon's Flute has yet to be recovered.

****

“Have you located the flute, captain?”

“No, sire, but we are close,” affirmed Bretton. He pointed to a pile of human remains. “It appears to be the corpse of Lord Radik Shade, sire. We also recovered the remains of the dragon, Trisadez, who had this durenthium sword embedded in his middle skull.” The captain handed Siris the sword.

Siris’ eyes lit up. He swung the sword around admiring its authenticity.

“That’s definitely the blade of Lord Radik Shade,” confirmed Demonis.

King Siris handed his own sword to Kelar and sheathed Lord Shade’s as his own.

“My gift to you, Kelar.”

Kelar swung his new sword around. “This sword will do just fine.” Testing his resolve, he pointed the blade’s tip toward Breton’s throat. “You broke my wrist.”

Breton raised his hands in surrender. “I was ordered to do so. It was a ploy to humiliate the Komalsh and detour the peace talks.”

“Yes, Lord Kelar,” confirmed Siris, “we’ve been purposely trying to prevent Drakonia from uniting. It’s all part of our improvised plan to conquer the Komalsh.”

****

Thus, Siris showed his hand. It was now apparent how it came to be that all the misfortunes they endured were part of a bigger plan. And, hence, the reason why he now calls it his improvised plan.

****

"At the time, Kelar," continued Siris, "I wasn't aware of your shadow spirit. It had been too dormant to detect. It wasn't until you entered the Mystique Forest that it did reach out to me."

Demonis grabbed Kelar by the shoulder and looked into his eyes. "You are right about this one, Cretes. His shadow spirit is vibrant."

"What of this plan, King Siris?" The question detoured Kelar from Demonis' eye contact.

"To conquer the Komalsh is a difficult task," explained Siris, "and even more so if all the kingdoms formed an alliance. Ten years ago, with the help of Fenka Rek and Malores, we assassinated the Sykanian king and his family. The ploy was to keep the kingdoms divided. Unfortunately, Lord Demonis and I were caught stealing the music for the Dragon's Flute. Lord Demonis was imprisoned, and I spent the last ten years trying to find him. During that time, and with the aid of Malores, I eventually took the mantle of king to the Sykanian people. After all, Sykania was my birthplace."

"So, it took Fenka Rek ten years to find Lord Demonis?" Kolos' curiosity was engaged.

"No," replied Siris. "It took ten years to find Fenka Rek. The last I saw him he was pulling me from the swamp of Karnagins believed to have killed me. Fenka Rek hadn't been seen since. Without Lord Demonis and the Dragon Flute's music I couldn't carry out our plan. So, I spent the years training and developing the Sykanian army while secretly preparing for our war on the Komalsh."

"That's why we're here? To find the Dragon's Flute?" guessed Kelar.

"That's correct," answered Siris. "We been mining this area for the last couple of years without any success."

"So, your plan is to conquer the Komalsh?" Neasha tries to emphasize the ridiculousness of the idea. "What about the return of the Darkstar? What about Malshidiel?"

"If the Komalsh awaken Malshidiel, they will destroy the Darkstar, and life will continue the way it always has," answered Siris.

"What's wrong with that?" defended Neasha.

"Allow me to explain." Demonis wanted the floor. "What you perceive to be life is really a prison. Our souls are trapped in these mortal bodies in constant fear for our demise. We live in pain and suffering only to accept it as normality. When we die, it starts over again reincarnating us in a new body with no memories of our previous life. It's all part of an endless cycle of eternal imprisonment. The Darkstar offers us immortality and an end to all suffering."

"Why would a loving god punish his children?" Puzzled Neasha.

"We were all once angels who questioned a malevolent god," answered Siris. "Our sentence here is life."

"That seems inconceivable." Neasha could not subscribe to the idea of being virtually imprisoned.

"When your shadow spirit awakens, Neasha, you, too, will understand the truth." Siris clutched his fist. "With the power of Castle Malshidiel, we will unite Drakonia under one order and with the power of the Darkstar we will rule eternity!"

"But first we first need to find the Dragon's Flute." Kelar piped in.

"We will find the flute, Kelar. It's only a matter of time," affirmed Siris.

Terrified, Neasha secretly grabbed Kelar's hand and telepathically haled him. "They're insane!"

Kelar nodded his agreement. "We must follow for now. Trust me." He whispered in thought.

With both hands she squeezed his. "I trust you, Kelar."

Two weeks had passed and the whereabouts of the Dragon's Flute remained a mystery. During that time, the Sykanian slaves dug up the remains of two bodies which they claimed to be the wizard, Marlyn Cosmos, and the Komalsh, Lady Mia Cosmos. They were Savita's parents. Frustrated yet undeterred, King Siris had his Sykanian Knights search local villages for more slaves in the hope of doubling their efforts.

Back at Castle Malshidiel, the young Lords settled into the charm of Utopia. They met many other Komalsh and Earth creatures alike. Their new home was a paradise of its own, filled with knowledge, insight, and wonderment where everyone shared in a spirit of harmony.
Over the last couple weeks, the young Lords psychic abilities expanded exponentially as they all graduated to higher levels of consciousness. Each new Lord adapted quickly.

Lord Arias Jackyle found an interest in the Metalsmiths shop. He spent most of his time with the dwarves, Burlok and Grundy. There he quickly mastered the fine art of weapon design. Arias had also adapted the ability to levitate and move objects so precisely he could mold durenthium while in its melted state. The dwarves spent much time helping him develop his special gift. When Arias showed enough confidence Burlok placed Ashes, the dragon, before him. She stood there confused as to what was going on when she hiccupped a ball of flames. Arias trapped the flames in a cocoon of psychic kinetic energy. He moved it around the room then suffocated the flames.

Lord Terex Gungnir was most comfortable in the combat training area. He spent his time sparring with the Komalsh Elite. Terex was by nature a warrior. His reflexes and strength were enhanced by the forest's venom—a strength equaled by no other. Arias had made him durenthium knuckle and foot armour to prevent his newfound strength from shattering his bones when punching and kicking. Terex had also gained a precise aim; he could throw stones, knives and axes and hit every target. He never, however, got the hang of returning objects to his hand. This was a weakness that had little effect upon him but was found to be a hazard to those around him.

Lord Kris Tarius divided his time between the library and the archery. He developed a keen eye and an appreciation for the art form. As his mind expanded, he become powerful in almost all aspects of psychic ability. He had spent long hours in the library with Lady Dunlam learning and understanding his array of gifts. Kris was among the most gifted of Komalsh.

Late at night, he'd hold on to his silk handkerchief and yearn for his beloved Bella Flora.

Lord Trayke Basa took life casually. He found himself enjoying the social life, harmlessly flirting with all the women of Utopia. Upset by his immunity to alcohol, he was introduced to a plant that grew in the Mystique Forest. The herbs from the plant were either smoked or eaten and were widely used by the Komalsh for calming their minds and aiding a peaceful sleep. An open mind is a busy mind.

As Trayke's psychic abilities expanded. He started to see the dark shadows of people no one else could. They hid from him like the spirit he saw inside the Mystique Forest. After researching this gift in the castle's library, he discovered that he had the ability to see spirits of the recently deceased—a gift that left him on edge and he decided it was best kept to himself.

Lord Nyte Shade was by far the strongest of all the Komalsh. His psychic power had developed beyond Lord Drakus' expectations. His only weakness was a barrier of doubt preventing him from bursting through his own full potential. Lord Drakus reassured him that time would be its only remedy.

Nyte also felt a guilt about the loss of Kelar. Often, he separated himself from the others by getting lost in the Mystique Forest searching for answers that never appeared. His unicorn, Loki, never left his side.

Nyte's dreaming had abated for now. The forest and its herbs alleviated his anxiety allowing Nyte the time to process and develop his amazing array of psychic gifts.

In the early morning hour, Lord Hirum Drakus awoke from a terrible dream. Trembling with anxiety, he reached for a jug of water at his bedside. After slaking his thirst, he walked out onto his balcony. There he found peace listening to the soothing sound of the ocean disappearing into the bottomless ravine. Rubbing his eyes, he recalled his dream of a disturbed future. Visions of a brutal battle flashed through his mind. Then there was only peace. Drakus went back inside and stared at the painting above his fireplace—the portrait of his wife, Kayla, painted before she passed away. He loved her so. She was the beacon of all hope in his eyes.

"I miss you so much," he told the painting.

A knock echoed from his door. Drakus opened it. On the other side stood the skeletal cook, Twiggins. “Bad dreams my lord?” inquired the peculiar cook.

“What do you want, Twiggins?” he demanded curtly. Drakus did not like being disturbed when he was in his private chambers.

“You have guests in the waiting lounge,” he announced cheerfully. “They wish to speak with you.”

“At this hour! Who dares to awaken me?”

“I thought you were psychic,” poked Twiggins.

Drakus closed his eyes and felt the guest’s heartbeats in his waiting lounge. He identified who they were, especially their leader. He knew that presence well. Drakus despised him. “Lord Jarestt!” Drakus pushed Twiggins aside and marched toward the waiting lounge stark naked.

“Perhaps you should get dressed first, my lord,” suggested Twiggins.

Drakus was too angered to care. He marched into the waiting lounge and tossed his water jug at Lord Jaresst who telekinetically placed it gently onto the table.

****

Lord Jarestt was a rugged looking pale-skinned man with long black hair. He stood six feet and weighed over 200 pounds. He never saw eye-to-eye with Drakus or the Komalsh religion. Although he was no fool, his stubbornness blinded him toward other views and opinions. He was commonly portrayed as an adversary of blind debate—an unwelcome personality trait in the peaceful village of Utopia.

Lord Jarestt was easily recognized by his wooden prosthetic leg, a war wound he suffered as a Komalsh while transporting a Manticore to haven. It was but one in a series of many incidents where his stubbornness placed him and others in danger.

Behind Lord Jarestt stood a dozen renegade Komalsh who shared his radical views and fought loyally by his side. This was a group of rough-edged rogues who spent their lives on the road roaming about like Drakonian gypsies. Although they maintained their loyalty to Malshidiel, their views differed from the Komalsh religion.

Among the renegades was Lady Tazi Asheika. In her younger years, she was romantically involved with Lord Cable Demonis, a rare love shared between two Komalsh. The relationship ended the day Demonis' shadow demon awoke. Within a mere moment, he became estranged to her. After Demonis' stone imprisonment, Asheika started a new life with Lord Jarestt. Because she was still heartbroken, by the loss of Demonis, a hurt she couldn't hide, the spark of jealousy was inflamed within Jarestt.

Together Lord Jarestt and Lady Asheika formed their separatist legion under Malshidiel's order. Drakus abbreviated it as the S.L.U.M. gang. The Komalsh had banished their legion from Castle Malshidiel. They weren't enemies but they also weren't allies.

****

Lord Jarestt sat at the table. His arrogant smile infuriated Drakus.

"Well! What do you want S.L.U.M?"

"Please sit down. The sight of your penis is making me uncomfortable." Jarestt was not amused.

"Uncomfortable or intimidated?" glared Drakus while sitting down. "Well, speak, rogue!"

"Lord Demonis has been freed. I've intercepted their conversations telepathically," revealed Jarestt with a sense of superiority and cunningness.

"I know," replied Drakus deflating his adversary's ego.

Jarestt's eyes widened. "Then why haven't you done anything? It's obvious they're in lead with the Darkstar!"

Drakus rose from his chair angered. Jarestt covered his eyes.

"I need not explain myself to you. You're reckless without insight nor wisdom which makes you poisonous to others. Now, get out of my castle!"

Jarestt rose from his seat. "My knights and I are going to end this war once and for all!"

"Your knights are nothing but renegades and misfits." Jarestt returned the glare. "We know where they are," he bragged.

"Of course, you do," ridiculed Drakus. "They allowed you to and when you follow their breadcrumbs, all you'll find is death."

"I don't think so," snickered Jarestt.

Drakus shook his head. "Your arrogance has blinded you. If you think for a moment that killing Lord's Siris and Demonis will end the Darkstar's uprising, then you're simpler than I thought."

Angered from insult, Jarestt telekinetically tossed the large conference table across the room shattering it against the wall. He pointed his finger at Drakus with rage. "When I finish with them, I'm coming for you, and I'll take my rightful spot as a Lord of the Komalsh."

Drakus wound up and punched Jarestt in the nose. Jarestt dropped to the ground hard.

"Why wait?" glared Drakus.

Jarestt stood back up. His broken nose reset then healed. He wiped the blood from his face, then unsheathed his sword in anger.

"Your jealousy of Lord Demonis and Lady Asheika is the card King Siris plays," warned Drakus. "He's luring you into a trap."

"You're a fool, Lord Drakus. We will end this war soon. Then I'll ask the Komalsh who should be leading them." Jarestt tapped his thumb against his chest. Then he and his rogue's left.

"It's never too late to work on your social skills, my lord," suggested Twiggins standing quietly in the corner.

"Indeed," mumbled Drakus marching back to his room. "Replace that table, Twiggins!"

"Yes, my lord."

The following morning the sun rose over the Avila Mountain Range. Kelar awoke next to his Neasha. Their naked bodies embraced under a domed tent.

"Last night was special," whispered Neasha.

"I love you." Kelar had no reason to keep his feeling to himself.

"I love you, too," smiled Neasha.

Lately, Kelar and Neasha had very few moments alone together. They cherished each one.

"Where do we go from here?" Neasha worried about their current predicament.

"I don't know Neasha; we must be patient."

"I know, it's just we've studied all our lives to be Komalsh. We failed and now we ride with the enemy?"

"I know. But the Komalsh tried to kill us, Neasha. Fate has brought us here and we're safe for the time being. Most importantly, we have each other."

"That's right," she purred.

"Between us, Neasha, I don't believe Malshidiel destroying the Darkstar is a bad thing. But for now, we'll remain allies to King Siris until an opportunity arises."

"I agree, Kelar, I don't care for any of this insanity. I just want the two of us to run away from this life and start fresh. Change our identities, get married…raise a family?" She winked, then kissed him on the nose.

"I think that's a great plan. Just be patient for now Neasha, my love."

Neasha held him close. "I guess we're Sykanians for now."

"That's the spirit, Neasha. Now all we need to worry about is finding that flute?"

Neasha got up and dressed in her stolen Komalsh robes and light armour. Kelar, who was gifted Sykanian robes and light armour by Siris, dressed and took a fancy to his new appearance. Neasha smiled at her handsome man, then paused a moment in thought.

"What are you thinking about?"

"We've heard the story of Radik Shade and the Dragon's Flute many times," answered Neasha.

Kelar stood puzzled, "Yeah, so?"

"What I recall is the flute wound up in the hands of Lord Radik Shade before he was buried under the rock," hinted Neasha.

"Are you suggesting the guards didn't search his body?" asked Kelar.

"That's exactly what I'm thinking."

Neasha and Kelar were suddenly alerted to the distinctive sound of dragons outside their tent. Then the shouts of panicked Sykanians followed.

Kolos entered their tent in a panic. "We're under attack!"

Kelar and Neasha went outside with their swords drawn. Dragons swarmed the skies above. They were aggressively attacking the camp by snatching Sykanians one at a time flying high into the air and releasing them to their deaths.

A dragon landed near Kelar. It stood 10 feet high with feathered wings spread wide. A Sykanian knight defended Kelar and attacked the dragon head on. With a quick snap the dragon's tail pierced the knight's shoulder filling him with poison. The knight's body swelled unrecognizably. Puss oozed from his ears and mouth and after a few uncontrolled twitches his body fell limp in the dragon's grip. She flew off to her nest where her hungry younglings waited.

Kelar, Neasha and Kolos reached for their swords. They backed toward each other forming a circle of defense. All around them Sykanian Knights fell from the skies.

"Where are they coming from?" asked Kolos.

Neasha pointed to the Avila Mountain Range. "Beyond that mountain is Jirasab, the dragon homeland. They must be out pack hunting. If we hurt enough of them, they'll leave for easier prey."

"How do you know all this?" asked Kelar.

"Some of us didn't sleep through school!"

"I thought dragons were supposed to be larger than this?" confessed Kelar.

"They're big enough!" shouted Kolos.

"These are Wyverns," explained Neasha. "They are the smaller of the species, yes, but don't let that fool you...and be aware of their tail stingers, they are deadly poisonous!"

****

The Wyvern is of the dragon family but unlike their reptilian cousins they only have two legs. Both legs of fowl decent were feathered as were their wings. The body of these lethal lizards varied in brownish orange and reddish colours. Their triangular head and curved fangs added to an already hideous looking creature. Armed with talons the length of a person's forearm and a poisonous stinger on their tail, these pack hunters made for a lethal predator.

****

A Wyvern swept down grabbing Neasha, then took back off into the sky.

"Kelar!" she screamed.

Kelar leapt into the air and grabbed onto Neasha's legs. He climbed up to the dragon's leg and stabbed his sword through its feathered thigh. With an agonizing screech the dragon released Neasha to the ground. Kelar dove down after her. He grabbed onto Neasha and used his body to cushion the impact. When they hit the ground Kelar screamed in agony as his lower spine snapped over a rock.

"Get up, Kelar, it's coming back!" screamed Neasha as she was rising to her feet.

"I can't move my legs, Neasha!" grimaced Kelar.

The wounded dragon flew back around and swooped toward them with its talons stretched outward.
Neasha stood between Kelar and the attacking dragon. Her sword in one hand with the other reaching forward. As the dragon approached, she threw her sword as hard as she could. Its blade stuck deep into the dragon's head killing it instantly. It slid along the ground stopping just before her feet.

Kelar picked himself up slowly. His spine healing fast. "That was very impressive, Neasha."

Using her telekinesis, she returned the sword to her hand. "My mind is opening, Kelar! I can feel it!" She was excited. "Are you okay?"

"I'm in pain, really stiff. But getting better quickly." He groaned.

A dragon landed next to them and snapped its venom filled tail at Neasha. With unnatural speed Kelar raised his hand and with a mere thought snapped the dragon's neck. It dropped to the ground dead.

Both Kelar and Neasha looked at each other in disbelief. Their minds were expanding exponentially as their psychic abilities heightened.

King Siris ordered his knights to take cover along the mountain face. "Protect the wizard!" he shouted while thrusting his sword into the chest of a dragon.

Kolos grabbed Malores and ushered him to safety inside a mountain crevasse. A dragon landed close behind them and reached its head part way through the narrow crevasse. In a frustrated frenzy the dragon clawed and snapped viciously toward them. It roared revealing a full set of sharp salivating fangs. Malores and Kolos' hair blew straight back. Kolos fell to his knees before the dragon's mouth. His mind expanded exponentially as his psychic abilities heightened. The dragon snapped its mouth inches from Kolos' head. Kolos opened his eyes and screamed while thrusting his hands forward. His voice exploded into a sonic blast shredding the dragon to pieces.

Siris ran out into the open, his sword stained in reptilian blood. Two dragons soared toward him flying barely 10 feet above the ground. Siris levitated a fallen tree and tossed it striking one to the ground. The other dragon maneuvered around it. Siris waited patiently as the dragon flew toward him. In the last moment he swung his sword around and decapitated the attacking dragon. Its head and body slid along the ground colliding into the mountain behind him. Siris walked toward two other dragons. His sword dripping in blood, his cloak blowing in the wind. Frightened, the two remaining dragons flew away.

Lord Demonis stood by the mine site with sword stained in blood. The sky above him was shadowed with swarming dragons. Demonis placed his sword away and held his hands outward. All the mined boulders and rubble started floating around him. With an evil grin he launched the projectiles toward the swarm of dragons. Defenceless in the face of Demonis' bombardment, the dragons retreated to Jirasab.

Neasha helped the recovering Kelar to his feet. His fractured spine had completely mended.

"How are you feeling now, Kelar?"

"I'm feeling better by the second," he amazed. "But this has me thinking, Neasha."

"About what, love."

"If those were the smallest dragons, I'm not looking forward to meeting a large one."

"Looks like there's dragon on the menu boys!" shouted King Siris with a hint of insanity.

"Is the wizard alive?" Lord Demonis demanded deflating Siris' ploy for humour. "I said! Is the wizard still alive?"

"He's right here," replied Kolos escorting him out from the mountain crevasse.

"Excellent work, Kolos." Demonis grinned. "From this day forward, make Malores your highest priority. Only a conjurer of magic can play the Dragon's Flute." Malores brushed the dust from his robes elegantly. Demonis' words had given him a regained sense of importance.

"As you wish." Kolos bowed as he spoke.

After regrouping from the dragon onslaught, the Sykanians stacked their dead and set them ablaze to prevent the spread of disease. As ordered by Siris they also skinned the dragons and butchered the meat.

Neasha, still contemplating the whereabouts of the Dragon's Flute, walked over to the decayed corpse of Lord Radik Shade, and searched through his robes. Unsuccessful, she placed her hand down his boot where she felt something. Her eyes widened. "King Siris!" She hollered. Neasha raised the Dragon's Flute above her head for all to see.

Both Siris and Demonis ran over to her in disbelief. Neasha handed the flute to Siris who admired its intricacies. The enchanted flute was carved from the talon of a Silverback dragon. Siris handed it to Demonis who, too, was captivated by its beauty.

"Captain Korrigan." King Siris summoned him to come forward.

"Yes, your majesty."

"I need a messenger."

"As you wish, your majesty." The captain ordered a random Sykanian Knight to come forward.

"What's your name, Sir Knight?" asked King Siris.

"I am Sir Riclean Messenger, your majesty."

"That's too funny." Siris looking around to see if anyone else got it. "Come on you guys, his name is Messenger and I'm asking him to be a messenger. No one finds that just a tad funny?"

"I do, your majesty." Spoke Captain Korrigan in a serious tone.

"You don't seem humoured." Siris was unconvinced.

"I'm laughing on the inside, your majesty."

Siris shrugged him off and addressed the messenger. "Sir Messenger, I want you to deliver this letter to Lord Drakus." Siris released a mild chuckle still appreciating the humour.

"Where will I find Lord Drakus, your majesty?"

Collecting himself he answered. "Wait for him at the Elvin Ocean docks. There will be a ship setting sail on its maiden voyage. Lord Drakus will be overseeing the ceremonies."

"As you wish, my king. Consider the job done." The messenger mounted his steed and galloped off.

Demonis revealed the Dragon Flute's scroll of music he stole from the Arkonian castle a decade ago. "Put this scroll in your purse, Malores. I will hold the flute."

"As you wish my lord."

Demonis placed the flute within his robes and smiled as he and Siris watched as the messenger rode off on his quest.

"Soon Cretes…soon all will unfold."

Chapter XXI
Six Demons.

On a clear night, Milita gazed toward the star-lit sky. Her time with the Elves had proven insightful. Yet, deep inside she still felt betrayed by God and the universe. She felt her anger was grounded in self-justification because of the brutal murder of her parents. Milita desired vengeance, not peace, and held God accountable for her loss.

"May I join you?" Savita spoke as she approached.

"But of course." Smiled Milita as she gazed into the stars.

Savita admired the starlit night as well.

"How are you holding up, Mili?"

"I'm doing okay."

"The Elves worry over you. They say you have much hate."

"I guess." Milita had no interest in talking about this. She let her mind drift off into the stars.

"I, too, lost my parents. I can relate to your pain."

"It's not right, Savita!" Mili was quick to let her anger show and then retreated with, "I mean, it's just not right."

"The Elvin elders tell me you haven't found peace with the universe."

"How can anyone ever find that peace, Savita?"

"I did."

"How could you believe in the creator of all life when it takes away the ones you love? When it allows such atrocities to unfold?"

"The universe is far more complex than that Mili."

"Is it? Is God even willing to prevent evil, Savita, or is it unable? If so, that would make it less than omnipotent. Or is it able, but not willing? Wouldn't that make it malevolent? And if it's both able and willing then why call it a god?"

"You have a strong case, Mili. However, you lack understanding of how the universe works."

"Understanding? All I see is a god who does nothing while endless people suffer, while religions conquer and divide one another over false divine righteousness. All are killing one another for the blessing of God's grace! Where is God now?"

"God is all around us, Mili."

"Then where was God when my father was murdered? Where was God when my mother was being raped? Where was God when her throat was slit? She bled out slowly, Savita, and don't you dare tell me that God works in mysterious ways! That is no answer. It's just a line used by those who fear falling from God's grace!"

"You seem to have it all figured out, Mili."

"I don't mean to sound rude. But I've never felt God's presence…nor do I want to."

"I see." Savita showed no judgment and listened.

"Just the idea of God puts me in a dark place. The world is a dark place, Savita. God, the universe, is supposed to be our hope yet it asks me to awaken Malshidiel. It asks me to defeat the Darkstar. I am not hope! I'm only me," she surrendered.

Savita stared back into the star-lit sky.

"The darkest of nights bring out the brightest of stars, Mili. You are not hope. You're the star that leads us to hope."

Milita fell silent.

"Come, Mili, follow me. There's something you need to see."

Savita led her to a domed room deep within the Elvin castle. Inside the visibility was limited. It's only light coming from a large purple gem displayed in the middle of a round table. Surrounding the table were reclined chairs. Three of them were occupied by the Elvin elders: Nym, Respen and Eldrin.

"Have a seat, Mili." offered Nym. "You are about to witness the truth of the universe."

Savita and Mili sat into their reclining chairs and stared toward the ceiling. The light within the gem expanded and the room filled with a storm of multi-coloured mist.

"I want you to focus on my voice," instructed Nym. The room fluctuated with light that slowly dimmed to darkness. "Before time existed, there was only a vast celestial entity commonly referred to as God."

"What was before God?" interrupted Milita.

"Time did not exist. Therefore, nothing was before nor after," explained Nym.

The purple gem's light expanded into an energy cloud hovering over the table. Then Nym continued to narrate. "Lonely, God created from its own body of energy, a group of immortals known as angels."

The purple gem formed several angels within the cloud of energy.

"There was only peace in the realm they called heaven—a place of absolute perfection until a group of angels craved more."

The purple gem focused on six fallen angels.

"Lucifer, Hades, Belial, Beelzebub, Asmodeus, and Baelin rejected the perfection of their existence and raged war amongst the heavens. The angels fought back and defeated the demons. They imprisoned the six fallen angels into a sphere known as the Darkstar."

"Why didn't God just destroy them?" asked Milita.

“Angels were created by slivers of God’s own energy. To destroy them would be to destroy a part of itself. Instead, God realized the utopia created for its angels was inherently unstable. Each angel was different, and no two desires could be simultaneously satisfied.”

The purple gem’s light formed into a black hole of dark matter hovering over the table. “So, God decided to change existence and created an enormous implosion.” The sphere’s image of the black hole imploded into a unique matter of absolute gravity.

“Then the universe was born, and time began,” narrated Nym.

The purple gem’s illusion sped up time showing the formation of stars and planets. Billions of galaxies expanded exponentially with each galaxy forming their own solar systems rotating in their respective gravitational pulls.

“Billions of years passed,” continued Nym. “In each dimension, planets evolved life from single cell organisms until evolution reached consciousness. The awakening of the first naturally created souls blessed with free will. God understood that only by experiencing a life of mortality could the soul appreciate the utopian perfections of heaven.”

“So, God’s growing angels?” interrupted Milita. “What about babies and children who die young? How are they to learn life’s gift?”

“There are some who live full lives and never understand a glimpse of life’s truth,” answered Savita, “which others grasp fully in the short time of their existence. However, none of God’s children learn from one cycle of life.”

“So, we’re reincarnated?” asked Milita.

"Not reincarnated, Milita," corrected Nym. "We're born in every dimension concurrently. Each fraction of our soul living a different life under different circumstances. In the afterlife, the fractional soul remains in their dimension for the time needed to let go of their physical form. From there our fractional souls from each dimension gather in the depths of the afterlife where we unite as one collective soul, sharing each self's memories and experiences. When conflict is resolved from our hardships, our united soul submits to the heavens."

"I can't imagine how full heaven must be," poked Milita.

Savita smiled. "When you stare into the night sky Mili, can you count how many stars you see? Yet, despite so many stars, you can see that there are plenty of spaces in between."

"No, I can't count them and yes, there are spaces." She admitted. "What about the ones who commit murder or suicide? Do they just walk into heaven, too?"

"There is no hell, Mili. Everyone knows the difference between right and wrong. However, evolution has its mishaps. Sometimes we are born with mental illnesses or depressions. Sometimes life itself sends you tumbling down a dark path. In death we are released from our physical barriers and the souls who lived violent lives often spend more time dwelling in the afterlife. Once our soul fragments from each dimension unite as one, our combined energy creates a balanced soul much needed to appreciate the perfections of heaven and the forgiveness of our sins."

"But my mom and dad," cried Milita, "why did they have to leave me? Why would God allow this?"

"Divine intervention alters a future only God could see. You must trust in God's wisdom, for the universe is holistic."

Milita paused in distaste. "What about animals? They have consciousness."

"Yes, Mili," answered Savita. "Any creature that shows love or compassion is driven by a soul."

"So, if a dog has a soul, then I guess God's making inferior angels." Milita sized the opportunity to make the jab.

"Indeed," answered Savita, "but, don't worry, the animals think nothing less of you."

Milita's eyes widened.

Nym continued to narrate the story of the gem's images. "During the creation of the universe, the Darkstar was pulled into the realm of time." The purple gem displayed a glowing image of the Darkstar spiralling down to Earth.

"Not knowing its whereabouts, God divided its angels amongst the billions of galaxies in search for the Darkstar. Earth and Drakonia were two planets in the many galaxies Malshidiel had been assigned. With the aid of we Elves, we located the Darkstar on Earth holding five demon captives."

"I thought there were six demons?" queried Milita.

"There were. While entering the Milky Way, Baelin managed to separate from the Darkstar. The demon landed on Earth and took the form of flesh and blood. He scorched the Earth searching for the Darkstar."

The purple gem reflected the image of the Elvin castle on Earth.

"After the energy of the Milky Way released one demon, we Elves decided to reinforce the Darkstar with a spell in the form of a scroll, a Scroll Key that if destroyed would release the demon captives. It is the very scroll hidden within Castle Malshidiel and Baelin searches endlessly for it."

The purple gem showed images of Baelin's army of men attacking the Elvin castle. The castle walls tumbled, towers fell, and the Elves were decimated.

"After the inevitable loss of the war on Earth, Baelin retrieved the Darkstar," continued Nym. "Malshidiel recovered the key scroll and brought us to Drakonia as a refuge."

"I'm told that I will help Malshidiel destroy the Darkstar. Won't that be destroying a part of God?"

"No, the demons have been stuck in time for billions of years. Their connection to God has long since diminished," answered Nym.

"Then why doesn't God kill them?"

"The spirit world is a dimensional barrier separating heaven from the realms of time. God's abilities here are limited. Only the angels can pass through the gateway of time. However, they need mortality to walk this world. That is why Malshidiel started the Komalsh."

"What will happen if the Darkstar is opened?" asked Milita.

"The demons will rise, and mankind will be enslaved. The fabric of our reality will intertwine with the spirit world and time will cease to exist. Eternal slavery under demonic order will be the result."

"How could one angel defeat six demons? Even with an army of Komalsh, we stand no chance."

"Malshidiel is not alone, Milita. God created an army of beings born to the realm of time. This army is comprised of a group of uncanny creatures separate from the natural evolution of life. We were created for one reason—to destroy the Darkstar."

"The Mythicals…"

"Yes, Milita, we are Malshidiel's immortal army," answered Nym, "and you are the one to awaken Malshidiel. You are the one to lead our army."

"What of the other angels God sent?" asked Milita.

"They're all trapped in different dimensions," answered Nym. "They cannot help us."

The purple gem lit up the room. Milita's eyes slowly adjusted.

"How do you feel, Milita?" asked Nym.

"This is much to process. I need time."

"Time, my dear, is a luxury we don't have." Nym was most firm.

Chapter XXII
The Purple Flower.

Lord Drakus and his unicorn, Mythra, wondered aimlessly through the Mystique Forest. They had no sense of urgency and no place to be—a rare occasion to enjoy the simpler things in life. Lord Hirum Drakus appreciated these moments he had with Mythra. Over the past three decades of serving Malshidiel they had seen much adventure and great wonder. They had also suffered much loss, heartache, and pain. They'd become cold to the world of Drakonia but never cold to each other.

"We are getting old, my friend."

"Speak for yourself." Mythra was having none of this.

Lord Drakus stood silent as though sarcasm had no place. Mythra had noticed his darkened demeaner as of late. He'd seen him go through many difficult times but never had he seen him in such a state of turmoil and depression.

"You don't seem yourself today, Hirum. Are you feeling, okay?"

"Mythra…" Drakus hesitated. "I would like you to know everything as I do. With your permission I will share my precognitive dreams."

"I thought we agreed sharing your insight could jeopardise the future?" reminded Mythra.

"I'm afraid, old friend, the future as I see it is already set in stone. Therefore, I want you to see it as I do."

"As you wish," agreed the unicorn.

Drakus placed his hands over Mythra's head and closed his eyes. He opened his mind and shared his prophetic dreams. Mythra scrolled through his memories and for a long moment there was only silence. When Mythra returned, he gasped as though the very air from his lungs was taken. Slowly processing all he witnessed, Mythra could now understand his friend's recent behavior.

"I am terribly sorry, Hirum. I assure you; we will carry this burden together."

"Thank you, Mythra." Drakus patted his neck. "You are my closest friend."

"Friends for life," reassured Mythra.

Drakus grinned. "I remember the first time you said that."

"I, as well. It was the first day we met in this very forest."

Lord Drakus and Mythra carried on with their stroll through the Mystique Forest. They enjoyed their quiet time together.

"Come Mythra. It's time to meet the future."

When Lord Drakus and Mythra returned to Utopia they went straight to the combat training grounds. The rumours going around spoke of Lord Terex Gungnir's success in the Komalsh's Elite combat training. Currently he was competing in hand-to-hand combat and Drakus was eager to watch.

Since his arrival, Terex was undefeated in all aspects of combat. Always a good sport in every competition, Terex's positive attitude made him a fan favourite among his Komalsh brothers and sisters.

Lady Tori Preddy was the head instructor of the Komalsh's Elite combat training program—a position she had held for over a decade since the former instructor Lord Siris' defection. She was a well-respected Komalsh who took a quick shine to Terex's natural ability.

"Excellent work!" She complimented Terex after he defeated his opponent at wrestling. "Now this time I want you to spar with your sword, Terex. Lord Mack, you're up."

"Good morning, Lady Preddy." Lord Drakus and Mythra greeted her adding, "Lord Gungnir has impressive skills."

"Good morning, Lord Drakus. Good morning Mythra. Terex is my greatest student. Come, watch with me."

****

Lady Tori Preddy, like Lord Drakus, was of Dosanian culture. She graduated from Olemeeze the same year as Lord Soren Kyros. Tori stood five foot nine inches tall and carried 175 pounds of toned physique. She proved to be a worthy replacement to Lord Cretes Siris shortly after he defected. She and Lord Kyros were close friends.

****

Lord Mack, a seasoned Komalsh, entered the combat circle with his sword drawn. Terex and Mack respectfully bowed to each other and then proceeded to take their combat stance. Circling each other, they began clashing blades. Mack was quick to get the upper hand and separated Terex from his sword. Mack then thrusted his blade toward Terex's heart stopping inches away from contact. Frustrated by his opponent's skill, Terex slapped Mack's blade away with his durenthium plated knuckles and then punched him hard in the chest. The impact sent Lord Mack sailing backwards through the crowd. With a thud he slammed hard into the stone wall and dropped to the ground face-first.

"Ah, sorry about that," apologized Terex. "My strength seems to be increasing by the day."

"That's okay!" moaned Lord Mack sprawled out on the ground.

"We all share the same abilities, Lord Gungnir." explained Lady Preddy. "However, the forest's venom amplifies who we were. Our will becomes our strength. Your will has gained you physical power."

"I feel it, Lady Preddy, I feel very powerful." Terex picked up his sword and waved it around. "I need something heavier than this. It doesn't feel right."

Lord Arias Jackyle and the metalsmith Burlok brought out a larger version of the Komalsh sword designed by Arias.

"After building your fist and foot armour, Terex, I figured a stronger, heavier sword would complement your increasing strength. So, the dwarves and I built you this."

Arias handed Terex a two-handed broad sword. Terex admired its size and weight. He smiled with gratitude. "Thank you, Arias." Then grabbing his old sword, he tossed it deep into the Mystique Forest.

"That is a remarkable sword, Lord Jackyle." complimented Drakus.

"He is a quick learner, Lord Drakus," Burlok was happy to boast about his most capable student. "Show him what you made for yourself, Lord Jackyle."

Arias revealed an X-shaped durenthium boomerang. "Watch this!" He threw the boomerang and without control, it sailed through the air cutting down everything in its path. Tree branches, flowers and hedges fell to the ground as Komalsh, and Earth creatures alike dove for safety. Then the X came to a halt by embedding itself into a large rock.

Everyone fell silent.

Arias looked at Drakus feeling a little embarrassed. "Needs a bit of work, I think." He chuckled hoping laughter would be the cure. Then the rock in which the boomerang was embedded broke in half.

Lady Preddy put her hand on Arias' shoulder. With great admiration she suggested. "Instead of focusing on its design, guide it with your mind."

Lady Preddy opened her hand, and the boomerang flew to her grasp. She handed it to Arias.

Arias wound up and threw it again. Using his telekinesis, he maneuvered the boomerang through buildings weaving in and around obstacles. He did loops around locals and chased a dog down the path. Then gracefully he returned it to his hand.

"Where Terex excels in strength, you excel in telekinesis. Know your strengths Arias and use them to your advantage," encouraged Lady Preddy.

Terex felt a vote of confidence from Lady Preddy's words and held out his hand. "I think I have the hang of this now." Using his telekinesis, he pulled the boomerang from Arias' hand. With no control, the boomerang flew by Terex and punctured deep into Trayke's shoulder.

Trayke staggered backward. He stared in absolute disbelief at the boomerang protruding from his body. Then blood started squirting from his wound.

"What's wrong with you!" glared Trayke.

"I'm sorry," apologised Terex.

"You're sorry! What the hell, man!" angered Trayke.

"Come on, Trayke. I said I was sorry. Here, let me pull that out for you."

"No bloody way! You just stay the hell away from me, man!"

"Don't be a baby, buddy. You'll heal." Terex's words were calming but his sincerity was lacking.

"It bloody hurts, Terex!" gasped Trayke.

"Lord Basa!" commanded Drakus. "When you are done bleeding all over the place, I'd like you to locate Lords Tarius and Shade immediately. I request everyone's presence in the castle's waiting lounge."

"Yes, Lord Drakus," answered Trayke while removing the boomerang from his shoulder. He returned it to Arias while glaring at Terex balefully.

Terex shrugged his shoulders. "I said I was sorry."

Trayke mounted his unicorn, Charley, whose features caused both Arias and Terex to wince. Then they rode off into the Mystique Forest in search of Nyte and Kris.

****

Unicorns were elegant and beautiful animals. But Charley wasn't. His larger than normal ears, his one crossed eye and his over-sized tongue which hung to the side of his mouth showed that the beauty of unicorns is sometimes a myth.

****

"There's something wrong with that unicorn," said Terex with a snicker.

"Yep, something wrong with Trayke, too." Chuckled Arias.

"Terex, Arias, come, walk with me," ordered Drakus. His words were sharp.

The two young Lords joined Drakus and headed toward the castle.

As they walked along, Terex and Arias noticed several Komalsh scattered about on a grassy field. They were praying in their own cultural manner - each one born of a different kingdom - each one raised with different rituals.

"Lord Drakus," wondered Terex. "Why are there so many different religions in Drakonia?"

"We all seek our own path to God and our own paths vary because we vary," answered Drakus.

"But as Komalsh our teachings differ from the traditional biblical religions. Why would these Komalsh practice biblical rituals instead of our own?" Terex asked curiously.

"Our teachings view God as an energy, the universe, where most feel comfortable viewing God as a man," answered Drakus. "When really it is one God, one universe no matter how you perceive it. We encourage our Komalsh to talk to the universe in the way they feel most comfortable."

"Don't all Drakonian religions derive from one bible?" asked Arias. "I heard somewhere that the bible came from Earth, too. Is there any truth behind that Lord Drakus?"

"Yes, Arias, all Drakonian religions are different translations of the same bible. A bible not only from Earth but from Earth's future," Drakus added.

"Then how did it get to Drakonia?" Dumbfounded Terex.

"That is better off asked of the ones who brought it here." Drakus was deliberately evasive.

"And who might that be?" wondered Arias.

"You'll meet them soon enough," assured Drakus while entering the castle.

Terex and Arias followed close behind.

Nyte Shade spent his afternoon wandering aimlessly through the Mystique Forest. He stopped by a stream to refill his gourd then carried on down a path through old growth trees and brightly coloured brush. The summer air was sweetened by pollen and the singing from the birds was like a melodic theme for a dream. His aimless stroll was a peaceful trek on most occasions.

However, the deeper into the forest Nyte wandered, the darker his thoughts became. Those sounds and smells of the forest receded in the face of the doubt that clouded his mind. He sat against an enormous tree where pixies flew about carelessly curious to his presence. Disconnected from his surroundings, Nyte sank deeper into his troubled mind.

"What's bothering you, Nyte?" asked Kris leaning against the tree.

"What do you mean?" Nyte was startled.

"Don't answer a question with a question, my oldest friend. I know you too well, Nyte, and if I can sneak up on you, I know there's something eating you inside." Kris sat down next to Nyte and started tossing rocks. "Remember when we were kids, Nyte? That large boulder we used to climb?"

"Yeah, I remember."

"I remember you could never climb that rock, Nyte. I used to encourage you to try yet you always fell to the ground before you could reach the top. You used to get so frustrated. I saw it in your eyes then like I see it in your eyes now." Kris stood up from the ground. "Remember that day, Nyte, you got so close to the top of that boulder. You were about to lose your grip and fall. That's when I extended my hand to you. You grabbed my wrist, and I helped you to the top. After that, Nyte, you climbed that rock every day."

Kris reached his hand down to Nyte. "I'm here for you, brother. So, I ask once again, what's troubling you?"

Nyte grabbed his wrist and Kris helped him to his feet. “Sorry, Kris. I should never shut you out. It’s my dreams. They’ve become intense. The only trouble is they’re filled with riddles.”

“You mean like you right now?” snickered Kris. “Look, I know you dream of the future. You’ve been doing it since as long as I can remember. So, explain your dream and maybe I can help.”

“Well to sum up the dream it basically says without faith, without destiny, I will die.”

Kris expressed deep thought and concern. “Loki told me you saved a baby named Faith.”

“Yes, we actually did.” Nyte was quick to verify the truth.

“So then, all we need to do is find out who or what this destiny is.”

“That’s what worries me, Kris. What if I don’t?”

“Listen to me, old friend. You found Faith by making the right decision, helping someone in need. You will figure out this destiny too. Do you know how I know? Because you have good friends like me to help.” Kris being a larger man compared to Nyte, wrapped his arms around him and squeezed out his breath. “We are brothers!”

“Brothers!” gasped Nyte.

“Come now, let’s get back to Utopia. I’m starved!”

While the two old friends headed back toward the castle, Nyte’s curiosity about Kris’ sword came to the fore.

“So, you say you received that sword from inside the Mystique Forest?”

“That’s right, an older version of me handed it over as a gift. I just can’t figure out if he was real or not.”

“May I hold it?” asked Nyte.

Kris handed the sword over to Nyte who waved it around.

“Seems pretty real to me.”

“I was referring to the old man,” reminded Kris.

"Well, friend…real sword, real man."
Nyte handed the sword back to him.
"Yeah, good point Nyte."
"Is that why you're out here?" pondered Nyte.
"Searching for your older self?"
"No, I just asked Loki where you went."
"Loki talks a lot."
"Loki just cares about you," defended Kris. "He's one of us, brother."

Trayke Basa and his unicorn, Charley, burst out through a nearby bush. "There you are. Lord Drakus summons you!"

Both Nyte and Kris stared at the peculiarities of Charley. His larger than normal ears, his one crossed eye and that tongue which hung from the side of his mouth freely were, indeed, odd.

"I'm sure he'll grow on us." Kris cringed at the thought.

Inside Castle Malshidiel, Lord Drakus, Terex, and Arias sat around a new table in the waiting lounge. Twiggins had replaced the old table shortly after Lord Jarestt destroyed the original during his recent visit. Lord Drakus liked the old table. He despised Lord Jarestt. The three waited quietly for the others to arrive.

"What happened to the old table?" asked Arias breaking the awkward silence.

"It broke," replied Drakus coldly.

The room turned awkwardly silent.

Twiggins entered the room with a huge platter of lunch. Following behind him were Nyte, Kris, and Trayke.

"Nice new table!" admired Trayke while sitting down. "What happened to the old one?"

Drakus stewed in anger.

"It broke," answered Arias.

Lord Soren Kyros entered the room holding two bottles of Arkonian wine. The young Lords rose immediately in respect.

"Please seat yourself," he commanded while pouring wine into each of their goblets. "We've gathered you here for two reasons, new Lords. First, to congratulate you on your acceptance to Malshidiel's knighthood." Lord Kyros raised his goblet in the air. "A toast to our newest members. Cheers!"

After the cheers, Drakus set his goblet down and took over the meeting. "Now then, the second reason for our assembly. We are all aware Lord Kyros will be setting off to sea tomorrow on the Elvin ship, Excelsior. This will be an important exploration voyage and he may not return for some time. In his absence, I will need to choose a replacement as second in command of the Komalsh. Lord Nyte Shade, please rise." Drakus rose from his seat and drew out his sword.

Nyte stood perplexed. He turned to his friends for support. Kris, Arias, Terex and Trayke rose from their seats each holding a smile bigger than the next.

"We will follow you to the end, Nyte," said Kris.

His friends drew their swords and knelt on one knee. In this way each was showing their confidence in Lord Drakus' decision.

Nyte was dumbfounded by the decision. "I don't understand. Why me?"

"Like your mother and father, you, too, possess the Komalsh's greatest gift. To dream the future. I can see it in your eyes, Lord Shade, and one day you will see it too. When that day arrives, you will become the most powerful Komalsh of our generation."

Nyte shook his head. "I'm only as powerful as the people who stand by me."

Lord Kyros smiled at Nyte's response. "A leader is not one who demands respect. A leader is one who earns it."

Nyte looked back to his friends kneeling on the floor.

"Well!" grumbled Terex. "My knee hurts. Hurry up!"

Reluctantly, Nyte knelt before Drakus.

"Today I choose the next leader of the Komalsh."

Raising his sword, Lord Drakus placed his blade on Nyte's right shoulder. "As a Lord of psychic enlightenment to Malshidiel's order, as you kneel in deference to your lord, I confer the honour of serving as my voice when I am distant. Remember your allegiance to my command and all the Komalsh. His voice is the same as mine when I am not there to speak. Rise Lord Nyte Shade, as my successor, as servant of Malshidiel."

"I accept with great honour."

"Rise Lord Shade."

Lord Nyte Shade turned back to his friends. "Rise, my brothers. You shall never kneel before me again." Kris Tarius, Arias Jackyle, Terex Gungnir and Trayke Basa stood with their swords raised high.

"To Lord Shade!"

"This is exciting, buddy!" Trayke cheered.

"It's only temporary," Nyte just wanted to downplay it all. "I doubt I'll have to worry about much."

The uncanny cook, Twiggins, placed his skeletal hand on Nyte's shoulder. "Exciting news, indeed! Lord Shade, your parents would be proud of you!"

Drakus placed a small wooden chest on the table.

"Your first quest, Lord Shade, is for all of you to deliver this chest to the Cluricaun Tavern. There you'll find two Earth beings by the names of Brian and Lee-Ann. They're the owners of this ancient establishment. Once they open this chest, you will listen to what they say. Are my orders clear?"

"Yes, my lord," acknowledged Nyte.

"Brian and Lee-Ann?" laughed Terex. "Those are the strangest names I've ever heard!"

"They've been around for over a thousand years." explained Lord Kyros. "They're nothing like the Earth beings you're used too."

"When do we go?" asked Nyte.

"Immediately," replied Drakus. "Head straight there and avoid all contact with anyone. It is crucial you waste no time." Drakus' directions were assertive.

"Understood," replied Nyte. "Lords, let's ride!"

After seeing the new Lord's off on their quest, Drakus and Kyros walked along the inner edge of the Mystique Forest. There stood a tall tombstone. Engraved on it was the name, Kayla Drakus. Below that read Tessa. Lord Hirum Drakus knelt on one knee and placed a purple flower on their grave. "My wife, my stillborn child. How I miss you so."

"How long has it been, Hirum," asked Lord Kyros.

"Fifteen years, Soren. I remember how happy she looked while pregnant. That was supposed to be the greatest day of our lives. Instead, it was the worst day of my life."

"It was a tragedy, Lord Drakus, their deaths due to complications from the pregnancy. She was a great woman, my lord." Lord Kyros tried to be understanding.

"She was a great wife."

"I'll leave you to your privacy, my lord."

"Thank you, Soren."

"One question puzzles me, Lord Drakus. Why did you never remarry?"

"Man spends his whole life looking for that one right women. I found mine. There was no need to keep searching. When I die, she will be there waiting for me as I have waited for her."

“I understand, my lord.”

Kyros left him to his privacy.

“I miss you so much, Kayla. Every year on your birthday, I’ve placed a purple flower on your grave.” Drakus placed his hand on her tombstone. “I miss you so much my love.” A tear rolled down his cheek and splashed onto the purple flower.

Since her passing, Hirum had become jaded, cold, and distant to the world. She was the fire that warmed his heart. Now only embers remained.

Hirum whispered to her grave. “In life we sleep, in death we awaken. I will see you soon my love.”

Chapter XXIII
Whispers from the Dead.

After a few days of riding, Nyte and his friends arrived along the forests edge of the Soapstone hills. The young Lords set up camp and ate around a blazing fire. Their unicorn counterparts, exhausted from travel, slept hidden in the nearby forest. Tomorrow they were to arrive at the Cluricaun Tavern to deliver the chest as instructed by Lord Drakus.

For now, only food and rest mattered.

Trayke lit up his pipe and smoked its sweet herbs.

"So, what do you think is in the chest?" he timed his breathing poorly and coughed.

"I don't know," answered Nyte staring at its simple design, "but whatever it is, it must be important."

"Why do you say that, Nyte?" Trayke choked again from the pipe smoke.

"Well, it's locked for one and why else would Lord Drakus have it delivered by five Komalsh?"

"Yep, seems like overkill if you ask me," said Arias.

"Can't we just smash it open and see what's inside?" suggested Terex.

"Or even better, added Trayke, we'll just get Terex here to use his telekinesis. I'm sure it'll be broken in no time!"

"You're still mad about the boomerang, aren't you?" razzed Terex.

"We're not smashing anything." Kris appointed himself protector of the box. "This is our first quest, and we will deliver it as Lord Drakus requested."

"Yeah, what Kris said," agreed Nyte. "Still, I can't say that I'm not curious."

All of them stared at the chest. Only the sound of crickets could be heard.

"Oh, come on you guys!" Kris was disappointed that they were even talking about breaking open the box. "We will find out tomorrow. You can wait."

"You are right. We can wait." Said Nyte with a trace of doubt.

All of them once again stared at the chest. The crickets were loud tonight.

"Well, I know what I can't wait for." Stood Trayke breaking the silent stare. "I need to go take a leak."

"Don't piss into the wind," warned Arias.

"No, no, I won't do that again!" replied Trayke.

Trayke wandered off into the forest. His vision was limited by the moonlight. He started to pee when off in the distance he noticed a dark figure. It ran from one tree to the next, blending in with the shadows. Startled, Trayke closed his eyes and searched the area with his psychic gift. Other than some birds sleeping in their nests, he detected no other heartbeats. Unconvinced of his findings, he stared toward the tree where the shadow had stopped. As his eyes adapted to the darkness, he started to see the vague silhouette of a person standing still. Trayke looked closer to identify what he was seeing if anything at all.

Frightened, the shadow bolted before Trayke's eyes and hid behind a nearby bush. Trayke followed the shadow behind the bush where he saw a figure kneeling over a decaying corpse. She appeared to be a young girl with colourless features—a mere reflection of the deceased on the ground.

Startled, she stared back at Trayke. She couldn't understand how he could see her. Confused and afraid, she turned to run away.

"Stop! It's okay, I won't harm you!" To show his respect, Trayke went down on one knee.

"I'm afraid," whispered the shadowed girl.

“I can help you,” offered Trayke reaching out his hand.

She reached out in return. Her ghostly fingers passed through Trayke’s hand giving him chills that he felt to the bone.

“You’re a ghost?” This fascinated Trayke.

The ghost pointed to the corpse which had been brutalized by a predator’s hunger.

“Is that me?” she whimpered. “What’s happening to me?”

“I believe you’re in the spirit world,” answered Trayke.

“Then how is it you can see me?”

“I’m a Komalsh with special abilities. I can see and evidently communicate with the recently deceased. However, I’m still figuring it all out.”

“What do I do?” She believed she was lost.

“What’s your name?” asked Trayke to soothe her fears.

“Isabell,” she replied.

“That’s a beautiful name. I’m Trayke.”

“Thank you, Trayke.”

“Well, Isabell. I don’t have an answer for you. I’m new at this myself. In fact, you’re the strongest spirit I’ve encountered.”

Isabell worried. “I’m all alone?”

“No, you’re not alone. You’re welcome to stay with me until things sort themselves out.”

She smiled with renewed hope. “Thank you, Trayke.”

“Trayke! You still alive buddy?” shouted Arias from the fire.

Trayke turned toward the fire and answered Arias.

“I’ll be right there!”

When he turned back, Isabell was gone.

“Isabell?” Trayke searched the area briefly, but her spirit was nowhere to be seen.

Trayke felt perturbed with his own psychic ability. As a child he remembered seeing ghosts of the recently deceased. But since his introduction to the Mystique Forest's venom, this gift, this curse, had escalated. Trayke shook it off and returned to the campfire.

"Wow Trayke!" Arias laughed. "You look like you just saw a ghost!"

"What do you mean…ghost?" stammered Trayke.

"Well, you're awfully pale bud," he answered.

"Yeah, Trayke." Nyte added, "Maybe you should go lay down. Perhaps we should all get some rest."

The young Lords concurred, and they all went to sleep.

Under a sheet of stars, the tired young Lords slept around the smoldering campfire. Trayke snuggled into his blankets. Undecided whether to be disturbed or humbled, he stared off into the shadows of the forest waiting for Isabell to appear. Exhausted, his eyes grew heavy, and he drifted off to sleep.

Hidden in the shadows of the forest, Isabell watched over Trayke and the young Lords.

In the early morning hour, a dark witch stood on an open field. Her burgundy tattered cloak floated in the breeze. She lowered her hood revealing long black greasy hair and golden-brown skin discoloured and decayed. Her eyes were demonic.

From a distance she watched over the young Lords while they slept. Behind her thirteen hell hounds slowly approached. Cerberus, the pack leader, sat next to the witch.

"I need Lord Nyte Shade alive," she instructed. "Kill the rest."

"As you wish, Enchantress," growled Cerberus.

The hellhounds ran stealthily down the hill toward the unsuspecting Komalsh.

The young Lords were fast asleep around a dying campfire. Trayke, lost in a dream, started to smell a strong odour of soil and mildew. Its pungent scent was potent enough to waken him. As his eyes opened and came into focus, above him stood the spirit of Isabell staring back.

"What the hell!" shrieked Trayke as he struggled to his feet.

"Wake the others, Trayke!" warned Isabell. "You are in grave danger!" She whispered while vanishing into the shadows.

Trayke went over to Nyte and shook him awake. "Wake up, Nyte! Wake up! We're in grave…" From behind a hellhound bit onto Trayke's head and viciously dragged him backward. Trayke grabbed onto the hound's powerful jaws and struggled to hold them open to keep the dog from crushing his skull. The hound squeezed harder and slowly sank its long fangs into Trayke's throat. Trayke screamed for help as the hound started whipping his body about.

Terex awoke from Trayke's screams. He grabbed his two-handed broad sword and decapitated the hellhound attached to Trayke.

Trayke returned to his feet and pulled the dogs head off his own. His neck and throat were ripped apart by the hound's sharp fangs. Dark red blood gushed from his neck as he fell to his knees gasping for air.

Arias quickly wrapped his cloak around Trayke's neck and applied pressure. He slowed down the bleeding allowing his healing abilities the time needed to catch up. Nyte stood guard beside them with his sword drawn. His senses ran wild. He searched the forest with his psychic gift but could only feel the heartbeats of his friends. "That must be the only one!"

Another hellhound leaped through the bush toward Kris who was still reaching for his sword. Nyte swung his blade and decapitated the hound. With the second swing of Nyte's sword, he decapitated another who attacked him from behind.

"Where are they coming from?" Kris was unable to sense their heartbeats.

Yet another hellhound leaped out of the bush toward Terex. Terex grabbed it from out of the air and snapped its neck in one swift motion. After tossing it to the ground, he raised his two-handed broad sword and leaped into the air splitting the fifth attacker down the middle. Blood sprayed across Terex's smiling face.

Arias dragged Trayke to his feet. He removed his cloak from around his neck. Trayke's wound had mended enough for him to breathe.

Another hellhound leaped from the bush behind Arias snapping its massive jaw inches behind his head. Kris grabbed onto its tail before it could reach Arias and tossed it into the bush.

The hellhound leaped back from the bush and was joined by another. The two dogs attacked Kris head on. Arias threw his X-shaped boomerang and as the hellhounds leapt toward Kris it slit both their throats wide open. By time the boomerang returned to Arias' hand, both the pack hounds lay lifeless on the ground.

Arias, Kris and Trayke drew their swords and formed a circle of defense.

Terex attacked Cerberus head on.

Cerberus bit onto Terex's shoulder and dug his fangs deep inside his flesh and bone. Terex dropped his sword in pain while trying to release his opponent's clenching jaw. But Cerberus was too strong and Terex's wounds too deep. Cerberus overpowered him and then tossed his limp body at Kris, Arias and Trayke who all tumbled to the ground.

The five remaining hellhounds herded Nyte toward his defeated friends. They circled the young Komalsh growling as Cerberus stood before them.

"What do you want?" demanded Nyte.

"We only want you, Lord Nyte Shade." growled Cerberus. "Come willingly and we'll spare the lives of your friends."

Terex knelt on the ground, his wounds deep. His pain was unbearable, and he bled profusely. Angered, he stared Cerberus in the eyes. "I'm going to kill you."

"So be it," replied Cerberus.

The remaining five hounds opened their jaws wide and snapped toward the backs of the young Lord's heads. Through Nyte's eyes, everything went into slow motion. He saw the hounds in mid air targeting his friends. Their mouths opened and fangs extended. There was nothing he could do.

From out of the early morning darkness flashed five bright white lights. When the flashes faded five unicorns appeared. Loki, Chaos, Dusty, Shiloh, and the peculiar looking Charley thrusted their horns up into the chests of the five attacking hellhounds. Blood exploded over their heads as they gutted the dogs in mid air then tossed their lifeless corpses to the ground.

Terex, still on his knee, smiled at the mayhem. His wounds were now healed. With renewed confidence he rose to his feet and tackled Cerberus to the ground. Cerberus bit onto Terex and ripped him back and forth several times before tossing him aside.

Terex's unicorn Chaos stabbed Cerberus with his horn and tossed him against a tree. Both Kris and Nyte stabbed their swords through the hellhound's chest pinning him to the tree. The young Lords and their unicorns surrounded Cerberus.

"Who sent you?" demanded Nyte.

Cerberus gasped for air.

"Who sent you!" Kris repeated the question twisting his blade.

Cerberus's eyes closed. Then he wheezed his dying breath.

"They had no heartbeats, Nyte. How were we warned?"

"A spirit warned me," admitted Trayke. "She saved our lives," he gasped.

"You see ghosts?" Arias was impressed.

"Yes, I always have," replied Trayke, "but now it's more intimate."

"You have a welcomed gift," gasped Nyte regaining his breath. "A welcomed gift indeed."

The birds of the forest started to sing, the sun began to rise, and dead hellhounds stained the ground in red. Trayke wiped the blood from his neck and then fell into shock over his near-death experience. Although Komalsh possess the ability to heal rapidly, it was now clear that this ability wasn't strong enough for the enemies they'd face. Trayke declared, "Those are the biggest dogs I've ever seen!"

Nyte and Kris inspected the dogs.

"They're definitely pack hounds, Nyte, but with enhanced features," examined Kris. "It's like they have been turned into killing machines."

"Why did they want you, Nyte?" Arias could not make sense of it.

"I don't know," confessed Nyte. "At first I thought they were after the chest."

"These dogs are huge!" Trayke was dumbfounded.

"We get it, Trayke!" snapped Terex still healing from his latest wounds.

A high-pitched scream escaped one of the dead hounds. A shadow demon slowly clawed its way out of the corpse. It was in extreme pain as it struggled to escape its host. Amidst its escape the shadow demon evaporated into a black mist.

"That's not normal! What the hell is going on, man?" Trayke was scared. Death was real.

"If you ask one more unanswerable question, I will rip out your spine!" threatened Terex.

"Everyone, calm down!" ordered Nyte. "Kris, Arias, any guesses?"

Arias shook his head back and forth. "Nope."

"This seems familiar somehow," answered Kris. "I just can't explain why."

"Familiar? Do you even know what that word means!" Trayke was very near his breaking point. "There's nothing familiar about any of this!"

"Calm down, Trayke," asked Nyte calmly.

"Calm down! Our lives were saved by a dead person! That doesn't even make sense!"

Terex grabbed Trayke by the throat and thigh. He picked him up over his head and tossed him thirty feet into the forest.

"Was that really necessary?" asked Nyte.

"Probably not," replied Terex, "but it sure felt good."

All around them, shadow demons started clawing their way out of the hellhound corpses. Loud screams echoed through the forest ending sharply as they evaporated into black mist.

Now standing alone in the distance, Trayke raised his arms into the air. "What the hell man?"

Terex moaned. "I hate that guy."

In moments, the shadow demon cries of pain and suffering ended as they evaporated into black mist. The forest was now peaceful and quiet with only the sound of a gentle breeze in the background.

Nyte packed the chest onto his unicorn, Loki, and then mounted himself. "Komalsh, mount up! We're getting the hell out of here now!" ordered Nyte.

Kris, still looking around the bloodied field of slaughtered hounds, tried desperately to piece together his suppressed memories. "Why does this seem familiar?" he thought. Unable to recall anything, he mounted his unicorn, Dusty, and joined the others.

Their next stop, the Cluricaun Tavern.

The Enchantress walked through the forest of hellhound carnage. She knelt before the fallen Cerberus. Placing her hand on his head she summoned him back to life. His shadow demon shimmered across his face fading away as his eyes opened. "I'm sorry Enchantress." He rasped. "I have failed you and now I lay in the shadow of death."

"Not yet, Cerberus," whispered the Enchantress. "You shall rise again."

The Enchantress stood up with her arms spread out—her eyes swirling with darkness. Her skin bubbled and oozed as a burst of energy snapped from her body. Two other hellhound corpses rose into the air and were placed carefully on either side of Cerberus. After releasing another snap of energy, the three dogs melded together. Cerberus' painful howls echoed through the forest as the three hounds merged.

After moments of excruciating pain Cerberus arose from the ground. He now weighed over 1200 pounds and stood 10 feet tall. His hide was like armour, his claws, and fangs like steel blades and on his shoulders sat three hellhound heads.

"We are Cerberus!" The creature snarled and snapped.

His eyes swirled in darkness, steam escaped from his hide and an odour of decay lingered. Cerberus was the hound of hell and evil was its master.

The Enchantress mounted the three headed hellhound. “Follow the young Lords, Cerberus.”

“As you wish, Enchantress…then I kill them and retrieve Lord Nyte Shade?”

“Not this time, Cerberus. I have underestimated the young Lords’ abilities. There are, however, alternative methods for acquiring what I need. Follow them from a safe distance.

“As you wish, Enchantress.”

Chapter XXIV
Kill the Messenger.

In the early sunrise, Lord Jarestt, Lady Asheika and the rogue Komalsh awaited patiently along the eastern side of the Kabi River, one that feeds an enormous lake named Fylen, the main water supply for the Famorian kingdom. Lord Jarestt had intercepted telepathic communications between Lords Siris and Demonis. The most recent gave him an insight as to their whereabouts. After consulting with Lord Drakus and receiving no aid by the Komalsh, Jarestt and his rogues took it upon themselves to use this insight and orchestrate an ambush.

Along the western ridge, King Siris and his Sykanian Knights galloped toward a blockade of rogue Komalsh. The Sykanians were forced to halt their horses before the proud Lord Jarestt and his barricade.

Both Siris and Demonis dismounted from their horses. When Captain Korrigan and the others followed suit, Siris calmly stopped them.

"Stay on your horses. This will be brief."

Demonis and Siris approached Lord Jarestt who struggled with the discomfort of his wooden leg. Beside him stood Lady Asheika and behind them were a dozen Komalsh rogues and their unicorns.

"We've been expecting you." Jarestt pompously announced, "Today we will end your tyranny, King Siris."

"Well, if it isn't lord shit-on-a-stick!" taunted Siris. "I knew you couldn't resist our lure." Siris' comical expression instantly turned to rage. "You're a fool for coming here, Lord Jarestt. But a fool you've always been."

"I'm wise enough to find you two," Jarestt rebutted arrogantly.

"It was Lord Demonis who gave you our whereabouts, nitwit. Could you ever guess why?" Siris chastised Lord Jarestt as though he were nothing more than a child who needed a lesson.

"A reunion of old friends," toyed Lord Demonis. "Do you miss me, Lady Asheika?" He sent her a mocking wink. Lady Asheika stood repulsed. "You are nothing of the man I once loved."

"I'm twice the man he is." Demonis resented being compared to Jarestt.

Jarestt returned the glare while unsheathing his sword. "I have been waiting a long time for this, Cable."

The Komalsh rogues drew out their swords, their unicorns ready for combat.

"You're outnumbered, King Siris. Surrender or die!" Siris and Demonis looked to each other and smiled. Then they returned their glares to the rogues. Their shadow demons shimmered across their faces. Their eyes became engulfed in rage.

"I want his wooden leg," grinned Siris.

On the southern coastline of Drakonia overlooking the White Sea. Lords Drakus and Kyros led their army toward the Komalsh ocean docks. The most advanced ship in the Elvin armada, the Excelsior, was preparing for its long maiden voyage.

On arrival they were greeted by the ship's captain, an older Elvin named Kroloth. With him were two well-armed Elvin sisters named Norika and Renka.

"Welcome, Lord Drakus," said the captain. "Would you care for a tour through the most advanced ship ever constructed?" Behind him at the dock was a massive ship dwarfing all that anchored in the harbour.

"It's very impressive, captain. I've never seen such a vast vessel. I, however, prefer to have both my feet on land if you don't mind. I'm merely here to say farewell to my dear friend." Drakus gestured to shake the hand of Lord Kyros. "Be careful out there."

"Thank you, Lord Drakus, for placing your faith in me. I'm certain we'll find the remaining Earth artifacts on our journey to the undiscovered lands."

"If such land exists!" The sorcerer, Kudos Nexus, who too had shown great interest in these explorations, arrived in the nick of time. "This land could be no more than a myth, my sea-loving lord."

"Kudos! I'm glad you could make it!" smiled Kyros.

"And you are as optimistic as usual."

"I suppose there's only one way to find out," replied the sorcerer while taking a drink from his gourd. "That's to sail until you hit land!"

"Into the drink a little early, don't you think, Kudos?"

"Don't knock it, Lord Drakus. This stuff makes you interesting. But enough hen pecking, I would like to introduce you to my brightest pupil. Come here, boy!" yelled the sorcerer to a skinny lad dressed in a white robe and a pointed hat. He was no older than 13 years of age, a short brown-haired kid who stood awkwardly in his sandals.

"Hello there. I'm Lord Drakus."

The kid gave a strong handshake but showed little eye contact. "It's an honour sir. My name is Merlin."

"This kid's going to be a great wizard one day." Kudos sounded most certain of his prediction.

Merlin approached Captain Kroloth and Lord Kyros. "The island you seek does exist. I've dreamt it."

Lord Kyros gazed upon him in disbelief. "I too have dreamt it, son."

"It would be a great honour if I could join your journey, Captain Kroloth."

"The boy would be a great asset," added Kudos.

"I have these powerful images of an island." continued Merlin. "I believe I know where it is."

Lord Kyros nodded in agreement. "I believe a wizard would make a great addition to the crew. Don't you agree captain?"

Captain Kroloth stared at the skinny little wizard. "Are you sure you're seaworthy? These long voyages can be troubling to the mind."

"I'm prepared, Captain," assured Merlin.

"So be it. Gather your things and meet us on the bridge."

"I, too, would like to join your crew," volunteered Lady Tori Preddy. "Lord Drakus. Lord Mack is quite ready to take over my position with the Komalsh Elite. I would so love an adventure like this." She bartered with the captain. "You could use my sword…my Komalsh skills."

"You don't need to convince anyone of your worth, Lady Preddy," interrupted Drakus. "Gather your things and report to Lord Kyros."

Confusion swept through the group.

"Well, I won't complain…are you sure you're not leaving yourself short, Lord Drakus," wondered Kyros.

"We will be fine," assured Drakus.

"We could really use her help," agreed Captain Kroloth.

"I'm confused here, Lord Drakus." Kudos wrinkled his brow and scrunched his mouth as if to be thinking hard.

"Why would you let go of your most skilled Komalsh during these unsettling times?"

"It's not confusion you have, Kudos. You're just drunk."

Kelar, Neasha Sentrix, Malores Barnett, Kolos Dreken and the Sykanian Knights watched with horror as King Siris and Lord Demonis slaughtered the rogue Komalsh. Even their unicorns could not escape their wrath. The massacre left most of its audience sick to their stomachs. The rage, power, and speed that Siris and Demonis displayed were driven not by their Komalsh abilities but rather fueled by the shadow demons within them. At the battles end, Lord Jarestt and Lady Asheika, the only survivors, lay mortally wounded.

Demonis thrusted his sword through the chest of Jarestt's unicorn. It dropped to the ground dead.
Siris threw Lady Asheika over a boulder. Her mortal wounds immobilized her as she bled profusely.
Jarestt lay defenceless on the ground with both his hands severed from Demonis' blade.

"Look at me!" screamed Siris viciously. "Look at me!" His shadow demon shimmered across his angered face.

In agonizing pain, Jarestt struggled to focus.
Siris shook Asheika around till her neck was revealed. With a clean swing of his sword Siris decapitated her.
Jarestt closed his eyes and screamed in horror as King Siris and Lord Demonis approached him joyously.

"You two don't look right!" uttered Jarestt. "You look possessed!"

Siris cackled, "But I feel so good!"

Demonis didn't smile. He wore the look of psychotic rage.

"You want to see hate? I'll show you hate!"

Lord Cable Demonis stepped on Jarestt's chest and grabbed his wooden leg. With a couple of pulls he managed to remove the wooden limb. Then gripping it by the ankle he smashed Jarestt's forehead repeatedly.
Jarestt's skull popped like a grape.

Blow after blow Demonis caved his skull in deeper and deeper. Blood splattered across his face as he continued to hit it again and again. Each swing harder than the last. Each blow driven by psychotic rage. Jarestt's body twitched and shook until finally the wooden leg got lodged into his skull.

"It's stuck!" blurted the exhausted Demonis.

Siris grabbed onto the ankle of the wooden leg. He placed his foot on the dead man's chest and with a couple of tugs managed to break it free from Jarestt's skull.

"That is one strong piece of lumber!" Siris admired the limb while swinging the wooden leg around like a bat.

"Just feel the weight of that bad boy!"

Demonis lifted himself up from his knees and gasped to regain his breath. He looked at his audience of disturbed Sykanians staring at him silently. They could see Demonis' shadow demon shimmering across his face until it slowly flickered away. Demonis' dark expression softened and all that remained of his rage was the blood splattered across his face.

Siris studied the mutilated corpse of Lord Jarestt. He cackled sarcastically. "Yeah, I'm pretty sure he's dead!"

"I never liked that guy!" said Demonis.

"I never could have guessed," teased Siris.

They both looked back down at the mutilated corpse. His face unrecognizable.

"Do you think he'll pull through!" Cackled Siris at the top of his lungs.

A legion of Sykanian knights rode over the western ridge to rendezvous with Demonis and Siris. Their plan was unfolding.

"King Siris!" Demonis wanted to keep his attention on the mission at hand. "It's time for you to take Captain Korrigan and the Knights Elite to the Cluricaun Tavern. There you'll find Nyte Shade and his clan of adolescent Komalsh."

"We have a hundred Knights Elite, your majesty. How many should I assemble?" inquired captain Korrigan.

"We will assemble them all, captain. I want all the archers too," replied King Siris.

"But sire, there are only five of them to be slain. Should we really be leaving our castle this short of protection?" queried Captain Korrigan.

"I'll decide!" Siris was angered at the challenge.

"As you wish." The captain bowed as he spoke.

Siris admired Jarestt's wooden limb. "I'm keeping the leg." He cackled with sort of childish joy.

Demonis grinned, "As you wish, my king."

"Captain! Prepare the Knights Elite, we leave immediately," ordered Siris. "Soon, Cable, the young Lords will be no more."

"Kill them all, Cretes!" Demonis' utterings had the sound of grit and determination that could only come from someone whose voice had been silenced in stone all those years.

King Cretes Siris and the Sykanian Knights Elite rode off leaving a trail of dust behind.

Curious, Kelar asked Demonis. "How are you so sure that's where they'll be?"

"We have eyes and ears everywhere," answered Demonis coldly. "The great war is about to begin."

Kelar feared for his friends especially for Nyte Shade. Neasha's voice hailed him in thought. "We have to do something, Kelar!"

Kelar reached out to Nyte with a psychic hail, warning of Siris' approach. Demonis felt his attempt and blocked their connection. The two exchanged dirty looks. Then Kelar surrendered. He turned to Neasha with an expression of his failure. Neasha closed her eyes and lowered her head. There was nothing they could do.

"Malores!"

"Yes, Lord Demonis."

Gather the remaining troops. We are taking Kelar and his friends to the Sykanian castle."

"As you wish, my lord."

At the Komalsh ocean docks Kudos, Drakus and the hundred plus Komalsh all waved and cheered as the Elvin ship Excelsior set sail on its journey.

"Lord Drakus." Lord Mack approached. "There is a messenger here to see you. He's Sykanian, my lord."

"Bring him before me," replied Drakus.

Lord Mack escorted the messenger before Lord Drakus.

"Who are you?" he asked.

"My name is Sir Riclean Messenger. I'm under direct order by the King of Sykania to deliver this letter to Lord Drakus in person."

Drakus grabbed the letter and looked it over. Furious he ripped it in half and tossed it to the ground.

Drakus glared at the Sykanian.

"Look!" Riclean backed away. "I'm just the messenger!"

Drakus unsheathed his sword and with one swift swoop severed Riclean's head clean off. It bounced on the ground twice before his body collapsed.

"Komalsh, mount up!" ordered Drakus. "We're taking this war to the Sykanian castle!"

The Komalsh responded quickly.

"I thought killing the messenger was frowned upon in the rules of war," heckled Kudos.

"There are no more rules, old friend. The rise of the Darkstar is upon us."

"But Raine still guards the passage. Baelin cannot pass into Drakonia," reminded Kudos.

"That's a secret best kept unspoken. For now, our top priority is to protect the chosen one," warned Drakus.

"And who might that be?"

"Mili is the chosen one. You must go to the Elvin castle, Kudos. You must protect her from the Darkstar's assassins."

"Milita Drakus…your niece? Not the wisest choice from Malshidiel, was it?" Kudos was not impressed.

Lord Drakus handed Kudos a hand-sized cube of black glass wrapped in a silk handkerchief. "We have no time for humour, my friend. The Darkstar is aware of her identity. My prophetic dreams have revealed the letter I received from the messenger today coincides with her discovery. Milita will only be safe in the cube's realm of the Hidden Night."

"I understand, Lord Drakus." Kudos stared into the enchanted cube. Carefully using the silk handkerchief to prevent his skin from touching its surface, he paused in thought. "All this time you knew she was the one and yet you never mentioned it to me?"

"My dreams and visions warned me to keep silent. The Darkstar has eyes and ears everywhere. Until now, she was best kept a secret. But in your heart, Kudos, you must have known it was her?"

"Funny, my heart still doesn't see it." Kudos felt mind boggled. He could not wrap his head around Milita being the chosen one.

"Nevertheless, this is goodbye, Kudos."

Kudos and Lord Drakus shook hands. "Farewell, Hirum."

"Kudos…" Drakus paused. "Milita is a difficult child. She won't go inside the Hidden Night willingly. You may need to be creative."

"Understood, old friend," replied Kudos.

Lord Drakus mounted his unicorn, Mythra, and led the Komalsh army toward the Sykanian castle.
The old sorcerer wrapped the glass cube in the handkerchief and placed it carefully into his saddle bag. On the ground he noticed the two torn halves of the letter the messenger had delivered. He picked them up and placed them together. Interestingly, both sides were blank.

"Actions speak louder than words." The sorcerer contemplated what would come of that. "Well Hocus, things are going to get pretty nasty around here."

Kudos mounted his old horse and rode off toward the Elvin castle.

Chapter XXV
The Cluricaun Tavern.

Riding over the mountain range with the sun trailing behind, Nyte Shade and his friends rode the final stretch toward the Cluricaun Tavern.

On route they approached a wagon parked on the side of the road. Nyte recognized the wagon and the scruffy looking horse that pulled it. It belonged to the gypsy who'd given him the never-ending horn of beer.

The young Lords rode over to the wagon and searched the area. Nyte searched the back of the seemingly abandoned wagon where he found the body of an elderly woman laying in her bedding. Her skin was cold and blue—her eyes devoid of life. Her partially opened mouth revealed a full set of sharp teeth.

"Her name was Jasmine." Nyte remembered her. Arias crawled into the wagon and examined the body.

"She's been dead for days, Nyte. There are no signs of foul play."

"Perhaps it was a natural death," suggested Kris. "Those do happen from time to time."

"It was a heart attack," confirmed Trayke.

"How do you know?" Wondered Terex.

"She told me," Replied Trayke.

"She told you?" Arias asked.

"Yes Arias, her spirit is right beside you."

"Well, uh, how is she doing?" asked Arias nervously.

"I'm not about to ask a dead person how they're doing." Trayke was annoyed.

"Yeah, good point." Arias gave out a nervous laugh.

"Hey Trayke," said Nyte diverting his attention.

"When I saw Jasmine last, she was with another person, a young girl with one green and one blue eye. Would you ask Jasmine's spirit where she went?"

“Jasmine’s pointing toward the Teasian town where we are headed,” answered Trayke, “she said she’s in danger or she’s dangerous. I couldn’t quite make her out.”

“What do you mean couldn’t?” Nyte was perplexed.

“Her spirit just vanished, Nyte.” Trayke concluded, “She must have crossed over.”

“That would make sense,” agreed Kris. “Her spirit remained behind long enough to seek help for her friend.”

“Komalsh, mount up,” commanded Nyte. “We have a little girl to find.”

The young Lords rode toward the Teasian town.

****

The Cluricaun Tavern was located next to the Riegan River where it spilled into the Eastern Sea. Beyond the tavern, along a horseshoe-shaped bay, was a small-town containing five dwellings of business. This town was built next to an enormous ocean dock that hosted dozens of boats. This was a fishing town under the rule of Teasian King, Monty Devon.

****

The young Lords tied their unicorns to a hitching rail outside the tavern’s entrance, exhausted from their ride and still unsettled by their hellhound encounter. The weary riders unloaded the chest from Loki’s saddle.

“Who do we know that’s Teasian?” asked Terex.

“Lord and Lady Dunlam are,” answered Kris.

“Trayke, come grab this,” ordered Nyte struggling with the chest.

Trayke held onto the chest and as the weight shifted to his arms he staggered backward and fell on his ass.

“Be carful, Trayke!” warned Nyte.

"You're a little late on that one, Nyte!" He grumbled with exhaustion.

"That was a long ride," Kris was weary and ready for food and rest.

"Yep." Arias agreed. He was exhausted. "Damn hot, too." He wiped his forehead with a handkerchief. "You need help with that, Trayke?"

"No, of course not!" Trayke grunted sarcastically. They ignored him.

A sharp scream from a girl's voice was heard from behind the building.

"I'm going to look into that," alerted Nyte. "I'll meet you all in the tavern."

"I'll join you," volunteered Terex.

"Yeah, me too," added Kris."

"Well, Arias! Are you going to help?" muttered Trayke pinned to the ground by the chest. "I'm too tired to move!"

"Why don't you just use your telekinesis?" suggested Arias.

"I hate you." Trayke was genuinely embarrassed.

Another sharp scream ripped through the air as the young Komalsh ran behind the tavern. There knelt a battered young girl no older than nine. Above her was a skinny middle-aged man. He raised his fist high in the air and punched her face. The young girl dropped to the ground hard. There she lay weakened—her face battered in blood and tears. The short skinny man grabbed her by the hair. He pulled her back up to her feet then punched her back down to the ground.

"Komalsh law forbids us to intervene," reminded Kris.

Terex was angered. "So, we're supposed to just stand and watch! That's not going to happen, Kris!"

"Hold up, Terex!" ordered Nyte. "Kris is right. We're not supposed to intervene. Perhaps I can come up with an alternative solution. You two wait here."

Nyte walked up to the man and grabbed his arm before the next punch could land. He ushered him away from the crying girl with little effort.

"This woman is my slave!" The man jerked himself free from Nyte's grasp. "It is my right under Teasian law to do whatever I deem fit!" He pointed his finger into Nyte's face. "So, back off mister!"

The commotion attracted a large crowd of local fishermen and villagers alike. They scowled in defence of the slaver's rights.

Terex was infuriated. He stepped forward to intervene but was quickly intercepted by Kris' arm.

"This is not the right time, Terex. Our laws cannot be compromised."

"I could end this quick!" scowled Terex.

"Yes, however, explaining your violent intervention to the Teasian King would put unneeded pressure on the Drakonian peace talks. Remember Terex, the Komalsh are trying to become ambassadors of peace, not avengers."

"Why would we defend slavery?" Terex was enraged.

"Once we are declared the embassy power over Drakonia, the Komalsh will have diplomatic power to put an end to slavery permanently," answered Kris. "We will save countless lives, Terex. Do not jeopardise that over one."

Frustrated, Terex backed down.

Lord Nyte Shade stared the middle-aged man up and down. He had a balding forehead with long, coarse hair and a big nose with a crooked arch. His lips were sunken from tooth decay and his dark blue eyes were as cold as the ocean behind him. Nyte recognized his clothing differed from the crowd of fishermen and women who gathered behind him. This man was no local boat owner. He was a slave gatherer.

"What's your name, friend?" asked Nyte politely.

"I'm Dicklifentaisly," he answered gumming his words sternly.

"That's a mouthful." Nyte tried not to sound too condescending. "Why do you strike your slave Diclifent…Dicklide…can I just call you Dick?"

"Cause she's a witch!" claimed Dicklifentaisly. He turned and addressed the villagers who crowded around. "She's a witch, I say!"

The crowd of villagers muted their rage in murmurs until a woman finally bellowed out. "Burn her!"

Nyte quickly addressed the crowd. "Calm down, my friends. She is no witch, I assure you."

"How do you know?" Dicklifentaisly disapproved of the interference.

"I'm a Komalsh. We are educated in such affairs." Nyte spoke confidently to the crowd.

The surrounding crowd of murmurs lightened.

"He's right!" hollered a fisherman. "I heard the Komalsh deal with all kinds of weird Earth critters!"

The crowd nodded in agreement.

"She's still my slave!" defended Dicklifentaisly.

"Good point, good point." The fisherman had no comeback.

The persuadable crowd nodded in the slaver's defence.

Dicklifentaisly stood nose to nose with Nyte. He was aware the Komalsh would never intervene. He puffed out his scrawny chest and warned Nyte with a glare. "Back off, Earth lover!"

The crowd fell silent in suspense.

Nyte kept calm. He wanted to strike him. He wanted to watch him bleed. Instead, he resisted the temptation and focused on a diplomatic approach.

"I tell you what…Dick. How about we cut a deal?"

"I'm listening?" Dicklifentaisly was intrigued.

Nyte removed the second golden egg from his robes and watched as the man's greedy eyes widened.

"Well…Dick. I propose a trade. This egg for your slave."

Kris approached Nyte. "Lord Shade, owning a slave is forbidden by Komalsh law."

"It's a deal!" grinned Dicklifentaisly revealing his decaying teeth.

Nyte handed over the egg and the slaver snatched it from his hand.

The village crowd cheered and clapped as emotions of good will spread among them like a prairie fire.

"Thank you!" The beaten child still on her knees sobbed between her words. "Thank you! I'll do whatever you want, my master."

Nyte helped the young girl to her feet. As tears struggled to escape her rapidly swelling eyes, Nyte noticed something familiar. One green eye, one blue. This was the missing girl who travelled with the gypsy, Jasmine.

"What is your name?" he asked.

"My name is Des."

"That doesn't sound like the name of a witch," teased Nyte.

Des produced a half smile on her swollen, bloodied face. "Well…it's short for Destiny."

Nyte's eyes widened with astonishment.

"Well, Nyte," grinned Kris ear to ear. "Looks like we found your destiny."

"Hello, Destiny. I'm Nyte, this is Kris and the mean looking one over there is Terex.

The young girl gave a sweet smile through bruised cheeks.

****

Destiny was a tall and lanky nine-year-old girl with one green and one blue eye. Her hair was black with silver streaks reaching down her back. Her skin was golden brown—her clothes tattered and dirty. She was alone in this world.

****

"Destiny, how did you become a slave?" wondered Kris.

"My keeper, a gypsy named Jasmine, passed away in her sleep. That man found our wagon. When he saw I was alone, he took me into slavery." She whimpered and continued, "I was hungry. I didn't know what to do."

"What about your parents?" asked Nyte.

"They died."

"I'm sorry for your loss. It was recent, wasn't it?" There was an air of empathy in Nyte's voice.

Destiny stared at the ground and made a hesitant nod.

"Well, I guess I can leave now!" The slimy slaver was looking for an easy exit.

"Not so fast!" Terex grabbed Dicklifentaisly by the scruff of his neck. "Hey Destiny! How would you like to punch this worm?"

Dicklifentaisly panicked and squirmed. "A slave who strikes anyone is beheaded in these lands!"

“This is true, Terex,” informed Kris disapproving of his actions.

“Truth or not, it no longer matters,” announced Nyte. “I’m releasing Des from slavery.” Nyte opened his cloak revealing the last of his golden eggs and gave it to Destiny.

“This will help you start a new life.”

Destiny’s eyes softened with tears of joy. “Thank you, Nyte.”

“I’ll hold him, Des!” persisted Terex. “Just come over here and release your rage!”

Des walked up to Dicklifentaisly who cowered to avoid her eye contact.

“He’s all yours,” Terex announced coldly.

Destiny stared right through the slaver. Her face was black and blue. Blood dripped from her nose and tears ran down her swollen cheeks.

“I hate who you are!”

With both hands she raised the golden egg high above her head. She scowled at him with vengeance. Her hands trembled and arms weakened. Then, in a split moment of compassion her eyes teared and her anger subsided. Destiny lowered the egg and whimpered.

“I promised my mom and dad I wouldn’t live in this world with anger and hate! I promised that I wouldn’t let the wrongs of this world change me! They made me promise them just before they died. I won’t let a weak, pathetic man like you make me break that promise! I’m better than you!” Des broke into tears. “I’m better than you!” She ran into Nyte’s opened arms and released her pent-up anger in a down pour of tears.

Nyte could feel her pain, her loneliness. She lost her parents. He could relate. But Nyte had Savita to raise him. Destiny was all alone.

“Come with me, Des. Let’s go get something to eat.” Nyte placed his arm around her, and they walked toward the tavern. While escorting her away from the madness, Nyte turned to greet Terex’s eyes. “We will meet you inside, my friend. Take your time.” Nyte nodded giving Terex silent consent.

Terex nodded in return with a devilish grin. He gripped tighter onto Dicklifentaisly’s scruff.

Kris followed Nyte to the tavern. “I’m not sure it’s wise leaving Terex alone with him.”

“I don’t care.” What Nyte did not see was fine with him.

Dicklifentaisly started to laugh at Des as they walked away. “You stupid bitch slave! Even now you were given your freedom, and you still act like a slave. You think you’re better than me, huh? You say you’re better than me! Ha!” Dicklifentaisly shook free from Terex’s grip. “Piss off, you stupid son of a bitch,” He snarled.

“You know,” said Terex calmly, “Destiny may be better than you.” Then placing his thumb on his chest, he finished coldly. “But I’m not.” Terex grabbed Dicklifentaisly by the collar and thrust his forehead into the slaver’s face. Dick’s big nose broke, and his eyes swelled with tears. Terex picked him up over his head and tossed him 30 feet into the Riegan River.

The villagers watched as the slaver sailed through the air and splashed into the river. Then looking back to Terex, the crowd murmured with confusion.

Terex stood there quite pleased with himself until he noticed the villagers staring at him. Terex pondered a moment for an excuse. After finding one he was proud of, Terex spoke his defence. “It’s okay! I’m a Komalsh. There was a witch inside that man. That’s right, a witch!” Terex struggled not to laugh. “But don’t worry folks, he’s going to be alright now.”

Terex nodded at the crowd reassuringly. The crowd nodded contagiously in return. Then they applauded Terex's good deed.

"Should we burn him?" asked the lady.

Terex rubbed his chin. "Well…"

Inside the Cluricaun Tavern, Trayke and Arias were sitting at a table feasting on fish and mead. Nyte and Kris escorted the battered Des through the front doors and joined their table.

"Des, this is Trayke and Arias."

"What happened to you?" Trayke asked.

"She was beaten by a slaver," explained Kris.

"Where is this slaver?" Arias stood ready to defend. "I'll go have a word with him!"

"We left him with Terex," answered Nyte calmly.

"Oh." Arias sat back down to eat. "I feel sorry for the slaver." He chuckled.

"Yeah, especially if he shows him his telekinesis." poked Trayke.

The young Lords broke out into laughter as Terex entered the tavern.

"How are the villagers taking it?" asked Nyte.

"They are fine," answered Terex. "They're just starting a fire."

"A fire?" Kris was not connecting the dots.

"Yeah, you don't want to know, Kris." Terex heaved a huge sigh while sitting down to the table. "Des, honey, I just want you to know you'll never have to be afraid again. You've just adopted five big brothers."

Des teared with joy. "Thank you, Terex."

"How did you guys get food?" Terex was starving.

"All this violence has worked up my appetite!"

Trayke pointed across the empty tavern to one of the staff of Cluricaun's. "Just ask one of them."

****

Cluricauns are cellar spirits who resemble mini-innkeepers. They dressed in green shorts with red stockings and pointed hats. They wore black buckled shoes, white aprons, and shirts. Their daytime drinking habits were on public display as they staggered around to perform the tavern's upkeep. Although they had a weakness for the drink, their hard work ethics were reflected by the well-maintained tavern.

****

Nyte Shade grabbed the attention of a Cluricaun walking by. "I would like to speak to Brian and Lee-Ann."

The Cluricaun glared at him, took a drink from his pint then spat on the floor. The glaring cellar spirit walked away with his shoulders held high.

"He has quite the attitude," said Kris.

"I know, right!" Nyte nodded his offence. He approached the bar and looked behind the counter where another Cluricaun had passed out drunk. "What's with these guys?"

"They're just drunks," explained Trayke placing the chest on the bar table. "You have no idea how envious of them I am."

"Brian! Lee-Ann! Is there anybody here?" yelled Nyte. But no one other than the Cluricauns were around.

"Have something to eat, Nyte. The food is amazing!" said Arias expressing his pleasure.

Nyte surrendered to his appetite and joined his friends at their table. Together they sat down and ate as a family would.

Des felt a strong sense of belonging with the young Lords and for the first time since her parents' passing felt the warm feeling of family. Her adopted brothers kept her in the loop of their conversations, never leaving her out, never letting her feel lonely. Trayke laughed at Des for having fish juices on her nose. She laughed at all of them for having the same.

After their meals were done, they moved to the stools at the bar. Displayed on the shelves behind the bar was a plethora of bottled Drakonian spirits.

"I wish I could get drunk," said Trayke.

"Yep," Agreed Arias.

"Yeah, me too," Sighed Terex.

"Not me, I'm too young to drink," added the battered Des.

"You are one tough little girl," complimented Kris. "After all you been through, you can still smile."

"Smiles are important, Kris. Smiles spread joy."

Nyte placed his hand on her shoulder and smiled into her swollen eyes. "Do you remember when we first met, Des?"

Des nodded with a grin. "On the river crossing barge. Jasmine read your palm and gave you the never-ending horn of beer."

"A never-ending horn of beer?" Trayke was all ears. "Where is it?"

"I gave it to a sorcerer named Kudos Nexus. It's a long story. I was with Kelar at the time." The memory of his friend caught him off guard. Sadness waited in the wings if given the chance.

Their conversation was interrupted when the tavern's front doors creaked open. In walked two people robed in clean, almost glowing white robes.

"Cluricauns! Come grab our bags, please," asked a beautiful and elegant woman in her forties. Her hair was blonde and curly—her eye lashes long and seductive. Her divine curves were almost hidden by her cloak.

"Yeah, little buddies. Chop, chop!" ordered a handsome man in his forties—lean with ravishing blonde hair and bright blue eyes.

"Oh, look babe. We have guests!"

"Hello guests. I'm Brian and this is Lee-Ann. We already know who you are so no need to introduce yourselves."

The couple walked behind the bar peeling off their hooded cloaks. "Oh, look pumpkin. They brought us a chest!" Brian was excited.

"Oh, that's cool!" admired Lee-Ann.

"Cool?" Kris was confused. "Is the chest cold, Trayke?"

Trayke shrugged his shoulders.

"You'll get used to our lingo, Kris. We're not from around here," explained Brian. "Well, originally anyway. We've been stuck in Drakonia for over a thousand years now."

"What happened to you, sweetie?" Destiny's appearance had caught Lee-Ann's attention. "You poor thing! Let's get you cleaned up." Lee-Ann grabbed a wet towel from behind the bar and catered to Des's wounds. "Don't worry honey, auntie Lee will take care of you."

Destiny instantly trusted Lee-Ann. She adored her beautiful hair and vibrant loving glow. She was mesmerized by her aura.

"So then, where are you from?" asked Kris.

"We are from Earth," answered Brian, "a place called Vancouver, British Columbia, Canada. It was October 31st, 2018, when we crossed over to Drakonia."

Brian had a cheerful disposition. His facial expressions and hand movements could tell a story without saying a word.

"How did you get here?" asked Arias.

"When Malshidiel opened the portholes that transported the enchanted Earth creatures to Drakonia. They didn't just open in one moment of time on Earth but in fact opened across several timelines. You see, the Earth creatures Malshidiel brought over to Drakonia are from many different time periods. For some unexplainable reason one opened during our first date together."

Lee-Ann glowed in the background over the fond memory of their first date while Brian continued telling the story.

"We drove straight into the porthole and when we came out the other side, bam!" Brian slapped his hands together. "We are permanent residents of this medieval draconian culture."

"I miss the internet," reminisced Lee-Ann.

"I miss hockey," countered Brian.

"You don't look a thousand years old," said Terex.

"Why thank you!" Lee-Ann glowed at the thought.

"That's not where I was headed with that." explained Terex. "I meant; shouldn't you have died from old age?"

"We are immortal," explained Lee-Ann still wiping Destiny's face clean.

"Yes, we are, pumpkin," agreeing with Lee-Ann and adding his pet name for her whenever he could pepper it into the conversation.

"So, if I pushed my sword through your chest you would live?" asked Terex.

"No…we'd die," answered Brian with a disturbed expression. "We're a different kind of immortal, Terex. You see, the universe just wouldn't allow your sword to go near me. We can never be harmed."

"We have many other gifts too," volunteered Lee-Ann. "Come, see for yourself."

The young Lords stood amazed. "Des, your face, it's healed!" Trayke was mystified.

Des stood up and looked in the mirror. "My face is better!" She was amazed. "You healed me!"

"Pretty cool, eh?" Lee-Ann applauded her.

"Is everything cold to you two?" Kris did not have a clue.

"I don't understand why you keep saying things are cool but the miracle you just showed us is similar to our own Komalsh healing abilities." Nyte noted the comparison.

"We've been allies with the Komalsh since they first came to pass under Lord Duren," according to Brian.

"Then why haven't you fought with us?" Terex asked.

"We aren't allowed to," answered Lee-Ann.

"Says who?" Terex couldn't understand.

"Says, the universe. Any of our powerful interventions could accidently disrupt Drakonia's timeline creating an alternate reality," explained Lee-Ann.

"Our actions, if not approved, could even disrupt the very fabric of your existence," spoke Brian in a deep solemn voice.

Lee-Ann winked at Brian. "Did you just lower your voice?"

"Yes, pumpkin. I was going for a dramatic effect."

"You're a weirdo! Anyway, the change we've accidently caused already shows in modern-day Drakonia," admitted Lee-Ann.

"You're not bringing up the bible thing again, are you pumpkin?" Brian was embarrassed.

"That mishap altered Drakonia's social and religious structure dividing its people into a thousand years of war!" reminded Lee-Ann.

"What about that magic eight ball you traded for those shoes?" reminded Brian.

"Oh yeah, I forgot about that!" giggled Lee-Ann. "I can't believe a religion was formed from that!"

"Wait, are you saying you two are the reason Earth's bible is on Drakonia?" Nyte wanted clarification.

"He is." Pointed Lee-Ann to Brian.

"How was I supposed to know it would be translated differently by every culture and transcribed for their social structures while dividing kingdoms with conflict that would cost countless lives in the name of God?" defended Brian.

"Oh, like it never happened on Earth," poked Lee-Ann.

"You gave out the bible purposely?" Flabbergasted, Nyte was beginning to understand the magnitude of the potential consequences they could cause.

"Well, not exactly," admitted Brian. "It was actually stolen from me when we first arrived."

"I thought you two were powerful immortals?" questioned Terex. "How could you let someone rob you? It makes no sense."

"Well, at the time we crossed over here, we weren't aware of our abilities. We weren't even aware what the hell happened! One moment we were on Earth and then boom! We are here!" said Brian with his hands waving in the air.

"Are you a religious man, Brian?" asked Nyte.

"God no, why would you ask that?"

"Well, you had a bible for one."

"No, no, a guy gave it to me just before we crossed over. He said it would enlighten my life. Oh man. If he could see me now!"

****

The young Komalsh had a hard time comprehending Brian and Lee-Ann's strange lingo and peculiar behavior. Their names were odd. Their spirits were seemingly careless and free. They were also exceptionally clean and well dressed compared to the average Drakonian. Their hair was perfect, their skin youthful. Lee-Ann even wore make-up.

****

"So, what's in the chest?" asked Lee-Ann changing the subject.

"It's a gift from Lord Drakus," announced Nyte. "After you open it, we're to wait for your further instructions. We don't, however, have a key so I'm not sure how you'll open it."

Brian stood before the chest with his hands waving over his head. "Open Sesame!" he commanded in a deep voice. The chest unlocked and opened.

"You're such a nerd," chuckled Lee-Ann.

"Sorry, pumpkin," laughed Brian. "I can't help myself.

Inside the chest was a lone scroll. Lee-Ann picked it out and unrolled it. The two read it together quietly. A moment passed while the young Lords stood silently awaiting the scroll's message. When they were done reading, Lee-Ann snuggled into Brian.

"It's really happening." Lee-Ann's expression went from light-hearted to sadness written all over her face. Brian placed his hand on her cheek, "I love you." he whispered.

"What's happening?" Nyte was not happy being held in suspense.

"How would you guys like to get drunk?" asked Brian changing the subject.

"Quit teasing us!" Trayke was disappointed by his sobriety.

With both hands Brian hoisted a methuselah-sized bottle of moonshine onto the bar table.

"No teasing. Lord Drakus instructed you to listen to us for further instruction did he not?" reminded Brian.

"Yes, but..."

"No buts, Nyte, drinks are on the house!" Brian was excited to have Komalsh Lords to entertain.

"But as Komalsh we heal too quickly for alcohol to affect us, so what's the point?" Trayke was frustrated.

"This is my special brew." Brian stretched his mouth so everyone would notice his exaggerated wink and added,

"You'll get drunk."

"Oh yeah!" Lee-Ann gave a two-thumbs up. "Be careful with that stuff!"

The skeptical young Lords eagerly accepted the tavern owner's offer. Lee-Ann placed five goblets on the bar table and Brian filled each one.

"Aren't you two having a drink?" asked Terex.

"We don't drink," answered Brian.

The party came to a grinding halt.

"You own a tavern...and you don't drink?" That baffled Arias. "Why not?

"Well, that's a long story, so I'll make it short," answered Brian. "It starts with one drink and ends with chaos, madness, and destruction in the midst crazy love connections!"

"Yeah, not a great combination!" Replied Lee-Ann.

The young Lords shrugged their shoulders and cheered to the tavern hosts.

As the festivities progressed, Lee-Ann brought Destiny a dress to wear in replacement of her dirty garb. She sat her at a table and brushed her long black and silver hair.

"Does this feel better, honey?"

"Yes, thank you Lee-Ann." Des was glowing.

"I know your secret Des," whispered Lee-Ann.

"What do you mean?" stuttered Des.

"Don't be afraid of what you are." Lee-Ann reassured her with a loving squeeze. "I'm not afraid of you."

Des teared up as she cuddled her back. "I know. I trust you."

"You have a special gift, honey. I could help you learn to embrace it," offered Lee-Ann.

"It's not a gift." Des' tears became sobs.

"What gift?" asked Nyte.

"Why Des here is gifted with therianthropy." explained Lee-Ann.

"She's a shapeshifter?" Kris asked.

"Yes, a very rare one indeed," bragged Lee-Ann.

"Is she a werewolf?" Arias was all ears.

"No, no. That is a simpler version by comparison, Arias. Des can metamorphose into any animal. I saw the energy when I first laid eyes on her." Smiled Lee-Ann. "But it's her eye discolouration that gave it away." Turning to Des, she said, "Oh honey, your energy is so pure, so beautiful!"

"Is that why the slaver claimed you were a witch?" Nyte wondered who else might have detected Des.

Des nodded quietly.

"Can you give us a demonstration?" Arias was in the mood to be entertained.

Des moved into the protection of Lee-Ann's arms. "I don't like changing. It scares me."

"That's okay, you don't need to do anything that frightens you," affirmed Arias.

"We won't be able to care for her, Lee-Ann." Nyte could see the complexity of the situation.

"That's okay!" smiled Lee-Ann. "We have plenty of room here if Des doesn't mind helping with the tavern chores."

"Happy to. I'm a hard worker!" Des was excited. Lee-Ann grinned. "I'm sure you'll do better than the Cluricaun's. All they do is get drunk. Sheesh! Some of them can be nasty drunks, too! But nothing a good swat from my broom doesn't fix."

Des' giggle was swallowed up by a sudden yawn. "The food in your belly has made you sleepy, Des. How would you like to see your new bedroom?"

Des nodded her tired approval.

"Come dear, follow me." Lee-Ann held her hand and the two went upstairs.

Nyte and his friends returned to the bar where Brian poured them each another drink.

"You know," said Brian, "I've poured a drink for every Komalsh who has ever passed through the Mystique Forest."

"Then you've met my parents?" asked Nyte.

"Yes, sir. Radik and I spent much time chatting over this bar. He always sat in the chair Kris is in which, coincidentally, was the same spot Lord Duren preferred."

"I can't believe I'm sitting in the same spot as Lord Duren." That excited Kris. "What was he like?"

"Well," explained Brian, "he was nothing like the man depicted in history books. But he had a big heart, he worked hard, and he never quit. Those are the qualities of a hero, gentlemen."

"What about my mother?" asked Nyte.

"Your mother," interrupted Lee-Ann coming down the stairway, "was a true blessing to be around."

"Where's Des, pumpkin?" Brian wanted to steer away from the topic.

"She's sleeping in her new room."

"So, I can assume she'll be staying with us then?"

"Yes, it's best she does for now, hon. She's too dangerous to be on her own."

"But you never asked me." Brian teased with a rather phony pout.

"I knew you'd agree." Lee-Ann softened her voice while batting her eyelashes.

"You know, pumpkin, if this were the other way around, you'd be giving me trouble for not asking."

"Yes, but you are smarter than that love."

"Oh pumpkin, how can I argue with that?" surrendered Brian sarcastically.

The two kissed. While they were lip locked, Brian retrieved a hockey puck from his pocket.

"Why do you have a hockey puck in your pocket?

"Don't you?"

"No! You weirdo!" Lee-Ann giggled with an eye roll.

"What's a hockey puck?" asked Terex.

"It's used in a sport called hockey which is played on a sheet of ice. Two opposing teams battle each other with grit and teamwork trying to move this puck behind a goalie and into the net to score a goal. The one with the most goals after three periods of play wins!" answered Brian nostalgically.

The young Lords gazed in confusion.

"Maybe you should keep it simple, honey." suggested Lee-Ann.

"Yeah, okay. On Earth we have knights called hockey players who use this hockey puck to defeat their enemies."

"So, it's a weapon?" asked Trayke while the others were rapt with intrigue.

"Yeah, sure." Brian gave up trying to explain it further.

"Oh boy." Lee-Ann did another eye roll.

"What?" wondered Brian to her eye roll.

"This is exactly how the whole bible thing got out of hand!" She shook her head unimpressed.

"It's a hockey puck, pumpkin. What's the worst thing that could happen?"

"May I have it?" asked Terex.

"Sure, here!" Brian handed the puck to Terex.

"What do you do with it?" asked Terex while feeling it's weight.

"You defeat your enemy with it. Then you raise your arms in the air and shout he shoots he scores!" roared Brian.

"Oh boy."

"Stop saying that, Lee-Ann," giggled Brian.

"What?" defended Lee-Ann.

"Oh boy!" said Brian. "This isn't an "oh boy" moment?"

"This is definitely an "oh boy" moment!" She looked into Brian's eyes and kissed him on the lips.

"Geeze, you two have been together for a thousand years and you're still in love?" Kris liked what he saw.

"We have our moments," admitted Lee-Ann.

"Anyway," She yawned, "you guys enjoy your night. I'm off to bed, it was so nice to meet you all."

"Yeah, I'll join you, pumpkin. It's been a long day. The Cluricauns will take care of you guys. Good night!"

"Good night!" replied the young Lords.

With the tavern owners off to bed, the young Lords continued to drink and to their surprise, they got drunk. They laughed and joked, bugged, and teased one another. They recalled fond memories of school and the days they all first met. As the night sky darkened their conversations grew louder.

While on their way to a relaxed inebriation, they were alerted to the tavern's front entrance by a sharp creaking sound. Then the doors burst open with a gust of chilly wind and through those doors entered a person dressed in a burgundy cloak. The young Lords stared with silent intrigue as the figure removed her cloak slowly. There before them stood a beautiful young woman dressed in a snug black lace outfit. The young Lords fell silent seduced by her soft pale brown eyes, her silky golden-brown skin, and her long dark red hair. It was her pointed ears that aroused Nyte's curiosity.

"She's Elvin." Nyte was astonished.

The silence of the room was disrupted by a wolf whistle exiting Trayke's lips followed by an immature laugh from Arias. Encouraged by their attention, the Elvin walked gracefully toward the young Lord's table.

"Hello." She smiled. "My name is Moya, Moya Blynn. May I join you?"

"If you can drink, you can join," said Nyte.

"I can drink, boys." The Elvin princess moved her head to make eye contact with each one as any experienced flirt would do.

All through the night, the Elvin princess matched goblet to goblet with the young Lords. She held her own with little sign of impairment. The beautiful Moya's intentions unfolded through the night as her eyes targeted Nyte with flirtatious desire. By the late hour of the eve, intoxication sent Trayke, Kris, Arias, and Terex to their rooms for rest. Moya now had the inebriated Nyte all to herself.

Under the candled light she kissed his lips softly. Nyte kissed her in return. The passion escalated and they undressed one another tossing their clothes carelessly. Moya spread her burgundy cloak out on the tavern floor. There they lay lustfully seducing one another touching, kissing, and biting. Moya straddled Nyte guiding him inside her. She placed his hands over her breasts and moved her hips to a slow steady rhythm. The candlelight shimmered revealing their shadows along the tavern walls as she moved faster and faster. Lost in the moment, each instant seemed like a beautiful eternity. A shriek burst from Moya's lungs as her body shook and trembled in euphoria. Overrun with desire, Nyte swung her over on all fours and entered her from behind. He grabbed her hips, eagerly thrusting himself deep inside her. As the intensity grew so did the forcefulness. Nyte's primitive nature quickly overtook what started off as a gentle moment. Moya was now at the mercy of Nyte's animalistic lust, much to her enjoyment. Soon he collapsed into climax and rolled over onto the cloak beside her, his body vibrating as he attempted to catch his breath. Moya wrapped her arms around Nyte and kissed him passionately on the lips—their bodies layered in silky sweat. Nyte smiled still catching his breath. He stared into her pale brown eyes. So beautiful, so enticing. Then the whites of her eyes swirled like a darkened storm. Nyte felt her anger and pain as it overwhelmed him with a dark anxiety.

"Sleep." She spoke with a serpent's hiss.

The candles blew out and Nyte drifted off to sleep.

Moya Blynn dressed in her burgundy robe and left the Cluricaun Tavern. Outside, her silky dark red hair turned greasy. Her golden-brown skin withered and decayed, and her pale brown eyes stormed into darkness. Cerberus walked out from the shadows and growled. "Did you succeed, Enchantress?"

Moya Blynn placed her hand on her belly. “Time will tell.” She mounted the enormous three-headed beast. “Take us home, Cerberus.”

"As you wish,” he rasped.

Chapter XXVI
Dark Anxiety.

Underneath the stars, hidden within a forest, Lord Drakus and his Komalsh army gazed across the Field of Blood. The Sykanian castle was in their sights.

****

The Field of Blood was a stretch of open land surrounding the Sykanian castle. It was given the name, "Field of Blood," not due to the bloodshed of war but rather a rare red flower which carpeted the ground. Following a heavy rain fall, the field would puddle with red stain. The Sykanians were commonly identified by their red stained boots and the red hooves of their horses.

****

"We wait till dawn," instructed Lord Drakus. "Then we attack the castle head on."

"Understood my lord," replied Mack.

"Lord Mack, I cannot express the importance of retrieving the Sykanian chapter to *The Book of Dragons*. It is vital to the Drakonian peace talks."

"I'll see to it personally that the Komalsh are informed my lord," assured Lord Mack

"We are at war for peace. How ironic." Mythra was just putting two and two together.

Inside the Sykanian castle, Kelar, Neasha and Kolos sat down to a royal feast hosted by the wizard, Malores. They sat proudly upon their thrones while being served as though they were royalty. Hungry from their travels, they overindulged themselves with fancy food and drink.

Few words were exchanged during the feast. Malores sat quietly by himself at the head of the table. He picked at his plate slowly while scrolling through the music for the Dragon's Flute.

Finished with her dinner and tired from their travels, Neasha rose from the table and kissed Kelar on the cheek.

"I'm going for my bath," she winked.

Kelar smiled at her. "I'll see you shortly."

Kolos rose from his seat as well, patting his swollen belly. "I'm going to go find a woman to bed."

"Shouldn't you bathe first? I can smell you from here!" grimaced Kelar.

Kolos smelled his armpits. "What do you mean?"

"Never mind, I'm sure the woman you lay with won't mind."

Malores, too, left the dining table with his eyes still glued to the flute's tablature.

Kelar wandered around the dining room admiring the demonic sculptures and artwork King Cretes Siris had chosen for decor. He noticed a larger than average-sized painting dominating the back wall. A likeness to the Door of Duren. However, this one was opened and inside the darkened doorway were two glowing red eyes.

An audible whisper entered Kelar's thoughts.

"Come to me."

Kelar looked around the empty dining room.

"Come Kelar," repeated the voice.

Kelar left the dining room and made his way down a hallway. He stopped before a large wooden door.

"Come to me," repeated the whisper.

The door opened to a long narrow balcony under a starlit sky. Kelar walked through the doorway. On his left was the castle's front yard known as the Field of Blood and to his right was the castle's protected grounds. Ahead of him stood Lord Cable Demonis.

Kelar approached him. "You wanted to see me, Lord Demonis?"

"Yes, Kelar. I am aware you and Neasha have doubts about our ideals."

"I mean no disrespect, Lord Demonis. We just want to live simple lives," assured Kelar.

"Come here, son." Demonis ushered him toward a view of the citizens of Sykania safely protected behind the castle walls. "Look at the villagers roaming about Kelar. They are living simple lives. Like sheep they sleep, they eat, and they go about their daily routines oblivious to the nature of existence. They occupy their minds with tedious tasks to subconsciously avoid the inevitable outcome of mortality. They live under a blanket of ignorance, never grasping their full state of consciousness. That is the simple life, Kelar. We are not simple. Our minds have been opened. Our sixth sense has been awakened. We could never find peace in simple."

Kelar stared down at the simple life. He knew Demonis' words to be true. His mind had been opened to a psychic array of knowledge beyond imagination. He had nothing in common with the people who mingled below.

"There are two psychic abilities which I'd like to share with you, Kelar." Demonis pointed inside the castle grounds to a couple of villagers in friendly conversation.

"Observe." He closed his eyes and released a negative vibe piercing the minds of the two villagers. Their spirits instantly darkened. They became irritated and argumentative with each other until their bickering sent them off in different directions.

"The Komalsh code forbids psychic influence." reminded Kelar.

"We are not Komalsh," reminded Demonis. "Do you want to learn how to motivate the simple life?"

"Don't you mean manipulate?"

"Point of view, Kelar. All I did was amplify what they truly felt for each other. Isn't that purer than watching them hide behind false pretences?"

Kelar stared off into the crowd of Sykanians. They now seemed petty to him. "Alright, show me."

"You already possess the ability, Kelar. Your years at the school of Olemeeze have steered you away from this gift. Allow me to guide you back."

Demonis placed his hand on the back of Kelar's head. Darkness momentarily engulfed Kelar's eyes. Then his pupils returned.

"It is done, Kelar."

Kelar looked over the crowd of Sykanians until he came across two laughing with each other. He closed his eyes and released a negative vibe.

The two men stopped laughing. Their spirits darkened. They started glaring at one another then exchanged harsh words. One pushed the other leading to a fist fight. They continued to beat each other bloody until a guard patrol separated and arrested them.

"Very impressive!" grinned Demonis.

"It felt like I had power over them," admitted Kelar distastefully.

"Indeed. It was this very ability that Lord Cretes Siris used to influence the Sykanian people in the process of becoming their king. After the assassination of King Hennessy and his family, Malores gained temporary control over the Sykanian people. He would allow Cretes to hide under his care until gaining enough prestige to be crowned. Being of Sykanian ancestry made it easy for Cretes. With this gift I've shown you, he would manipulate his way to becoming the first elected King in Drakonian history."

"Now our plan moves forward, Kelar. With the Dragon's Flute, the Sykanian's chapter of, *The Book of Dragons*, and Siris' personally trained Knights Elite, we are a force to be reckoned with."

"Now then," he continued, "for the second forbidden fruit."

Once again Demonis placed his hand on the back of Kelar's head. Again, darkness engulfed his eyes and as that darkness faded, his pupils returned.

Demonis pointed to the wizard, Malores Barnett. He wandered through the crowd of villagers.

"Kelar, I want you to read the wizard's mind."

Kelar focused on Malores' thoughts.

"What do you see?" asked Demonis.

"He's anxious. He awaits a lover."

A young man approached the wizard. He had a gentle posture and his eyes sparkled flirtatiously.

"Yes, Kelar, our wizard leads a private life with a sexual preference for younger men. But there's more, much more. Search deeper into his memories."

Kelar focused deeper into Malores' memory. What he saw disturbed him greatly.

"What do you see, Kelar?"

"Malores beds with young men. Then he kills them slowly. This excites him but then afterwards he feels remorse and regret. So, he cuts their bodies into pieces."

Kelar was disturbed by what he had just learned. The visuals repulsed him.

"Yes, strangely enough he hides the body parts in an airtight room beneath the castle."

"He's sick!" Kelar lamented.

"We all have our secrets, son. That is why we read everyone's mind to know who we can trust. The Komalsh are ignorant in creating laws forbidding this gift."

Kelar could understand where Demonis was coming from. To rule a prosperous Drakonia, you must first control it. The sheep don't know better. All they desire are the comforts of a simple life. A controlled environment gives their lives much-needed structure.

"There's something else you should be aware of, Kelar." Demonis led him to the other side of the balcony overlooking the Field of Blood. "Close your eyes and search the forest beyond the field."

Kelar obeyed. "I don't feel anything."

"That's because they're blocking you," explained Demonis.

"Who is?"

Demonis placed his hand on the back of Kelar's head. "Search the forest again."

Kelar did as Demonis asked. He closed his eyes and searched the forest with his mind. But this time Demonis' shadow demon shimmered across the old lord's face. Its dark power amplified Kelar's psychic abilities revealing to him the beating hearts of over a hundred Komalsh and their unicorns.

Demonis placed his arm around Kelar. "It's the entire Komalsh army, son. They're waiting until morning to attack us."

"What are we going to do?"

"We will fight back, son."

"We cannot defeat the Komalsh?"

"We won't need to, Kelar," grinned Demonis.

Early the next morning, Lady Savita Cosmos stood on the balcony of the Elvin castle overlooking the Western Sea. In this dark hour, a sliver of sunlight stretched across the horizon. Soon the sun will rise and with it a new day. Beside her approached the Elvin high priest, Nym.

"Trouble sleeping, Lady Cosmos?"

"Something feels very wrong, Nym. I feel a dark anxiety running through my veins."

"The Darkstar is reaching out," replied Nym. "It grows stronger each day."

"Is Mili ready, Nym?"

"In body, yes. However, I'm afraid her mind still has much conflict."

Savita felt overwhelmed by her anxiety. "I don't feel well, Nym."

"This dark anxiety you feel—it lures you away from seeing the truth. Focus, Lady Cosmos. Breathe as you were taught. Then reach out and see the truth it hides."

Savita closed her eyes. She started to breathe as taught by the Elvin priest. Her anxiety slowly diminished. She found peace and tranquility…then she saw war. "Mili's in grave danger, Nym!"

Savita looked over the wall to the front drawbridge. It was being closed while Elvin guards scurried about. Then a bell clanged with a sound so alarming it felt like it could tear a hole in the sky.

"The castle is under attack!" warned Nym.

In the distance a single rider on horseback galloped toward the castle leaving a trail of flames behind him.

"It's Fenka Rek." Savita recognized him immediately. "We need to get to Milita now!"

Fenka Rek and his undead horse, Apocalypse, ignited the mountain ridge in flames. On his approach to the drawbridge, he avoided Elvin arrows hissing by his head. Fenka Rek raised his hand and telekinetically forced the draw bridge down. The force of his telekinesis was so powerful the drawbridge chains shattered and whipped about killing several nearby Elvin guards.

With the bridge lowered over the Triton River, Fenka Rek and his undead steed galloped into the Elvin castle leaving a trail of flames behind.

Sleeping in her bed, Lady Milita Drakus awoke abruptly to the sound of bells. In the corner of her room hiding in the shadows stood a cloaked figure. Milita reached for her sword telekinetically summoning it to her hand. "Reveal yourself!" she demanded at sword point.

"You won't need that my lady." Spoke a familiar voice. With a snap of his fingers all the candles in the room lit.

"Kudos! What are you doing here?"

"We don't have time for that, my dear. Come with me. You are in grave danger."

Milita donned her robes and Komalsh light armour. Armed with her sword and dagger she followed Kudos through a hallway of panicked Elvin guards.

"What's going on, Kudos?"

"I'm afraid your identity has been revealed, Milita. Fenka Rek has come to assassinate you."

"Mili!" Shouted Savita and Nym running toward them.

"Kudos? What are you doing here?"

Kudos explained, “Lord Drakus has made me aware of Malshidiel’s chosen one. He’s also mentioned spies who walk among us. I’m afraid Milita’s whereabouts has been compromised, Savita. She must be hidden and hidden well.” Kudos revealed the hand-sized cube of black glass given to him by Lord Drakus. He held on to it with a silk handkerchief to prevent it from contacting his skin. Nym’s eyes widened. “It’s the gateway to the Hidden Night.” He gasped. “Quickly, we must reach the balcony!”

Inside the Elvin castle, Fenka Rek and his undead steed rode through the castle yard. Surrounded by impossible odds, his undead horse’s hooves exploded into hellfire, incinerating all in a 50-foot radius. The infamous assassin leapt off his steed and ran through the singed Elvin corpses toward the nearest staircase.

Archers shot arrows from balconies above.

Fenka Rek slapped them away with his sword. He reached out his hand and crushed the archers with a squeeze of his telekinetic grip—their heads squashing as their bodies crumpled to the ground.

Fenka Rek continued up the stairs and toward the balcony guided by Milita’s heartbeat beacon. Gathered on the balcony were Kudos, Milita, Nym and Savita.

“What’s going on? Why don’t we just fight him?”

“We cannot win, Milita. He will kill us all.” answered Kudos calmly. “There are other ways to win this war, none of which we possess today.”

"Reveal the cube, master Kudos,” ordered Nym. “Milita, the only place you’ll be safe from detection is in the realm of the Hidden Night.”

“You want me to hide in that cube?” pointed Milita to Kudos’ hand.

“It’s your only chance of survival!” pleaded Nym.

“But together we could stop Fenka Rek! Right here, right now!” The idea angered Milita.

"There are only two in Drakonia that can defeat Fenka Rek. Unfortunately, they are more interested in serving drinks." Kudos had more important matters to address and so he suppressed his tongue.

"I am not going into that bloody cube!" Milita raised her voice. She was adamant.

"I cannot force you to!" shouted Kudos back at her. "Here, just take it and throw it away then!"

Milita grabbed the cube from the silk handkerchief. As she was about to throw it, her body turned to smoke and was vacuumed into the black glass cube. It dropped to the ground like an anvil.

"That was very clever, Kudos," said Nym.

"Lord Drakus warned me of her obstinacy."

Kudos picked up the glass cube carefully with the silk handkerchief and placed it at the end of his staff. "Be hidden!" he shouted while thrusting it into the air. Like a shooting star the cube launched from Kudos' staff and disappeared into the night.

Kudos whistled for Pegasus who landed on the balcony. "You must leave, Savita. Live to fight another day."

"I'm not leaving without you, Kudos!"

"This isn't a request, my dear. This is an order." calmed the sorcerer in Kudos. "The only way you'll survive is if I stay behind and stall Fenka Rek."

Savita had never seen the look Kudos now displayed. The sorcerer was frightened, and that fear disturbed her greatly. Her eyes filled with tears as Kudos helped her onto Pegasus.

"How will we find Mili, Kudos?" asked Savita.

"Only her closest friend can lead you to her. Now run!" Kudos slapped Pegasus' ass sending him jolting up into the air. "Fly Pegasus, fly!" he screamed.

Fenka Rek ran out onto the balcony while launching an arrow toward the back of Savita's head. Kudos slapped it out of the air with his staff then sent a sorcerer's blast of energy toward Fenka Rek. The villainous assassin took the full impact and the entire balcony erupted into smoke and flames.

Savita watched helplessly as the castle's balcony crumbled to the ground. Both Kudos and Nym disappeared in the debris and dust.

"Kudos!" She screamed in terror.

Savita searched the area with her mind but couldn't detect any signs of life. "Oh no." She wept. "No, no, not you Kudos. Please no."

"Lady Cosmos!" interrupted Pegasus. "Where do we go?"

Savita reached out telepathically to Lord Drakus, but he never responded. The dark anxiety returned through her veins silencing her psychic abilities. It crawled into her thoughts and darkened her soul. But the sorceress would not give up. She calmed her mind by breathing as instructed by Nym. Then she created a psychic barrier forever protecting herself from the dark anxiety's influence. Savita's psychic strength was restored.

"Pegasus, I sense Nyte is in great danger." announced Savita.

"We won't reach the Cluricaun Tavern in time, Lady Cosmos. It's too far!" replied Pegasus.

"I know who can warn them."

Savita reached out her telepathic thought and focused on Kudos' cottage. Inside sleeping beside two gremlins was the phoenix, Blythe.

"You must warn Nyte Shade!" hailed Savita. "You must warn Nyte Shade!"

With a sudden sense of urgency Blythe pecked away at her splinter then spread her wings. She leaped through the window and flew toward the Cluricaun Tavern.

"Pegasus. Take us to the Sykanian castle. We must find Lord Drakus!"

"As you wish, Lady Cosmos."

Pegasus changed course and headed toward the Sykanian castle.

Chapter XXVII
War: Part I.

Nyte's vision blurred in and out of focus. His head throbbed and his mouth was dry as a desert. He lay naked in the middle of the tavern floor discombobulated and confused. Slowly, he got up and looked around. Moya Blynn was nowhere to be seen. Evidently, she'd been a one-night Elvin love affair, but not his most pressing concern. He was spitting dust from dehydration and the quest for water became imperative.

Nyte heard a loud shuffling sound coming from the rafters above. Before his unconvinced eyes, a phoenix landed beside him. "Blythe? Is that you?" asked Nyte unconvinced.

"Yes, Lord Shade," she whistled.

"Hey, I understood what you just said!" slurred Nyte still feeling the effects of Brian's moonshine.

"We have little time, Nyte. I've come to warn you!" whistled Blythe.

Nyte rose to his feet and put on his pants. He fumbled toward a chair and sat down planting his face on the table.

"Well, what is it?" he moaned.

"King Siris and his Knights Elite will be arriving here shortly. They're coming to kill you all!" warned Blythe.

"How? What? I mean…how do you know this?" Nyte still felt the cloud of inebriation in his head and his tongue felt the thickness of thirst.

"Lady Cosmos summoned me to warn you!" whistled Blythe.

"What's the phoenix whistling about?" Trayke staggered from his room feeling the remnants of a drunken stupor.

"She says King Siris is on his way to kill us." Nyte's mumble was still able to relay the message.

"Really! Whatever happened to good morning!" Trayke grumbled while rubbing away the pain of too much alcohol from his left eye socket.

The phoenix whistled again.

"Now what's she saying?"

"She said good morning, Trayke," conveyed Nyte.

"What a smart ass!" said Kris leaning over the bar counter. "Oh, my head hurts, where's the water?" Kris rubbed his temples. "Why haven't we recovered from this yet?" he moaned.

"I don't feel very well." Terex entered the room struggling with balance.

"Where's Arias?" wondered Kris.

"He won't get up. He refuses to." answered Terex. "Is there any water?"

Trayke noticed a closed door behind the bar. "Maybe there's water in there."

He struggled to unlatch the door then peered inside. "It's awfully dark in here." he squinted in an effort to get his eyes to work.

A deep grumbling sound purred from the depths of the darkened room. Trayke peered in closer to investigate. He noticed two yellow eyes staring back at him. Trayke squinted and leaned in closer. The yellow eyes winced. Then a burst of flames engulfed the doorway jolting Trayke backward to the floor.

"What the hell was that!" said Terex as he was driven back from the flames.

Lee-Ann and Brian trampled down the stairs to the opened doorway. Stepping over Trayke, Lee-Ann glowed with excitement. "Oh honey! Baby's first flame!"

She walked into the dark room where a baby dragon sat thrilled to see her. Lee-Ann wrapped her arms around him and kissed him on the cheek. "I'm so proud of you, Clarence!"

The baby dragon purred while snuggling back.

Trayke lay flat out on the floor. His frontside had been singed to a crisp. "There's no water in there," he whimpered.

"Of course not!" proclaimed Lee-Ann closing the door behind her. "Can't you read?" She pointed to the door. Kris looked at the door and leaned forward. "Read what?"

"The sign..." Lee-Ann pointed in the direction of the door suddenly noticing it was gone. "Brian. What happened to the warning sign?"

"It's over here, pumpkin." Brian grabbed it from under the bar table and displayed it. Caution, dragon inside. "I used, it under this table leg to stop the wobbling."

"Oh, babe. Put it back on the door before someone gets hurt."

"Okay, pumpkin!"

"Someone already got hurt!" scowled Trayke slowly rising from the floor. He tiptoed away from the door in agonising pain.

****

Although his Komalsh healing abilities would regenerate flesh and bone, Trayke's ravishing hair would take time to grow back.

****

"Ha, ha!" laughed Terex while pointing at Trayke. "You're bald!"

"Oh, very funny!" Trayke patiently waited as his skin finished regenerating itself. "Why is there a baby dragon in your cellar? Who does that?" Trayke looked at his reflection in a wall mirror. He wiped the ash from his bald head. "What kind of a name is Clarence, anyway? Who names a dragon Clarence?"

The phoenix, Blythe, flew around the interior of the tavern and then out the front door. "I'll show you where they are, Nyte," she whistled.

Nyte followed her to the doorway and watched as she flew toward Siris and his army. In the visible distance, Blythe circled around the Sykanian ambushers revealing their location.

Nyte rubbed his tired eyes. "Hey guys, someone go wake up Arias. There's going to be an army of Sykanians outside the tavern soon."

The sun started to rise over the Field of Blood's red flowered meadow. Hidden within the outer rim of the forest, Lord Drakus sat on his unicorn, Mythra. They observed the Sykanian castle from afar as its draw bridge slowly opened. Behind him all along the treed area, his Komalsh army and their unicorn counterparts awaited Lord Drakus' command. They stood in silence while anticipating the war to come.

Lord Demonis stood on the Sykanian castle's balcony overlooking the Field of Blood. He reached for the Dragon's Flute hidden within his robes. With both hands he held it under the sun's morning light. The flute absorbed its radiation and started to glow.

In the distance, dragons occupying the Avila Mountain Range were awakened by the lure of the Dragon's Flute. They rose from caves and mountain peaks stretching their wings and taking to the skies.

Sykanian Knights mounted on horses assembled in the castle grounds below led by Colonel Wile Stella. When the drawbridge opened, the army assembled outside the castle in their assigned combat positions.

Kelar, Kolos and Neasha were dressed in a new design of Sykanian Elite cloak and light armour. The uniform was a solid black decorated with the head of a red dragon on the chest plate. Their new look was a gift from King Siris who had Demonis appoint them as Lords of the Red Dragon.

The three dark knights gathered beside Lord Demonis on the castle's balcony where Demonis made a request.

"Kelar, would you be so kind as to retrieve the wizard."

The wizard, Malores, lay in bed beside his lover. After a night of intimacy, they awoke in each other's arms. Malores offered him a drink from his bedside table. Parched, his lover swallowed it down while smiling cheerfully in return. Moments after ingesting the juice, his body started to twitch, and his muscles cramped and stiffened. Drool ran down his cheek while he lay paralysed and confused. He could see Malores sitting above him smiling with anticipation. The wizard revealed a dagger from his bedside table and with both hands raised it over his head. His lover's eyes filled with confusion and terror.

Kelar kicked open Malores' door. "You sick bastard. Get your clothes on and come with me now!"

The startled Malores jumped back from his bed dropping his dagger to the floor. With widened eyes and a pounding heart he cowered as he moved toward Kelar. "It's not what it looks like, Kelar!"

"Save it, wizard. Lord Demonis summons you!"

Drakus and Mythra observed the Sykanian soldiers taking their formation on the Field of Blood.

"Well, so much for a surprise attack." Mythra was not sure what was going to take place next.

"This was always a planned battle," reminded Drakus.

Drakus gave Mythra a gentle pat on the neck and repeated the words he said before every battle. "You are my best friend, Mythra. It has been an honour to ride with you."

"The honour is mine, Hirum." snorted Mythra.

"Then let us ride into battle."

Lord Drakus raised his sword and with a gallop led the Komalsh army onto the Field of Blood.

The young Lords and their unicorns gathered before the Cluricaun Tavern awaiting King Siris and his Sykanian army. Being the last one out of bed, Arias left the tavern still strapping on his armour. He stopped as Brian, pulling a heavy wagon with little effort, passed him. Hungover and confused, Arias watched as Brian positioned the wagon in front of Lee-Ann's garden.

"What are you doing, honey?" asked Lee-Ann standing in the tavern doorway with Destiny under her arm.

"Just making sure no one wrecks your garden, pumpkin," answered Brian cheerfully.

"Oh, thanks, babe! Good thinking!" Lee-Ann was pleased with Brian's thoughtfulness.

"Hey, Nyte." Arias was still baffled by the simplicities displayed by Brian and Lee-Ann. "How do you know King Siris is ambushing us this morning?"

Nyte paused. "Well...a little bird told me."

"A little bird?" repeated Arias.

"It was a phoenix named Blythe. It's a long story, Arias, but she flew to me with great urgency to deliver me a message."

"Hold on right there, Nyte. Did you say she?"

Nyte paused. "Yes, I did."

"Didn't we learn in school that all phoenixes are male?" Was Arias remembering correctly?

"Yeah, Nyte," added Trayke, "and they're not a little bird by any means. More like a medium-size bird."

"Why are we having this conversation?" Kris was confused. "Shouldn't we…, I don't know…, prepare for battle?"

Terex raised his hand in the air feeling awkwardly left out of the conversation.

"Why do you have your hand up?" asked Nyte.

"Well, Nyte," explained Terex. "We all know that phoenixes don't breed. They burst into flames and from the ashes rises a baby one."

"Yes, and your point is?" asked Nyte patiently.

"So, having a sex type would be altogether pointless."

"This whole conversation is pointless!" Kris was agitated.

"So, what came first?" queried Trayke. "The fire or the bird?" he chuckled.

"I read this philosophy book about that," continued Terex. "It went on about what came first, the chicken or the egg."

A moment passed in silence.

"Well!" asked Trayke in suspense. "What came first?"

Terex nodded with a smile. "Oh yeah, uh, I never read that far into it but I'm pretty sure it had something to do with a tree falling in the woods."

The phoenix, Blythe, swooped down and landed on Nyte's shoulder. "Listen up!" said Nyte. He pointed to the bird on his shoulder and spoke loud enough to grab everyone's attention. "This medium-size female phoenix told me that those guys," Nyte pointed to a thunderous cloud of dust coming from the west, "are coming here to kill us!"

The five of them stared quietly at the Sykanian army as it grew larger and larger.

"That's a pretty big army," noted Trayke.

"Yep. It sure is." Arias agreed. "Do you think they left anyone at home?"

"I always imagined our first sword fight to be smaller," admitted Nyte. "…you know, a gradual flow into it kind of thing."

"You think we can talk our way through this?" asked Arias. "You know, …a peaceful negotiation?"

"I don't think that will be an option, Arias." answered Kris. "But I can say my hangover doesn't feel as bad now. Hey, boys!"

The young Lords all nodded in agreement when Arias noticed Trayke's bald head. "What the hell happened to you?"

"I had a run in with a dragon named Clarence."

Terex chuckled. "You look so funny bald."

The others joined Terex in an uncontrollable laughter that they seemed unable to stop. Trayke stewed.

Overlooking the Field of Blood from the castle's balcony, Demonis firmly gripped the glowing flute. Malores, now in attendance, waited patiently for both armies to assemble into their battle formations. He rolled out the Dragon Flute's music and nodded to Demonis.

"You can hand me the flute, my lord."

"Not yet, Malores."

"What do you mean? We must play the flute now or our army will be vanquished! They're no match against the Komalsh!"

"There's a method to my madness, wizard. Be patient."

"Yes, my lord," surrendered Malores helplessly.

On the battlefield below the Sykanian colonel, Wile Stella stood nervously.

"We cannot win this battle, sir." advised his lieutenant. "No one can defeat a unicorn let alone the entire Komalsh army. This is suicide!"

"It's quite fine, lieutenant. Lord Demonis has assured us we will be victorious. We're only here to spring a trap."

"Do you trust Lord Demonis, colonel?"

"Of course, I do! The king speaks highly of him, and I would never question our king."

Riding up to the Sykanian castle the Komalsh army assembled in a row fronted by Lord Drakus. On either side of him stood his newly appointed generals, Lords Mack and Kloken.

United by telepathic communion, Lord Drakus whispered to his Komalsh. "This is textbook warfare gentlemen. Attack their defence line straight on. The three of us will penetrate the barrier and take-out Lord Demonis. Understood?"

The Komalsh raised their swords and cheered, "To victory!"

King Cretes Siris halted his Sykanian Elite a couple of hundred yards from the Cluricaun Tavern. Five young Komalsh stood before it.

"Lord Nyte Shade!" hailed King Siris telepathically for all to hear. "Surrender now or die!"

"We will not surrender, King Siris!" replied Nyte. The young Lords beside him nodded in agreement.

The king turned to his captain, Breton Korrigan. "That was a close one. For a second there, I feared he was going to surrender. I never even anticipated a surrender speech."

Siris hailed again. "Okay then, this is good!"

Inside the tavern, Brian and Lee-Ann stood before the window waiting for the battle's outcome. Destiny hid behind the bar.

"Brian, I think they're too close to the tavern. They're going to get arrows and thingies littered everywhere," said Lee-Ann.

Brian opened the window. "Hey Nyte!"

Nyte turned around to the tavern. "What?"

"Can you guys move further away from the tavern? Lee-Ann doesn't want you guys making a mess."

"What! Are you kidding me?" yelled Nyte.

"Do I look like the type of guy who would kid?" yelled Brian trying to be as polite as possible.

"We should probably just move further out." suggested Kris.

"Yeah, okay. Is it just me or is there something really off about those two?"

"They've been here for a thousand years, Nyte. I'm sure that would make anyone a little off," replied Kris.

"Good point, good point," agreed Nyte as they cautiously moved further out.

"They are moving out." Announced Brian.

"Oh…, thanks, babe, I don't mean to sound like a nag but if we can avoid the mess, then why not, right?"

"Absolutely, pumpkin!"

Entering the town along the riverside was a group of farmers travelling by horse and carriage. They were led by Eli and his wife, Lindy, who held their baby girl, Faith.

"Eli! Look, it's Nyte and Loki." She waved.

Eli sensed the tension of battle and halted the convoy.

"This doesn't look good, Lindy. Get inside the wagon, honey!" Eli steered his wagon behind the tavern leading the other farmers to safety.

"So, what's the plan then, Nyte?" asked Kris.

"I'm not sure," sighed Nyte.

"We can still try to talk things out?" suggested Arias.

Terex stood impatiently. "Let's just take out the king and the rest will fall!"

He grasped the hockey puck from his light armour and threw it as hard as he could toward Siris' head. The king ducked and the puck hit the knight behind him. The knight fell off his horse and snapped his neck on impact. Terex raised both his arms in the air and shouted. "He shoots, he scores!"

Inside the tavern watching from behind the window, Lee-Ann stood beside Brian. She shook her head at him, rolled her eyes, and merely said, "Oh boy."

"Did you see that?" Siris was in disbelief.

"Yes, your majesty," answered the captain dully.

"Have you ever seen anyone die like that before?"

"No, sire. Not like that."

"What a humiliating way to go!" cackled Siris.

"I'm sure he doesn't care any more, my king."

"I guess you're right. When you're gone, who really gives a shit…speaking of which…" The king gagged from the stench of the foul odor. "I think he just soiled himself!"

"Yes," agreed the captain. "This sort of thing happens when you die suddenly."

"Well then, let this be a lesson!" spoke the king to his surrounding knights. "No more heavy meals before battle." His cackle sounded anything but serious.

"Well spoken, my king," calmly nodded the captain.

King Siris drew his sword and gave the order, "Archers to arms!"

Captain Breton Korrigan repeated the order, and a blue flag was raised indicating that the archers were to take the line of offense. Now that they were positioned, Siris lowered his sword and the blue flag followed. The Sykanian archers released their arrows and blanketed the sky in a sheet of darkness.

The young Lords looked up to see the bombardment of arrows heading toward them.

"About that plan, Nyte?" inquired Kris.

Gathered on the Field of Blood, the Komalsh and Sykanian armies collided in combat. This one-sided battle led to an onslaught. The Sykanian numbers decreased rapidly, and their front line collapsed. The Komalsh skill and psychic abilities proved an advantage from the start. Lord Drakus and his unicorn, Mythra, charged through the weakened line with Lords Mack and Kloken trailing behind. Their unicorns exploded into a bright white flash engulfing them and their riders. Reappearing on the opposite side of the Sykanian defensive line, they galloped fiercely toward the castle.

"It's Lord Drakus! He's coming for us! I beg you my lord," panicked Malores, "hand me the flute before it's too late!"

Lord Demonis stood fearlessly with both hands firmly gripping the glowing flute. "Not yet, Malores."

"But my lord…"

"Enough!" snapped Demonis.

Kelar pointed off to the horizon where dragons by the hundreds engulfed the morning sky.

Demonis grinned devilishly.

Lord Drakus rolled backwards off his unicorn, Mythra, while unsheathing his sword. Effortlessly he struck down colonel Wile Stella and then killed his lieutenant. Mythra leaped toward the castle and vanished into a bright white flash. He reappeared with his front legs hanging over the balcony wall. With a snap from his jaw, Mythra bit on to Demonis' shoulder. The two vanished in another bright white flash reappearing on the battlefield below. Mythra aggressively tossed him against the castle's outer wall. He lowered his horn and charged the renegade lord. While he was in full stride charging toward him, Demonis dropped the illuminating flute steering Mythra's attention away. Before impact Demonis unsheathed his sword and thrust his blade through Mythra's skull.

Lords Mack and Kloken left their steeds and joined Drakus' efforts to break the Sykanian hierarchy. With unmatched skill they effortlessly slaughtered the Sykanian guards.

Drakus pulled his sword from the chest of a Sykanian knight. He watched helplessly as his unicorn, Mythra, fell to the ground dead. Enraged, he ran at Demonis raising his blood-stained sword. Demonis pulled his sword from Mythra's skull and blocked a downward swing from Drakus' blade. The two clashed swords in a flurry of blows.

Back at the Cluricaun Tavern, what seemed a nightfall of arrows drove down toward the young Lords. The Sykanian archers released a second and third wave of arrows.

"Maybe you should sit this one out, Terex." Suggested Nyte hinting to his poor telekinesis.

"Yeah, okay." Terex agreed.

Telekinetically orchestrated, the young Lords raised their hands and stopped the first wave of arrows in mid descent. Using their telekinesis, they returned the arrows to the archers killing them all before a fourth wave could be released. The second and third wave of arrows were stopped by the young Lords and were redirected toward the Sykanian Knights Elite who hid protected under their shields.

King Siris ordered a strike. Captain Korrigan raised the red flag and the Sykanian Knights Elite charged into battle.

"That worked out well!" grinned Arias.

"It's not over yet," reminded Kris. "What's the plan now, Nyte?"

"Well, we're outnumbered. We need to take this battle away from the townspeople." Nyte hoped it would prevent the bloodshed of innocent people.

Terex glanced around. "There's a ravine over the top of that ridge, Nyte, and to the north is the river. Behind us is the ocean. Our only option is to fight head on."

"Then that's just what we'll have to do, Terex. It seems we are low on options."

"We have another problem, Nyte." Loki was picking up a scent from near the river.

Out from the Riegan River emerged the Minotaur. His bull head and massive rippled body dwarfed the Sykanian threat. Downwind, his nostrils flared as he inhaled Nyte's familiar scent. He looked directly at Nyte. The Minotaur drooled and huffed as he hunched over and started to charge.

Loki's ears raised. "Why does it feel like he's coming for us, Nyte?"

"He's after me, Loki. But that's okay. I have a plan." He grinned.

The Minotaur gained full momentum as he charged toward the tavern.

"Everyone, wait here. We'll return shortly. Come Loki!" uttered Nyte.

The two galloped away with the Minotaur closing the gap behind them. They headed straight toward a hundred plus Sykanian Knights Elite who charged toward them. Loki questioned the intelligence of Nyte's decision. "This doesn't seem like a solid plan, Nyte!"

"Trust me!" Nyte smiled intensely. "This will work!"

The Minotaur was gaining ground, getting closer and closer to Loki's backside. Loki's hooves tore up the ground as he galloped as fast as a unicorn could. The Minotaur reached out his hand, coming just inches away from Loki's tail. The Sykanian army was now only moments from impact, their swords drawn and horses in full stride. The Minotaur's clawed hand reached from behind again almost touching the hairs from Loki's trailing tail.

"Now Loki!" commanded Nyte.

Loki and Nyte became engulfed in a bright white flash and vanished. The Minotaur collided with the Sykanian Knights Elite. He savagely ripped their horses apart. The bull-headed beast massacred all in his reach.

Loki and Nyte reappeared next to their Komalsh brothers. "Who thought war could be this much fun?" Nyte was pleased with the way he had handled this.

"That was brilliant!" grinned Kris.

"Wow, so that's the Minotaur," nodded Terex. "I like his style."

Trayke cringed at the horrific violence. "He sure has anger issues."

"Yep. He's awfully angry alright," added Arias with a chuckle.

The window to the tavern opened again and Brian stretched his head out. "Hey, fellas. Lee-Ann doesn't want that monster anywhere near her garden. Okay?"

"Yeah, okay. Hey, would you two maybe want to help us, you know, being immortal and all?"

"One second, Nyte," answered Brian.

He went outside the front door and yelled into the sky.

"Hey, universe! Should we, like, help them?" A moment passed and the universe didn't reply. Brian shrugged his shoulders. "I'm sorry, guys. You're shit out of luck." He went back into the tavern and locked the doors.

"That is a special kind of crazy," nodded Kris.

King Siris sat on his horse while watching his Knights Elite being slaughtered by the Minotaur's rage.

"Should we retreat, sire?" inquired captain Korrigan calmly.

Siris' shadow demon shimmered rage across his face. He thrusted his hand forward levitating the Minotaur high above his army. Effortlessly he tossed him over the ridge and into the ravine. A third of his Knights Elite lay dead. Angered, King Siris demanded retribution. "Attack the town and kill every living creature!"

Siris and his captain galloped toward the tavern. His Sykanian Knights regrouped and followed.

As the battle unfolded before the Cluricaun Tavern, the young Lords were immediately overwhelmed by the Sykanian numbers. The first rows of knights attacking the young Lords were easily disposed of by telekinetically tossing them far into the ocean. Siris put a stop to that by clouding the young Lord's minds with a dark anxiety weakening their psychic influence. It was now up to their skills in combat.

The Sykanian Elite charged into the young Lords with swords drawn. Separated from his unicorn Charley, Lord Trayke Basa's sword skills struggled against six attacking Sykanians.

Dismounting from his horse, King Siris ran toward the struggling Trayke while wielding the late Lord Jarestt's wooden leg. With a powerful swing Siris cracked open the side of Trayke's skull.

Trayke dropped to the ground unconscious. From above, Siris raised the wooden leg for the final lethal blow when the ghost of Isabella appeared between them. She flickered in and out of sight like a haunted strobe light. Spreading her arms outward her head rattled about spasmodically as she reached toward Siris screaming for vengeance.

Siris staggered backward startled at the spirit. He tripped over a dead knight and fell to the ground. A half dozen Sykanian Knights, unattuned to the spirit world, charged through her ghostly body and attacked the fallen Trayke. Trayke awoke having healed from the blow to his head and crawled on his back desperately blocking each oncoming sword attack. Discombobulated by his concussed head, his life flashed across his eyes. Trayke could no longer defend himself and his enemies overwhelmed him. Then, when hope was all but gone, an elegantly flying X-shaped boomerang swooped around and decapitated each attacker leaving Trayke under a pile of heads and bodies. Trayke pushed the bodies aside and staggered toward Arias for cover.

"Thank you... Arias." he gasped attempting to catch his breath.

"That's just what we do, Trayke." He spoke while pulling his sword out from a Sykanian knight's chest. Terex and his unicorn, Chaos, rode through the swarm of Sykanians, swinging his two-handed broad sword. Each rage-filled swing decapitated multiple enemies. Chaos thrust his horn through a knight's chest plate and tossed him into the wagon Brian had placed in front of Lee-Ann's garden.

Inside the tavern, watching from behind the window, Lee-Ann smiled at Brian lovingly. “Awe, you saved my garden! Thanks, babe!”

The unicorns Loki, Charley and Shiloh ran to the aid of local villagers who had been confronted by Sykanian knights. The steeds tore them apart with their horns and hooves. When the Sykanians surrounded the unicorns in large numbers, the villagers supported them in battle by throwing pitchforks, buckets, shovels and whatever else they could find to fight the Sykanian threat.

Charley thrust his horn through the chest of a knight and tossed him aside. “Hey, Trayke!”

“What?” yelled Trayke decapitating a Sykanian knight.

“When I close one eye like you taught me, I hit every target!” Charley was proud of his newly found ability to contribute and tossed another dead Sykanian to the side.

“Good job, buddy!” Cheered Trayke.

A dozen knights attacked the already overwhelmed Trayke and Arias who stood back-to-back, the Komalsh way, fending them off.

“There are too many of them, Trayke.” Arias was reaching his limit as his boomerang returned to his hand dripping in blood.

Kris and Nyte stood back-to-back sword fighting Sykanian knights. Kris telekinetically lifted the wagon from in front of Lee-Ann’s garden and crushed all the Sykanians who were overwhelming Trayke and Arias. Kris then unsheathed his dagger and tossed his blade toward King Siris. Siris caught the handle of the dagger inches before his face then quickly threw it back toward Kris.

While leaping out of its way, still defending himself from Sykanian swords, Kris ended up with the dagger in his own shoulder.

"Kris!" shouted Nyte who, too, was being overwhelmed.

Kris fought with all his might. His hope slowly dwindled as the enemy surrounded him. A Sykanian knight stabbed Kris' left leg. Weakened from pain Kris defended himself while falling to one knee. Another sword struck down into Kris' shoulder rendering his sword arm limp. Then a third Sykanian raised his sword and chopped down toward Kris' neck.

As his blade dropped a flash of bright white light blinded the Sykanian attackers. From the flash appeared Kris' unicorn, Dusty. With a flurry of kicks, Dusty crushed the faces of all who threatened him. Screams pierced Kris' ears as skulls shattered from Dusty's powerful hooves. The relentless fury of defensive tactics from his unicorn cleared Kris from harm's way.

And when it was all over, "Are you okay, Lord Tarius?" asked his steed.

"Yes, thank you, Dusty. Help me up, my friend. Where is Nyte?"

"Over there!" Dusty pointed with his horn."

Nyte was backed up against the tavern. His psychic enhanced speed and hand-eye coordination was reflected through his skilled swordsmanship. He held off five Sykanian Knights Elite. Kris watched as Nyte made his sword play look elegant and graceful. In apparent slow-motion, he witnessed Lord Shade kill all five of the knights simultaneously. And now there he stood stained in the blood of his enemy. The young Lord Shade walked over their dead bodies and confronted King Siris.

Siris grinned while cackling softly. He raised his blood-stained wooden leg and warned. "You cannot defeat me, Lord Shade." Siris entered Nyte's mind and whispered a trace of fear and doubt. Nyte squeezed his eyes desperate to shake it off. But Siris was too powerful.

Chapter XXVIII
War: Part II.

In front of the Sykanian castle, Drakus and Demonis clashed swords in a frenzy of hatred. Fueled by the death of Mythra, Drakus' attack grew more violent with every swing of his sword. Desperate to achieve an advantage, Demonis used his telekinesis to pick Drakus up and toss him aside. But Drakus only slid mere inches. His mind was too powerful to overcome. His desire for vengeance equally so.

Drakus defended himself from Demonis' burst of sword strikes that followed. In the process, he found the advantage and separated Demonis from his sword. Drakus kicked him to the ground and with both hands raised his sword above his head for the final decapitating blow. Kelar and Kolos leapt down from the castle balcony and attacked Lords Mack and Kloken. Kolos screamed while thrusting his hands forward. His high-pitched sonic blast shredded Lord Kloken, his shattered body dropped to the ground dead.

Lord Mack leapt away from the sonic blast swinging his sword down onto Kelar's blade. They sparred clashing swords back and forth. Mack swung his blade downward. Kelar blocked his blade, then raised his hand and telekinetically snapped Lord Mack's neck. His head twisted right around backwards. Mack dropped his sword and held his head screaming in pain. Kelar swung his sword sideways and cut off his head.

As the oncoming Komalsh started breaking the Sykanian defence barrier, Kolos shot out as many sonic blasts as he could unseating the attacking Komalsh from their unicorns.

Kelar watched as Demonis fell to the ground. He saw Drakus raising his sword over his head. With enhanced speed, Kelar bolted behind Drakus and swung his sword sideways. His blade severed both of Drakus' arms at the elbow preventing Demonis' demise. The Komalsh Lord screamed in agony as his arms and sword fell to the ground. He dropped to his knees; his eyes squeezed shut. His arms bled profusely. Drakus' skin whitened as he fell into shock. Then, after a moment, all fell silent for Lord Hirum Drakus. Time itself slowed to a halt and his pain diminished. The great Komalsh Lord reopened his eyes. There were dark purple flowers scattered around him. The same he had placed each year on his wife's grave. With his eyes he followed the trail of flowers slowly looking up. There before him stood the spirit of Kayla Drakus. She smiled at him with reassurance, hope and love. Drakus returned the smile, tears rolled down his weathered cheeks. All he ever wanted was to be with her. His wife's spirit knelt before him. She wrapped her arms around the broken knight, then kissed him on the lips.

With a two-handed thrust, Kelar pushed his sword through Drakus' back and out his chest. The blade piercing through his already broken heart. Hirum Drakus. Lord of the Komalsh, was dead.

Trapped inside the glass cube of the Hidden Night, Lady Milita Drakus heard a whisper.

"I love you, my niece."

Her eyes filled with tears. She could feel her uncle's dying breath. Milita screamed at the top of her lungs. A sharp scream that would never escape the Hidden Night.

Savita, who approached the Sykanian castle with Pegasus, grasped her chest. "Lord Drakus, no not you, too." She teared.

Demonis watched the life within Drakus' eyes fade into nothingness. He picked up the Dragon's Flute and stared off into the Field of Blood. The Komalsh were killing the last of his Sykanian army.

Neasha lowered a rope down from the balcony above. Kelar, Kolos and Demonis climbed urgently to the top.

"Hurry, Lord Demonis! Give me the flute!" Malores was losing his patience.

Demonis glanced across the battlefield. Dragons had gathered in the skies above lured by the illuminating flute.

"Excellent! Finally, something went as planned!" Demonis was pleased.

Malores was taken aback. "Are you mad?" "We lost the entire Sykanian guard!"

"Just shut up and play the damn flute, wizard!" snapped Demonis handing him the enchanted instrument. Malores started playing from the written music. The glowing flute's soothing sounds captivated the reptile's sensitive ears. Once the skies above swarmed with dragons, the flute's melody changed. It darkened with hatred. Its haunting sounds induced rage in the reptiles. Like an angry tornado, the dragons swarmed above the Komalsh below. Flying high over the Sykanian castle, Savita and Pegasus circled the chaos below.

"This is unusual behavior for dragons, Pegasus." observed Savita. "Wait a moment, over there! Fly over the castle's main balcony. I'll leap off and you can get out of here. We can't afford to lose you, too, my friend."

"As you wish, Lady Cosmos."

In front of the Cluricaun tavern, Nyte Shade and King Cretes Siris circled each other—Nyte with his mother's sword and Siris with his wooden leg.

"You're all grown up, Lord Shade. But you are no match for me. Even you know that don't you?"
Nyte resisted the fear released into his mind by Siris. The fear cast enough doubt to make a constant attack on his confidence which Siris never eased.

The king cackled as he tossed his wooden leg to the ground. Then slowly unsheathed his sword for Nyte to see.

"Do you recognize this blade, Lord Shade? It belonged to your father. I found it while retrieving the Dragon's Flute."

Nyte's bold expression contained traces of fear.

"That's right, Nyte. Lord Demonis has the flute and is using it on the Komalsh as we speak."

Nyte could sense his words to be true.

A shadow demon shimmered across Siris' face for a split moment. "Do you feel that, Lord Shade? Do you feel the death of Lord Hirum Drakus?"

Nyte struggled with focus as Siris' seeds of fear flourished throughout his mind.

"That's right, Lord Shade. Soon you and your friends will be the last of Malshidiel's knighthood. A knighthood I end here today!" Siris swung his sword down onto Nyte's defending blade.

The wizard, Malores, continued to play the flute's enchanted music. Rage filled the skies above as dragons spiraled down toward the Komalsh below.

"Don't worry, Kelar," assured Demonis. "The spell of the flute has no effect on those within its perimeter. Just stay close to the wizard and let the dragons do the work."
Kelar, Kolos and Neasha's eyes sickened to the onslaught of dragon's ravaging the Komalsh below. Even the Sykanian villagers in the protection of the castle's walls were victims to the flute's melodic rage.

Savita and Pegasus flew over the violent skies high above the Sykanian castle. Fearlessly, Lady Cosmos leapt from her flying steed and dove down toward the castle below. Feet first, she landed on the head of a dragon in flight. After the dragon slowed her momentum, she did a back flip past its tail. Once again freefalling toward the castle Savita noticed another dragon swooping toward her. Her sorcerous hands started to glow as she conjured a simple spell. Thrusting her fists forward Savita released a bright flash of light blinding the attacking dragon. She grabbed onto the blinded dragon's tail and swung down to the castle balcony. Savita landed on her feet then engaged Demonis.

Kelar, Neasha and Kolos quickly intervened and attacked Lady Savita Cosmos. Kolos screamed his sonic blast toward her. The sorceress absorbed it with a spell and redirected it back toward him. Kolos flew backward into the wall—his body shattering to near death.

Neasha swung her sword at Savita who stepped out of harm's way. Neasha swung again throwing herself off balance. Savita grabbed on to her head and swiftly snapped her neck. While Savita let Neasha drop to the ground, Kelar's blade swung dangerously close missing the first time and blocked by Savita's now drawn sword the second. Kelar swung his sword repeatedly only to be matched effortlessly by Savita's defensive skill. Now on the offensive, Savita swung her sword and sliced halfway through his throat. Kelar dropped his sword and grasped his neck. Blood sprayed from his jugular veins as he fell to his knees gasping for air.

Unchallenged, Savita confronted Lord Demonis. Demonis revealed, *The Book of Malshidiel*, from his robes—the book Savita lost to Siris a decade ago. Savita pointed her sword toward Demonis' face. "Give me that book," she demanded.

Behind Demonis, Malores continued to play the Dragon's Flute.

"Take a look around, Lady Cosmos." Demonis grinned. "All is lost."

On the Field of Blood, dragons slaughtered the last of the Komalsh. The massacre from above sent several dragons to their demise. However, the ravaging lizards were proven victorious for no Komalsh nor Sykanian was left alive. Even within the castle's protected walls its villagers perished from the intense heat of dragon's breath. No one survived the deadly influence of the flute's melody.

"You want your book, Lady Cosmos?" teased Demonis. "Then go get it!" He tossed, *The Book of Malshidiel*, off the balcony.

Savita telekinetically summoned it to her hand when Demonis lifted her over his head and tossed her down to the Field of Blood. Savita grasped the book while skillfully landing on her feet outside the castle's wall.

Malores continued to play the flute orchestrating the dragons above. They circled the castle targeting Savita. The sorceress looked around desperately to find a way out. She looked back up into the sky hearing the screams of dragons spiralling toward her. Savita was trapped.

In front of the Cluricaun Tavern, Lord Nyte Shade and King Cretes Siris clashed swords in a fury of psychically enhanced swordplay. Nyte's connection with his mind and blade impressed Siris. Drakonia's greatest swordsmen struggled to get the upper hand. But Siris was clever and knew tricks that only experience could teach. While their swords were locked, Siris used his free hand and punched Nyte in the nose. With Nyte's vision blurred by tears, Siris kicked him in the groin and knocked him to the ground. The young Lord regained his footing while blocking several lethal blows from Siris' relentless attack. Nyte thrust his sword toward Siris' face. Siris slapped it aside then punched him in the throat. Nyte dropped to the ground gasping for air.

Terex leaped off his battling steed, Chaos, and ran to Nyte's aid. As Siris picked up his sword to finish Nyte off, Terex tackled him to the ground. He got on top of Siris and delivered a bout of powerful punches.

Siris' shadow demon shimmered across his face absorbing each punch that Terex threw. Siris grabbed Terex by the throat and snapped his neck. He picked Terex up over his head and tossed him effortlessly aside.

Siris picked up the wooden leg and walked over to the fallen Lord Nyte Shade. With both hands he raised the leg over his head and smacked the back of Nyte's head. The mortally wounding blow left Nyte momentarily unconscious as his healing abilities struggled to engage.

Lindy placed baby Faith down into the wagon. "Eli! He's going to kill Nyte! Do something!"

"Like what?" Eli frantically looked around for a weapon, but his wagon carried only farm supplies.

Then, out of the blue, baby Faith started to giggle. She giggled louder then ever before. Eli and Lindy stared in confusion to her happiness. There in her hands was the golden egg. They turned back to each other, and both nodded.

Inside the tavern Destiny screeched in terror. "He's going to kill Nyte!"

Brian and Lee-Ann stood watching through the window. "It doesn't look good, does it?" Observed Brian. Two Sykanian Knights Elite smashed through the locked tavern doors with their swords drawn.

"Holy frick, buddy!" Lee-Ann was taken off guard. "Take it easy on the door!"

Destiny took refuge in Lee-Ann's arms.

"Oh, honey, there's no reason to be afraid." She reassured Des as best she could. "Brian, will you do something about our uninvited guests."

"Like what, pumpkin?"

"I don't know but they are scaring Destiny."

"Okay, pumpkin."

Brian approached the Sykanian Knights with his hands up. "Okay guys, you win. Do you want our gold?" he offered encouragingly.

The knights stared to each other and then nodded in agreement.

"It's behind the bar. See that door. Yeah, that's it, Look back there."

"You must save Nyte, Lee-Ann! Please!" Destiny pleaded in terror.

"I'm sorry, but we can't love." Lee-Ann frowned as she spoke. "But you can!"

"No!" Destiny felt boxed in. "Bad things happen when I change."

"Say it, Destiny. What bad things happened?"

Destiny's stomach collapsed and tears rolled like rivers down her cheeks as she blurted out, "I killed my parents! It was an accident. I never changed before." Destiny's tears turned to sobs. "Because of me, they were laying there on the ground dying. They said they forgave me and that I should never be afraid of my gift—that I should never let this world make me cold. I promised my mom and dad I'd make the world a better place!"

"This door here?" asked the Sykanian.

"That's the one!" smiled Brian deviously.

"But there's a sign here that says beware of dragon?"

"Oh, come on!" "Who in their right mind would put a dragon in the back of a tavern?"

The two Sykanians shrugged their shoulders and opened the door. "It's dark in here."

A deep grumble sound purred from the depths of the darkened room.

The knights peered in closer.

They noticed two yellow eyes staring back at them.

"What's that?"

The yellow eyes blinked, and the room erupted into flames. The two Sykanian Knights fell to the ground burnt to a crisp.

"Awe! Clarence's second flame!" Lee-Ann cheered.

"Nyte's going to die!" cried Destiny. "You have to do something!"

"This is your destiny, Destiny. It's time for you to keep your promise and make the world a better place."

"But how?" whimpered Des.

"By embracing your gift."

"It's not a gift. I keep telling you it's a curse!"

"Then embrace your curse." Brian felt compelled to weigh in while dragging a burnt corpse out the busted front door.

"Oh, Brian you're making a mess! Your spreading ashes everywhere, hon."

"Sorry, pumpkin!" Brian was hopelessly smitten with Lee-Ann. He adored her and would do anything for her.

"I'm sure the Cluricauns will be up soon."

"Those cellar spirits always sleep in. They think the world revolves around them." Lee-Ann had no respect for their lackadaisical attitude.

"Well, I don't know what makes the world revolve but it definitely stops turning every time I look into your beautiful eyes, my sweet Lee."

"Awe, thanks, hon. You're so sweet!" Lee-Ann grabbed Brian to kiss him.

"Where's Destiny?" Brian had lost track of her whereabouts.

"Destiny is unfolding in the front yard, dear," answered Lee-Ann.

Nyte Shade struggled to rise to his knees concussed. He felt warm wet blood running from his ears and nose. His fractured skull and protruding left eye blinded him in pain while Siris' seeds of fear haunted his thoughts.

"How are you…still alive?" rasped Siris. "Your ability to regenerate is impressive, Lord Shade. But you will die all the same. Good night, Nyte," cackled Siris raising the wooden leg over his head. Siris paused a moment. "Wasn't that funny? Night, Nyte." Siris cackled again. "Don't I have the greatest sense of humour?"

He raised the wooden leg high above his head.

Eli ran out from behind the tavern and threw his golden egg. It sailed through the air and struck Siris in the temple. The king lowered the wooden leg and covered his head. "That smarts!" He winced while looking to the ground to discover what hit him. "Is that a golden egg?" Then he glared at Eli. "Who the hell throws golden eggs?" Eli stood there awkwardly.

Siris shook his head at him. "What were you thinking?" Destiny ran out from the tavern. "Leave Nyte alone!" She ran toward Siris transforming into a giant tiger. With her powerful jaw she snapped onto the head of a Sykanian knight who blocked her way and crushed it like a grape. She leaped toward Siris biting her fangs down into his chest, ripping his body apart and tossing him around ferociously.

The attack on Siris' body awakened the shadow demon within him. He grabbed onto the powerful cat and tossed her hard against the tavern wall. "Aren't you an odd creature?" He said in an eerily inquisitive manner. Siris' was then interrupted by a golden egg striking the back of his head. Behind him stood Nyte Shade with his sword drawn.

****

Given plenty of time to heal, Nyte Shade rose from the ground. Within his mind whispered the dream he never understood. "Without Faith, without Destiny, Lord Nyte Shade will die." Empowered with regained hope, his mind escalated to its highest plateau of psychic enlightenment. He could hear baby Faith's giggling through his enhanced hearing. He felt Destiny's unconditional love nourishing his mind and spirit. Siris' invading whispers of negativity withered into silence.

Nyte found himself experiencing everything in slow motion. He watched Siris reaching for his father's sword—the one his mother's spirit mentioned in the Mystique Forest. "The sword would find me." He remembered and he was astonished. Everything is as foretold. Lord Nyte Shade has awoken.

****

Nyte grinned with revitalised hope.

"What are you smiling about, boy?" Nyte's grin instilled a twinge of rare nervousness in Siris.

"I can smell your fear," answered Nyte swinging his sword at Siris.

Siris blocked Nyte's attack and reattempted to invade his mind. But Nyte was different now. His mind was far too powerful to manipulate. All Siris could see was his own fear which weakened his spirit.

Nyte delivered a relentless barrage of sword attacks forcing Siris backward. Nyte levitated dirt up into Siris' eyes and then punched him in the nose blinding him with his own tears. Siris' shadow demon shimmered rage across his face as he thrust his blade toward Nyte's chest. Nyte blocked the blade then punched Siris in the throat. Siris gasped for air.

Angered, his shadow demon resurfaced. With enhanced speed and power Siris now swung multiple sword attacks from every angle desperately trying to penetrate Nyte's defence. Nyte blocked each blow with ease.
Siris overextended on his last attack. Nyte's blade redirected Siris' swing, throwing him off balance. Then Nyte swung himself around and decapitated King Cretes Siris. His headless body collapsed to the ground.

After witnessing the death of his king, Captain Breton Korrigan ordered the retreat of the remaining Sykanian Knights Elite. Frantically, they scattered on horseback.
"The king is dead!"

Nyte and his friends stood over King Cretes Siris' body. A shadow demon clawed its way out of Siris' head. Screaming in pain, it evaporated into a black mist.

Nyte looked around at his friends. They were blood stained and battered, but no worse for wear. Terex, with his broken neck now fully mended, patted Nyte on the back and handed him the golden egg.

"Hockey pucks are more effective." He laughed.

Nyte waved to Eli, Lindy and baby Faith who stood before their wagon waving in return. He tossed the golden egg to Eli and nodded with gratitude.

In front of the tavern Destiny transformed back to herself. Nyte knelt before her placing his cloak around her naked body. "Thank you for saving my life little sister." Something had changed. She now had a note of confidence in her smile. "I'll always take care of you, big brother. I promise."

Kris handed Nyte his father's sword.

Nyte Shade raised both his parent's blades above his head—his thoughts reaching out to the universe.

"Mother, father. I no longer hide in the shadow of Shade...I make the shadow!" he decreed.

The two swords released a vibration resonating through Nyte's soul…then a whisper with a warning followed.

"The Darkstar awakens."

A vision flashed through Nyte's mind forming into a black sphere. "The Darkstar!"

Nyte felt paralyzed with fear in its elusive aura. The image expanded and the dark sphere sank into the chest of a red dragon. The dragon's eyes opened and glowed red. The red dragon started to wither and decay into an undead dragon known as the Dracolich. It rose from the ground and spread its decayed wings. The Dracolich screeched a violent scream scaring Nyte from his vision. Lord Shade fell to his knees gasping for air.

The young Lords gathered around him.

"Are you okay, Nyte?" Kris was like a watch dog paying attention to Nyte's every move.

"Yeah, come on Nyte. We won the war! Let's celebrate." Trayke wanted closure.

Nyte turned to Trayke pale as a ghost. "The war has just begun." He turned back to Kris. "Lord Drakus is dead…all the Komalsh are dead!"

"How do you know this?" Kris was startled by the news.

"Siris told me and deep inside I know it to be true. I fear Savita is also in grave danger. We must find her, my brothers!"

"You heard, Lord Shade!" shouted Kris. "Komalsh, mount up!"

"Destiny," ordered Nyte. "Stay here with Brian and Lee-Ann. I will return for you. I promise."

"Be safe," said Destiny as she waved goodbye.
Nyte sheathed both his parent's swords across his back then mounted Loki. The young Lords mounted their unicorns and followed Nyte toward the Sykanian castle. The phoenix Blythe trailed from a distance.

Brian and Lee-Ann held hands outside the Cluricaun Tavern.

"There are dead people all over the place, Brian!"

"I know, Pumpkin."

"Well, who's going to clean them up?"

Brian looked to the sky and yelled. "Hey universe, should I have to clean…"

Lee-Ann punched his shoulder. "Don't you start with that, you little bugger!"

Behind them a huge flame burst out from the tavern's entrance setting it a blaze.

Lee-Ann rolled her eyes and giggled. "Oh Clarence!"

Lady Savita Cosmos held *The Book of Malshidiel* close to her chest. Above her a swarm of dragons crashed downward. Lord Demonis watched with joyful anticipation as Malores continued to play the Dragon's Flute.
Above the attacking flock of dragons, a larger dragon appeared. With its broad and powerful wingspan, it plunged its way through the onslaught of diving dragons. The vicious dragon opened its drooling fang-filled mouth and targeted Savita.

Savita looked at Malores who still played the flute. She held out her hand and telekinetically summoned the flute from Malores's grasp to her own. She gazed in wonder upon the talon carved flute. Then, with a snap, the enormous dragon swallowed Savita whole. It lifted itself back into the sky and flew off into the horizon.

With the flute silenced, the surrounding dragons scattered, and the skies were clear. The battle was over.

The aftermath of carnage littered the Field of Blood and fires blazed within the castle grounds. The only survivors stood wounded on the castle balcony.

Kelar and Neasha, whose injuries healed quickly, stared off in terror at the mayhem that surrounded them. Sickened by the horror, Neasha collapsed into Kelar's arms.

"They're all dead!" she cried.

Chapter XXVIIII
The Green Mist.

As Malores gazed upon the massacre of his people, he could not help but be distraught. They perished while he played the flute unaware. He cried out, "There are no survivors."

"A necessary evil, Malores." Demonis commented coldly.

Malores stood weakened in despair.

Neasha and Kelar helped Kolos to his feet, his body still mending from the sonic deflection he endured from Savita's sorcery.

"That bitch will die!" cursed Kolos. "My voice? Its changed!" he rasped.

"Although we possess the ability to heal, Kolos," explained Demonis, "extreme wounds never quite mend the same."

Demonis stood with his hands behind his back overlooking the carnage on the battlefield below.

"What do we do now?" Malores felt lost.

"Now, we go to Castle Malshidiel and claim the key scroll," answered Demonis confidently.

Malores shook his head unconvinced. "With what army? Everyone is dead, Lord Demonis! Dead!!"

Demonis reached inside his robes and revealed the Sykanian chapter of *The Book of Dragons*. He scrolled to a saved page. "In order for this spell to work Malores, I needed your people dead."

"You've gone mad!" accused Malores.

Demonis' shadow demon resurfaced across his face as he chanted the spell's written words. By the sixth repetition a green mist rose from the bloodstained battlefield and absorbed itself into the fallen. Slowly, the dead began to rise.

Sykanians, Komalsh, unicorns, horses, and dragons alike slowly reanimated while rising from the ground.

"Zombies?" Malores was mystified.

The dead walked slowly toward the castle. Their orchestra of moans was melodically disturbing. They gathered below Lord Demonis awaiting his instruction.

"Our new army, Malores." Demonis' shadow demon flickered from sight. "You see, wizard, Cretes and I had always intended on turning the Sykanians into zombies. To be honest, I don't see much of a difference. For this spell to succeed they first needed to die. However, even as zombies they would not prevail against the Komalsh army. So, we used the Komalsh to kill the Sykanians and the Dragon's Flute to kill the Komalsh."

"Two birds with one stone!" Malores was beginning to grasp the plan.

"Even better, wizard," continued Lord Demonis, "the Mystique Forest will have no effect on the undead. With the Komalsh defeated the few remaining to protect the castle will be no match for me and my undead army." Malores started understanding the possibilities.

"Does that work for you, wizard?"

Yes, the Darkstar's return would bring eternal life." Malores added, "I would be most grateful to serve."

"Malores!" Shouted his lover who was somewhat disoriented while shaking off the effect of the drug Malores had fed him earlier. Running out on the balcony, he called out, "What's going on?" He staggered backward to the outer wall and then turned in the direction of the noises of Demonis' undead army. His eyes widened in terror.

"What's going on?" He repeated.

Malores could tolerate him no longer. He grabbed him by the scruff and tossed him off the castle balcony. The gentle man fell to the ground snapping both legs on impact. He screamed in agonizing pain as the undead ripped him apart while feeding from his flesh.

Malores watched over the savage execution. It excited him in ways he couldn't explain. He turned to Demonis and kneeled. "My lord, I am at your disposal."

On the opposite side of Drakonia, Nyte Shade led the young Lords galloping through a field, he felt a sudden increase in his psychic enlightenment. His senses peaked as his mind graduated to the final plateau. Nyte reached out with his thoughts and hailed Kelar's mind.

Kelar could feel Nyte reaching out to him.

"What is it?" Demonis never seemed to miss a beat.

"It's Lord Nyte Shade. He killed King Siris."

Demonis gazed in disbelief. "The young Komalsh still live?"

"Yes, and they are coming for you, Lord Demonis."

Demonis turned back to overlook his army of the undead. Unperturbed by Kelar's words, he carried forward with his plan. "Gather your horses. We leave for Castle Malshidiel immediately."

After gathering their horses and gear Demonis, Kelar, Neasha, Kolos and Malores rode ahead of their undead army leaving the Sykanian castle behind.

"The soldiers travel so slowly." Demonis sighed in a tone of defeat. He hadn't considered how long it takes the undead to get anywhere. Too late now.

"What are we going to do about Lord Shade, sire?" queried Malores. "A man capable of killing Drakonia's finest swordsman should not be trifled with."

"You need not worry, wizard. I have a contingency plan."

Neasha shared a horse with Kelar. She could've had her own. But she chose to be close to him. Sickened by recent events, she held him close worrying about their future and terrified by their past—Kelar was equally worried. "I killed Lord Drakus."

The five of them rode ahead slowly with hundreds of undead soldiers, dragons, unicorns, and horses following behind. As they left the Field of Blood, one last zombie trailed behind. It was a Komalsh with no arms.

The unicorns were in full stride when Nyte started to feel Savita's heartbeat. He slowed the others to a stop and searched the area.

"What is it, Nyte?" Kris was just being his usual vigilant self.

"Savita is here. I can feel her."

"There's nothing but an open field here, Nyte." Trayke pointed out the obvious. "Do you see anything Arias?"

"Nope," answered Arias. "I don't see Savita either."

An enormous Silverback dragon swooped down and landed before them. A cloud of dust followed. When the dust cleared, the dragon stood before them. He lowered his body peacefully.

"I see a dragon," said Arias brushing the dust from his clothes.

The young Lords left their steeds and approached him with caution. The dragon gently released Savita from his mouth onto the ground.

Nyte knelt by her side. "Savita! Savita wake up! She's not responding. What have you done, dragon?"

"She will be fine," reassured the dragon. "Our saliva has a sleeping agent which disables our prey—a defence mechanism enabling us to feed our young a living meal. In time it's effect will subside."

The dragon peered closer. "You are the young Lords I've heard so much about…interesting."

The Dragon's Flute rolled out from Savita's grasp. With his own telekinetic abilities, the Silverback dragon levitated it before, Nyte.

"This flute is dangerous." Nyte knew of its history and its power.

"Yes, I am aware, young Lord. I created it from my own talon. That is why the Dragon's Flute has no influence on me," admitted the dragon. "It's my flute."

"Why would you create something like this?" asked a disheartened Nyte.

"It was a necessary evil during a dark time," said the saddened dragon. "I fear it will always be sought out by the wrong hands, young Lord. It would be wise for you to hide it within the safety of Castle Malshidiel."

Nyte accepted the flute and its burden. Curious as to Savita's rescue, he asked. "Why did you save Savita?"

"She recently saved my life. It was only fair to return the favor. Just be thankful I arrived when I did."

"Thank you for saving her life. My name is Lord Nyte Shade."

The dragon responded, "I am Stratos."

"Stratos!" repeated Nyte. He was star struck. "You're legendary!"

"So, I've heard." Stratos liked to downplay his reputation. Intrigued by the surname of Shade, the Silverback asked the young lord, "Are you related to Lady Raine Shade?"

"Yes, she was my mother."

"Interesting. You talk of her as though she were dead."

“My mother is dead.”

“Interesting.” Stratos gave pause and then continued. “I knew your mother, Nyte. I was the one who gave her, *The Book of Dragons*. How unfortunate she divided the chapters to all those unworthy kingdoms.”

“Her intentions were for the greater good,” defended Nyte.

“Yes, but her decisions were poor and caused much grief,” snapped Stratos.

Nyte wrapped Savita in a blanket from his saddle.

“I mean not to offend you, Lord Shade. In my heart your mother is a hero.”

“Was a hero,” reminded Nyte.

“Interesting.” Stratos stood and prepared for flight. “Lord Nyte Shade, I need to ask a favour of you. If achieved, I will share valuable knowledge regarding your mother.”

“What is this favour you wish of me?”

“Collect all the chapters to my Book of Dragons and return them to me at the highest peak of the Avila Mountain Range.”

Nyte accepted the offer. “I will return your book, Stratos.”

“If you are truly a member of the Shade bloodline, then I have no doubt in my mind you will. Until then I bid you farewell.” Stratos lifted off into the air and flew out of sight.

“Nyte, look at this!” Kris removed, *The Book of Malshidiel*, nestled in Savita’s grasp.

“She did it! She got it back!” laughed Nyte. “She never stopped talking about this damn book!”

“So, what’s the plan, Nyte?” asked Terex. “Should we hunt down Lord Demonis?”

“Yeah,” agreed Kris, “revenge does seem fitting.”

Thinking ahead, Nyte said, “I think it would be wisest for us to regroup at Castle Malshidiel.”

Arias was quick to respond. "Who is left to regroup with? All the Komalsh are dead."

"Lord and Lady Dunlam reside at the school of Olemeeze," reminded Kris. "We could try hailing them telepathically."

"Let's keep silent for now, Kris." ordered Nyte. "We will wait for Savita's counsel before making any decisions." Nyte lifted Savita onto Loki and held her close in his arms. Her eyes struggled to open; her speech had been weakened and had not been available.

"Nyte," She gasped suddenly.

"What is it, Savita?"

"Nyte. You must find the hidden night." She garbled.

"I don't understand, Savita?"

"The hidden night." She repeated while drifting back into unconsciousness.

"What do you suppose she means?" wondered Kris.

"I don't know," Nyte replied.

"She must be delirious. How would you find a hiding night?" Arias was not sure if this was a puzzle that was to be solved.

"Maybe she thinks Nyte's hiding," chuckled Trayke.

"Or maybe she's referring to a warrior knight." suggested Terex. "We are in desperate need of allies."

"She just needs some rest," assured Nyte. "I'm sure everything will come to light. Let's just get home."

"Komalsh, let's ride!"

Nyte held her close while returning to Castle Malshidiel. Occasionally, she'd awaken for a moment saying repeatedly, "The hidden night. The hidden night." Under a starlit sky, the weary young Lords made their way back through the Mystique Forest and returned to Castle Malshidiel.

Chapter XXX
Rise of the Dracolich.

In the backyard of the desolate Kelasian castle the Enchantress, Moya Blynn, walked gracefully up it's stone steps toward the Door of Duren. Behind her followed the three-headed hell hound Cerberus.

The Door of Duren slowly opened. Walking out from its darkness approached Fenka Rek followed by his undead steed, Apocalypse.

"Did you succeed?" rasped the infamous assassin. Moya Blynn placed her hand gently onto her belly. Her fingernails started to glow. "The spawn of Nyte Shade grows inside me."

"Excellent, the warlock awaits you."

Moya Blynn and Cerberus entered the Door of Duren and vanished into the cave's darkened corridor. The door closed with an echoing clang.

Fenka Rek mounted his undead stead. "Come Apocalypse, the search for Milita Drakus continues."

Beyond the closed Door of Duren in the dark depths of the mountain, the decayed corpse of a red dragon lay dormant. Her bones lay exposed from rotting flesh and the horrible stench of decay reeked the already toxic air. Inside her chest beat not her own heart, but that of the dormant Darkstar. The dragon's eyes momentarily opened revealing the glowing red eyes of a soulless beast. Then they closed and the dragon, the Dracolich, returned to her hibernation. On a stone throne before the resting Dracolich sat a darkly cloaked warlock. Moya Blynn and Cerberus approached him on either side. No words were spoken, none were needed. The warlock rose from his thrown and then bowed before the Dracolich.

"Rest, my master. Soon you will rise."

To be continued…

About the Author

Rylo Kinn, hailing from Sechelt, British Columbia, Canada, found his passion for storytelling in the midst of the town's natural wonders. His childhood explorations ignited his imagination, nurturing his creative talents from an early age. As he matured, his affinity for writing and weaving tales only deepened, culminating in the publication of his poetry under an undisclosed pen name and the beginning of his journey as an author. Today, Sechelt, remains a wellspring of inspiration for Rylo Kinn, infusing his work with the charm of his upbringing. Blending real-world experiences with elements of magic, he crafts captivating narratives that enchant his readers, keeping them enthralled with every word.

Look for @rylokinn on Instagram, TikTok, LinkedIn, Facebook.

Special thanks to Riegan Lowe for everything you did to make my book possible. Additional thanks to Lee-Ann Page for encouraging me to write, as well as my family and friends, for their ongoing support. It's been a long journey and without them I'd have never succeeded.

I love you all.

Northern Sea
Mount Maximus
Lake Maximus
Lake Anastasia
Lake Aeron
Titan River
Flat Lands of Izon
Elvin Castle
Desolation Valley
Soapstone Hills
Eastern Sea
Western Sea
Whispering Woods
Dragon Marshlands of Jirasab
White Sea

Manufactured by Amazon.ca
Bolton, ON